A Roll of the Dice:

Book One - We Who Endure Series

J. A. Quarles

HISTORIUM PRESS

This is a work of fiction inspired by historical events and family stories. Names, characters, places, and incidents are products of the author's imagination or are used fictitiously, with some names changed to protect privacy. While certain historical elements are based on true events, the narrative has been fictionalized to explore themes creatively and is not a literal account of history.

HARDCOVER ISBN: 979-8-950078-15-6
PAPERBACK ISBN: 979-8-950078-14-9
EBOOK ISBN: 979-8-950078-13-2

Historium Press
Printed and Published in the USA
2026

Table of Contents

Preface

The American Civil War, known in some circles as the War of Southern Independence, the Second War of Independence, or the War of Northern Aggression, is one of American history's most debated topics. Why is this? Why is a war fought over 150 years ago still captivating Americans to this day like no other conflict in American history? As a native Louisianian, my answer is simple. It happened here.

There is an easy way to prove this point. If you drive through the old Union States, there are a few Civil War battlefields to visit. Excluding the border states of Missouri, Kentucky, and Maryland, there is one infamous battlefield outside of the Confederacy: Gettysburg, Pennsylvania. Pick any Southern state outside of Texas; plenty of Southern battlefields exist. Many of these battlefields are within easy driving distance of my home in Louisiana. I have walked the battlefields of Port Hudson, Shiloh, and Vicksburg. I have even stayed the night in a Baton Rouge home where a Union cannonball fired from a gunboat remained embedded in a wall. For my Northern friends, try as they might, there are no Civil War battlefields to tour in New York, Chicago, Ohio, or Minneapolis.

In many ways, the Civil War is a distant memory in the northern states, a memory in which the righteous troops of the Union defeated the evil slave-owning Southerners. However, the war was a catastrophe if one were to view events from the Southern or Confederate perspective. For Southerners, the war was nothing less than a foreign invasion in which ¼ of the total adult white male population of the South died, the region's entire economy was destroyed, whole cities and towns were raised, and tens of thousands of civilians, both white and black, were killed. Hundreds of thousands were left homeless and destitute. And to add insult to injury, all 11 former Confederate states had to go through Reconstruction in one form or another.

Not only was the Civil War the most transformational event in American history, but it also occurred mainly in the South. Though more Union troops fell in battle than Southern troops, per Capita, the South's losses were far more significant. Demographically, the South was utterly wrecked by the war and would take well over a century to recover. Some even argue the South has never recovered.

This work is not a conventional historical study of the War Between the States. Instead, it ventures into the realm of speculation, exploring an alternate reality in which the South emerges victorious and secures its independence.

Few are eager to undertake such a project in today's social and political climate. Why so? For starters, with the Union victory in 1865 came the victor's version of history. According to the North, the South was lazy, immoral, and evil in its society and culture. The culmination of these traits was the institution of slavery. In essence, the South was an evil slavocracy that had to be punished and destroyed for its many sins.

Let us imagine a scenario in which we examine the Civil War and its causes without preconceived notions. It becomes evident that while slavery was a significant issue, it was not the sole or primary cause of the war. Samuel Mitcham's 'It Wasn't About Slavery: Exposing the Great Lie of the Civil War' presents a compelling argument. I concur with Mitcham's perspective that the conflict was fundamentally a struggle for economic and political power.

The Civil War between the North and South loomed for decades. Over the first half of the 19th century, the more populous and industrialized Northern states accumulated more power, wealth, and influence than the Southern states. Four of the first five United States presidents were Southerners, while Zachary Taylor was the last

Southern president before the outbreak of hostilities, an entire decade before the war.

However, Southern representation extended beyond the presidency on the national level. Throughout the first half of the 19th century, the Northern States attained a permanent majority in the House of Representatives. At the same time, the Southern States relied on the occasional admittance of new slave states to gain new Senators to check Northern political power. However, this strategy had mixed results and only forestalled eventual conflict.

This Southern vs. Northern conflict was inevitable due to the political and economic policies implemented by the Northern Whigs and later by their successors, the Republicans. The Republican Party carried on the Hamiltonian traditional platform of high tariffs, the desire for a national bank, and crony capitalism for their Northern industrial friends.

These policies were detrimental to the South and highly advantageous for the North. The rural South, which accounted for 30% of the United States population, paid 80% of the country's federal taxes. To compound this arrangement, with the Northern states controlling Congress, most federal tax revenues were spent on projects and improvements in the Northern States, while employing Northern companies to carry out the work. The South was being exploited economically for the North's sole benefit.

With Lincoln's election in 1860, many in the South decided they had had enough and wanted to go their separate ways. And the rest, that's history, four years of the bloodiest war in American history. America embarked on a markedly different trajectory, one of centralized federal power and curtailed State (Southern) rights.

The premise of this work is twofold. First, I present a scenario, based on extensive research, in which the South, through a combination of military and political victories, can achieve independence from the North. Second, the South can maintain that independence, enter the family of nations, and determine its destiny.

Do not get me wrong; there is an ever-growing market for alternate history these days. There are several well-written works concerning an alternate American Civil War, and many are not worth reading. I hope my work falls into the former category. My sales pitch is simple: I do not propose a Disney- or fairy-tale-like utopian vision of a Southern victory. If the South were to win, and they could have, it would have been a bloody, savage affair. In this work, I will demonstrate how the South could have achieved independence, despite limited manpower and resources.

Before I conclude, I must mention the writers who, before me, blazed the path of Alternate History. Harry Turtledove first introduced me to alternate history, and through his work, the impulse to seek divergent points on the historical timeline became second nature to me.

In more recent years, I have discovered the works of Peter Tsouras and Newt Gingrich. Although I do not always agree with their conclusions, their alternate histories, especially of the Civil War, made me realize how much research was required to produce a credible account.

Research is the most critical aspect of writing a believable alternate history. I prefer an alternate history that is believable both on the surface and in its depth. It's not dependent on time travelers or aliens to change the course of events. Instead, subtle shifts in decisions and events create a butterfly effect that alters history. A notable example of this is Harry Turtledove's "Order 191 Timeline." The premise of that entire series was what if, instead of Robert E. Lee's battle plan for the Battle of Sharpsburg (Antietam) being discovered by Union forces and alerting General McClellan of Lee's intentions, those plans were found by Confederate soldiers, allowing

Lee to implement his strategy without McClellan knowing the better. One action/ event changes history.

The challenge with deviations from our timeline is the butterfly effect. The further a story diverges from the initial event, the more the author must extrapolate what would happen in history as a result. At this juncture, the alternate history genre becomes the most challenging, as it predicts outcomes that occur years or decades after a divergent event. Well-researched alternate history combines our knowledge of the past, current cultural norms, and informed conjecture.

Another reason I was drawn to this project is that, in general, I find attitudes and portrayals of the South in fiction and nonfiction unflattering. I can admit that, by being a native Southerner and half of my family being from the South, I tend to be perhaps oversensitive to how the South is perceived. However, many mainstream historians and authors have created almost cartoonish versions of the South that they portray, holding the heroes and people of the South in low regard. At times, this portrayal alludes to Southerners as being Proto-Nazis, which historically could not be any further from the truth.

In this work, I wish to represent the South as it was, for all its good and shortcomings. Slavery played a critical role in the cause of the war, and I have tried my utmost to address the institution of slavery and the plight of black and enslaved people in the South. If the South had been independent in the 1860s, approximately 40% of its population would have been of African descent. If anything, Southern independence would have meant Southerners would have had to confront the end of slavery and a civil rights movement that occurred 100 years earlier than in our timeline.

And let me make this very clear, I in no way support slavery or discrimination based on race or ethnicity. However, in this book, I have sought to present the perspectives of people who lived during that period, regardless of race. At times, we may be exposed to perspectives that are not aligned with contemporary moral or cultural norms. One of my primary goals in writing this book was to immerse the audience in the characters' time and world, allowing readers to confront the same dilemmas and difficult decisions our characters faced. Ultimately, my readers will decide if I was successful in my efforts.

1863 was a critical year in the War of Southern Independence. The South was at its peak in military manpower and had won several key victories during the first two years of the war. However, the Northern blockade was in full effect, and the Confederacy had lost critical pieces of its territory. Much of Tennessee lay under Union occupation. New Orleans and most of the Mississippi River Valley were under Union control. Another Union attempt to capture Vicksburg was underway, the Army of the Potomac lay encamped 60 miles north of Richmond, and the Emancipation Proclamation was in effect. If the Confederacy were to win the war and gain independence, the strategic dilemma it faced would have to change.

I am a firm believer in the premise that history is not fated or predetermined. Indeed, historical trends can become forces in their own right, shaping history in specific directions. But humans have inherent gifts of free will and self-determination. Mystical forces or some magic do not determine history. History is determined by the actions and decisions we make every day. Is humanity flawed? For sure. But there is also humanity's inherent goodness, a determination to make the world better for future generations. The following work, *A Roll of the Dice,* examines how the Confederacy could have begun its journey to ultimate victory and independence from the Northern States.

Author's Note:

I want to thank everyone who, behind the scenes, made it possible for me to write this book. Without the time and generosity of others, I could not have accomplished much. Special thanks go to my wife, Jenni, and our wonderful kids, Ella and Benji, whose love and tolerance of me make my life truly blessed.

This book is dedicated to the nations and peoples of the South, the civilization they have built, and the freedom they still strive for.

Prologue

May 6, 1863: Confederate Presidential Study, Confederate White House

Jefferson Davis studied the papers on his desk and paused for what must have been a dozenth time. The fifth month of 1863 began with significant battles fought in Virginia, Alabama, and Mississippi. Generals Lee and Forrest proclaimed spectacular victories in Virginia and Alabama, while a massive catastrophe occurred in Mississippi. Hundreds of miles separated these battles, yet President Davis knew that the ultimate responsibility for defending the Confederacy rested on his shoulders.

With his one good eye, he turned and quickly read the dispatch from General Lee. Was it true? Had Lee and Jackson destroyed two whole Corps in Hooker's Army of the Potomac? Even if it was not two entire Corps, Lee had won a great victory. The feat was even more impressive because Longstreet and two of his divisions had not participated in the battle at Chancellorsville. Most of Pickett's division was en route to Mississippi, while Hood's division could not reach the fighting near Fredericksburg and Chancellorsville in time to participate. What could this mean for the Confederacy moving forward? What options would be available for Davis to make now?

He then turned to a report, scant on details, by General Nathan B. Forrest. Again, it was hard to believe what he was reading. With his independent command separate from the Army of Tennessee, Forrest had annihilated a Union force of 1,700 cavalry troopers in northern Alabama. Forrest consistently delivered victories in a theater devoid of major Confederate victories for two years.

Lastly, Davis sighed and looked at the reports from Mississippi and Louisiana. Not only were the butchers Grant and Sherman driving on Vicksburg, but a new name was burned into his memory. A General named Grierson had led a large Union cavalry force through Tennessee, Mississippi, and Louisiana. Not only had this cavalry formation defeated handily every Confederate force it had encountered, but the Yankee marauders had also devastated the surrounding countryside and caused untold millions in damage. With Grant's massive army closing in on Vicksburg, Grierson's raid was the last thing Davis had the resources to deal with.

There was no other way to describe the situation in Mississippi other than a complete and utter catastrophe. However, Davis felt secure with the Confederacy's position in Virginia; a thousand miles away, however, the last two Confederate strongholds on the Mississippi, Vicksburg and Port Hudson, were nearly surrounded.

"Can we hold the river?" he asked himself out loud. "What would be the cost?"

There had been much discussion within his cabinet and with high-ranking Confederate generals on the course of action going forward when he had authorized General Pickett's division in Virginia to go to Mississippi to be under the command of General Joseph E. Johnson. The dice were cast, and Pickett was expected to arrive in Jackson, Mississippi, within the next several weeks. Between Pemberton's army in Vicksburg and Johnson's gathering army in Jackson, Mississippi, Confederate forces in the department would be near parity with Grant's army. For now, and that was if Johnson was ever willing to risk a battle.

Davis ran some calculations in the margins of a parchment sheet and considered the results. He knew all too well the criticisms directed at his management of the war effort, namely that he interfered too much or that he allowed personal preferences and prejudices to dictate his decision-making.

This time, he knew no one could honestly question his decisions. He wrote a direct Presidential Order, sealed it, and marked it

'Urgent.' He wrote several more orders, sat back in his chair, and wiped his forehead when he finished.

President Davis had just made three decisions that he knew would ultimately decide the fate of his nation. His first order was to give General Forrest an independent cavalry command and to report for action to General Johnston in Mississippi. The second was to peel away General Patrick Cleburne and his division from the Army of Tennessee and transfer them to Johnston as well. If that old fool could not figure out how to dislodge Grant with an additional nearly 16,000 crack infantry and cavalry from Pickett, Cleburne, and Forrest, Davis would fire him and find someone else to do the job. Hell, he would even be willing to give that damn annoying Creole General Beauregard another chance to fight Grant.

His third decision was to call a meeting with Generals Lee, Jackson, Longstreet, Stuart, and Secretaries Benjamin and Seddon. Davis could have included additional generals and government officials on the list, but he knew that more attendees would mean less would get accomplished. He still had reservations about Longstreet, but Longstreet's attendance would go a long way toward gaining General Lee's cooperation and blessing to adopt the chosen strategy.

A general sense of relief washed over the president. Having made the necessary and crucial decisions, he felt confident in leaving his office and going to Varina for the evening. The war was aging him rapidly and devouring much of the time he could have dedicated to his family. Still, Davis knew the only way the Confederacy could achieve victory was to receive his undivided attention.

He looked one last time at the dispatch from General Jackson's headquarters and nearly fell out of his chair when he realized he had missed the name of a young Confederate officer mentioned at the end of the report, "*Therefore I recommend Captain Lutze, after escaping captivity from the enemy and returning for duty to General Hays's 1st Louisiana Brigade, provided great service to General Jackson in his knowledge of the enemy's dispositions and by heroically saving the General's life."*

The fatigue momentarily had left Davis's mind. First, did he read that correctly with his one-functioning eye? Second, was Captain Johan Lutze of Louisiana, his godson, still alive and returned to action? Grabbing a fresh sheet of parchment, Davis added one last order to his stack of Presidential Orders.

Chapter 1

May 2, 1863, Conclusion of General Lee's and Jackson's Midnight Meeting

The hour was late, but everything had been necessary to implement the proper plan. General Jackson was exhausted from the day's marching and fighting, yet he also knew that he was under the weather and that the constant flow of days in the saddle would not improve his condition. All he needed was a few hours of sleep beneath the shade of the trees outside Army headquarters, and he would be ready for the day.

As if in a fog, there was a distant voice he had trouble understanding, "General Jackson, Sir."

A younger man in a brilliant gray officer's uniform saluted him. Jackson saw the captain's insignia on his collar, "Captain?"

"General Jackson," the young Captain stuttered, "If II Corps is to march for 4:00 AM, should we not send dispatches to your divisional Commanders, Generals Hill, Heth, Early, and Colston?"

The fog lifted from Jackson's mind, and he nodded his approval: "Thank you, son. It is indeed Providence that you brought that issue to my attention. Send riders to all four divisional commanders at once. They are to be ready to march at 4:00 AM sharp."

Satisfied that his divisional commanders were to be notified of his commands, General Thomas "Stonewall" Jackson laid down and ran the calculations of his daring flanking attack in his mind. It would be a sight to see the entirety of the II Corps hitting with everything it had, the exposed position of the enemy's XI Corps.

12:45 PM, May 2, 1863, the XI Corps Main Camp, 45th New York

It was another summer morning in the God-forsaken state of Virginia. The heat did not prevent Karl Schultz from enjoying a slow, well-paced brunch and coffee with his brother, Frederick, and their friend, Jacob. Another young man who had become attached to their group, Johan Ludwig, had a most peculiar accent for a native German speaker. The boy acted as if he had never seen a fight before, whereas Karl and Fredrick had seen fighting at Cross Keys and Second Bull Run. If Colonel Von Amseberg, Commander of the 45th New York, felt no need to dig entrenchments and or the like, why should they not have their gear stowed away and rifles stacked while they cooked breakfast?

Johan kept his rifle slung over his shoulder or close to his side all morning. Karl shook his head, "If he feels like carrying that ridiculous rifle around, why should it matter to me?"

No sooner had Karl uttered those words to himself than the sound of artillery and thousands of muskets firing ended his introspection. Dozens of blue-clad men around the camp fell to the ground silently or screamed bloody murder, grasping at ghastly wounds.

The carnage was surreal, and Karl gaped at the catastrophe around him. A strong pull at his arm brought him to his feet. Young Johan yelled at him in his ridiculous accent, "Hör auf zu träumen, mein Freund. Zeit zu rennen." What was Johan saying? "*Stop dreaming, my friend. Time to run.*" Karl had to agree with Johan's assessment.

12:45 PM, May 2, 1863, Confederate General A.P. Hill's Division

Something had been different about General Jackson that morning. Perhaps, despite the early hour, Hill had his division ready to move out before 4 AM and earned back some of General Jackson's endearment. Whatever the reason, General Jackson had commanded Hill to lead the 2nd Corps march and the attack on the Union's right flank.

It had taken much longer than usual to deploy the entire 2nd Corps for the attack due to the problematic terrain of the Wilderness. The 2-mile-long attack line was a testament to the generals, officers, and NCOs of the 28,000-man II Corps. What shocked General Hill the most was that, despite the long march in which there was skirmishing with Yankee forces along almost the entire march, there was no sign of any defensive works in the camp. In addition, the XI Union Corps was deployed in one of the few flat, open areas of the Wilderness, with few natural features to anchor a defensive effort. He continuously scanned the camp, looking for anything out of place. And yet, even with the effort and noise it took to deploy the II Corps, the Yankees did nothing to prepare for an attack beyond a few officers gathering work details.

"General."

General AP Hill looked to his aide, "Colonel."

"The division is deployed."

Hill breathed a sigh of relief. Somehow, the Yankees had no idea that 28,000 men of the finest Confederate infantry and artillery were about to unleash a hurricane upon them.

"You have done well, General Hill."

General Jackson's voice was unmistakable, and when General Hill turned in his saddle, Jackson bowed his head and touched his cap.

Since the two Generals had been feuding until the past morning, Hill was taken aback by Jackson's praise. "General Hill," continued Stonewall Jackson in his typical confident tone, "you may begin your attack."

With a look to his aide, General Hill drew his saber and commanded, "Colonel, pass the word quickly; time to attack!"

Moments after a cannon signaled, the first volleys of musket fire erupted into the federal camp, thousands of Confederate foot soldiers charged forward with the rebel yell announcing their presence. Within 30 minutes of the initial Confederate volleys, the Union XI Corps ceased to exist as a fighting force. After the first hour of fighting, over half of the 11,000-man Corps would be taken prisoner, on top of the thousands killed and wounded. General Hill almost felt sorry for them.

2:00 PM, May 2, 1863, General Dan Sickles, III Corps Commander, Old Plank Road

General Dan Sickles was itching for a real fight, not this silly skirmishing he had been engaging the Rebels in for the last few hours. If they were to destroy Lee and his rebel army, why could he not forcefully pursue the retreating rebel rear guard and their baggage train? Had he heard more skirmishing up the road an hour ago? Little did he know how soon his answer would come.

A fatigued blue-clad rider galloped up to General Sickles and his staff. The rider saluted and began without introduction, "General Sickles, you must report back to the main body of III Corps. The Rebels attacked our right flank in force about an hour ago."

General Sickles turned red when he heard the news. "Damnation, an hour ago? Why didn't anyone come to find me? What of Howard and XI Corps?"

The courier's face turned dark. "General, there isn't much of XI Corps left. As for General Howard, he is believed to be either captured or dead."

Sickles immediately led the courier and his staff back to the main body of the III Corps. As his horse galloped towards the apparent sounds of battle, he berated himself and the damnable army, "Within an hour, we lost an entire Corps! An entire Corps! My God, what will be left of III Corps when I reach them?"

Late Afternoon of May 2, 1863, the Reformed Union XI Corps

Johan had no idea how he had managed to survive the day's events. The only answer was by the grace of God. To complicate things further, his former corps, the II Corps of the Army of Northern Virginia, had attacked this morning and routed his mostly German-speaking companions of the XI Corps. That was why he was determined to affect the battle when General Sickles, the III Corps Commander and acting XI Corps commander, had set up new defensive positions.

Johan had been a Captain in the 6th Louisiana Infantry Regiment and had served with distinction in every campaign in the East since the beginning of the war. With Generals Taylor and Hayes as brigade commanders of the Louisiana Tigers, the name associated with many Louisiana troops in the Army of Northern Virginia, Johan had known nothing but victory. However, in December of last year, during the Fredericksburg campaign, Johan, along with several men from his company, was attacked and captured during the battle.

Since his capture in December, Johan had spent months in captivity, passing through the Union-controlled cities of Washington, Baltimore, Philadelphia, and New York. His escape from New York, a city teeming with Union sympathizers, was a testament to his ingenuity and good fortune. Assuming a false identity, Johan navigated New York's underworld and thrived briefly, all in his effort to return to the Army of Northern Virginia.

Johan was only able to pass as a German immigrant for so long. But thanks to Mr. Lincoln's bounty of $300 to enlist as blue belly cannon fodder, Johan enlisted in the Union Army as Mr. Johan Ludwig. As fortune would have it, in early May 1863, he was a corporal in the XI Corps. Since the XI Corps was composed primarily of native Germans and other Central Europeans, his fellow soldiers mainly ignored Johan's odd German accent. But everything had changed around noon.

Johan attended the Louisiana Military Academy the year before the war and served as an officer for two years in the Army of Northern Virginia. However, he only needed some of his training and battlefield experience to know that General Howard had left XI Corps, the right flank of the entire Army of the Potomac, completely exposed and unprotected.

The army of bluebellies had boasted that they had Lee and Jackson outsmarted and whipped this time. Johan did not believe that for a moment. Enough rumors circulated through the camp from couriers and returning pickets that Rebs had been seen on the road to the Southwest. If Johan were a betting man, and he was, he would bet all the money that he didn't have that Jackson was going to attack.

Everything about the camp was lazy that morning. Most troopers had their rifles stacked and were more concerned with sleeping and eating breakfast. If anyone attacked, including Jackson or Old Man Lee, the XI Corps would afterward need to be referred to in the past tense.

Johan faked his identity and joined the Union Army to return to the 1st Louisiana Brigade. However, the last thing he wanted was to be killed by his former comrades in arms, who would believe by his blue uniform that he was a Yankee.

His behavior was not much different from his blue-bellied comrades that morning, besides eating a lighter breakfast and finding excuses not to stack his rifle. Vigilance on Johan's part had paid off because, a little before 1:00 PM on May 2, Jackson's attack came. Combined Confederate rifle and artillery fire caused instant chaos, confusion, and hundreds of casualties throughout the XI Corps' exposed position. But Johan did not inwardly panic. He merely shouldered his rifle and joined a gang of panicked Germans to the safety of the III Corps position. Undoubtedly, he felt he would return to his old Louisiana Brigade. Still, Johan would do it in a way where death was not inevitable and bring any intelligence he could obtain to the detriment of the Yankees.

Around 4:45 PM, May 2, 1863, Hazel Grove, Generals Jackson and Hill

A table was erected in a clearing next to Hazel Grove, and a map of the region covered its top. Generals Jackson and Hill studied the map to determine where to attack the Federals next. The day so far had been a spectacular victory, one of the most incredible single days in any Confederate Army's history. But Jackson knew that the purpose of this battle was to destroy the Federal army, if not at the very least cripple it. Two entire Corps, the XI and III, had been effectively destroyed, leaving the Federals with an effective army of almost 110,000 men. There was much still to be done, and Jackson wanted one more crack at the Federals to consolidate the Confederate gains so far.

General Hill spoke first, "General Jackson, each division has almost completed reforming. The battles this afternoon confused everything. However, after accounting for our losses of killed and wounded and men to guard," he paused as he read the dispatch and continued, "the 10,000 Federal prisoners, it still leaves us with almost 25,000 effectives."

"And thanks to our Northern cousins, the men have resupplied," smiled General Jackson, his eyes twinkling with a hint of mischief.

It was a stroke of strategic brilliance for the Confederate armies to utilize captured Union supplies. However, this time, capturing almost two Corps' worth of supplies, weapons, and ammo in nearly pristine condition was genuinely remarkable. Jackson's men wasted no time using these, a testament to their resourcefulness and adaptability. It was, in every sense, Jackson's manna from heaven.

Jackson shrugged, "We need to send scouts forward and know what the Yankees are up to. There is no way they will just let us stay here unmolested after we have thrashed them so. If they can get the jump on us in the morning, they could easily reverse today's outcome. General Hill, perhaps we can assemble a small entourage and observe their lines and launch one last attack before nightfall." He pointed to a location on the map, "If we could make it to the Chancellor's house..."

A sudden commotion off in the distance caught Jackson's attention. Men shouted and pointed, their voices carrying a mix of excitement and apprehension. A dozen Confederate infantrymen, their faces etched with determination, escorted a bedraggled man wearing Union blue. The small group made its way straight for Jackson, its purpose clear, but its intentions unknown.

"What on earth?" questioned General Hill.

A dozen armed Confederate infantrymen, along with their blue-clad prisoner, cautiously approached as Generals Jackson and Hill and saluted.

The group leader, a sergeant, hesitantly saluted and received the two generals' salutes in return. Sensing the man's unease, Jackson said, "Sergeant, it is unusual for a dozen of my men to bring one Yankee prisoner to me, so I assume this is important?"

"General Jackson, Sergeant McKay of the 18th North Carolina," the sergeant said. "Sir, this man, clearly clothed in the uniform of a corporal in the Yankee army, claims to be a certain Captain Lutze of the 6th Louisiana."

The usually stoic Jackson was taken aback at the sergeant's words. Captain Johan Lutze of the Louisiana "Fighting Tigers" Brigade had been either captured or killed during the Fredericksburg Campaign back in December. How would a Yankee corporal come up with the correct name, rank, and unit of a fallen officer?

General Hill looked at the Union prisoner and said, "What do you have to say for yourself, son?"

The young prisoner smiled and wiped his hand over a bruised eye, "I made a bet with the sergeant here that if he didn't shoot me and General Jackson wouldn't hang me, I'd get him and his boys an accommodation from you, General Jackson. And if I ended up dead, well, he wasn't losing out on anything."

The young man's ridiculous Louisiana accent was a dead giveaway, along with the grin on his face, which made Jackson blink. The man's hair was light brown, darkened only by the need to wash. He looked the right height, around 5'8", and appeared to be in his early twenties. All the while, Jackson looked him over; the mischievous look in the boy's eyes convinced him.

"Captain Lutze, it is my pleasure to see you again. Since your departure in December, your brigade and the II Corps have sorely missed your presence."

Johan smiled amiably. "It's been a while, General Jackson. Once we win this battle, I would like to share with you the tale of my travels over the last several months. However, I went through all this trouble to give you the information you need to win this battle."

Before Jackson could respond, General Hill said, "Go on, Captain Lutze."

5:05 PM, May 2, 1863, Within the Union Picket Line, several hundred yards away from Chancellor's House

"This was not the accommodation I had in mind," complained Sergeant McKay as they lay in the underbrush.

Johan grinned at McKay. "Look at it this way, Sergeant; at least you still wear a butternut uniform." Johan then gestured at the blue coat he still wore. "But remember, even though I killed the man who had been on picket duty with me, the men at this picket are honorable. And above all else, they are friends of mine. We give them a chance to surrender, and then we release hell."

Johan's story was hard to believe, and he experienced it firsthand. After the virtual destruction of XI and III Corps, General Sickles rallied the survivors and formed a new defensive line near the Chancellor's House. Johan, Karl, Frederick, Jacob, and Jones, a man who always had it out for Johan, were all put out on picket duty. Johan had managed to get placed by himself with Jones and, when they were left alone, knifed him in the kidney before the man knew what happened to him. Johan then made his way to the Confederate pickets, where he encountered the 18th North Carolina and was taken to General Jackson. And now, Johan returned to the scene of his betrayal.

"Alright, Sergeant. If my friends shoot me, it was nice meeting you this afternoon."

Johan then crawled towards where Karl, Frederick, and Jacob were picketed. It took time to get close, but Johan wanted to make sure he was not seen or heard and did not want to spook anyone into shooting at him. Several times, he cursed as thorns and brambles stabbed him in the hands and knees, yet Johan persisted. This mission was too critical.

Following a depression in the ground, he got to within 30 yards of his former companions and called out in German, "Karl! Fredrick! Can you hear me? Don't shoot!"

He heard rustling in the underbrush and heard Fredrick's voice respond in German, "Johan, is that you?"

"Yes! Something terrible has happened! I am about 30 yards in front of you. I am going to rise slowly and walk towards you."

"Alright, Johan," Karl answered this time. "Take your time, my friend; we are keeping watch."

In Johan's mind, this would be the most dangerous part of his mission. With his original position compromised by his killing of Jones, once his friends had surrendered, a gap of at least 250 yards would be made in the Union lines. And that was all General Jackson would need to attack.

With his hands raised, Johan slowly rose and walked towards his former companions, who had their muskets at the low ready. After a few brief tense moments of the three unsuspecting men looking around, Karl motioned for Johan to hurry.

Johan reached the three men and gasped for air. "Are you alright?" a concerned Fredrick asked.

"I think so," Johan tried to look over himself and look even more disheveled. "I just don't know what happened. One moment, Jones was sipping his canteen. Next, he was on top of me, trying to poke his knife in my ribs."

Karl groaned. "What happened next? And does this mean your picket is now unoccupied?"

Johan leaned into the act, "I had to defend myself. I know Jones, and I did not get along very well, but the thought of him attacking me at the first chance of us being alone together, well, it just never occurred to me."

"This is bad," Karl lowered his musket and looked around. "With your picket gone, that leaves a hole in the lines. General Sickles just finished reassembling what is left of XI and III Corps; if the Rebs knew of our situation here...," Jacob and Fredrick had lowered their muskets and were looking to Karl while they had completely lost focus on Johan. And that was all that the Confederate Captain needed.

"I am sorry to do this, my friends," Johan had pulled out his hidden Colt Navy revolver, courtesy of General Hill, pointed, and cocked it before any of his three German friends could register what had happened.

Karl looked white-faced at Johan, "What is this all about, Johan?"

"Listen to me carefully." Johan's voice was firm, and he spoke perfect German. "If the three of you, whom I consider my dearest friends, wish to live, lay down your weapons and make not a sound. Surrender peacefully and in silence, and you will have my protection. On my honor as a Confederate officer."

He had acted and said the words. Now, it was up to his friends to decide how to respond.

Betrayal and anger flashed in Karl's blue eyes, but the tall blonde German did not move. Jacob remained frozen in place but looked at Fredrick.

"How can you make that promise?" asked Fredrick with skepticism.

Johan gave his friend a sad smile, "Let's just say there are several important people who will owe me lots of favors. And, because of my affection for the three of you, I wanted to give y'all the option to surrender rather than," he gestured to his revolver. "However, my friends. Time is short. I hate to put you in this position, but your decision must be made now."

For a moment, there was silence other than the sound of the forest. Then, a musket fell to the ground. Karl stood tall with his hands raised, and Fredrick and Jacob followed his example.

Johan let out a breath he didn't know he was holding. Lowering his revolver away from his friends, he let out a long whistle. Within moments, that call was returned, and gray/butternut-clad Confederate infantrymen emerged from the surrounding area and began to file past Johan and his companions.

***

Sergeant McKay could not believe his eyes when he saw the young Captain approach the Yankee picket and disarm all three men. Even though he could not understand the German spoken, he knew that the young Captain Lutze had spoken to the men, his friends, from the heart. The fact that Lutze had risked his own life for this mission and had the men of the 18th North Carolina swear that they would give the Yankees a chance to surrender touched McKay's soul. As young as the captain was, Sergeant McKay knew that Captain Lutze was a man he would gladly follow to the gates of hell.

Chapter 2

5:30 PM, May 2, 1863, Chancellor's House, Union Army Headquarters

"We reform and dig in," said General Hooker, Commanding General of the Army of the Potomac, though he did not feel the courage he was projecting. "The rebels stung us this afternoon. But we will bring the full force of our army into them tomorrow. Let's see how old Bobby Lee and "Stonewall" like those odds."

General Dan Sickles chimed in, "They are out there right now! There are still a few hours of daylight left; we hit them now before the rebels can consolidate their gains."

"If I am correct," interjected General Couch, Commander of II Corps, "the rebels took 10,000 of our men alone captive, many of them being from III Corps. What are we attacking, General Sickles? We have no idea what strength the rebels have. We know we faced Jackson today, but Lee and Longstreet are still out there. What of those forces?"

"I thought Longstreet was south of Richmond," quipped Sickles. "And even if he miraculously made it here, is not General Pickett's Division being shipped out west?"

"A rumor," General Meade, Commander of V Corps, spoke up.

"What on earth is going on here?" exclaimed an exasperated Sickles. "We must stand and fight and deliver a blow to the rebels. If Longstreet is here, so much the better; we can bag the whole damn Army of Northern Virginia."

"Like the rebels bagged XI and III Corps," General Slocum, Commander of XII Corps, asked in an almost mocking voice.

The room erupted into more arguing and finger-pointing, and it took General Hooker several minutes to calm everyone down. With no actual decision being made, Hooker decided to step outside onto the porch of the Chancellor's home. He struck a match on a column and lit his pipe, now dangling from his mouth.

"May I join you?" came the voice of General Sickles.

Hooker looked at Sickles and nodded. The man was a pain in his ass, but despite not being from West Point, he had proven to be an adequate, if not even talented, Field Commander. And if anything, Sickles's tenacity and stubbornness had saved what remained of XI and III Corps from being completely annihilated.

As Sickles reached for a cigar from his coat pocket and Hooker lit another match, there was a deafening explosion, and debris flew everywhere. General Hooker found himself on his back and unable to move. And then the world went dark.

May 2, 1863, 10:00 PM, Chancellor's House, Confederate Staff Meeting

With joy in his voice, General Lee congratulated General Jackson. "General Jackson, I must say the events of this afternoon and evening were nothing short of spectacular. The damage your men have caused to those people, with minimal losses of our own, is close to a miracle."

Not wanting to take the credit for his men's accomplishments, General Jackson adjusted his sling and responded, "You are right, Sir. Our men were magnificent. And though we did not cause as many casualties as before, our final attack on this very home put the entire command structure of the Army of the Potomac in disarray. But alas, we know they will be back tomorrow."

General Lee nodded in agreement and looked about the room. General Stuart stood a respectable distance away while Generals Hill and Rhodes sat on darkened benches. Hill sported a bandage around his head while Rhodes nursed a badly sprained ankle. Next to Hill and Rhodes sat the intrepid hero from Louisiana, Captain Lutze. Lee's gaze only lasted a minute on the young man who had fallen asleep where he sat.

***

Johan had been given a gray officer's jacket and ran forward along with the men of the 18th North Carolina. The underbrush of the Wilderness was hell to get through, and Johan was thankful to have two pistols instead of an officer's sword. His adopted unit served as a sort of bodyguard for General Jackson, and their presence proved necessary in the final battle of the day.

After the outer Union pickets had been subdued in an area of their lines of around 250 yards, Jackson sent his entire Corps in for one more attack against the Yankees. The Confederates achieved surprise and rushed past many rifle pits that the Yankees had dug, but the men in blue, this time, stood and fought.

The noise and smoke almost overwhelmed Johan's senses. As the Confederates poured volley after volley into the Union ranks, the Yankees returned fire, inflicting heavy losses on the Southerners.

What gave Jackson's men the edge in the fight was the incapacitation of General Hooker at the beginning of the battle. However, fresh troops had been rushed from the V and XII Corps to reinforce the Union position before the fighting, preventing the Union line from breaking again.

Johan felt terrified and energized to be part of General Jackson's security detail. With the battle raging all around, Johan kept his two revolvers drawn, constantly scanned his surroundings, and directed the men of his adopted squad to clear obstacles for General Jackson.

However, General Jackson, being mounted on little Sorrel and being "Stonewall" Jackson, made it difficult for him to always be by his side. For a time, Johan did little other than run to keep up with General Jackson.

A disaster nearly occurred when Jackson and his detail encountered a pocket of Union soldiers in green uniforms. These were the men of Berdan's Sharpshooters, and they were all armed with the infamous Spencer repeating rifles.

The green-coated Yankees were almost as surprised as Johan and his men. Two of his men went down almost immediately to the Spencer repeaters, and several bullets flew past General Jackson. Realizing the disaster that could befall the army, Johan yelled for his men to charge, and he ran forward, firing both of his revolvers. Being only feet away from the Yankees, Johan's shots found their targets and launched their victims backward.

Mechanically, Johan fired repeatedly into the small mass of green-coated Yankees, decimating their numbers. He tried not to think of the carnage he inflicted and the screams of the men as the bullets maimed and killed them. All he focused on was saving General Jackson and his men. Luckily for the men of the 18th North Carolina, they had their bayonets fixed and made quick work of what was left of the sharpshooters. After the brief battle, General Jackson remained unfazed and urged Little Sorrel forward.

There was no time for Johan to aid the fallen Yankees. Still, he paused long enough to pilfer a Spencer rifle, bayonet, and cartridge box that contained several of the tubular magazines that held the rifle's ammunition. Johan had never fired a Spencer before, but had seen enough soldiers carrying them around while he was in Howard's XI Corps to understand how they worked. He was confident he could figure out how to use the damn rifle. With a quick check, he verified that the gun was loaded and led his men after General Jackson.

The battle raged on as Jackson directed his forces forward. The Confederates were having the better of the Yankees, but it did not stop the bluecoats from launching repeated counterattacks. Jackson put himself everywhere within the battle, helping to reform Confederate lines or pushing the men forward to take a Yankee position.

Johan gasped for air as he and what was left of his security detail chased after Jackson, but he felt only admiration for the man. Through his sheer will, Jackson changed the dynamic of the precarious Confederate position from the day before and handed the Yankees their worst defeat of the war so far.

They had pushed the Yankees back and reached a more level and cleared area, and a large house loomed several dozen yards away. This house, Johan correctly assumed, was the Chancellor's House, and it was Jackson's obvious objective. General Hill had somehow joined their entourage with some of his staff, and the Confederate line surged forward to consolidate the day's victories.

Unfortunately, unable to keep up with the two generals, Johan's squad had become separated from the main Confederate force. Though he felt relief when he reached Jackson and Hill, Johan believed they were still too exposed.

Upon reaching the house, Johan's fears proved true when a mass of Union infantry rushed from the nearby woods towards the two generals. The unmistakable whistle of a cannonball registered with Johan, and then there was a loud explosion. To his horror, he saw both generals thrown from their horses.

"Follow me," Johan screamed without looking back as he raced to the fallen generals. To his relief, he saw both men moving, but General Hill was the only one of the two able to stand.

Sliding into position in front of the two injured generals, Johan threw on his Spencer's bayonet. He worked his Spencer like he had seen Union cavalry troopers do, taking a kneeling firing position to shield Jackson and Hill as best he could. As the Union infantry closed in, Johan sought out the gold shoulder bars of an officer and fired, dropping the unfortunate man. He then furiously worked his rifle, chambering another round and firing into the mass of Yankees. His men, directed by Sergeant McKay, let off a volley from their single-shot muzzleloaders at almost point-blank range into the Yankees. The advancing line froze, stunned by the shock of the volley before they could close in on and capture what had to be in their minds: two high-ranking Rebel generals.

"Charge," Johan screamed as he emptied his rifle into the mass of Yankees and jumped up. The small squad around him followed suit, and as they crashed into the unlucky Yankees, General Hill, along with a few of his staff, managed to stand and draw revolvers. As General Hill stood over General Jackson, he and his remaining officers emptied their guns into the attacking Yankees.

A desperate fight ensued with Johan and what remained of his squad hacking and stabbing into the Union ranks. Johan did not bother to count the number of men he dispatched at that moment, but encouraged his men to move forward and keep fighting. Every minute any of them could stay on their feet, the better chance Generals Jackson and Hill could escape.

Johan conceded that he had arrived at his last action as his men began to fall. Luckily, enough time had been bought for an entire Confederate infantry company to rush forward and push the Yankees away from Generals Jackson and Hill. Little did Johan know that General Hill, using his body as a shield for Jackson, would set the reconciliation between the two generals in motion.

As quickly as the fight had started, it ended. Knowing his primary responsibility was to protect General Jackson, Johan gathered

Sergeant McKay and the few remaining men and assisted their two battered generals.

***

Johan opened his eyes and realized he was back in General Lee's headquarters.

"General Jackson, I know your men are exhausted, but they must dig in tonight and prepare for tomorrow's onslaught. General Hill, how are your injuries?"

As General Hill began to stand, both Johan and General Heth arose to help him. "I have a godawful headache, Sir. But it is nothing compared to what many of our boys have experienced today."

Lee gave a satisfied nod and then looked at Johan, who was nursing his injuries. "Very well. If everyone can gather around the table," he gestured at the slightly burned table whose top held a new map. The greatest general of the Confederacy then waited patiently as his fatigued and injured officers gathered around the table.

"First," Lee pointed to a spot on the map, "General Jackson, your II Corps will dig in along the intersection of Plank Road and the Orange Turnpike. Hooker will want to retake this home for honor's sake, so make him pay dearly for that decision. While your Corps will take most of Hooker's attention, I will have my own surprise. McLaws and Anderson's divisions are en route from Fredericksburg, marching as fast as possible to take up positions here, just south of Orange Turnpike.

He waited a few moments while the men around him processed his plan. "Now, this will only leave General Early's division to cover our right flank at Fredericksburg. Facing them are Sedwick's entire XII Corps and perhaps additional reinforcements. Now, I understand this will be unlike the fight in December, and I have no intention of having Early face down an entire Corps. I have given orders to both Generals Early and Stuart. Early is to deploy part of his division as skirmishers and have the rest available for counterattacks when practicable. He is to perform a fighting retreat and not be overwhelmed. I have instructed General Stuart to assist General Early and strike the Yankees where vulnerable."

"Gentlemen, a great victory was won today. In fact, it might be the greatest victory our forces have ever achieved. But this battle is not over. It is my understanding that we have inflicted over 20,000 casualties on those people. General Hooker will want blood. Everything he has will be thrown at us tomorrow. I do not need to instruct any of you on how to dig defensive positions, but please ensure we can bring everything we have to bear for tomorrow. General Jackson, your Corps captured dozens of cannons today. Ensure that all are ready for the fight in the morning. And General Stuart," Lee gave something that resembled a smirk to the Commander of all cavalry forces for the Army of Northern Virginia, "reserve some of your men's finer exploits until the Yankees have decided to retire from the field."

"Why, General Lee, my men are always on their best behavior," answered Stuart theatrically. "Since the Yankees have been such gracious guests, I would only want to give them the proper send-off.

The meeting ended shortly afterward, and General Lee asked General Jackson and Johan to stay back. "General Jackson, I must commend you again for your actions today. And I must ask, how is the arm?"

Jackson shrugged, "It is a sprain of the left elbow and wrist—minor compared to other past injuries."

Lee nodded. "I am glad to hear you escaped what could have been far worse. You have injured your left arm, but you, General Jackson, act as my right arm. This army would not be the same without you.

Therefore, I must ask that tomorrow you take a more," Lee paused, "distant view of the action."

Not waiting for Jackson to respond, Lee addressed Johan, "Captain, Lutze, how have your injuries fared?"

"Well, General," Johan winced and rubbed his backside where shrapnel from an exploding shell had 'injured' him. "I think my pride suffered worse than my body."

Lee let out a rare laugh, "Captain Lutze, you and your kin from down on the bayou provide this army with a certain flavor that it would otherwise lack." He held out a hand with a folded paper and two major stars.

Johan's eyes widened when he saw what was in Lee's outstretched hand. "General Lee, I feel there are many more worthy than I to wear those stars."

Lee put the paper and stars in Johan's hand. "Son, what you did today to direct our forces through their picket line was enough for you to be promoted to Colonel. Saving General Jackson's life, I would make you a general for that. So, take this battlefield brevet promotion in stride. This war will not end tomorrow, and I can't put you back with your old brigade right now. So, humor me and serve this army by shadowing General Jackson tomorrow. It seems good fortune comes when you are in his presence."

Chapter 3

May 10, 1863, 10:00 AM, City of Washington, White House

"It's a catastrophe," said President Lincoln somberly.

Edward Stanton, Secretary of War, cut in, "Our losses were high, Mr. President. But we inflicted heavy losses on the rebels as well."

"We suffered over 30,000 casualties, Mr. Stanton. The rebels suffered under 10,000, probably closer to 8 or 9,000. Going by that math, I would have handily beaten Douglas for the Senate back in '58 if a win was for me, only to have a third as many votes as him."

General Halleck, General-in-Chief of the Armies of the United States, tried to restore peace to the conference. "It was a defeat—a bad one. However, Hooker did manage to recover whatever brains he had left after his concussion and extracted the Army of the Potomac from Lee's little trap. Our forces are now back on the north sides of the Rapidan and Rappahannock Rivers."

Secretary of State Seward asked, "What are we doing to replenish our forces and ensure Lee cannot move on Washington?"

Halleck was ready for the question, "The garrison for the city has been strengthened with a combination of Marines and 5,000 regulars. We are also mobilizing the state militias in Pennsylvania and New York. We are hoping to convert 7,500 from each state into regulars. So that is an immediate 15,000. We are also pulling forces from the Atlantic Seaboard. We will have to scale back our operations in the Carolinas, especially around Charleston. However, winding down those operations won't significantly impact our overall war effort. We can redeploy 10,000 to 15,000 troops immediately, with more available later if needed. So, more or less, we have immediate replacements for Hooker's losses at Chancellorsville without affecting any other theater of operations."

"So, it will not affect the Gulf Coast or Mississippi River Valley Campaigns?" Lincoln asked with eagerness in his voice.

"No," said Halleck confidently. "Chancellorsville was a disaster, but we have calculated our adjustments not to affect the Vicksburg and Port Hudson campaigns. Operations in middle Tennessee under General Rosecrans can also continue going forward."

Lincoln tapped his fingers on the table, "So we do some card shuffling and move forward."

May 10, 1863, 1:00 PM, Fredericksburg, Virginia

Every step his horse took caused him to grimace. So embarrassed by his condition, Johan pulled down his wide-brimmed officer's hat to cover his face better and make it difficult for anyone to recognize him. General Jackson's staff had proclaimed him a hero once again for saving Jackson's life a second day in a row on May 3rd. But that mattered little to Johan. He did not feel much like a hero for getting shot in the backside again.

The extra padding he had put in his pants did little to help, especially since he had injuries to both butt cheeks. He stood in his stirrups after a few strides on his borrowed mount. This decision only exacerbated his other injuries from the battle, making them more bothersome.

The Major's star on his collar made it easy for him to navigate through the crowded streets of Fredericksburg. Soldiers and citizens busied themselves rebuilding the town less than half a year after the last battle in this place.

Not too far away from here was where Johan had been captured, and his Northern odyssey in captivity had begun. He put that thought out of his head and went about finding General Hays, his former brigade commander of the Louisiana Tigers and his former employer in New Orleans before the War.

There was no luck in finding General Hays, but Johan did run into a few officers who greeted him with excitement and joy. Johan was not well known outside the 6th Louisiana, but most within the brigade respected his skill and bravery as a junior officer. Apparently, 'Buns of Providence and Steel' was his new nickname, courtesy of General Jackson's staff. And more than one old acquaintance greeted him with the moniker.

Unable to locate General Hays, Johan continued to his second objective. He found the large Episcopal church that had been converted into a hospital that cared for both the Confederate and Union wounded. Slowly dismounting, Johan handed his reins to a young boy dressed in a drummer boy's uniform and placed a coin in his hand.

Johan spoke in French, "This horse is not mine, son. So, do me a favor and hold on to it while I attend to my duties." Johan gestured to the church. "But," he held up another coin, "I will give you this when I return."

The boy smiled from ear to ear and answered in French, "Why, Major, sir, thank you! If you would like, I can go water and feed your mount while you attend your duties."

"Thank you, son. That sounds wonderful."

After watching the boy lead the horse away, Johan processed the scene within the churchyard and limped forward. Men in blue and gray with various injuries were sprawled all about the churchyard. Orderlies came to and fro, along with several townswomen providing aid and comfort to the wounded men.

Even though the battle for Chancellorsville had ended a week ago, this scene in front of the church reminded Johan how high the butcher's bill was, and in some ways, it was never-ending. He had heard from General Jackson himself that the Yankees' casualties were around 30,000. It shook Johan to his core that their foe could absorb that many losses in three days and still have an effective army almost twice the size of the Army of Northern Virginia.

After walking around the churchyard, he found the man he was looking for. In an area where wounded men were laid on the ground, staged in neat rows for either surgery or transport to another building, Johan approached an orderly wearing a blue Union Jacket.

"How is it going, Karl?" Johan asked sympathetically in German.

Wiping his face with a dirty sleeve, Karl Shultz looked in Johan's direction. "My, my. Excuse me, Major, if I do not salute you. My hands are full."

With a forced smile, Johan waved away the veiled insult from the man who had been like an older brother to him for the last several months. "Karl, if you have a moment, I want to talk with you."

Karl looked to the other orderly across from him, and the man shrugged. "Alright," Karl responded in a slightly more polite tone.

Though Karl was a prisoner, no one challenged him while leaving the churchyard since it was a Confederate officer who was pulling him away. They walked to a large oak tree that had seen better days, and Johan gestured for them to sit on some large logs left at the tree's base. Sitting gingerly, the young officer produced a small flask and offered it to Karl.

The German's eyes widened just enough for Johan to notice, and he gladly accepted and took a sip.

"Oh my," Karl said as he handed back the flask. "What you Rebs call whiskey can take the edge off."

Johan smiled at his friend, "How have they treated you three? I could not find Fredrick or Jacob."

"Better than I expected. The other two might be on a burial detail," Karl grimaced and quickly continued, "but we are getting fair treatment compared to what some of the other prisoners are facing. They are at least feeding us as well as they can."

"I am glad to hear that. Karl, I am sorry for how things have gone for you three. I regret how long I misled you, for you have truly been a friend. The way I captured your picket, I only did that so the three of you could not get hurt."

Karl softened his tone, "I'm still mad as hell at you, but I appreciate what could have been our fate. How did you fare in the fighting? It seems you are moving a bit slowly."

"I would say my pride has suffered more. Shrapnel hit me in the backside on two different occasions."

"So, you are the one they say has the buns of steel?" Laughed Karl.

The tension was broken, and they chatted for a few more minutes. "Well," said Karl somberly. "I think I've taken a long enough break. I guess I will see you around, Major."

Johan touched Karl's shoulder, "Karl, listen to me. I'm getting shipped out to Richmond tomorrow to meet with President Davis. Given how things have transpired here, I may be able to call in some favors. Some opportunities may be open to three loyal Germans who know how to fight."

The confusion and then intrigue in Karl's eyes were all Johan needed. He left his friend to attend his duties and went inside the church. Inside was more organized chaos, and he politely approached an older woman holding linens.

“Excuse me, ma'am,” he said as he bowed slightly. I was informed that Corporal Andre Breaux was housed here. He is with the 6th Louisiana Infantry.”

The woman momentarily contemplated, “Major, I think if he is here, he will be bedded down by the altar.”

Johan thanked the woman and quickly strode down an aisle, taking him to almost the foot of the altar. And there, lying in a bed with one arm and leg bandaged and propped up, was a man with darker hair than Johan, though his face was similar enough to Johan’s that there was no doubt that Andre Breaux was his cousin.

The bored look on Andre’s face quickly went away when he recognized the man standing in front of him. “Well, I’ll be if it is not my dear familial relation. Tell me, Johan, were you bending over when the Yankees decided to shoot you in the ass again? Haha.”

Luckily, the whiskers on his face helped hide the redness he felt, and Johan grabbed a short chair and pulled it up next to Andre. “They felt they wanted another crack at it since they had not gotten it right the first time. But how did you hear about that?”

“Johan, you are the talk of the entire brigade. I know you did not serve with us during the battle, but we will gladly take the credit for your exploits.”

“It's good to see how my memory lives on in the brigade.” Johan let out a laugh. “But Andre, you were still a sergeant when I left for my… sabbatical up North in December. Who did you piss off this time? And what on earth put you in this?” he gestured at the semi-body cast Andre was in.

“Where to start? There was a green lieutenant who ordered us to do something stupid. He was trying to impress his daddy or some rich socialite in Richmond. The pup was so stupid I didn’t bother to learn his name because you know what happens to dumb officers.”

“They die,” agreed Johan.

"Exactly. Well, I told him to go pound rocks, and this mule that was looking really lonely. Well, what do you know, he didn't like that much. His head got blown off not too long after, but it was already too late."

"I wouldn't expect anything different from you, Andre. But, again, what about…"

"Oh, it was during one of our 'tactical withdrawals' on May 3rd. That's when our fearless lieutenant got his head blown off trying to be a hero. And like our company was going to stop a whole goddamn Yankee Corps. Anyway, I twisted my ankle pretty badly and wrenched my shoulder so that I couldn't even lift my arm above my head. The surgeon at some point mentioned amputation for some dumb reason, and that's when I pulled out my bowie knife and told him two could play at that game."

"That doctor must have been as confused as you, Andre. How long will you be laid up?

"My ankle already feels a lot better. This shoulder, though, it's my left arm at least, but they wanted to keep an eye on me in case of infection and all that. I can walk around pretty much all I want with just some pain. My shoulder will keep me from active duty for a while, though."

"That's understandable. I am headed for Richmond tomorrow to meet with Uncle Jeff."

"You don't say," Andre said with a twinkle in his eye. "Not everyone can say that their godfather is the President."

"Don't say that out loud," Johan shushed Andre. "I don't think I will be reassigned back to the 6th; General Jackson told me as much. I've been attached to his staff for the last week, but now that the battle is over, they mostly have me running errands and sending messages. I think when I go to Richmond, there will be a new assignment for me."

Andre understood what Johan said, "And you might need a good Sergeant to tag along with you."

Johan chuckled as he realized how much he had missed Andre's company.

"Oh, and I almost forgot," said Andre sheepishly. "Jacques joined the regiment at the beginning of the year."

Johan snapped his head back and looked at Andre, "What! He is 15!"

"Johan, you are forgetting that your baby brother just turned 16 and is an excellent shot. He has this way of effectively and efficiently…shooting Yankee officers."

Chapter 4

May 17, 1863, 9:30 PM,
Richmond, VA, Confederate White House

President Davis seethed angrily as he paced his office. He was tired, but he could not rest after the news he had just received. The Confederacy had just achieved its most significant victory at the beginning of the month at Chancellorsville. Now, they were facing the real possibility of catastrophe in the West, along the Mississippi at Vicksburg.

On May 14th, Grant and his army attacked General Johnston and his forces at Jackson, Mississippi, and soundly defeated the Confederates. But it was more than just a military defeat; Jackson was now another state capital that had fallen into Yankee hands. And though it was abandoned soon after by Grant's army, a large part of Jackson had been burned to the ground. Johnston had given his usual excuses, and it was the final straw for Davis. He decided to replace General Johnston with General Beauregard to command all Confederate forces in the Mississippi/Western Department. But to make matters worse, before Davis could even notify Johnston that he was to be relieved of command, another defeat had been suffered by Pemberton's Army of Mississippi at the Battle of Champion Hill.

Vicksburg was under siege. If nothing radical were done, Vicksburg would fall, and the Confederacy would be split in two, making the war that much more challenging to win.

Davis rang one of the wall bells, and a black servant entered the Presidential Study. "Yes, Mr. President," the refined black gentleman asked, "how may I be of service?"

"Thomas, please go fetch me, Colonel Lutze. He will still be up working. Tell him it is urgent."

"Yes, Mr. President. Right away."

A short time later, Johan entered the room. He was groomed and shaved and sporting a brand-new officer's gray uniform. "You asked for me, Uncle Jefferson."

Davis handed Johan the dispatches he had just looked over. "Read these."

"This is bad," Johan stated when he finished reading.

"The conference with General Lee's staff and my cabinet is still scheduled for tomorrow. I need you to update your report so that we can factor in how we will respond to this catastrophe." Davis waited as Johan reread the dispatches and handed them back. "I know how much time you have devoted to your report, but we must consider this before tomorrow's meeting."

Johan agreed, "No worries, Uncle Jefferson. "My report will be ready."

***

May 18, 1863, 12:00 AM, Confederate White House

The memory of the heated arguments of the last two hours between Johan and the President still hung in the room. Johan had volunteered for Andre to be his personal secretary, but because he could not be on active duty, Andre had no choice but to accept. By being with Johan almost every waking minute of the day, he had a front-row seat to Johan's new "ideas" and Uncle Jefferson's anger at many of them.

Andre sat uncomfortably at Johan's desk while his friend paced the room. Andre felt he would be on at least easy duty with his left arm in a sling. Well, when your cousin's godfather is the goddamn president, that does change things, he thought. With his good hand feeling his collar, Andre could not believe he had been promoted to

First Lieutenant. The highest rank he had ever held was Master Sergeant, and Andre's big mouth had assured him that any promotion he received was always temporary. But hell, something momentous had to be happening if his past indiscretions were overlooked and he was made a junior officer, no questions asked.

"Are you ready, Andre?" asked Johan in an exasperated voice.

"Sorry," Andre rubbed his eyes with his good hand. "Must have drifted off." He picked up the ink pen and dipped it in the ink well. "Where do you want me to start?"

Johan stopped pacing momentarily to look out a window into the darkness of the night. "Where do you think?" He gave Andre a seditious smile. "Let's rewrite the section about enlisting negros into the army."

"Alright", thought Andre. "It's your hide on the line."

Johan began again, oblivious to Andre or the servant Thomas entering the room to replace their empty water pitcher. "This report recommends that a bill be presented to Congress authorizing the enlistment of Confederate Negros. As an incentive, Negro soldiers will be given emancipation upon honorable completion of their enlistment as well as the emancipation of their families."

Letting out a breath, Andre finished writing, "This will be interesting tomorrow."

***

Thomas froze when he heard the young officer standing by the window repeat what he had said to President Davis earlier that evening. Hearing the man mention Negro enlistments and emancipation once, he could have blown off as a young man trying to be bold and challenge the President. But on hearing the conviction in this young man's strange accent, Thomas knew the young officer meant every word he spoke.

Unsure of how he felt, Thomas quickly finished his tasks and made his way to the door as quietly as a house negro was supposed to. As he reached the door, the young officer was still dictating his words to the other young officer at the table.

Not wanting to interrupt, Thomas looked to the young man at the table to ask silently if these two strange young men required anything else. The man with his left arm in a sling looked up to him, having put his pen down and raised a glass of water, silently thanking Thomas.

Closing the door quietly behind himself, Thomas walked down the hall, contemplating the look of sincere gratitude the injured officer had given him, along with the words of the other young man. If more white men looked at him and his people the way those two young officers did, things were going to change. Thoughts raced through Thomas's mind of the possibilities for his people and family, and what it meant to live in the Confederacy.

May 18, 1863, 9:30 AM, Richmond, VA, Confederate White House

For such a momentous gathering, Johan longed to immortalize it, whether through a painting or a photograph. The giants of the Confederacy were assembled in the Presidential Study. President Davis presided over the session, with Generals Lee, Jackson, Longstreet, Stuart, Secretary of State Judah Benjamin, and Secretary of War James Seddon in attendance.

Positioned in a corner a few paces from President Davis's side, Johan was acutely aware that this meeting held the fate of the Confederacy in its hands. He vowed to exert every ounce of his influence to secure the Confederacy's independence. Uncertain that his ideas and potential criticisms would be well-received, he steeled himself for the task.

The room was pregnant with anticipation as President Davis cleared his throat. The sound reverberated, and the room was enveloped in a tense silence. “Gentlemen, I extend my deepest gratitude for your unwavering service to the Confederacy. These past few years have tested us all, but our mission is far from over. With this meeting, we lay the groundwork for our people's independence, a task I approach with unwavering conviction.”

All the men present murmured their agreement and waited for President Davis to move the conference along. General Longstreet, known for his stoicism, surprised the room by turning to President Davis and asking about his family. The tension dissipated as the two men exchanged a few friendly words. Johan, witnessing this moment, felt a glimmer of hope. He understood the importance of fostering such relationships amid war and silently urged his godfather to continue this practice. Additionally, the young colonel surmised that General Lee had encouraged Longstreet to bury the hatchet with President Davis and end the dispute that the two men had with one another. Knowing both men could harbor a grudge for the slightest offense, Johan wondered if the whole feud between the two men was based more on pride than anything else.

After a few moments, General Lee delivered his report on the Battle of Chancellorsville, the current state of the Army of Northern Virginia, and his assessment of the Army of the Potomac. The room was filled with a palpable sense of awe and admiration, and well-deserved praise was heaped upon Generals Jackson and Hill for their conduct during the battle. Their stunning victory was still fresh in everyone's minds, profoundly impacting the atmosphere.

Lee’s report then evolved into his proposed strategy for the future. Johan had read much of the correspondence between Lee and Uncle

Jefferson. He was not surprised that Lee's proposal entailed a significant reorganization of the Army of Northern Virginia, a move that could potentially reshape the course of this war. The plan involved transforming the existing two Corps into three. General Longstreet would continue to lead the 1st Corps, while General Jackson's 2nd Corps would be split into two. Returning to active duty after his severe wounding and leg amputation at Second Manassas, General Ewell would take command of the newly formed 3rd Corps. But what Lee had in mind was modifying the entire structure of the army. Each Corps would be rounded out to 20,000 men, facilitated by both Longstreet and Jackson handing over certain brigades to Ewell and by bringing in additional brigades from the Carolinas.

General Lee's vision was not merely a desire but a pressing necessity for Confederate victory. He proposed a bold move to force a decisive battle on Northern soil. This strategic maneuver not only promised relief to Pemberton's besieged men at Vicksburg, moving the fighting out of worn-torn Virginia, but also could compel the North to seek peace. The urgency in General Lee's voice was palpable, reflecting his shared desire with all present to end the war as swiftly as possible.

Silence fell upon the room when Lee finished speaking. President Davis looked to all the men seated at the table and asked if anyone had anything else to add. Taking a sip of water from his glass, he continued the meeting, "General Lee, on behalf of this government, I wish to give you my heartfelt thanks for your devotion to our cause. Without your audacity and fortitude, we would not be in the position we find ourselves in today."

Pausing, Davis looked to Johan, then back to the table, and continued, "There is no doubt in my mind that we must seize the initiative. But there are other considerations. Gentlemen, early this morning, copies of Colonel Lutze's report were made available for all of you to read and become familiar with." Davis raised his hands slightly to prevent several generals from speaking up, "To be clear, this report is not gospel, but I do feel that the Colonel, who most of you know by this point, is my godson, has brought several important issues to the forefront. This report is the best strategic assessment I have seen to date. Though I have some misgivings, which Lieutenant Breaux and the household servants can attest to, I feel it is best to allow the newest Colonel in the Confederacy to explain and defend his work."

Chapter 5

May 18, 1863, 10:00 AM,
Richmond, VA, Confederate White House

With the confidence in his smile he did not feel, a trait he had mastered at the Louisiana Military Academy before the war, Johan stood and walked to the large map of the Confederacy on the wall.

Johan collected his thoughts with a humble smile that belied his true feelings. Addressing the esteemed men gathered before him, he began, "I am deeply grateful, Mr. President, for this opportunity to speak. I also extend my thanks to Secretaries Benjamin and Seddon for their presence at this historic meeting. And to Generals Lee, Jackson, Longstreet, and Stuart, I am honored that you value the perspective of a newly appointed Colonel still finding his way."

Most of the men acknowledged Johan's lack of hubris and focused their attention on the president's godson. "As the President mentioned, my report was circulated before this meeting. And let me be the first to say," and Johan gave a sheepish grin, "that I did take advantage of my relationship with the President. That is, I pushed forward several ideas that others would not have the leverage to do so, and some that even the president would disagree with."

General Stuart lightly elbowed General Jackson, "I say, Thomas, do you think I could borrow some of your boys from the bayou state?" He winked at Johan and said loud enough for the whole room to hear, "If I had a handful of these mad Louisiana Tigers, I could ride straight to the Canadian border and back!"

Most of the tension left Johan with General Stuart's compliment, and he continued, "But let me begin with our strategic situation. First," he pointed to an area north of Richmond on the map, "Little over two weeks ago, the Army of Northern Virginia routed the Army of the Potomac at Chancellorsville. It is estimated that the Yankees suffered some 30,000 casualties and that the III and XI Corps were virtually annihilated. Our casualties were just under 9,000. These factors have left us in a position to take the offensive into Northern territory. Second, in middle Tennessee, General Bragg and the Army of Tennessee are holding the line against General Rosecrans and his forces around 30 miles Southeast of Nashville, for now."

Johan placed his pointer directly on Vicksburg. "It is without a doubt that Vicksburg is our most pressing strategic issue now. General Pemberton has roughly 30,000 men within the city facing down General Grant. Vicksburg is surrounded and cut off by General Grant's army. General Johnson was in command of the Army of Relief and the Western Department; however, following the events in Jackson, he has been replaced by General Beauregard. The combined strength of Beauregard and Pemberton should be approaching 75,000 men, almost matching Grant's strength. And here is where an opportunity presents itself, for it has been quite infrequent in this war that our numbers came close to matching the enemy's."

Looking around the room, Johan checked whether everyone present was following him.

General Jackson spoke, "Colonel Lutze, what you have stated is correct, but all these facts are well known to those gathered here. I assume you have a point that you are trying to make."

"Yes, General Jackson. I do." Johan looked to President Davis and pushed forward, knowing this would be his last chance to give an opinion in a setting like this: "If the Confederacy is to win this war, our strategy must change. Our territory is too vast, and our numbers too small, to defend every inch of land. I know firsthand from the president the pressure he faces to respond to every incursion. We no longer have the manpower to do this."

"The Union armies in the field are what we must focus our efforts on. I have seen reports from the Carolinas that most Yankee forces have evacuated via steamer back north. This evacuation can only mean that Mr. Lincoln and his cronies are stripping forces from non-essential theaters and sending them to reinforce the City of Washington and the Army of the Potomac. But what if we leaned into this? What if instead of the Yankees having the forces necessary to launch attacks all along our borders and waterways, what if they were forced to react to our forces in Mississippi and Virginia?"

"Colonel Lutz," General Longstreet spoke in a polite voice. "A short time ago, I had suggested that we focus our forces on Kentucky to liberate the state and threaten Ohio. With a large Confederate Army threatening to cut Union territory in half, I suggested that this would force my old friend, U. S. Grant, to abandon his campaign for Vicksburg. Following Generals Lee and Jackson's victory at Chancellorsville, my thinking has now changed in light of our new strategic situation. I do favor a campaign in Maryland and Pennsylvania under specific parameters."

Longstreet paused and looked around the room, and, with no interruptions, continued, "I read your report, Colonel. I found parts intriguing but lacking in detail. This is your chance to win us over and provide those missing details."

Johan rose to the occasion, "Thank you, General Longstreet." With a deep breath, Johan rolled into the lecture he had so furiously practiced, "Let me begin with a lesson I learned from my time in the military academies of France and Louisiana. I know my time does not compare with an education from West Point," Johan grinned, knowing all four generals had attended the U.S. Military Academy and that, at one point, General Lee had been its commandant. "Our friend General McClelland fashions himself the Napoleon of the West, and in New Orleans, streets such as Jena and Austerlitz commemorate the French Emperor's greatest victories. But what my francophone relatives in Louisiana would hate to hear is that Napoleon himself acknowledged Fredrick the Great was the better general."

Johan walked to another wall where servant Thomas had attached an enlarged map of Europe. With the pointer stick, he circled the kingdom of Prussia. "100 years ago, Frederick the Great found himself in a situation similar yet different from our own. While the British were supposed 'allies,' Prussia was surrounded and at war with France, Austria, Russia, and Sweden. In such a dire predicament, most believed Prussia would be conquered and dismembered. But Prussia was never defeated, and King Fredrick never lost a battle. How did small Prussia, practically alone, take on all the major continental powers of Europe and win?

The room was silent as everyone focused their attention on Johan. General Lee, practically the patron saint of the Confederacy, bore down on Johan with his gaze as he walked back to the map of North America. "We have no allies presently. France and Britain tiptoe around the issue, waiting for us to secure victory before committing to our cause. But we have our own Fredrick to ensure victory."

"First, we will challenge Grant at Vicksburg. Can we lift the siege? For a time, maybe. But we will bleed Grant's army and have his campaign absorb the men and material at such a rate that the Yankees will be too slow to react to our right hook."

Johan circled Vicksburg. "General Longstreet, Vicksburg will be a static campaign that the North will throw everything at to split the Confederacy in half. Our goal in Vicksburg would be to either destroy Grant and his army or bleed it so severely that it would take months for it to be operational again if Vicksburg were to fall. And instead of defending Vicksburg until the last man, when defending the city is no longer feasible, we will evacuate with our army intact, alive, and ready for the next battle."

The pointer moved to middle Tennessee and then to Virginia. "General Bragg will hold the line in middle Tennessee while the crippling blow is thrown in the East. Never afraid of his own shadow, Frederick the Great used speed, agility, misdirection, and daring to win his victories." Johan smiled, "I can think of a few Southern generals who operate along those lines."

"General Lee has proposed reorganizing the army of Northern Virginia from two corps to three. General Longstreet would retain command of I Corps, while II Corps would be split between Generals Jackson and Ewell."

Johan paused for effect, "But I must disagree with General Lee at this juncture, for his reorganization does not go far enough. It must be with certain objectives in mind if we are to reorganize the Army of Northern Virginia."

General Lee interrupted Johan's lecture for the first time. "What would your organization and objectives look like, Colonel Lutze?" Johan did not miss the hardness in General Lee's voice, for few men in the Confederacy would have challenged Lee openly. But Johan did not take General Lee's harshness personally. Instead, he treated it like an exam question back at the military academy.

"We make the Yankees react to us, General Lee. My reorganization would be as follows: First, General Pickett's division from General Longstreet's I Corps is replaced by reinforcements from the Carolinas and two of his brigades that were detached for a secondary police assignment in Virginia. Next, II Corps is split into II and III Corps, with Generals Ewell and Hill in command." Johan smiled as he continued, "Since the threat to the lower Atlantic seaboard has been greatly reduced, an additional 18 to 20,000 troops can be transferred from the Carolinas to Virginia to form IV Corps, with General Joseph Johnson in command."

Murmurs broke out in the room as the men present took in Johan's proposal. Johan looked to General Jackson and, with a wink, went in for the conclusion of the lecture, "General Lee, I further propose that the Army of Northern Virginia be split into effectively two independent forces, or, dare I say, wings, with II and III Corps under the overall command of General Jackson, while I and IV fall under General Longstreet and you, Sir."

Johan spoke confidently, leading the pointer stick through the Shenandoah Valley on the map. "General Jackson will lead II and III Corps through the Shenandoah Valley, across the panhandle of Maryland, and into Pennsylvania. With General Stuart's cavalry as a screen, General Jackson's army would march quickly and give every appearance of threatening Harrisburg. Instead, General Jackson's army would seize Gettysburg, Pennsylvania, and dig in. I've studied maps of the area, and Gettysburg has no fewer than 11 roads converging on it, plus a railroad; thus, it acts as a wheel, and if our forces seize it, it jeopardizes the entire Union effort in the East. The topography would allow II and III Corps to build a natural fortress that the Army of the Potomac would pay dearly in blood attempting to take back."

"And while the Army of the Potomac is occupied with General Jackson."

"I and IV Corps would slip in between the Army of the Potomac and Washington," General Longstreet grinned.

The room fell silent as Johan's strategy became clear. "Gentlemen," cautioned Johan, "understand the objective I have laid out before you. It is a risky endeavor to split the army in half against a superior foe. But it is not what the Yankees expect, and they would panic, having been defeated on their own soil and having their main army cut off from the capital. It could cause them to make some hasty and unwise decisions."

"General Lee," stated President Davis, "obviously, this is the outline of a campaign. If we move forward with this, your blessing, organization, and leadership would be required."

Lee leaned back in his chair and grinned at Johan. "Colonel, I must say it took some imagination and daring to devise this plan, and perhaps some of my correspondence with the President made its way to your desk. There are many factors to consider and details to work out, but you have my attention. If we were to successfully either severely defeat the Army of the Potomac or outright destroy it, what next? Washington, Philadelphia? This has been on my mind since the beginning of the year. What would be the ultimate objective if we were to invade Northern Territory? I know you spent some time as an unwilling guest of our foe. What did you glean from that experience?"

Memories flooded Johan's mind, but he pushed them back and considered General Lee's question. "General Lee, my time as a prisoner of war up north has colored my outlook on the war. I was able to escape captivity and pass myself off as a German immigrant only because hundreds arrive every day, just in New York Harbor. Throw in the other nationalities of Europe that flood Northern ports every day, and it gives Mr. Lincoln a virtually unlimited supply of manpower. Any victory we achieve must not only militarily cripple the Union but also put political pressure on the Lincoln administration."

"If we can trap and destroy the Army of the Potomac, I would recommend focusing our efforts afterward on securing Maryland, including seizing Baltimore and Annapolis. However, I would not recommend attacking Washington after passing through that city earlier this year. It is a virtual fortress, and even if we were to take the city, the cost would be one we could not afford after gaining so little. Instead, I would allow Mr. Lincoln to reinforce the city and assign a detachment from our army to surround Washington and tie down as many Union forces as possible. If we build the proper entrenchments, 10,000 troops could tie down 50-60,000 Union forces. The more troops in Washington, the fewer will oppose us in the open field."

General Stuart slapped his hand on the table and patted General Jackson on the shoulder, “Thomas, I must revise my opinion of Colonel Lutze. His plan is madness.” The cavalier laughed, “This boy’s plan is mad. It is either pure mad genius or a path to our doom. I must admit, though, it will be a lot of fun either way!”

Chapter 6

May 18, 1863, 6:00 PM,
Richmond, VA, Confederate White House

Varina Davis's modest reception in the presidential mansion fondly reminded Johan of the peaceful time before the war. With both of his parents deceased, his father having been mortally wounded at the Battle of Shiloh, and his mother dying after a brief sickness from yellow fever, this reception reminded Johan of how much Aunt Varina had been like a mother to him during his childhood.

Across the room stood General Longstreet and his wife Louise, who were talking amiably with General Jackson and Secretary Benjamin. Johan could not help but think of the tragedy that had befallen the Longstreet family, having lost three of their four children the previous year. The first time Johan saw any inkling of joy returning to General Longstreet's eyes was tonight. General Jackson would always have Johan's unending loyalty, but the young colonel knew he would gladly follow Ole' Pete into battle.

"It's almost like being back home and attending your parents' parties," said Andre as he shoved some delicacy into his mouth in a less-than-sophisticated way. "The pride of the Confederacy," Andre said with no excitement.

"They are better than anything the North has," Johan said confidently.

"For better or worse, they are ours, I suppose. How many rounds do I have to make with you?"

Johan laughed. "I knew there was a reason you were so dismissive. Well, we do need to say hello to everyone at the very least; it's the polite thing to do."

"At least we have the excuse of needing to catch a train." Andre paused and produced a pocket watch, something Johan was unaware of that he had. "Don't gape at me like that, Johan. I pilfered this here watch fair and squared off a dead Yankee who had no more need of it."

"I can tell a hand-crafted German watch when I see one. That thing is worth almost $300. That's double what you make in a year."

"And they said Paul was the smartest of the Lutze children." Andre laughed when he saw Johan's look on his face. "Now, don't you worry. We have a thousand-mile train ride, and I have more where that came from.

"Andre, one day you are going to piss off a general royally, and not even the grace of God will save you. But in the meantime, we have already spoken to Longstreet, Ewell, and Jackson. Let's give this another hour to exchange pleasantries with General Lee, Mrs. Lee, and Uncle Jeff. Then, we grab our gear and head to the train station.

"Sounds like a deal," Andre agreed.

The two young officers were soon entrapped by Aunt Varina, who introduced them to Mary Anna Jackson, General Jackson's wife, and their daughter Julia.

"I have heard so much about you, Louisiana boys," Mrs. Jackson said in a sweet voice as she swayed her less-than-year-old child back and forth. "And most of all, you, Colonel Lutze. Your actions saved my husband and have allowed him to hold his daughter and me in an embrace once again."

The emotion in Mrs. Jackson's voice touched Johan deeply. "Your words mean much to me, Mrs. Jackson. I have served under your husband in almost every battle I have fought, and I would gladly risk my life," he paused to smile, "or my pride again to keep him safe."

The evening wore on, and after socializing more, Andre looked at Johan and motioned to his watch. Understanding, Johan led Andre out of the main ballroom. As they were making their way to their shared quarters, Generals Lee, Jackson, Longstreet, and Secretary Benjamin met the two of them in the hall.

General Lee spoke first, “Colonel Lutze, Lieutenant Breaux, could you lead us to your quarters so we can discuss some matters privately?”

Johan knew that General Lee was essentially giving him an order, and with Andre leading the way, they led the small contingent to the room they had called home for the last few days.

As Andre opened the bedroom door, he looked at Johan and said softly, “I’m glad we tidied up before dinner.”

Once all the men were inside the bedroom, General Longstreet closed the door and looked at Johan and Andre. “Well, boys, Colonel Lutze had some intriguing ideas this morning.”

General Lee’s voice then filled the room. “Colonel Lutze, I will make this brief since you and Lieutenant Breaux have a train to catch. Do you still have your repeating rifle available?”

Thinking he knew what General Lee was getting at, Johan walked to his bed and pulled out the rifle that had been secured with his other luggage. Holding it out for all his audience to see, Johan responded to General Lee, “Sir, this is the Spencer Repeating Rifle that I obtained while attached to General Jackson’s staff.”

“What do you think about the rifle, Colonel? I have heard several accounts of men seeing it in action, including General Jackson,” he motioned.

“Well, Sir, I became aware of this type of rifle last year and even faced down some Yankees armed with these. But once I had escaped captivity and was enlisted in the Northern Army, I saw this rifle firsthand and even witnessed some troopers at target practice. I put this rifle to good use at Chancellorsville. It is no more complicated to operate than a muzzle-loading Springfield or Enfield. In fact,” he pulled out a tubular magazine from his luggage and held out the rifle, "the weapon is loaded by inserting this seven-round magazine into the stock. A well-trained soldier could fire this entire magazine, and at the same time, that man could fire one or two shots from a muzzle-loader."

General Jackson spoke next, "I can attest to that. There was a unit of Yankee sharpshooters armed with these rifles who were a particularly nasty bunch. We destroyed them with surprise and overwhelming force, but I can see that if they had had time to erect defenses, they could have caused much harm to our forces. And I saw how the Colonel put this weapon to excellent use during the battle."

"Colonel," General Lee spoke once more, "our forces currently are at parity regarding small arms with most of the Northern army. But I understand that Mr. Lincoln's factories are producing ever more of the rifle that you now hold. Our nation cannot produce these rifles, but we have captured several hundred from the field at Chancellorsville and many thousands of rounds of ammunition. What would be your recommendation to employ these rifles within the Army of Northern Virginia?"

Johan knew that his audience must have come to their own conclusions before this discussion, but they wanted to hear his opinion on the matter. "Well, General Lee, keeping logistics and supply in mind, I would follow the example of the Yankees and outfit one or two specialized units with these rifles. In my own experience, one man can cause much devastation, especially when he can fire at near point-blank range at massed troops. Entrench the men armed with these rifles; a single brigade could produce the firepower near to what a division with muzzleloaders could do."

May 18, 1863, 9:00 PM, Main Richmond Train Station

Andre nestled onto his bench seat on the train and grinned at Johan, who sat across from him. "You know, I can order you not to enjoy all this so much."

"Why, Colonel," Andre said mischievously, "I always enjoy being in your company, especially when you, not I, are the object of someone else's ire."

Johan inhaled deeply on his cigar, then breathed, "I knew Uncle Jeff and General Beauregard had their differences. But hell, the fact that General Beauregard is being given a hand-picked staff that speaks French by Uncle Jeff will most certainly rub the General the wrong way."

Andre leaned back and pulled his hat over his eyes. "Just be honest with him. It seemed to win over everyone here in Virginia." Without another word, Andre was asleep in a few moments.

Johan had always wondered how his cousin could fall asleep upon command and paid no mind as Andre let out soft snores. For a few minutes, he contemplated how much his life had changed in just under three weeks. Taking out a leather-bound journal, Johan jotted down a few pages of notes. There would be some expected awkwardness with General Beauregard for sure, but Johan wanted there to be no doubt about his loyalty. Johan was here to assist General Beauregard and serve as a valued member of his staff, not as a spy for President Davis.

Satisfied with his work, Johan stood and opened the compartment door to the narrow hall. Karl was seated next to the door with his back to the wall. Though he looked asleep, he quickly stood when Johan entered the hall.

"There is no need to do that," Johan motioned as Karl stood.

"No, Colonel, it is better for me to stand. Keeps me from getting too sleepy at my post."

Johan ignored the veiled dig. There was still a fair amount of awkwardness between him and his companions from XI Corps. Though the whole business at Chancellorsville was in the past and Johan had kept his word about the treatment his friends would receive, the three Germans were officially traitors to the Union, each of them now wearing Confederate gray.

"Neither of y'all spoke to anyone?" Johan asked Karl.

"Nein. Frederick, but especially Jacob, has barely spoken, even to me. Granted, their English is lacking, but I am glad I do not have to stress about that now."

With an outstretched hand, Johan offered Karl a cigar. Briefly considering, Karl accepted the gift and followed Johan to a window that opened onto the rapidly passing countryside. Lighting his cigar, Karl silently stood with Johan as the train traveled to their destination.

Karl broke the silence, "You still not going to tell us where we are going, Colonel?"

Johan smiled back, raising an eyebrow, "Not yet, my friend. I know the three of you have been kept in the dark about all of this; it's just how it will have to be for a bit longer. Too often in this war, highly secret information has reached the enemy just in time for them to thwart carefully orchestrated plans. No, we must use caution."

There was more silence between the two men, and Karl changed the direction of his questioning. "Well, I know we are heading south, not north, at the very least. Perhaps we will travel to the Carolinas, Charleston, maybe? I know before Chancellorsville, there was much fighting in the area."

"Karl, Karl. If you keep this up, they might just be forced to promote you past corporal. Anyway, when does Jacob take the watch?"

After some quick accounting, Karl responded, “He should be coming up in thirty minutes, but I think I will give him an additional half hour. They looked utterly exhausted, and I hoped they would be rested when we reached our destination.”

They spoke for a few more minutes, and Johan excused himself and returned to his private compartment with Andre. The man was snoring softly, and Johan quietly took the opportunity to sit down and quietly study several reports and maps that he had packed in his travel case. After some time, Johan packed away his papers and became lost in the moonlight that flowed into their compartment.

He could put on a good show for the world to see, but the war and all its accompanying stress had worn him down to his soul. The good fortune he ran into at Chancellorsville had somewhat revived his spirits, but the South's predicament was still uncertain. Chancellorsville had been an unprecedented victory, but it wasn’t enough to win the war. In fact, it could be argued that, until the last several weeks, the South was losing ground in all theaters except Virginia. So that was why they were to rendezvous with General Beauregard and head to the swamps and hills of Mississippi.

May 19, 1863, 3 PM, Columbia RR Depot, Columbia, S.C.

General Pierre Gustave Toutant-Beauregard stood annoyed and ramrod straight on the passenger platform, waiting for the locomotive to come to a complete stop. His black servant, Elijah, a young man of 20 whose services Beauregard had acquired in Charleston, stood several feet to the side and behind the general. The journey by train from Charleston to Atlanta had been tedious and bothersome on the decaying rail network of the Confederacy. And Beauregard looked like he had walked the distance rather than ridden the train.

But he was the general who had given the Confederacy its first taste of victory with the surrender of Fort Sumter and the first Battle of Manassas. Then, his star had begun to lose its shine in the night sky. Various disputes with General Joseph Johnston led to his transfer out west as second in command to Albert Sydney Johnson's Army of the West. And then there was Shiloh and Corinth. After the evacuation of Corinth, with his health failing and a complete breakdown in his relationship with President Davis, Beauregard thought that his military career could have come to an end.

Almost as a punishment, he was transferred to Charleston to oversee the coastal defenses of South Carolina, Georgia, and Florida. And he had done well. Steadily, Charleston's defenses were built up, and it had even repelled several Union attacks on the surrounding area. All the skirmishes and battles, if they could be called so, were small affairs and almost always involved Beauregard being on the defensive.

Then, not even two weeks ago, around May 8, Beauregard was informed of large movements of Union troops around Charleston. Initially, he believed a massive attack was about to commence. In a near panic, he hurriedly called up all his available units and began preparations for the Union attack that had been planned for Charleston for two years. But the attack never came, and Beauregard wanted to kick himself when reports came in from his cavalry that, indeed, many Yankee warships were in the area. Further still, they were taking away blue-bellied troops, not disembarking them.

It was simple. Back in Virginia, Lee and Jackson had once again mauled the Army of the Potomac, but at a scale that shocked even the proud Beauregard. In roughly three days of combat, 30,000 Union casualties were reported. How could that Yankee army absorb so many losses and still be a coherent/ effective fighting force? Pull forces from non-essential theaters and sail them back as fast as possible, reinforcing what was left of the army of the Potomac before Lee could slaughter another 1/5 of the army or worse.

Beauregard agreed with the reasoning behind the withdrawal. He would have done the same thing if he were in Lincoln's shoes. However, this massive withdrawal of Union forces presented an opportunity he would not pass up, especially since he had called up all his available units, which were ready for a fight.

At dawn on May 10, with nearly 10,000 gray and butternut-clad troops assembled and hidden over miles of territory, Beauregard attacked several preselected Union positions. He knew he could not bag the entirety of the Union force being evacuated, and that some stay-behind forces would remain. Therefore, that was not his goal. The objective, instead, was a limited attack to incite chaos within the Union lines and the destruction and capture of as many supplies as possible.

Beauregard was already popular in South Carolina, but his final victory on May 10 forever immortalized him among Charleston's citizens. Due to the complete surprise of the Confederate attack, in half a day of fighting, his troops inflicted over 1,000 casualties on the Yankees and captured another 700. Additionally, one transport ship had been sunk by artillery he had personally sighted, while another had been badly damaged, and another outright captured with 200 blue-bellied Yankee infantrymen aboard. Around $100,000 worth of supplies were also captured, including rifles and ammunition, uniforms, and foodstuffs. This victory would not win the war for the Confederacy, but it certainly improved the morale of his troops and the citizens of Charleston and the surrounding coastal areas.

Then, President Davis sent a message without mentioning his victory, stating that he had been relieved of his command and would catch a train without delay to head to Atlanta to assume command of an important theater of operations. The realization hit the general that President Davis had decided his talents were better served elsewhere and that there could be no doubt he would be given back his old command, the Army of Tennessee.

The next few days, Beauregard spent reorganizing his department to accommodate the new reality of thousands fewer Yankees threatening Charleston. Additionally, he assumed that, since there were fewer Yankees to defend against, thousands of the Confederate forces in the department would likely be sent to other, more urgent theaters as reinforcements. The following message from the President supported some of his assumptions, but not all.

Eyes Only, Read Then Destroy: "General Beauregard, our nation's strategic situation is dire. A small staff has been arranged to meet you in Atlanta and accompany you to your destination. Proceed with all haste to Jackson, assume command of the Army of Relief, and do everything within your power to salvage our forces within Vicksburg and inflict as much damage as possible on the besieging Union Army."

Beauregard was to have a field command again, with apparently hand-picked spies from President Davis. What was the bastard up to?

***

Johan saw General Beauregard standing erect on the train station platform, and he knew the general was ready to show that he would be giving the commands. Not, thought Johan unsympathetically, to some green snot-nosed lackey of the president.

After the train had come to a stop, Johan and Andre leaped from the train onto the station platform and set a swift pace toward their new commanding general. "General Beauregard," Johan spoke in French as he and Andre saluted smartly, "I am Lieutenant Colonel Lutze, and this is my associate, Lieutenant Breaux."

The general's demeanor did not change much other than returning the salute. In French, he also responded to Johan: "Colonel Lutze, I have been given some. " He paused, and a hint of anger and frustration crossed his eyes. "Unique and direct commands by the President. Perhaps on our way to Jackson, you and Lieutenant Breaux can clarify the President's desires so that I can better understand his desires."

Chapter 7

May 19, 1863, 10:00 PM,
Passenger car on Route to Jackson, MS

A haze lingered in the private cabin for General Beauregard and his two new staff officers. Taking a moment to savor his cigar, Beauregard let out a satisfied puff. "Colonel Lutze, that is the most ridiculous story I have ever heard. But I believe you are telling the truth. The President would not give a liar this much authority and responsibility, godson or not. Now, you must prove you are not a spy for that spiteful man."

Sitting across from Beauregard, Johan continued to speak in French: "Well, General, I won't argue the fact that Uncle Jefferson can be a tad persnickety at times."

Andre let out a loud laugh. "Johan, I always thought you were meant to be a lawyer. If you downplayed the personality of dear Uncle Jefferson anymore, a judge would charge you with perjury."

"I think I am getting a liking for your cousin, Colonel Lutze." Beauregard smiled sincerely, giving the first hints of his suspicions being cracked almost 10 hours after meeting his two new 'staff' members. "But back to the business at hand. Obviously, the President was unsatisfied with General Johnston's performance in commanding forces in Mississippi and the Western Department in general. My god, I requested my first transfer because of that man. But we are entering a delicate situation. I know the morale of Johnston's troops must have suffered from their defeat at Jackson. But I have no desire to pull the rug out from under him either. The last thing we need to do is arrive, and my first act of business is to destroy any of the morale remaining within the army."

As the train swayed, Johan expertly poured each man a moderate amount of bourbon in the mismatched crockery he had obtained. "Lieutenant Breaux and I both served under General Johnston in Virginia, Sir. We are aware of his command style. But, despite him being relieved of command out west, I know from my conversations with General Lee that he and General Longstreet desired General Johnston to command the new IV Corps. We are all mature officers, General. But it would behoove us to be conciliatory towards General Johnston. His immediate cooperation would help us facilitate any offensive operations and improve his attitude upon arriving in Virginia…"

"All the better for General Lee and the Army of Northern Virginia. Yes, yes, Colonel. I see the path you are trying to guide me towards." Beauregard took a small sip and gestured to the map on the table, "Do you think that is an accurate depiction of Pemberton's, Grant's, and Johnston's forces?"

"To the best we know, General. In Richmond, we were relying on reports from Johnston via telegraph. I believe by the time we arrive in Jackson, we can safely assume that Cleburne, Pickett, and Forrest will have arrived as well. Those are three quality divisions. Pickett is a fighter, and Cleburne has the best division west of the Appalachians. And you are familiar with General Forrest."

Beauregard stared at the map with fierce intensity. "And I am familiar with Cleburne; he was at Shiloh like your father."

The first several hours of the train ride were mainly Beauregard practically interrogating Johan and Andre about their service in Virginia and Johan's escape from captivity. But then Johan's family connections to President Davis were brought up. Johan's father and Jefferson Davis had been friends before the war. They had met while serving during the Mexican War and had developed a strong friendship. Their Louisiana and Mississippi units had fought well together, and after the cessation of hostilities, Uncle Jefferson and

Johan's father remained in contact and went into several business ventures together. And then this war had come about. Johan's father, Paul Lutze, brother, Paul Jr, and several Louisiana regiments were at Shiloh when Beauregard took command of the Army of Tennessee from the mortally wounded Albert Sidney Johnston. Both Paul Sr. and Jr. were seriously injured at Shiloh, with Paul Jr. losing the lower part of his left leg, and Pappa Lutze, an exploding artillery shell, had severed an arm and sent dozens of pieces of shrapnel into his torso. Paul Lutze Sr., the father who had firmly and lovingly guided the wayward Johan, had died a horrific death, and Johan had been hundreds of miles away, unable to see his father in his final moments. Johan was never the same after his father died. But General Beauregard was not to blame. It was the damn Yankees.

Beauregard pushed forward, not wanting to give the past any more time to materialize in his two subordinates' minds. "I was in command at Shiloh, and so was Grant." He leaned over the map and guided his finger along the Mississippi River. "To be honest, I am not at all that impressed with General Grant as a strategist or tactician. I had that drunkard beat at Shiloh on the first day, but…" he paused, but did break his gaze from the map of the Mississippi Valley. "He just keeps coming. How many attempts has he made to capture Vicksburg in the last year? Five or six, depending on how you count. But his defeats do not matter; he just tries again."

Johan broke into Beauregard's train of thought, "Sir, General Sherman was the commandant at the Louisiana Military Academy, the one year I was there, in '60. I got to know General Sherman well during my time there. Grant and Sherman are cut from the same cloth. They are vicious, brutal, and efficient in their conduct of war. It is no surprise to me that the Yankee armies have fared better in the West than what has occurred in the East. Add the fact that these great rivers act as indestructible transport networks. They can attack almost anywhere they want and send an inexhaustible number of troops and supplies. However," Johan smiled slightly, "those attributes can be used against our Yankee friends.'

"You have remained quiet, Lieutenant," Beauregard smiled when he saw Andre straighten up. "What are your thoughts on the objective of this campaign?"

"First, General Beauregard, we punch Grant in the face as hard as we can. Second, as the undersized fighter would understand, we keep our heads and don't allow Grant to suck us in and shatter us. We have the chance to trap either part or the whole of his army between us and Pemberton's entrenchments. But from everything I have read and what Colonel Lutze has told me, Grant will fight to the last man and not give up without one hell of a fight. Now don't get me wrong, we punch as hard as we possibly can, but make sure we don't get sucked into the trap ourselves." Andre paused to open his hand to look at the pair of dice that he held. "It's a gamble for sure, but it's a roll of the dice that Grant would not be expecting, Sir."

"General Beauregard," Johan said excitedly. "At Second Manassas, General Jackson's Corps acted as bait for General Pope's army. Pope took the bait, and General Longstreet struck his flank with an armored fist. We have the same opportunity here. We can take Pickett and two of Johnston's original divisions and strike Grant and Sherman north of Vicksburg." Johan pointed to the various points on the map. "We then hit the southern flank with the majority of our forces. This action likely would not destroy Grant's army, but if we could hit the Yankee center and left flank with 30,000 troops led by General Claiborne, we could eliminate almost 1/3 of Grant's army."

"Colonel Lutze," Beauregard yawned and pulled out a pocket watch. "You and Lieutenant Breaux have given me much to ponder. But I fear I am beyond exhausted. I propose we table this conversation until the morning and get whatever sleep we can steal. I can assure the two of you that I will be in great need of your services and recommend that you get plenty of rest right now while you have the ability to take it."

***

May 23, 1863, Early Morning, several miles west of Meridian, MS

General Nathan Bedford Forrest was not a man to be trifled with or have his time wasted. The state of the Confederate rail network left the frontiersmen in Forrest wanting to strangle someone. Forrest was a natural military commander without formal training, but his intuition and bold decision-making hinted at his military genius. The Confederacy relied on its rail network to keep commerce going and to transport troops. However, the Southern railroads were overused, neglected, and unable to obtain spare parts due to the Union blockade.

In a clearing, not far away from a small depot along the railroad, General Forrest sat mounted on his horse, waiting for his 50-plus-man cavalry detachment to finish getting into position. He had been apprised of President Davis's decision to replace General Johnston with General Beauregard, and Forrest was here to ensure that Beauregard could safely complete his journey to Jackson. Or what was left of Mississippi's state capital.

Soon, he heard the unmistakable sound of a train engine and the train's whistle. His troopers kept their horses controlled but were ready at a moment's notice to pounce on any threat to the new commanding General of the entire Western Department.

***

As the train began to slow down, Johan hung part of his body over the railing to get a better view of the men who awaited them at the small train depot. He counted several dozen riders, all clothed in various shades of gray and butternut. What caught his eye, however, was the number of black men that he saw mounted and armed to the teeth, also wearing Confederate Gray.

As the train stopped at the depot, General Beauregard joined Johan, with Andre, Karl, Jacob, Fredrick, and the general's young black manservant doing likewise.

General Forrest saluted Beauregard. "General, I'm glad my message found its way to you. The Yankee raiders have really done a number on this line, and this train could only have gone a few more miles without experiencing a catastrophe. We have the horses for you and your entourage."

Beauregard returned the salute. "General Forrest, it is my pleasure to have you under my command once again. I need commanders who know how to win. I look forward to our ride together."

General Forrest had brought six extra mounts for Beauregard and his entourage. Since there were seven men in Beauregard's entourage, Elijah, the general's young servant, and Jacob doubled up on a mount. Jacob did not protest since the youth had never ridden a horse, and Elijah had some skill. Once the newcomers were mounted and their limited baggage distributed between themselves and some of Forrest's men, they set off for Jackson.

The railroad to Jackson and the wagon road to Jackson paralleled each other, with the railroad to the north of the road. As they got onto the main road to Jackson, Johan observed the ease with which General Forrest commanded his men and how they instinctively knew what to do without specific orders. Several riders rode out ahead of the main body while others stayed further back along the road in case a Yankee patrol were to come up from behind.

General Forrest traveled near the head of his column, with General Beauregard close to his side. Johan initially rode a respectable distance behind the two generals, but to his surprise, General Forrest called for Johan to come and ride along his other side.

"Colonel Lutze," began Forrest, "I have heard some extraordinary things about you. I would very much want to hear your story tonight while we rest the horses. But for right now, since it appears you will be on General Beauregard's staff, I figured you needed to be included in this conversation."

General Beauregard was one for protocol, and Johan knew the general respected men like Forrest. However, he bristled at the irrelevance paid to rank and privilege. But Forrest knew how to fight and win; that was all that mattered in his mind. Hopefully, General Beauregard would come to the same conclusion on his own.

It was a long ride, and Johan made it a point to converse with the two generals while constantly scanning the road. It did not matter that Forrest had men out ahead; Johan would not get caught with his pants down.

The conversation began with Forrest filling his new commanding general in on the looming catastrophe that Confederate forces on the Mississippi were facing. Though General Johnston would never admit so, Forrest confirmed that Pemberton had taken the Army of Mississippi out of Vicksburg to confront General Grant's army at General Johnston's urging. Despite hard fighting from Pemberton's troops, the Battle of Champion Hill had been an unmitigated disaster for the Confederates. The fact that Pemberton had kept his army together and got most of them back to the fortifications of Vicksburg was a small miracle. To add insult to injury, Johnston had given up Jackson with not much of a fight, which, combined with Grant's victory at Champion Hill, had completely isolated Vicksburg from the outside world.

Beauregard puffed on a cigar while Forrest finished his rundown of recent events. "Though I find Grant lacking as a general when he is presented with an opportunity, he almost always attacks. What on earth was going through Johnston's mind?"

Forrest did not miss a beat, "He was scared, Sir. No one wins when they fight scarred."

General Forrest," interjected Johan, "to the best of your knowledge, how many men do you think Johnston has under his command now?"

"That's difficult to say." Forrest grimaced. "Everything is so scattered and unorganized now. There are Walker's and French's divisions and Gist's brigade at Canton, just north of Jackson. Loring and Breckenridge are just East of Jackson, but to my knowledge, marching back west to the capital. Then, there are the local militia and state troops. That puts Johnston around 25,000, maybe just under. My command has now arrived in full, giving me 5,000 mounted troopers. Pickett's 6,000-man division arrived just after the fight at Jackson and now occupies the city. Cleburne's men began arriving two days ago, and by the end of today, all of his 8,000 men or so should be at Jackson as well. So, all told, we have over 40,000 in the vicinity of Jackson, not including any other brigades or whole divisions that are still en route."

Though still outnumbered by Grant, the Confederates had amassed a sizeable force around Jackson that, combined with Pemberton's army inside Vicksburg, would be close to matching Grant's numbers. Johan and the two generals knew that they had a golden opportunity before them.

"General Forrest," remarked Beauregard, "that is some excellent information to know. Now tell me what the hell happened at Champion Hill."

***

Early Morning, May 24, 1863, thirty miles East of Jackson, Mississippi

Johan and General Forrest were sitting on a log, drinking coffee, looking into the small fire. Unconsciously, Johan let out a satisfied sigh.

"Glad you approve," joked Forrest.

"General, this is the first time I have had coffee since I extricated myself from the Army of the Potomac."

With the dim moonlight, Forrest's smile could barely be seen. "I told you earlier I would like to hear about that. Also, your last name is Lutze. I believe I remember a Colonel Lutze in one of the Louisiana regiments at Shiloh. He fell there, unfortunately, like so many others. Is he of any relation?"

The battle of Shiloh had been over a year ago. But Johan still felt the pain of losing his father and the regret he felt from their last meeting. He had obtained leave from his regiment in Virginia and traveled back home to Louisiana to see his mother before she passed away after suffering from a long illness. His father had been there and had been adamant about Johan getting transferred to his regiment, even calling upon Uncle Jefferson for the favor. That way, Papa had reasoned, Johan and Paul Jr. could all serve in the same regiment. Johan would have, in any other circumstance, been open to the idea, but he felt fiercely loyal to the 6th Louisiana. They had trained and fought together and been victorious at First Manassas. It was apparent that the Yankees would launch a massive campaign in Virginia to take Richmond, and Johan felt obligated to return to Virginia to be with his men. His reasoning was sound, but he still regretted how he and Papa had parted ways and the animosity they both felt.

"Well, sir, the short answer is yes to the latter question. The Colonel Lutze you remember was my father. He tried to convince me to transfer to his regiment, and I was dead set on returning to my regiment in Virginia. We said some things we later regretted, but unfortunately, those were the last words we ever spoke to one another."

"Sorry to hear that," stated Forrest with sincerity.

Johan shrugged. "I am not the first to lose a parent or loved one in this war. I cannot change what happened at Shiloh. But I do approach my personal relationships with more care now. As for my stay with the bluebellies, I was captured at Fredericksburg. We were in a tough fight, and I lost track of my company. Well, I found myself surrounded, and after emptying my revolver into a crowd of Yanks, I fought them off as long as I could using my sword and revolver as a club. Well, after a bayonet to the calf and a rifle butt to the side of my head, I gave up the fight. After a few months, I found myself in a prison on an island in New York Harbor. I was able to escape on a medical/supply boat and make my way into the city itself. I then had the bright idea to pose as a German immigrant and take a $300 bounty to enlist in the Yankee army. That was my ticket to get back to Virginia. In the confusion of battle, I jumped the lines and brought myself before General Jackson during Chancellorsville. And the rest, I'm sure you have heard the tall tales about."

Forrest laughed. "It is a strange war. Those three Germans with you must be from the XI or German Corps. Are they trustworthy?"

"They are committed to me. Don't get me wrong, they are all stubborn Teutons. But they are loyal as hell and were the only true friends I had while with the XI Corps."

Both men stood shortly after, and as the first light of day crested the Eastern horizon, the entire command, under Forrest, was mounted and riding hard for Jackson.

Chapter 8

May 24, 1863, 12:00 PM, General Johnston's Headquarters, Jackson, MS

The low rumbling of the bombardment at Vicksburg could be heard as General Johnston met Beauregard outside his headquarters. Their exchange was cordial, but below the surface, everyone knew Johnston had been relieved of command and ordered back to Virginia. Beauregard had been in the same predicament as Johnston the year before and made every effort not to say anything that could embarrass Johnston within public view. Johnston led Beauregard, Forrest, Johan, and Andre into the hotel to his office/meeting room, where his staff was waiting.

The room was generally somber, and all of Johnston's staff felt loyal to the man. After introductions, Johnston's staff were dismissed, with Andre following them out. Beauregard, Forrest, and Johan were then left with Johnston.

"Well, let's get on with it," Johnston said testily. He was 56 years old, balding, and vain in how he wanted to be regarded as a general. Johan felt no resentment towards Johnston and felt that while he had been under Johnston's command in Virginia, the general had done his best. Johnston was unfortunate enough to be wounded in action and replaced by none other than Robert E. Lee. And the rest was history.

Having served together in Virginia, there was familiarity and some animosity between Beauregard and Johnston. However, Beauregard, Forrest, and Johan had devised a plan to deal with Grant on their ride to Jackson. To increase their chances of success, they needed Johnston's cooperation. And that meant playing nice. The three men opposite Johnston knew this was the second time he had lost command of an army he had helped organize to someone else within a year.

Beauregard began, "General Johnston, let me first say I truly regret the circumstance that led us here. We all know you have done a marvelous job creating this army out of nothing and doing everything possible to counter Grant. The President is strong-willed and opinionated, often leading to misunderstandings with his generals."

Some of the tension had visibly left Johnston's face, and his attitude became slightly more cordial. "I understand that the President's godson is present, and by no means do I mean any disrespect, but that man interferes and interjects and knows exactly how to make one's task completely impossible."

"Sir, at least the President, godfather or not, has never called you a damn rat Yankee bastard to your face."

Everyone in the room got a laugh from Johan's joke, and Johnston seemed to settle more into the conversation. "Well, General Beauregard, the Army of Relief is yours. If there is anything I can assist you with, I am more than willing to be of assistance."

"If I might ask, General Johnston," asked Beauregard, "what was your plan before you received the President's summons?"

Johnston gave a huff but decided to humor Beauregard, "Since I knew General Forrest and his command were en route, I planned to gather all of my forces here in Jackson, and with General Forrest providing my screen, begin the approach to Vicksburg and relieve the garrison there under Pemberton."

The other three men present did not contradict Johnston, but they knew his claim had a somewhat revisionist history. "Well, Sir," responded Forrest, "we have a similar idea to what you just proposed."

"I cannot go against the President's orders," continued Beauregard, "but I feel it wise and would appreciate any and all assistance you could render us. Very few of our forces in Jackson are aware of the change in command for this army, and more importantly, Grant has no idea about the change in command."

Johnston shifted, "What are you proposing, General Beauregard?"

"The President has made two things very clear. First, this army is to attack Grant and relieve the Army of Mississippi, which is trapped inside Vicksburg. Second, you are to return to Virginia for consultations. It is Colonel Lutze's understanding that an IV Corps for the Army of Northern Virginia is to be formed from forces I was commanding in the Carolinas and that you are to assume the command of this newly formed IV Corps. But who is to say you cannot assist this army for a few extra days before you take a train back to Virginia?"

"In what capacity would you desire my assistance?"

Johan knew they had Johnston's cooperation.

Forrest then took the lead. "Colonel Lutze here is a student of military history and has a good memory of the battles he has fought in. Why, he suggested to General Beauregard, nothing less than a good ole' bushwacking of Grant."

"If I remember," Johnston said politely, "something like that was the idea behind Shiloh."

"Yes," responded Beauregard with a smile. "And I want Grant to think the same thing again. I propose you take a force of about 15,000 men, spearheaded by Pickett's Virginians, and attack a section of Grant's lines. You would stealthily approach under a cavalry screen and then attack with your entire force deployed. Grant is to be hit as hard and fast as possible. However, he will react quickly and throw everything he has at you. You would hold firm and slowly pull back as more Yankee reinforcements arrive. And then, once enough of one wing of Grant's army is engaged with you, I strike with 30,000 into Grant's exposed flank. Meanwhile, General Forrest will have deployed cavalry to the north and south of Grant's forces, and that might be enough to threaten his supply lines and force him to make some hasty decisions.

There was silence for a moment, and then Beauregard continued, "My understanding is that Grant has three Corps surrounding Vicksburg. I plan to contact General Taylor on the Louisiana side of the Mississippi and have him coordinate his attack with you. President Davis has given me orders allowing me to modify the chain of command between the Department of the West and the Trans-Mississippi. Thus, the coordination of your forces attacking simultaneously would surprise the Yanks. With my attack, I would attempt to trap at least one of Grant's Corps between Vicksburg and us. We would destroy almost a third of Grant's army and open Vicksburg to receive supplies. With this defeat, Grant might abort his campaign. That is probably unlikely. However, if he chooses to stay and continue fighting, our army, combined with Pemberton's, would almost match his numbers."

There was silence once more until Johnston responded, "It is a bold plan. And perhaps the viable option to save the Vicksburg garrison. I could assist in this battle, but I must leave for Richmond promptly once the outcome is decided."

Beauregard stood straight and shook Johnston's hand. "Well, then, general, let us call back your staff and start assembling our battle plan. Colonel Lutze, go retrieve Lieutenant Breaux and the rest of General Johnston's staff."

Johan saluted the generals and quickly left the room. Adrenaline rushed through his veins as he took in their victory in convincing Johnston to stay for the battle. There were to be some long days and nights ahead, but it seemed that something very tangible to help Vicksburg was about to begin.

May 24, 1863, 11:00 PM, Jackson, MS, General Cleburne's Headquarters

General Johnson had shown unwillingness to meet Grant in an open battle, but everyone in Jackson could feel the energy and excitement now that Beauregard was present. At last, something was to be done. It was no mystery to the rank and file of the army that many would fall in the upcoming battle. But these men took the risk in stride, knowing that they were to counterattack the invaders who meant to subjugate them and their families.

It had been a long and exhausting day, but Johan could hear the bombardment of Vicksburg even more clearly at night. That sound kept propelling him forward, and he was determined to do his part in relieving the besieged city. Only 10 days had passed since the Battle of Jackson and the subsequent destruction brought to much of the town. Given the rapid arrival of thousands of gray-clad troops and the rushed repairs to structures still standing, Jackson did not look like a town that had just been through a major battle.

Johan had spent most of the afternoon running errands for General Beauregard. Though Johnston formally held command of the Army of Relief on paper, in reality the army was a hodgepodge of units from various theaters throughout the Confederacy, scattered within a 20-mile radius of Jackson. Several brigades came from the Carolinas, General Beauregard's former command. General Pickett's division had been in Longstreet's 1st Corps of the Army of Northern Virginia. Most of the divisions present had been peeled off the Army of Tennessee, including General Cleburne's, much to the chagrin of Braxton Bragg, the commander of that army.

General Beauregard, General Forrest, Johnston's staff, and Johan had methodically studied the maps of the area around Vicksburg, formalizing a clear battle plan. What made matters so complex was the distance separating the Confederate units from Grant. The size and composition of Beauregard's command were also constantly changing, with new units arriving that afternoon or sending word that they were days away from reaching Jackson. Andre and several of Johnston's staff were sent out on fresh, swift mounts provided by Forrest to locate the various divisions and independent brigades en route. Out of necessity, the current location of these units largely determined where they would assault the Union lines.

As stated in the initial meeting with Johnston, the newly renamed Army of the Mississippi Valley under Beauregard's command, or Army of the MSV, would be split into two unequal infantry wings for the upcoming attack. In all, Beauregard would directly command over 30,000 infantry, and Johnston would command around 18,000. At the same time, Forrest was given command of all Confederate cavalry, including General William "Red" Jackson, which combined would provide Forrest with just shy of 10,000 mounted troops.

Forrest's scouts had determined that Grant's three Corps were arrayed with McClernand's XIII Corps south of Vicksburg as the left flank of Grant's army. McPherson's XVII was east of the city and formed the center of Grant's line. Sherman's XV was northeast of the town and the extreme right of Grant's line.

Johnston would command a force of roughly 18,000 infantry, the backbone of which would be Breckinridge's and Pickett's divisions. Johnston was to approach Vicksburg from roughly the northeast. Going through Snyder's Mill, as General Pemberton's correspondence had requested that Johnston belatedly share with Beauregard, and under the cover of Forrest's cavalry screen, Johnston was to approach the edge of Sherman's sector and attack, focusing mainly on McPherson's Corps and attacking ferociously. Though Johnston had verbally given the plan his blessing, Pickett's division served as insurance that Johnston could not back out at the last minute, and the attack would go forward. Pickett was a respected divisional commander recently transferred from General Longstreet's Corps in Virginia. If there was any divisional commander up to the task of possibly taking on an entire Yankee Corps singlehandedly, Pickett was the man for the job, and his honor and ego would never let him turn down this assignment.

In the current campaign, Grant bypassed Vicksburg by marching down the western or Louisiana side of the Mississippi and then crossing the river south of Vicksburg. After his victories at Jackson and Champion Hill, Grant invested Vicksburg, which allowed a more direct route for his resupply, one in which supplies and reinforcements could be delivered north of the city without running the gauntlet of Vicksburg's guns. To Beauregard, the northern section of Grant's line was the most substantial and best defended, especially when Forrest informed him of the firepower the naval fleet on the river could bring to action.

Beauregard had learned his lesson from Shiloh, and rather than attack Grant evenly, Beauregard would focus his attack on the weakest and most vulnerable portion of Grant's line, McClernand's XIII Corps. The Southern Railroad, the line that Beauregard and Johan had ridden through Meridian, went into Vicksburg from the east. This railroad also separated McClernand from the rest of Grant's army. The idea was to attack XIII Corps from both flanks while attacking its center. If it could be coordinated with the garrison inside Vicksburg, there was the possibility of attacking the XIII Corps from all four sides with overwhelming numbers and annihilating it. Once XIII Corps was eliminated, Beauregard would link up with Johnston, and the idea was to roll up as much of McPherson's Corps from the flank while the Vicksburg garrison attacked McPherson from the rear.

It was a bold plan, and Johan approved because it was the best chance of relieving Vicksburg and severely damaging Grant's army. The only way this could be pulled off was by stealth, secrecy, and the undivided cooperation of Beauregard's subordinate generals. It was akin to herding cats, but that was where Johan, Andre, and Johnston's staff came in.

***

Clearing his mind, Johan verified the house's address and knocked on the door. Shortly, an officer answered the door. When the captain noticed Johan's rank, he quickly saluted and asked politely, "How may I help you, Sir?"

"This is General Cleburne's headquarters?"

"Yes, Sir."

"Excellent. I am Lieutenant Colonel Lutze from General Beauregard's staff, and I need to speak to General Cleburne most urgently."

Johan was led into the home and brought to General Cleburne's study shortly.

The young man knocked on the door and heard a muffled, "Come in."

The office was well put together, with a fine desk and bookshelf. Behind the desk sat General Cleburne. He was a modest man dressed in a gray general's uniform devoid of almost all decoration. His face sported a trimmed mustache and goatee, and his sandy hair gave Cleburne the appearance of a man with much vigor and youth.

Another man was seated across from Cleburne. He wore a worn gray coat and had a youthful appearance. After the captain followed Johan into the room and closed the door behind him, Johan belatedly noticed various refreshments on the desk, along with a pitcher with some drink in it.

Johan came to attention and saluted the general, "General Cleburne, I am Lieutenant Colonel Lutze of General Beauregard's staff reporting, Sir."

Cleburne returned the salute and motioned for Johan to take a seat. "Colonel Lutze, it's good to meet you. I understand there have been changes to this army and our orders." Cleburne gestured to the Captain, who had let Johan into the home. Behind you is Captain Buck, my Assistant Adjutant, and my Inspector General. And seated here," he motioned to the man across from him, "is Lieutenant Colonel Fremantle of Her Majesty's Coldstream Guards regiment."

Johan had to do a double-take, "Excuse me. But not to be rude, you mean Queen Victoria? Of England?"

"None other, good chap," said Fremantle light-heartily. "In fact, General Cleburne was at one point in Her Majesty's service as well. It seems he has exchanged the scarlet jacket of a corporal he wore in Ireland for the gray of your Confederacy."

"The Queen should be proud," smiled Cleburne, "for a corporal in her army is worth being a general in this one."

All four men laughed and continued acquainting themselves with one another. Cleburne was easygoing, and Johan immediately knew why his men fought so hard for him. Captain Buck was a highly competent Inspector General and a fiercely loyal supporter of Cleburne, which helped create one of the best Confederate divisions anywhere.

Fremantle, on the other hand, fascinated Johan. The man had sailed from Europe and entered Mexico, then crossed into the Confederacy through Brownsville, Texas, on his own dime. He had then spent over a month traveling across Texas, through Louisiana, and into Mississippi.

"If I may ask, Colonel," Johan asked after Fremantle had finished his story, "if you had an opinion about the Confederacy before, what do you think about it now?"

"Well, old boy," Fremantle pondered, "I would say you Southerners, as wide and diverse as you can be at times, are a tough, ferocious, and inventive lot. There has been much hardship I have witnessed myself since entering your country, but the perseverance of your people is worth praise of the highest order."

Johan, Fremantle, and Buck shared a fine bottle of bourbon, but the general politely declined. Johan's respect for the man depended not only on that, but the story of Fremantle intrigued him. "So, I must ask, Colonel, what do you hope to learn while you embed yourself within our ranks?

Fremantle responded with a final sip of whiskey, "Well, Colonel Lutze, I know what war and battle look like. I was in Crimea and fought the Russians, and after that, I went to India with my regiment to put down the Sepoy Rebellion. I have been more than curious to see how you Confederates would fight a battle."

"Well, sir," Johan gave a wry grin, "within the next few days, you will have every opportunity to see how we fight."

Cleburne folded his hands, leaning back in his chair, "Colonel Lutze, I greatly appreciate that we are of the same mind. Now tell me, what message do you carry from General Beauregard?"

"Pretty straightforward, sir," Johan handed over the written dispatches from Beauregard. "Have your men wake up at their regular time tomorrow and break camp. The general wants your division on the march no later than 8:00 AM. Your objective is to encamp at Ramond tomorrow evening, then march to and encamp in Utica by the evening of May 26th. Then march to Antioch Church on May 27th. The objective is for all forces to be in a position to attack by the evening of May 30th. The attack on Grant's army will commence at 8:00 AM on June 1st."

A sardonic grin crossed Cleburne's face, "You can call it straightforward if you may. But my division will be ready."

Johan knew Cleburne was not excited about the plan. "If it helps at all, sir, General Forrest will lead the screening for your division. As for myself, General Beauregard has assigned me to General Forrest and your division. With so many of our forces spread over such a wide area, it was felt that having staff officers assigned to various divisions would ensure everyone made it to the proper jump-off point for June 1st."

"Well, Colonel," Cleburne gestured, "it appears we will see much of each other the next few days."

***

May 25, 1863, 1:00 AM, General Forrest's Encampment, outside Jackson, MS

Andre smiled at Johan, avoiding the question. "Johan, as matters are rapidly evolving, quick decisions must be made in the placement of our forces."

"Andre, where the hell did my three krauts go?"

"They volunteered for combat duty."

"With whom?"

"Why, Colonel, if you must know, General Forrest convinced our Teutonic friends to ride with him."

"Andre," Johan said with some annoyance, "Jacob had never ridden a horse until a day ago. Is he going to be in the cavalry now? Who came up with that bright idea?"

"If you want to know, Colonel, I did."

General Forrest came into view with the campfire behind his back. "The only way to win this war is to outthink the Yankees. Your friend, lacking any basic riding skills, seemed very interested in cannons and generally blowing the hell out of stuff, so I gave him a job with my horse artillery. The other two were competent enough to ride, so they got to have more fun."

It was obvious to Johan that he had been outmaneuvered, so he wisely dropped the issue and saluted, "General Forrest, before I ran into my insubordinate relative, I was looking for you to report. General Beauregard has made me his official liaison for you and General Cleburne. My cousin, currently Lieutenant Breaux, is assigned to Generals Pickett and Breckinridge."

"Colonel, much must be done before we roll out in the morning. I suggest you get some shut-eye for a couple of hours and be ready to hit the ground running." Forrest's mischievous smile gleamed in the firelight. "Your insubordinate cousin will take you to where your gear has been stowed. I will send one of my men to get you in a couple of hours."

Dismissed, Andre led Johan to where their gear had been stowed. Johan was relieved when he saw Karl and Fredrick sleeping nearby, with his Spencer rifle tucked beside his sleeping blanket. Andre teased Johan about being more worried about a rifle than more important things like food or a woman's touch, but the exhausted Johan ignored him and lay down with his boots still on.

It was a hot, late spring night, technically. For all practical purposes, it was summer in Johan's mind. But he was the closest to Louisiana he had been in a year. A mere stone's throw away. The time would come when he would go back home. But something else flashed through his memory.

Clearing his mind, Johan pulled out a photograph that had survived the war with him despite all the battles in the East and his nearly half-year imprisonment up north. He turned the picture towards the firelight to glimpse once more the sweet face and blue eyes of his Tesa. He was now closer to her in Mobile, Alabama, than he had been since last year, but the 200 miles that separated them now might as well have been 2000 miles. Nevertheless, he imprinted her image into his mind once more, remembering their last words with one another.

"I will return. Even if I must storm the gates of Hell, I am always yours."

"Just get yourself back to me in one piece. I will be here, soldier boy."

When Johan closed his eyes, all he saw was the face of the woman who had changed his outlook on life and stolen his heart.

Chapter 9

May 25, 1863, 4:00 AM, General Forrest's Camp

"Morning, Colonel. Name is Jack Clark, and General Forrest sent me to come to fetch you and your cousin, the lieutenant."

Johan woke up to see a dark face over his. Though the fire had died down, between the moonlight and what was left of the fire, he could make out the face of a black man wearing Confederate gray standing over him.

"Thank you," Johan muttered as he got up and began to pack his belongings.

Andre was also up, and in a few minutes, the two officers had packed their belongings. Jack was polite and more than helpful in carrying some of the gear the two young officers had to the horse pens, for which Johan was more than grateful.

At 4:00 AM, the camp was bustling, with riders constantly flowing in and out of the camp and men saddling mounts and loading munitions. There was not much conversation between the three men, but Johan was impressed with how Jack carried himself. But who was Johan kidding? By his upbringing, he had been around people of African descent, both enslaved and free, his entire life on his family's plantation and at their New Orleans home. Skin color had no bearing on what was in a man's heart or mind, or his desire to provide good and honest work.

General Forrest was not a trained professional soldier, but his camp ran like a well-oiled machine. Two horses were soon brought out to Johan and Andre, and Jack helped them load their gear onto them. Jack soon said goodbye, leaving the two cousins alone.

When Johan tied his Spencer rifle to his saddle, Andre asked, "How much do you think you'll need that rifle?"

With a side view look at Andre, Johan replied, "I think there will be plenty of Yankees for me to shoot. Not going to be partial to parting with it, my friend."

"Well, it was worth a try. Where are you off to now?"

"I'm going to meet General Forrest at Beauregard's headquarters first. After that, we head for Raymond. I'll be part of the cavalry screen for part of the day. Hopefully, the first half of the day is uneventful, and I can ride with General Cleburne. But we will see. How about you?"

Andre tipped his wide-brimmed hat at an angle, "I'm going straight to General Pickett. Grant is the strongest north of Vicksburg, so it's going to be a tougher slog getting through all the Yankee pickets over there. But, what the hell, we've got to sell this thing hard to Grant, right?"

Andre was right. With the number of troops Grant had under his command and the way they were arrayed, chances were slim that his entire army could be surrounded and destroyed. But Beauregard had come up with the next best option: the partial destruction of Grant's army. If McClernand's Corps could be isolated and destroyed, Grant could be forced to abandon his campaign for Vicksburg. But there was only one way to find out.

A short time later, as the first rays of sunlight emerged on the eastern horizon, Johan rode to Beauregard's headquarters. In the distance, he could hear the bombardment of Vicksburg, which quickened the steps of everyone about the headquarters.

Inside, Johan found General Forrest with General Beauregard. After quickly getting through saluting and other formalities, General Forrest began, "Well, Colonel, I'm glad you made it here this morning. We have our work cut out." He pointed to the map on the table, "General Beauregard wants us to make sure the road to Ramond is clear before General Cleburne's division begins its march. Then we will ride all the way to Utica. The goal is to create as much of a buffer between our army and Grant's."

Beauregard cut in, "The bulk of General Forrest's cavalry will be on the southern flank of Vicksburg. I will rely on you, Colonel, to keep me updated on the progress of the advance every day. I cannot stress the importance of getting our army into position before Grant knows we are here. If he were to strike while our forces were spread out over all of the back roads of central Mississippi, well, it would be a catastrophe of the highest magnitude."

When Johan looked down at the map, which showed the displacement of Beauregard's forces along with Grant's, it was apparent how correct Beauregard was. The Army of the Mississippi Valley would use every available road to get its nearly 50,000 troops into position. For all the brigades and divisions to march the 60 or so miles and then be in position in time for the attack was a monumental task. The logic of spreading out the divisions as they marched made perfect sense, for often, when multiple divisions used the same road at the same time, an accordion effect occurred, putting the army in grave danger.

"Everyone must do their part," continued Beauregard. "There is no going back now."

***

Johan departed, riding next to General Forrest and a detachment of several dozen troopers. The whole experience was surreal, and he contemplated just how much had changed in his life over the last month. Those thoughts only crossed his mind for a few seconds because, for all intents and purposes, he was no longer a line infantry officer but an officer within the command of General Forrest.

After they had ridden a few miles west of Jackson, Forrest let Johan in on his operational framework of the day. "Colonel, welcome to life in the saddle. Now, don't get your hopes up about facing any action this morning. One thousand of my men set out about an hour ago on multiple routes, so if there are any Yankees between here and Raymond, they will rough them up well before we will get there." A quick succession of cannon shots from the direction of Vicksburg emphasized Forrest's point.

"General, I've seen enough fighting for a lifetime. But I know we have one hell of a fight coming, so I feel no loss in missing out on a skirmish or two. Besides, your boys seem to really enjoy the Yankee chasing; I would hate to deprive them of the privilege."

Forrest laughed heartily, "Why, thank you for being so considerate, Colonel. But tell me, you served in the infantry back east?"

"Yes, Sir. I served with the 6th Louisiana Infantry in the Army of Northern Virginia and fought in every major engagement from First Manassas all the way to Fredericksburg. I was captured at Fredericksburg and then spent the next six months working on my escape back to my regiment. I managed to survive the chaos of Chancellorsville and even contributed to our triumph, all while saving General Jackson's life and getting shot in the ass twice for the trouble of it all."

"Haha, Colonel. Well, I would expect you to get shot at some point by the time this is all done, but being in the saddle, your backside should be somewhat more protected. You seem at home in the saddle, which speaks much for you, formally being an infantry officer. What made you decide to join the infantry in the first place?"

"At times, I am not sure myself, General. The cavalry did have its allure, for sure. However, I attended the Louisiana Military Academy the year before the war. General Sherman, of all people, was our commandant. I think while I was there, and I saw the clouds of war starting to form, I realized that any war that was to be fought was going to be won by the infantry. My father and older brother served in the 18th Louisiana and set the example for me as well. I probably went with the 6th to be my own man." He paused and chuckled, "And be with my idiot cousin, Lieutenant Breaux."

"The things we do for family, Colonel." Forrest laughed. "The things we do. Don't you worry about Lieutenant Breaux. My brother has been assigned to his sector with General Pickett. They should have a grand old time picking a fight with Grant!"

They reached Raymond just before 8:00 AM after a completely uneventful ride. A few squads of Forrest's troopers greeted them as they were the security detail for Cleburne's camp for the night.

"Well, Colonel, it was good getting acquainted with you this morning, but I am off to Antioch, and you should go find General Cleburne and report to him. It's safe to say that the first part of our operation today is off to a grand start!"

A few hours later, returning to the road he had just ridden on, Johan found General Cleburne and his division. Riding alongside the general was none other than Colonel Fremantle.

"Good to see you, Colonel," spoke Cleburne in a friendly tone. "How was the road?"

"Open and clear, sir. The rains have left some parts muddy, but it's, for the most part, a straight shot to Raymond. General Forrest plans to set up camp in Antioch early this afternoon and send out his pickets several miles in each direction. All signs point to us having the jump on Grant."

"That's encouraging, to say the least, Colonel. Well, ride with us to Raymond, and then I will send you to General Beauregard with my report."

"I must say, General Cleburne, you Southerners are running a first-rate operation here," spoke Fremantle sincerely. "This division would measure up to any force her majesty would have to offer."

***

May 26, 1863, 7:00 PM, General Grant's Headquarters, Outside Vicksburg, MS

General Grant placed the cigar back in his mouth and looked down at the report that General Sherman had just handed him. In the years before the war, Grant had fallen on hard times and was considered a failure by many. But now, at 41 years old, many Northerners and Southerners considered him the best general in the entire Union Army. That reputation was well deserved because he was the only Union general to consistently win. Fort Donaldson, Fort Henry, Shiloh, Corinth, Jackson, and Champion Hill. The fact that a Union army was besieging Vicksburg and within a hairsbreadth of putting the entire Mississippi back under Northern control was due to Grant's efforts and increasing list of victories.

But past victories meant nothing going forward. Though his army was besieging Vicksburg, the Confederates could quickly turn the tables, and Grant could easily find his army of 77,000 troops, the ones who were besieged.

"Alright, Sherm, Johnston is obviously up to something. He has gone from virtually no cavalry to thousands of cavalry. They are constantly harassing McClernand to the south, and they have rolled up every patrol or picket that was unlucky enough to be found by the rebels to the Northeast." He gestured to the map, "I've heard enough rumors, and I believe Forrest is now here with God knows how many thousands of troopers. They have caused enough mayhem, but it is so obvious a damn attack is coming."

General McPherson leaned over the map to have a better view. "This terrain must be dealt with as much as our forces here as does Johnston. With most of the cavalry attacks coming further north than to the south, is Johnston tipping his hand to us?"

"I think so," said Sherman gruffly. "The man doesn't want to fight and risk losing a battle. He is afraid of his own goddamned shadow. I would only think he is being slightly more aggressive now because Davis probably threatened to fire him if he did nothing short of launching an all-out attack on us. Or maybe Forrest threatened to shoot him if he stayed idle."

"Whatever is lighting a fire under Johnston, we know Forrest is operating north of Vicksburg. Enough stragglers came into our lines today, screaming about Forrest being on their tail. And apparently, they have set up hidden cannons at various points along the river to take potshots at our ships. Anyway," Grant paused to reflect for a moment, "after all of the fresh reports yesterday, I sent a message to General Hurlbut last night to bring XVI down immediately. He should be able to bring an immediate 15,000 troops, with the other 5,000 staying behind in Memphis for garrison duty. Those troops should begin arriving by June 1st and all be here by June 2nd or 3rd."

"Should we begin rearranging our forces for a possible attack to the north?" Sherman asked gruffly. "And where the hell is McClernand tonight? His Corps makes up 1/3 of this army."

McPherson shrugged at the question, "A message was delivered to me by one of his staff officers before I left to come here. Apparently, he was very concerned about the reports of large numbers of rebel cavalry to his south and west and thought it best to stay with his Corps this evening."

"Be that as it may," Grant said with some annoyance, "I would expect to see Johnston attack within the next few days. I've already ordered increased cavalry patrols at the Big Black River railroad crossing and in the area of Snyder's Mill. Sherm, I know you have already positioned forces to repel Johnston, but we need to be even more vigilant. Johnston, for sure, has more troops now than when we kicked him out of Jackson. Hell, the Southern papers are just as bad as ours in announcing when troops depart from one city for another. It will be a real fight when he decides to show up."

"We'll be ready," stated a confident Sherman. "I'm looking forward to it."

"And James," Grant finished writing an order and handed it to General McPhearson. "Give this to McClernand. If he were here tonight, I would explain to him why I am pulling away 5,000 of his troops, but that is just how it is. He can pick the two or three brigades he wants to send to you. Sherm, you and James, work out how to distribute your forces to face Vicksburg and Johnston. And with that, my friends, I will leave you to your work, and I need to go find Admiral Porter."

***

May 27, 1863, 3:30 AM, Vicksburg, Willis-Cowan House, Pemberton's HQ

A knock at the door woke General Pemberton, the Commander of the Army of Mississippi. Having slept in his uniform, he quickly sat up, put on his boots, and walked to the door. Opening the door, he was greeted by one of his staff officers.

"Sorry to disturb you, sir," said the young captain, who had not changed his uniform since the siege of Vicksburg had begun. "But you asked us to come and get you if another one showed up. And well, we have another one."

Both men, armed with holstered revolvers, went to the home's private study, where such visitors were received. Inside the study, three armed guards stood with a man in a worn gray uniform. Upon seeing Pemberton, the man came to attention and saluted Pemberton.

Returning the salute, Pemberton got to the point, "Well, soldier, what brings you to my headquarters at this hour?"

"Well, sir, my name is Sergeant Jay Thompson, and I come from General 'Red' Jackson's brigade, which now falls under General Forrest's overall command." Seeing an impatient look on Pemberton's face, he hurried along his story, "Anyway, sir, ol' Red offered $500 to anyone stupid enough to try and get through the Yankee lines and into this death trap of a city."

"How many took up ol' Red on this offer? And why was he trying to get men into Vicksburg?"

"There was maybe half a dozen of us. Some of us took our chances on horseback, like me. My pal, Eric Parsons, was in the same company, and he decided to take a boat down that godforsaken river. Anyway, we were to personally deliver a message to you if we survived getting in here."

"Who sent the message, and what is it? Do you have it written down?"

Sergeant Thompson looked around the room before replying, "I mean no offense, sir, but can you trust these men? I have very sensitive information."

Pemberton motioned for two of the three guards to leave while his staff officer remained by his side. Once the door to the room was closed, Pemberton motioned, "Alright, Sergeant Thompson. Now is your chance to share your precious secret with me. Just a reminder, though, if you are not who you say you are and are, in fact, a blue-bellied spy, I will ensure you are hanged by dawn."

"Well, damn." Thompson's Mississippi drawl was unmistakable. "Well, sir, first of all, none of us were given any written papers. If we were to be captured or killed, there was no sense in letting the

Yankees know what we were up to. Anyways, there has been a change in leadership of the Army of Relief, or whatever it is called now. General Johnston is no longer in command. Beauregard now commands the army, and he swears by the Catholic or Protestant Bible, whichever you prefer, that he is coming and coming in hot for Grant. He requests your cooperation in coordinating troop movements and actions."

Pemberton looked to his staff officer and then back to his visitor. "And what would he like to coordinate with me?"

Thompson smiled, "On June 1, General Johnston will take about 20,000 men and attack Sherman and McPherson by way of Snyder's Mill. It would be appreciated if you could have your boys demonstrate themselves all along Grant's right flank and center. However, while Grant will be occupied dealing with Johnston, General Beauregard will come with 30,000 infantry to the south and attack McClernand's Corps. It is requested that you put most of your attention and resources into this sector. The plan is simple, Sir. We want to isolate and destroy McClernand's entire Corps and roll up as much of Grant's now exposed flank as possible. In the best case, after destroying 1/3 of Grant's army, he withdraws. Worst case, Vicksburg can now be supplied via the Warrenton and Hall's Ferry roads, and Grant is put on the defensive after losing 1/3 of his army."

Pemberton soon dismissed the Sergeant, leaving him alone with his staff officer. "That is the third man who has come to us in the last day with essentially the same story. I even remember speaking to the water-logged Parsons." Pemberton chuckled. "Well, I think God has answered some of our prayers, Captain. Someone other than Johnston has been put in charge of relieving us. I don't care at this point whether it's Beauregard or the Duke of Wellington; I will take anyone over Johnston."

Not only had multiple men been sent to Pemberton in besieged Vicksburg, but multiple messengers had been sent to General Taylor and his small force on the west bank of the river. It was taking time, but Beauregard was assembling all the necessary pieces for his planned attack on June 1st. Hopefully, Grant would stay in the dark about the true objective of the Army of the Mississippi Valley until it was too late.

Chapter 10

May 28, 1863, 1:00 AM, Antioch Church, MS, Cleburne's Camp

"How much riding did you put in the saddle today, Colonel?" General Forrest asked as Johan held a lantern over the map for them and General Cleburne to see.

Johan took a few moments to calculate. "Probably close to 60 miles, sir."

"Well, I'm glad General Beauregard is getting some use out of you. Run across any Yankees?"

"Only once. But that was after your men had finished their ambush. There were a couple still conscious enough for me to get a couple of questions in. I am thankful for the information, especially since Grant seems to think the bulk of our army is north and not south of the city."

"How are the other divisions coming along?" asked Cleburne. Is Loring still to our right?"

"Yes, sir. He is. Claims he is ready for a fight."

General Loring was a one-armed general about whom Johan and General Forrest had deep suspicions. Loring had served back east, like Johan, and was famously unable to get along with either Generals Lee or Jackson. Subsequently, he was transferred to the Western Department. Most recently, he had commanded a division at Champion Hill, the battle in which Pemberton was badly defeated and forced into Vicksburg. Loring had managed to extricate his division from the battle without serious fighting or contributing to the Confederate cause. It was evident to Johan that whatever excuses Loring made, none added up, and that he was probably the most responsible for the Southern defeat in that battle.

"Keep an eye on him," Forrest commanded. "After what happened at Champion Hill, I have no patience for any more 'misunderstandings.' If he needs his memory kicked in the ass, remind him that I outrank him. And," Forrest lowered his voice and put his mouth near Johan's ear, "if he pulls that crap again in open battle, put a bullet in his goddamn skull."

Cleburne chuckled, "Alright, General, show me how General Walker is deployed to our left. And General French is to his left, on the Warrenton Road?"

"Correct, Patrick," Forrest smirked, finding it funny that Cleburne was uncomfortable with him ordering the possible murder of another general. Pointing to the map, he continued, "And most of Red Jackson's men will be to the left of French, and the river will protect their flank. The terrain will be hell, with plenty of woods, hills, and ravines. But McClernand has to deal with that as well. This is going to be a hell of a fight."

***

May 29, 1863, 12:00 PM, Richmond, VA, Secret Joint Cabinet/ANV Meeting

President Davis… As per your orders, I have reorganized the Army of Relief and am moving it to engage Grant. The strike will be swift and destructive. Attack on June 1.

General PGT Beauregard

General Longstreet opened the door to the conference room and walked in. There had been several of these meetings lately, but from the message General Lee sent last night, Longstreet knew this meeting would determine the outcome of the war. He knew that General Lee valued his opinion and considered him the second-in-command of the Army of Northern Virginia. But there was still President Davis.

For whatever reason, his relationship with President Davis had been strained for some time. However, things appeared to have improved somewhat at Mrs. Davis's small reception after the victory at Chancellorsville. Jackson was the darling of the Confederacy, and Longstreet was okay with that, for Chancellorsville was the most significant victory any Confederate army had ever achieved. Perhaps President Davis was generous because of Jackson and Lee's victory.

Longstreet had been conducting the siege of Suffolk, Virginia, while Chancellorsville was occurring. And then everything changed, for word of a great victory and Jackson's wounding had reached him. The Yankees must have been informed at the same time, for immediately, all around his theater, vast numbers of Yankee troops were withdrawn. Like Beauregard in Charleston, Longstreet acted. First, Longstreet left a small screening force around Suffolk and moved the majority of his forces into North Carolina. Using rail and forced marches, Longstreet's small army arrived at Elizabeth City, North Carolina, and surprised the withdrawing Union garrison.

At dawn on May 8th, Longstreet's army stormed the defenses of Elizabeth City and captured almost 400 Yankees for minimal loss of life to his men. However, what they gained in supplies, materials, ammunition, and weapons was priceless. The victory was a great morale booster for North Carolina and helped quell conflicts arising with the Richmond government. But Longstreet only stayed in Elizabeth City long enough to requisition all captured supplies for the Army of Northern Virginia. The city was turned over to N.C. State militia, and at 11:00 AM, Longstreet marched his men out of the city and back to Virginia.

On May 10th, he pulled the same stunt again, and his army stormed the Union defenses at Suffolk. For a short time, the Union defenders put up a stout defense, but after 25 minutes, they were overwhelmed. Longstreet suffered 80 casualties, while close to 250 losses were recorded by the Yankees, along with the 700 men who surrendered. Though it did not remove Union forces from southern Virginia altogether, it was a stunning victory that bottled up all remaining Union forces in Norfolk.

Indeed, the back-to-back victories of Elizabeth City and Suffolk were plum feathers to put in his hat. Not only had Longstreet completed his mission in foraging supplies and protecting rail and supply lines when he had been detached from Lee, but he had recaptured cities in two different states and removed over 1,000 Yankees from the war effort. Hopefully, someone would listen to him today.

Longstreet seated himself next to General Jackson. Generals Lee and Stuart, President Davis, and Secretaries Seddon and Benjamin were also present. When all were seated, President Davis began the meeting.

"I would like to thank everyone for attending today. Has everyone read General Beauregard's telegram?"

When all acknowledged, Davis continued, "In less than 48 hours, Beauregard will attempt to pull off a miracle. I pray that he is successful. Even if he cannot destroy or decisively defeat Grant, Beauregard's active campaigning should, for the near future, keep Vicksburg and that last section of the Mississippi within our control."

"Moving on to middle Tennessee, General Bragg is holding on at Tullahoma, but almost once a day, he sends a message begging for reinforcements. Secretary of War Seddon has been in contact with the governor of Georgia, and around 3,000 state militia may be enticed to move from the Atlanta area to reinforce Bragg. Unfortunately, that is all we can send right now, given the situation at Vicksburg."

"This brings us to the Eastern theater. General Lee, we formalized your army's reorganization last night. Please," Davis gestured to

Longstreet, Jackson, and Stuart, "fill in, you loyal lieutenants, what has been decided."

"Thank you, Mr. President." General Lee stood up and paced at the head of the table. "Generals, if you look at the papers you were provided, the reorganization of the Army of Northern Virginia is detailed. General Longstreet, you have been promoted. Congratulations. You are also receiving a replacement division in place of Pickett from two brigades that were previously in his division, along with some of the forces you commanded in North Carolina. The governor was very appreciative of the recapture of Elizabeth City. These men will need further training to be brought up to the standard of the ANV, but their prior service under you is a good starting point."

"General Jackson, as you will see, your Corps is being split into two, with Ewell commanding II Corps and A. P. Hill commanding III. You will retain command of both Corps as an army wing commander. General Longstreet, you will retain overall command of II Corps, but I do desire for you to begin grooming General Hood to replace you. As for right now, you will command II Corps, and General Johnston's newly forming IV Corps will be put under your command to make you my other army wing commander."

"General Stuart, you should receive another 500 riders from the Carolinas. Though they do not have the training of your Cavalry Corps, many of these men are superbly equipped, thanks to the recent actions of Generals Longstreet and Beauregard. About 400 of these men are equipped with brand new breach-loading rifles, so this will add considerable firepower to your Corps."

"This brings us to the purpose of this reorganization. When all its strength is gathered, the Army of Northern Virginia should be able to put almost 98,000 men in the field. This will be the largest army the Confederacy has ever put into action, and we are to use it."

Lee walked over to the map hanging over the wall and used a pointer to explain. "President Davis, in consultation with Secretary Seddon, has approved another invasion of the North. General Jackson, Army Wing J, will clear the way through the Shenandoah Valley. Hooker is still entrenched too far into Virginia, and your movement will force the near evacuation of all Union forces from northern Virginia. General Longstreet will follow behind with Army Wing L. The ANV will cross into Maryland and then Pennsylvania. It is my expectation to use this campaign to take the war out of Virginia and forage for any and all supplies this army would need to prosecute the war. I want special attention paid to requisitioning cattle and horses, without which this army cannot function. Though I would not intend to capture it, I would have some of our forces make it to the Susquehanna, capture Harrisburg if practicable, and pose a threat to Philadelphia."

"By such a large Confederate army operating on Union soil, it is my hope to bring Mr. Lincoln to the negotiating table or, at the very least, gain international recognition and put intense pressure on the Republican government. Additionally, I desire to box in the Army of the Potomac and force them into making such an error that we can destroy them on a field of our choosing."

Longstreet had listened to Lee intently, and he could not help having misgivings about what he had just heard.

"General Longstreet, do you wish to say something?"

Longstreet did not let his face show his surprise at General Lee's question. "Yes and no, General Lee. The fact that we will have almost 100,000 men on northern soil for the first time ever will surely send shock waves through the North. But I do believe, given the risks of this operation, clear military objectives should be defined."

"Go on, Sir." Lee's tone was polite but like a professor waiting for his student to prove he had studied the night before an exam.

Seeing General Lee's look darken and President Davis shifting in his seat, Longstreet continued, "General Stuart has led raids into Pennsylvania before, but our forces have never held a city or a town in a deep Unionist state. What if we were to capture Chambersburg or even Harrisburg? What if our flag flew over a northern state capital, even for a day? What would the Yankee newspapers say? Congress?" Longstreet asked Secretary Benjamin, "Our 'friends' in London and Paris?"

Secretary Benjamin's deep voice filled the room, "The capture of a state capital such as Harrisburg would change the diplomatic dynamic. England, I fear, is too afraid to lose Canada, so the likelihood of military aid or intervention on her part is almost nonexistent. However, certain political developments could lead to large British investments in our economy. France, on the other hand, has a more protected position in Mexico, and Napoleon III seems more likely than England to intervene. But perhaps the most significant roadblock to either of those powers formally recognizing us is the Emancipation Proclamation and the institution of slavery itself. I know this is a war council, and slavery falls outside of its purview, but when considering military action for political gain, the issue of slavery must be considered. Additionally, let's just say we were to achieve some great victory, and England and France were open to giving some type of formal recognition; since both of those powers have outlawed slavery within their empires, they, at the very least, would want some type of understanding from us on the institution."

There was a brief silence in the room until President Davis spoke, "The institution of slavery, however uncomfortable some may find it, is central to our national economy and war effort. Nevertheless, if either England or France were to request certain provisions from us, I would have to consult with Congress. Certain proposals have reached my desk before, and we could find some accommodation."

Davis paused momentarily as if lost in thought: “Getting back to operations in Pennsylvania, General Lee, could Harrisburg be seized, and how long could it be held?”

Looking at the map, General Lee responded, “I think it is more than feasible to seize Harrisburg, Mr. President. In the coming campaign, General Ewell’s II Corps would lead the invasion and, once through the Shenandoah and into the Cumberland Valley of Pennsylvania, could outmarch any regular Union forces to both Chambersburg and then Harrisburg. I would say that once we were in possession of Harrisburg, our foe would make a great effort to take it back. It would be advisable for the infantry to take the city, but for the cavalry to hold it and use it as a forward reconnaissance base. If an overwhelming force were to be brought to the city, cavalry could make an escape much easier than infantry could. Additionally, that infantry would be useful if we were to make contact with the main Union army.”

Longstreet looked back to Benjamin, “If we captured Harrisburg and held it even for a handful of days and gave the appearance of threatening Philadelphia, would that be enough to get the French involved? Obviously, nothing would be done to jeopardize the safety of the army, but would that really change the perception of our cause?”

President Davis answered, “I feel it is something we must try, for we have no choice. How many battles have we won on our own soil, yet the war continues to favor the enemy? How much longer can our land be drained of all its resources, and the flower of our nation’s youth be bled away?”

The room was silent until General Jackson spoke, “Mr. President, I feel that we all agree with your sentiment. What my friend General Longstreet is driving at is that we must be bold but prudent in our actions in the coming campaign. You and General Lee have entrusted General Longstreet, General Stuart, and me with a sacred duty. With

God Almighty as our protector, we shall enter the enemy's territory and defeat him."

***

June 1, 1863, 12:30 AM, a few miles outside of Vicksburg, Cleburne's Division

Johan stood in amazement as General Cleburne walked around his camp, greeting and talking to any soldiers he encountered. Beauregard had done something similar earlier in the evening, which greatly affected the men. But seeing Cleburne walk amongst and interact with the men made Johan realize that if he had ever lived long enough to become a general, there was the man he would model himself after.

Cleburne had a way that put his men at ease, and they knew he was truly concerned for their well-being. And apparently, to Johan's surprise, as he and Colonel Fremantle shadowed the general, Cleburne knew by name scores of his men. The affection that he showed was also returned, and the camp hummed with excited energy. These men, Cleburne's Division, the best Confederate division west of the Appalachians, knew what was expected of them on the morrow.

Days of marching had put the division mere miles from Vicksburg, with only a thin picket line and mounted patrols separating Cleburne from McClernand's XIII Corps. The men had been implored to keep quiet and make no unnecessary noises. Somewhat placated by Beauregard's and Cleburne's socializing, the entire camp lay still, waiting for Cleburne's orders to rise and close the distance on the nearby Yankees.

The Union bombardment of Vicksburg also helped to conceal the Confederates. For the last two days, Union ships in the Mississippi and Grant's land forces pounded the city continuously, throwing several thousand artillery shells of various calibers into it. So fierce were the explosions that the ground in camp continuously shook

In the early hours before dawn, as the camp lay still and the bombardment of Vicksburg continued, Johan, Fremantle, and General Cleburne sat on fallen logs facing one another. Fires had been forbidden to the entire division so as not to give away their presence to the Yankees. So, the three men sat, passing the last few hours before the division was to be assembled for battle.

Fremantle took a sip from his canteen and spoke in a low voice, "Well, I must say, you Confederates certainly know how to keep your spirits up before the big battle. Being with your division, General, why brings me back to my time in the Crimea with Her Majesty's Coldstream Guards."

The dim moonlight was enough to show Cleburne's smile. "No offense, Colonel Fremantle, but I will take my division over anyone else, including the Coldstream Guards."

"Right, you are, sir. Right you are," chuckled Fremantle. Hearing Johan fiddling with a small knife, he turned to him and said, "Well, Colonel Lutze, are you ready for the morning?" I think very few in Her Majesty's service have seen as many battles as you."

"The day of the battle does not bother me, Colonel. In fact, in the moment of battle, I can push aside most feelings other than the desire to defeat the enemy. But it is the night before I know a battle is to occur. It is when there is nothing else to do but wait for that time. In the darkness, my mind." Johan paused, his eyes looking past Fremantle and Cleburne to the south, hundreds of miles away. "My mind tends to wander. I think about my family and friends. The ones are still with the ones who are now with our heavenly Father. But mostly, since this damn war began, it is my love, my Tesa, who I never leave my mind."

"You have a sweetheart," spoke Fremantle in a softer voice. "If I am not intruding, are you married, Colonel?"

"No, sir. We had made plans to marry early in the war, but with the fall of New Orleans and most of Southeast Louisiana to the Yankees and my own stay in a Union prison camp, time got the best of us."

"The fortunes of war," spoke Cleburne. "This war has caused so much harm, torn so many families apart. I confess that some of my own kin settled in Ohio and are staunch Unionists. But tell me, Colonel Lutze, how is your Tesa? Have you heard from her lately?"

"Not directly, Sir. But she is staying with my family and is out of any direct danger for the moment. With all of this," Johan gestured at the camp, "communications are difficult."

"For sure, Colonel. It is my hope that someday, and someday soon, you are able to meet your Tesa once again, and in the meantime, as the two of us get to know one another, you can tell me more about the woman who has stolen your heart."

General Cleburne was one of a kind, and Johan was so grateful he was assigned to this sector of Beauregard's army. "I think we will have plenty of time for me to share our story with you, General. But I must ask, sir, is there a special lady in the General's life?"

A hand running through the scalp told Johan all he needed. "Well, Colonel," and Cleburne paused and grinned, "I cannot say that I am practically engaged like yourself, but there is a certain woman that I have befriended. Susan, Susan Tarleton is her name." Cleburne's voice trailed off as if his mind had gone somewhere else. "We met while I was in Mobile earlier this year. We became acquainted with one another, and our friendship blossomed."

The way Cleburne talked, Johan knew the man was in love. It was evident to Fremantle as well. "Well, sir," Johan chuckled, "I gave my godfather, the president, some advice, and he told me to shove it, so take this as you may. Sir, from my own painful experience, if you love Susan, which to me is very apparent that you do, do not hesitate to tell her how you feel about her. I knew my Tesa for some time before we became committed to one another. Through stupidity, jealousy, and pride, we both lost so much time that could have been shared with each other. If you can learn anything from me, sir, don't follow my flawed example."

"Well said," Fremantle gave a soft clap. "Colonel, when the time permits, I would very much like to hear the story of your wonderful Tesa."

"As would I," Cleburne eyes focused on something or someone who was not there, far away in the relative safety of Mobile, Alabama.

Chapter 11

The Battle of Vicksburg
June 1, 1863, 4:00 AM, General Pickett's Division

"Morning, General," Andre saluted General Pickett.

Pickett returned the salute, "Good morning, Lieutenant. My god, I thought Virginia was hot in the summer, but Mississippi has re-defined the word 'heat' to me. And it is only four in the morning."

"Well, sir, just take a boat down to New Orleans, and you would think Vicksburg frosty. I've met with 'General' Forrest," Andre chuckled, "the younger. He promised to give you a clear path. Grant knows we crossed the Big Black River, so they will be expecting us."

"Right." Pickett was still nervous about Beauregard's plan, but it was the only realistic option the Confederacy had to relieve Vicksburg. "Well, we still have a few surprises in store for them. After all, we old timers from the Army of Northern Virginia must represent that most famed army to the utmost."

Pickett's division and Breckenridge's had not set up much of a camp, and all the men left their heavy packs behind at the main camp, several miles behind them. They were implored to pack ammunition and carry canteens for the summer heat, with no excess baggage. The day would be hot and dry, and the Confederates needed every advantage over the Yankees.

The shelling of Vicksburg lit up the western sky as the eastern sky began to have the first rays of daylight. As Pickett's division assembled into battle lines, the constant rap of musketry alerted them to the heavy skirmishing between Forrest's cavalry and Grant's pickets.

Mounted, Pickett lifted the kepi from his head. "Men, Virginians! Today is why we have traveled so far from our sacred Virginia! We have come all this way to help defend our fellow Southerners! The people of Vicksburg and the men defending it believe in the idea of freedom, just as our forefathers did when they fought ole' King George. Today, we join together to fight another tyrant, but one much closer to home. Follow me, men! We know the task assigned to us! Let's do our part in rescuing this great city. Battalions, Forward!"

***

General Grant knew a sizeable Confederate force that had crossed the Big Black River. Though General Forrest's cavalry screen largely hid their numbers, there was no doubt that Johnston was bringing the majority of his force to Snyder's Mill and then down onto Sherman's and McPherson's Corps. Sherman had assembled a force to face the east to confront Johnston, and it was assumed that all the proper arrangements had been made to face both Pemberton's forces in Vicksburg and Johnston's.

It had taken Grant by surprise that the Confederates in the Vicksburg theater had gone from virtually no cavalry during the time of Grierson's Raid to almost 7 or 8,000. The Confederate cavalry had an immediate impact and greatly hampered Grant's operations, leaving his troops without the support of his main army. The pickets were being continuously rolled up as well, with several survivors racing back into camp screaming about the devil Forrest and his demon cavalry. The fight was coming.

What Grant did not know was that the Confederate attack north of Vicksburg was to begin at 5:30 AM on June 1.

***

June 1, 1863, 5:30 AM

Eric Daniels of the 21st Iowa pulled the coffee pot from the cook fire and poured steaming coffee into his cup and several of his friends. It might be summer in Mississippi, but it did not mean they could not have good coffee.

The first rays of the morning sun lit up the camp as men began their morning routines. Eric sipped his coffee along with his friend Michael. The entire regiment, along with 30,000 other troops, had been put on standby to counter any moves that Johnston might make to relieve Vicksburg. However, over the last several days, the only Confederate forces encountered were extensive cavalry patrols. They were a nuisance, but nothing that could not be swept aside.

Michael took a deep drink of his coffee, "Damn, that's good, Eric. So, what do you think the weather will be like today?"

Eric saw Michael's smirk and laughed, "It's going to be hot as hell and dry like any other day in this godforsaken place. But, as long as we are not the ones in the rifle pits facing the rebs in Vicksburg, I'm fine with being out in the open over here."

Seconds later, thousands of Confederate troops gave the rebel yell, followed by a sheet of volley fire. Eric quickly changed his mind.

***

Generals Pickett and Breckenridge had aligned their divisions into an inverted V formation. Other independent regiments and brigades were distributed along the edges of the formation, with a couple of regiments held in reserve for Pickett. General Armistead's Brigade of

Pickett's division formed to the tip of the V, and it was that brigade's job to pierce the Union line and lead the charge through their ranks.

Andre was seated atop his horse when the two divisions let out the rebel yell and unleashed a volley into the unsuspecting Union camp. With bayonets fixed, the Confederate infantry raced in and overwhelmed the first part of the Union line.

Pistol in hand, Andre urged his mount forward. "God damn, we pulled it off. Ha!" A sea of gray-clad Confederate infantry pushed forward as they routed all the Union forces before them, and Andre followed the trail. Jumping the horse over a narrow rifle pit, he located Pickett's divisional flag and mentally noted the progress of Armistead.

Inside the V, Andre followed Armistead's brigade but put himself in front of Pickett's reserve. Dead and dying blue-clad Union troops littered the ground, many of them still not fully dressed for the day, being caught off guard by the dawn attack. And already, scores of Yankee prisoners were being escorted back to the main Confederate camp.

"Damn, that is at least 50 right there." So far, 10 minutes into the battle, it was an undeniable Confederate success. But that initial success was only going to last for so long. Holstering the pistol, Andre rode up further and pulled out his field glasses. Beauregard's whole plan relied on using Grant's predictable response against him. The area they were in was wooded and hilly, and it would not take long for Johnston's army wing to begin to lose steam. However, Andre watched as Pickett's men crested a small ridge and surged forward in pursuit of the fleeing Yankees.

Smoke was beginning to hamper the view of Pickett's advance, but at least the smoke was mainly for the repeated volleys Pickett's men were getting off. As wounded Yankees writhed and screamed for help on the ground, Andre ignored them and the random mini-balls that occasionally zipped past him.

When Andre reached the top of the ridge, General Johnston and his staff rode up as well. "General," Andre saluted.

"Lieutenant," Johnston returned the gesture. He took out his own field glasses and followed Pickett's and Breckenridge's progress. "Well, I must say, it was providence that we were able to achieve surprise on this level." He did some quick calculations in his mind. "Lieutenant, when you return to General Pickett, watch the time as closely as possible. It will take at least half an hour for the artillery to reach this ridge and then set up. We need two hours to have all of the artillery ready."

"Understood, Sir."

"And, Lieutenant, there can be no debate about the success we have achieved so far, but do remind General Pickett that he is to begin his withdrawal as soon as it becomes evident Grant is rallying for his counterattack. If we are not careful, Pickett will find that his division will be facing almost two Corps by itself."

Beauregard's battle plan involved Pickett and Breckenridge making an all-out attack on the Union line. Then, after having thrown the Yankees into complete chaos, the two Confederate divisions would begin a controlled withdrawal to the ridge Andre had just left. Johnston was to arrange several batteries on the ridge so that when Pickett retreated, the pursuing Yankees would be hit by a score of cannon firing canister shot.

The battle flags out of view; Andre followed the smoke and caught up with Pickett. He rode past several clusters of dead Union troops, most probably men who had attempted to make a last stand only to be struck down by a concentrated Confederate volley.

The general was very animated atop his horse, urging his men forward and trying his best to keep them in formation both as a division and in conjunction with Breckenridge's division. While Armistead's brigade cut the hole in the Union line, other brigades fanned out and rolled up any remaining Union forces, which, as planned, turned the inverted V formation into more of a set of parallel lines.

Andre saluted, "General Pickett."

"Good man, Lieutenant Breaux. Glad you were able to find us." The constant musket fire made it difficult to hear. "How much time do we need to buy General Johnston? Things have gone exceptionally well so far, with minimal losses. I know Grant will counterattack, but my God, there is nothing else like watching the Yankees run!"

"Two hours, General. That is what Johnston asked for."

The worry in Pickett's eyes spoke volumes. "Alright. I don't know if we can do this for two hours, but we will give it one hell of a try!"

Pickett spurred his mount forward and raced to the front of his division. He called out to dress the lines, and like the veterans they were, Pickett's men, while loading and firing their rifles, reformed their ranks and continued to march forward. The terrain was rough and hilly, so Pickett's men would soon begin to lose formation once again, but Andre could not help but admire the Virginians. But there was no time to go sightseeing, and Andre turned his horse to the southeast and urged it forward to find General Breckenridge.

***

June 1, 1863, 7:30 AM, General Taylor's command, Louisiana side of the river

"I have the urge to have you shot on principle, Lieutenant Breaux."

Andre laughed, "General Taylor, will you let a few minor indiscretions on my part a year ago in Virginia? Let's have bygones be bygones and get to the business at hand."

"Breaux, whether you are a private sergeant or an officer, you are an insubordinate bastard who could give two damns about anything. Especially anything that had to do with taking orders from anyone. Including multiple generals. The more I think about it, I might just shoot you myself."

"Why, General Taylor, was our time together that much of an inconvenience to you?"

"Yes, Breaux. Yes. You were exceptionally good at killing Yankees; that was your one saving grace. And Davis's godson kept you in line, sometimes."

"Well, Sir, as much as you would like to shoot me, General Beauregard, as your commanding general, would not appreciate that. However, let's get past our good-natured banter." Taylor still looked like he was ready to grab his revolver at any moment and shoot Andre. "Beauregard has a request of you, sir. And I think it is something you will take a liking to."

Just like that, the annoying Frenchman detailed to Taylor General Beauregard's desired operations for the Louisiana side of the Mississippi. It was going to be a risky operation. Still, like everything else lately, Taylor, the son of former United States President Zackary Taylor, knew that something extraordinary had to be done.

It still sounded strange to Taylor about the meeting with Lieutenant Breaux and the idea of him being a commissioned officer; it had only been a handful of days ago. It was actually a good plan, in Taylor's estimation, but like everything else, timing would be everything.

Taylor's small army was technically within the Department of the Trans-Mississippi. However, President Davis, Taylor's former brother-in-law, had given Beauregard the authority to override his own rigid departmental structure and to command Taylor. Taylor was more than happy with this development, especially since he was no longer under the thumb of his department commander, Kirby Smith.

Beauregard was to attack Grant in two spots on the morning of June 1, and Taylor was to attack the Yankees on the Louisiana side of the river, nearly simultaneously at Milliken's Bend, about 15 miles above Vicksburg on the Louisiana side of the river. Milliken's Bend was a major supply depot for Grant's forces, and it was a strategic location along the Mississippi to attempt a cut-off of Grant's supply lines.

Taylor marched his small army the night of May 31 and got it within almost a mile of the Union defenses. His cavalry, mostly made up of Texans led by General McCulloch, provided the screen for the infantry led by General Mouton's Louisiana and Texas regiments. Once his troops were positioned, Taylor waited.

Vicksburg was bombarded through the night, but at 5:30 AM on June 1, Taylor thought he heard a battle from the east. Using his cavalry and his own field glasses, he kept a watchful eye on the Union camp and waited to see what their reaction would be. At a quarter to 7, the Union camp was in a frenzy, and troops formed into regiments and began to file onto various steamships, which then sailed downriver to reinforce Grant, who was now engaged with Beauregard, presumably.

He knew his men were anxious for a fight, but Taylor waited until he saw a third regiment begin to board a steamship. Orders were quickly issued, and the attack began with the rebel yell and a cacophony of rifle fire.

Though caught off guard, the union regiments present resisted Taylor fiercely. Most of these Union troops were black men from Louisiana and Mississippi, many of whom had not long ago been slaves on nearby plantations. These United States Colored Troops (USCT) regiments would give Taylor everything he could handle.

Having served with Stonewall Jackson in the Valley Campaign the previous year, Taylor's philosophy for fighting was very clear.

Get a jump on the enemy early and hit him with everything you have before he has time to react.

After the initial Confederate volley, much of the fighting was hand-to-hand with either bayonets or rifle butts. As brutal and brave as the black troops fought, because two of their regiments had already been taken out of line and shipped off, the opening volley had effectively broken any cohesion they had.

The Union troopers were violently pushed back but fought for every inch that they gave up. The camp had few formal defensive works, so the levee along the Mississippi served as the last line of defense. Past the levee, the land was flat and somewhat muddy, where the supply depot was positioned next to the riverbank.

If the Confederates broke their defensive line at the levee, the Union troopers knew the supply depot would be in jeopardy of either capture or outright destruction. It was also a matter of pride and principle for the black troops, most of whom feared capture by the Confederates. So, the black Union forces held their ground and, with the assistance of the two Union gunboats in the river, held Taylor's men to a brutal standstill at the levee.

General Mouton, sensing the Confederate line beginning to stall, raised his saber and called for his men to follow him. He rode his horse straight at the Union line and, with pistol and saber, jumped his horse onto the levee and cleaved a hole through the Yankees. Luckily for him, his men with fixed bayonets followed closely behind and, with the force of a tidal wave, broke the Union line.

Confederate troops poured through the gap, but what the United States classified as 'native' black troops held their ground and slowly retreated and even counter-attacked with bayonets. As heroically as the black troops fought, with the mixing of Confederate and Union forces behind the levee, the gunboats USS Choctaw and USS Lexington had to cease firing or risk firing into their fellow bluecoats.

It was all the break Taylor needed. With no longer active fire support coming from the river, more pockets of Union troops were isolated and then neutralized. It was a brutal affair, but surprisingly, the Confederates from Louisiana and Texas allowed the black Union troops to surrender when the opportunity presented itself.

Generals McCulloch and Mouton urged their troops forward into the chaos that was engulfing the riverbank. Mouton led a charge and had his horse shot from under him, and the Confederate infantry immediately began to lose its cohesion.

Watching his men get mauled, Taylor led his horse into the melee and rallied his troops. The Union gunboats began to fire again on the Confederates, and several Union troop transport ships were visible in the river. Taylor realized that his window for inflicting loss on the Yankees was waning. He acted by having his infantry seize several artillery pieces and direct them at the Union boats in the river.

Mouton was able to remount and, despite the broken hand, took command of his infantry back from Taylor. This arrangement helped Taylor immensely, for he was now able to direct the battle through Mouton and McCulloch once again. Taylor focused on getting as many cannons as possible pointed at the river and firing, and on preventing his men from looting the camp while they should have been fighting.

The last remnant of the Union forces massed at the riverbank and continued to fight back ferociously. The brutality of the fight on and off the water kept increasing, and though the Black troops were taking grievous casualties, they held their ground and ensured that the fight would be costly for Taylor.

Satisfied with the artillery fire, Taylor directed troopers to either carry away supplies or prepare whatever could not be taken away for destruction. And then the coup de grace occurred. As the Confederates had turned the captured Union guns on the river, several Union ships were caught in the crossfire. Unluckily for 500 men of the XVI Corps who were en route to reinforce Grant at Vicksburg, their aged transport was hit in its smokestack and paddle wheel.

The paddle wheel sustained severe damage, but the smokestack damage triggered a catastrophic chain reaction. The smokestack was hit by shrapnel, and instead of shearing off, it twisted around and fell over, making it hard for the proper amount of steam to escape from one of the engine boilers. The boiler overheated quickly, causing it to rupture and explode. This caused the other boiler to fail and catch fire. Once the ship lost its engine power, the untrained Confederate gunners began focusing on the ship, and within minutes, it was in flames. The order was given to abandon the ship, but as lifeboats began to be lowered into the Mississippi, the ship blew up, killing almost all of the 500 troopers on board and the crew.

As wooden shrapnel from the explosion reached Taylor and his men, he knew that was his sign to take his victory and leave. To the chagrin of the Union troops fighting to the last man on the riverbank, many fell to their knees in the river water as the Confederates disengaged and began to withdraw.

By 11:00 AM, Taylor's troops had withdrawn entirely. Though the Union still was in possession of Milliken's Landing, they had suffered nearly 1,000 casualties, with several hundred of those men now being Confederate prisoners of war, along with the additional 500 men who had died on the exploding transport ship. Taylor suffered 250 casualties compared to the 1500 Union losses, and the depot was wholly wrecked, so Taylor had achieved his objective.

***

June 1, 1863, 8:00 AM, Pickett's Division

It had been one of those mornings when Andre thought he was back in Virginia fighting under General Lee. Pickett and Breckenridge had worked seamlessly together under Johnston's direction, and every Union unit they faced, either regiment or brigade strength, had been routed. That was until ten minutes ago. Grant was doing what they had suspected he would do. After several Union units had been essentially sacrificed to slow the Confederate advance, it was clear that massive reinforcements were being sent to plug the gap that Pickett had created.

Andre looked at his watch and then galloped toward General Pickett. His entire division was now deployed, linked with Breckenridge's division. But now came perhaps the most dangerous part of Beauregard's plan, the part where 18,000 Confederate infantry executed a fighting withdrawal.

"General," Andre refrained from saluting so as not to bring undo the attention of Union sharpshooters. "Sir, enough time has passed for General Johnston to assemble his artillery. The time has come to pull back, Sir."

The smoke of rifle fire trapped in a wooded area made it difficult for Pickett to scan his lines. "Lieutenant, I believe you are correct. Captain," Pickett turned to one of his staff officers, "You just came back from Breckenridge, so I am sending you back to him. Tell him we need to begin our withdrawal."

***

The fighting northeast of Vicksburg had turned from essentially a Corps-strength Confederate formation routing several smaller and isolated Union units to a pitched battle between equal forces. Grant and Sherman had rallied their forces and now had 20,000 troops engaging Johnston.

It marked yet another time that Grant had been surprised by a Confederate army, but Grant held Joseph Johnston in even less regard than Beauregard. This fight was to be no Shiloh. Despite the heavy losses early in the morning, Grant, with Sherman acting as his bulldog, continuously poured fresh forces into the battle. Not only had the Confederate advance been stopped, but Grant was now retaking much of the land that had been lost that morning.

By 9:00 AM, Grant sat atop his mount while he puffed on a cigar, enjoying yet another soon-to-be victory. General Sherman rode up and gave a half-hearted salute. "We are pushing them back, Sam. Johnston, maybe for the first time ever, got the jump on us this morning. But we are quickly reversing all their gains. Hell, we might put a permanent end to that army by the end of today."

"Sherm, if that is the case, I might actually share a drink with you. But let's not get ahead of ourselves. Forrest is still a factor, and I would hate to get overconfident and have him blindside us somewhere."

One of Grant's staff officers galloped up and halted before Grant as an artillery battery unleashed a volley. With the ground shaking beneath him, the rider addressed Grant, "General, there is a situation at Milliken's Bend."

"Go on," Grant spoke calmly.

"Well, Sir. The report just came in. It seems like Richard Taylor led a small army undetected up to the depot and launched an all-out attack. The men are holding strong, but it's mostly the Colored regiments that are defending the depot. Unfortunately, Sir, even when Taylor is driven off, our casualties will be high, and much of the supplies within the depot will be looted or destroyed."

"Damn." Grant pulled off his hat in disgust. "Well, not much can be done about that right now. But it will probably redirect any troops en route on the river from the XVI Corps and send them to Louisiana instead of here for today. Well, I must hand it to Johnston; not only did he get the jump on us, but he coordinated with Taylor across the Mississippi. Major," Grant scribbled an order and handed it over," locate General McPherson and give this order. It's straight to the point. I want his entire Corps to shift and pull some more brigades from McClernand. We are going to finish off Johnston today. Then I want that city," he pointed back to Vicksburg, "taken without further delay."

Grant then paused and grimaced once more. Sherman did likewise. "I hear it, too. I think Pemberton is launching an attack as well."

Chapter 12

Beauregard's Surprise
June 1, 1863, Confederate Battery, Synder's Mill Area

Jacob heard the familiar sound of musketry slowly drifting his way. He had never been fond of muzzle-loading rifles, and the amount of rifle fire was breathtaking to him. Being part of an artillery crew seemed much more civilized to him than standing shoulder to shoulder and blasting away at the enemy.

"You gotta get your head out of the clouds, my man, Jake." Elijah, General Beauregard's former body servant, grinned at Jacob and pounded another stake into the ground. "The Yankees aren't that far now. Our little surprise needs to be ready."

Wiping his brow, Jacob sighed and spoke in his thick Prussian accent, "It's 'ucking ut out here, my friend. I thought Virginia was it, but Mississippi is one train station away from Hades."

"It's fucking hot, Jake. Fuck…ing." Elijah gave his blond Prussian friend a grin. "Remember to pronounce the f."

A year ago, if anyone had told Jacob the journey he would take from Posen, Prussia, to right outside Vicksburg, Mississippi, he would have said they were out of their minds. But now, Jacob wondered at times if he had, in fact, lost his mind.

Jacob could not deny that he had some privileges growing up. His father, who was tough and no-nonsense as a professional, was a loving and caring family man at home. Papa was mostly jovial and good-natured, but as Jacob grew into a young man, Papa would take Jacob out of earshot of Mama and give some hard life advice. "Jacob, my lad. Remember, I love you with all my heart. Never forget that. But, my lad, you are the idealist just like my brother. It's commendable, very much so. But he followed his ideals to an early grave in '48. I will never turn my back on you, son, but just remember there are your ideals and then the real world."

What had brought him here? It was a simple but long story. At heart, he was an idealist, just like Papa had said, maybe even a bleeding heart for those he felt were oppressed. His father was a civil administrator in Posen for the King of Prussia, which gave Jacob an upbringing in Prussian Poland. Jacob had just as many friends who were Polish as he did German back home, which gave him a unique perspective on the plight of the Polish people.

Everything changed in January when the January Uprising in Russian Poland began. Jacob, by his nature, had a soft spot for the Poles, especially those under the brutal rule of the Russian Tsars. But when Russian troops had murdered his best friend's sister and her husband in reprisal against Polish rebels, Jacob crossed the Prussian/Russian frontier with several of his Polish friends and volunteered to join the fight against the Russians.

Jacob soon fought in several skirmishes with Russian troops and even managed to shoot and kill a Russian Colonel. But in early March, Jacob had been captured by the Russians and was only saved from execution by virtue of his Prussian citizenship. Papa had taken care of the rest through his influence within the Prussian administrative state and through the outright bribes paid to multiple Russian officials for Jacob's release. More or less an outlaw in Prussia, Jacob signed on with a Union recruiter of all people because of the $300 bonus that was offered and the idea of helping to free the oppressed negroes of the Confederacy.

Jacob saw only $50 of the promised $300 bounty to join the Union Army and found his time in the XI Corps of the Army of the Potomac to be eye-opening. He was unlucky enough to have joined XI Corps, the 'German" Corps, just before the shit show of Chancellorsville. At Chancellorsville, XI Corps had been left hung out to dry and virtually annihilated by Stonewall Jackson's Corps.

The scale and violence of Chancellorsville was nothing like the fighting in Poland. Still, though Jacob had gotten a couple of shots off from his muzzle-loading musket, he made every effort to shoot over the heads of Confederate soldiers. In his brief time in the Army of the Potomac, Jacob realized that the propaganda he had been told back in Prussia was simply that. In many ways, he saw Southern civilians mistreated like the Poles in Russia. And then the story he had been told about the Negroes, was very different from reality as well. With all of that in mind, maybe that was why he was so willing to go along with Johan. After all, had the man essentially saved his life twice?

"Head still in the clouds," Elijah laughed.

Jacob's English had greatly improved over the last month, and his becoming good friends with Elijah helped, even if he still had trouble pronouncing certain words. "I've been wondering. You are a negro and fight for the Confederates. Why is that?"

The two men pounded two more stakes into the ground before Elijah answered. "It's complicated. I have a friend, a negro, as you would say, and his grandpappy owns a plantation back in South Carolina." Elijah grinned when he saw the reaction on Jacob's face. "That's right, us negroes are just as capable of owning slaves as white folk. Even better, my friend joined the state militia and is now an artilleryman. But I would say this: I saw the fighting in South Carolina. Hell, I witnessed friends of mine, white boys I grew up with, die. I helped bury some of them."

They continued down the ridge, helping to dig rifle pits and position artillery wherever needed. "What it comes down to, these people," Elijah gestured with the pickax, "these people are my people, Southerners."

"But you also know how to read and write, a skill not had by all enslaved negroes."

"You're right, Jake. To tell you the truth, though it was illegal, I was taught to read and write in Sunday school. And I was good with numbers. Plantation managers value those skills in a slave; it makes that slave more productive and valuable. And the crazy thing is, the first plantation manager to hire me to help with the books, well, he was a negro just like me."

"This whole system in the South just does not seem fair. You work and work, and still you are not a free man."

"Well, Jake, haven't you said anything to that effect about the serfdom that exists in Poland? Well, that's not much different than what we have going on here?"

"Ya. Ya, you are right." Jacob stood up and turned his head to the sound of increased musketry. "You hear that?"

Elijah nodded. "Time to get back."

***

10:00 AM, Pickett's Division

One of the benefits Johan had presented to Andre for joining Beauregard's staff was that he would get a horse and not have to march everywhere anymore. That thinking ended when the mare Andre rode was shot from underneath him.

"Damn it!" Andre flew a short distance and clipped a pine tree with his shoulder. He looked up and grunted, "Fuck." Riding through a battle was dangerous and confusing, and Andre had managed to get stuck between Armistead's brigade and an entire division of Yankees with bayonets at the ready, pointed at him.

Bullets whizzed by Andre's head and struck the tree above his head as he attempted to take cover. His back to the tree, he winced at the pain in the shoulder he had injured a month before, only to reinjure now.

"Come on, you Yankee bastards," Andre pulled out a revolver as the blue-clad troops unleashed a volley at the Confederate brigade 50 yards away. The sound of hundreds of muskets firing at once boomed like a succession of thunderclaps. As skinny as Andre tried to make himself behind the pine tree, he felt the impact of several bullets into the tree behind his back. Stiffly, he stood while crouching and ran towards Armistead's brigade, hoping that neither the Yankees nor his fellow Confederates would shoot him.

"Charge!" Andre heard several Yankee officers scream and felt the ground shake as the mass of troops lurked forward. "Damn it!" He pumped his legs, willing himself to go faster as he saw in between the trees the Confederate line lower their rifles. It helped to be battle-tested, and Andre was on the ground before the volley was fired. The heat and air displacement of the bullets brushed his face, and Andre stood as the smoke still hovered over the Confederate line. Several men saw him, and they waved to Andre to hurry as the Yankees quickly regrouped and began to surge forward again.

Half deaf, Andre stumbled into line with Armistead's men, grimacing, pulled out his other revolver, and readied himself. All the Confederates still standing were hurriedly ramrodding their rifles and fixing their bayonets as the Union charge neared. The command was issued to fire at will, and Andre waited until the Yankees were almost on top of the Confederate line to begin firing his two revolvers.

The woods trapped the heat of the day, and Andre was drenched in sweat as he made each of his 12 bullets count. The man next to him fell as a bullet ripped through the side of his head, sending blood and brain matter everywhere. Being an officer no longer mattered to Andre, and when his revolvers were empty, he holstered them, picked up his dead comrade's rifle, and joined the melee as a rifleman. The individual rifle drill came back to Andre second nature, and he quickly bayoneted two Yankees who handled their rifles hesitantly, even though his left shoulder screamed with every movement of his arm. The battle had now devolved into its most basic form, a brawl that would be won by the side that was willing to be more brutal and barbaric than the other.

He heard the command fall back 30 yards, and, not noticing that his section of the line was not moving, Andre shouted out the order himself. To his surprise, the squads around him complied. Though simultaneously giving the Yankees everything they had to provide, the Confederate line slowly disengaged and retreated for a final 30 yards.

***

"Damn, ain't that a sight."

Jacob agreed with Elijah. As they crouched behind the recently built barricade, they watched as what they thought were Breckinridge's and Pickett's divisions were pushed back by an endless line of Yankee infantry. The two Confederate divisions even lost contact with each other, and at least one Yankee brigade began to flood the gap.

"Battle stations!" called out their commanding colonel. Elijah and Jacob jumped up to their stations. Their cannon, a smooth-bore Napoleon, was loaded with grapeshot and ready to fire. Grapeshot had the effect of a large shotgun blast, consisting of 9 or 10 grape-sized metal balls inside a sack that was then loaded into the cannon. Both men covered their ears as the gun's "shooter" gripped the cannon's lanyard and awaited orders to fire.

The blue wave of Union troops continued to surge forward, but no order was issued to fire. The Confederate battle plan had called for Pickett and Breckenridge to attack the Yankees and push as hard as possible until Grant began pouring in reinforcements. Once the Confederates lost the momentum in their advance, they would slowly retreat until the flanks of the Yankees were brought into range of Johnston's hidden artillery.

The initial Confederate infantry attack's purpose was to buy time for the artillery to get into place and to pre-sight ranges for the 27 cannons arrayed along the ridge. And as more Yankees came into view, the more that entered the kill zone.

"Fire!" called out the section chief, a lieutenant.

The shooter gripped the lanyard hard and pulled it. Fire and smoke erupted from the front of the cannon as the grapeshot thundered toward the Union lines. All the other cannons fired simultaneously as well, and the volume of cannon fire pulverized the exposed Union troops. While a cloud of smoke hung over the Confederate artillery, as the grapeshot tore into the Union ranks, weapons, bodies, and body parts flew into the air. Pickett halted his division, and as the Union troops stood in shock from the sudden artillery bombardment, Pickett's men frantically fired, reloaded, and fired again into the Union ranks.

Jacob and Elijah were the ammunition handlers for their gun. After their cannon finished its recoil, they rushed to the limber and brought the ammunition and powder for the next shot. This time, canister, a tin filled with iron balls the size of regular bullets, was loaded and then fired into the regrouping masses of Union troops. It was a slaughter, as the crew for each gun had drilled incessantly over the last few days, allowing each cannon to be fired around three times every minute.

Staggering losses over such a short period did not deter the Yankees. Their attack continued to advance and close ranks even though the canister shot at close range cut huge holes in their formations.

Sweat ran down Jacob's back as he ran back and forth between the limber and the gun. The Yankees had taken notice of the entrenched Confederate artillery, and several of the gun crews were either put out of commission or had already suffered some losses from the near-constant fire that was being directed at them. But Jacob and Elijah watched every time their cannon was fired and the horrific damage it caused. It terrified Jacob that so many guns could fire and, despite inflicting terrible casualties, did not stop the Union troops' advance.

***

General Sherman rode back and forth, weaving around trees to push his troops forward. The entire morning had been a chaos of confusion, but his boys had stopped the Confederates cold. Better yet, with his counterattack, the whole Confederate force was steadily pushed back until Sherman retook virtually all the territory the Confederates had conquered that morning, just after 10:00 AM.

"Come on, boys," Sherman waved his hat in the air. "Not much more now; we have them on the run!" And it was true. Johnston had gambled and lost, and Sherman would ensure that Johnston's army was finished off as a fighting force today. However, even as an elderly man, Sherman would never forget what he believed was his greatest blunder of the war.

"General Steele, keep pushing the 1st Division forward! That gap between those two reb divisions is getting wider by the minute. I want it exploited now!"

Steele honored Sherman's order, but as his division poured into the gap between the two Confederate divisions, the ground shook as the 27 Confederate cannons raked fire all along the Union line. Some of the rebel cannons got off two or three shots within that first minute, and several Union regiments essentially ceased to exist after getting hit more than once by several cannons with canister shots.

Sherman sat dumbfounded atop his horse at the destruction of so many regiments in such a short period of time. But his inaction almost cost him his life as a canister shot hit a tree that sent shrapnel everywhere, and with enough force, a foot-long wooden stake impaled his horse in the neck. Sherman could not leap from his horse, but still had the wherewithal to pull out his legs so the poor animal could collapse and not crush his legs.

Spitting the dirt out of his mouth, Sherman yelled for another horse and was soon mounted and again directing the battle. He called for a Colonel on his staff, “That goddamn rebel artillery.” The ground shook as several cannons fired one after another. “I don’t care where you get them from, but we need to sweep that ridge,” he pointed, “with everything we have. Our boys are getting slaughtered!”

“General Sherman,” the colonel grimaced, “I will do what I can. Pemberton has launched an attack across his entire front. I just came from General Grant, and that fight is tying down a lot of men and heavy guns at the moment.”

His face turned nearly scarlet, and Sherman let out a guttural growl. “For Christ’s sake, I need cannons. In the meantime, give me a brigade so I can at least occupy the attention of those damn rebel guns!”

***

After the cannon finished its recoil, Jacob ran forward and pushed the long pole with a sponge on its end down the cannon's barrel. One of their crewmen had been killed by flying shrapnel, and another man had been hit in the shoulder by a sharpshooter. Feeling the sponge hit the back of the cannon, Jacob pulled the pole out of the cannon, thereby cleaning the gun and ensuring no embers were still lit inside the barrel. Elijah then inserted the powder charge into the muzzle and rammed it down the barrel with his own pole. The rest of the loading process was quickly finished, and the cannon was fired once more into the oncoming mass of Yankee troops.

The cannons had certainly evened the odds with the Yankees, but the Confederates were down to 17 functioning cannons, and each cannon was becoming less effective due to casualties. Still, all crews were firing canister shot, which was utterly mauling Sherman's troops. The thing was, Sherman kept sending wave after wave of men, hoping sheer numbers would break the will of the Confederates. There was chaos everywhere, and the Confederate battery was slowly returning fire.

There was an explosion above them, and pieces of metal and wood shot into their small crew, and everyone was hit. Luckily for Elijah, he had been close to the barrel of the cannon loading and was spared serious injury, but did get a piece of hot metal stuck in his arm. The boy almost fell over out of the pain, but he gripped his injured arm and moved out of the way of the remaining artillery crew.

Jacob ignored the blood that ran down his face, placed the canister into the muzzle, and rammed it down as shots began to land around his feet. As the sergeant aimed the cannon, Jacob looked to see dozens of blue-clad Yankee troops scaling the earthworks. More shots rang out, and as Jacob felt a pain in his calf and his left leg go out, he turned to his sergeant only to see the back of the man's head get blown off.

On his knees, as the battle roared around them, Jacob saw the lanyard that had been set for their cannon. He crawled, his calf screaming at every movement to the lanyard, and yanked it.

As Jacob saw the light begin to blossom, he cradled his head in his arms only to hear the thunderclap of the cannon. Even with his eyes closed and facing the ground, the brightness of the cannon going off still penetrated his shut eyes.

He waited to hear the fighting resume, but then he realized that everything sounded muffled. Daring to open his eyes, Jacob lifted his head and saw no one standing anywhere around him, only the ground covered in bits of red and blue. It was then that everything went dark.

***

10:15 AM

"Sherm, how are you progressing?"

General Sherman lowered his field glasses and turned with a nod to General Grant. "Better, Sam. But Johnston played us well. From what I understand from a few of the prisoners who have been questioned, we face about 15,000 rebel infantry, primarily made up of Pickett's and Breckenridge's divisions."

"You mean General Pickett from Virginia?"

"You heard that right. It probably explains why the Rebs were so aggressive this morning. Well, it seems their whole plan was to rile us up and then lead us into this little death trap." Sherman gestured toward the ridge, where as many as 15 Confederate cannons still fired into the Union ranks, the booms shaking the ground.

Grant stepped up next to Sherman with his own field glasses. "How many guns do you think are up there?"

"Less than there were. The rate of fire is much lower, so I would say we have maybe taken out 10 guns or so. Our own guns have been brought up and have begun pounding that ridge, but the rebs are so well dug in that our sharpshooters are more effective than cannon at silencing them, but we are taking heavy losses in that regard."

Taking a long puff on his cigar, Grant leaned against a tree and scanned the entire ridge the Confederates had dug into. "I sent word that Pemberton launched an attack along his entire front."

"I received that message." Sherman sighed. "I guess you have McPherson handling that. How long before I can get more reinforcements? The rebs are pushed back to where they started, but I don't have the men to take that ridge and drown the bastards in the Big Black River."

An artillery round slammed into the branches above them, which sent shredded pieces of wood everywhere. Grant swatted debris off his hat, "McPherson has Pemberton covered. The fighting has been tough, and the rebels even seized some of our rifle pits. But we had retaken most of our entrenchments by the time I had left McPherson. I did send another request for reinforcements from McClernand, so between his troops and McPhearson, hopefully, by this afternoon, the rebs will be trying like hell to recross that river back to Jackson."

"Glad McClernand can do something to help us. He has been a drain during this whole campaign.

"Sherm."

"I know Sam. I shouldn't talk of a fellow officer as such. But my God, can you see what our boys have been through? He sits on his pretty hands while my and McPherson's boys do all the dying."

Grant turned his head to the southeast. "Have any of those rebel prisoners told you how big their army is?

Sherman laughed, "They claim 40 or 50,000 while there are only 15,000 facing us here. Where are the other supposed 30,000?"

"Oh my God." Grant's face turned white with the realization he had just come to. "Sherm, keep the rebs pinned in place here. Damn it, I know where the other 30,000 Confederates are!"

Sherman realized at the same time, "I might actually say a prayer for that fool McClernand. He will need it, even from an apostate like me." Grant did not hear Sherman because he was already running for his horse and calling for his staff.

Chapter 13

Cleburne's Immortals
9:45 AM, Cleburne's Division

"You hear that?" Cleburne asked Johan.

"I do." There was no mistaking it for what it was. Within the last 10 minutes, there was the unmistakable sound of heavy musketry coming from their right, where Loring's division was.

All morning, they could hear the distant battle at Snyder's Mill. The plan had been explained to all the divisional commanders of the Beauregard wing, Loring, Cleburne, Walker, French, and Jackson, and all those men had assured Beauregard they understood only to attack McClernand when they received the command to attack. Apparently, Loring had decided to start a battle with McClernand's corps by himself.

Cleburne's entire division was deployed and hidden in the woods only several hundred yards from McClernand's outer pickets. But now, all the planning and effort it had taken to get 30,000 Confederate troops in a concealed position to attack McClernand seemed wasted.

"What now?" asked Cleburne. "What on earth are we to do now?"

A commotion to the rear of the division caught the attention of Cleburne, his staff, and Johan, and they turned to see General Beauregard and a couple of staff officers ride up.

Beauregard did not wait for Cleburne's salute, "General Cleburne, as you can hear, General Loring decided to start this battle without the other four divisions he was assigned." An uptick in rifle fire underscored Beauregard's anger. "General, I need you to deploy your division forward and begin your attack. I have sent word to all the other divisions to begin the attack, and you are to take command while I sort out Loring's mess. I swear, that fool better have a good excuse for this. General Cleburne, I must rely on you to help reconnect with Loring. I plan to assume command of his division if necessary." Within the next few minutes, Walker's division established contact with Cleburne, and all of Beauregard's divisions except Loring advanced forward as one to begin the attack.

Like Beauregard's plan at Shiloh the year before, all of Cleburne's men had been instructed to keep quiet and to only talk when absolutely necessary in a low voice. Mounted atop a chestnut mare, Cleburne drew his sword and spurred his horse forward, and his entire division followed.

Over the last year, Cleburne had gained a reputation as one of the best divisional commanders in the Confederate army. Part of that reputation had to do with his division's training, including sending out teams of skirmishers and sharpshooters to clear out Union pickets and take out Union officers before they could organize their troops. Today, Cleburne employed the same tactic as his division advanced in echelon. The Union pickets were quickly rolled up, and as several blue-clad brigades lined up to prepare a defense, Cleburne's men slammed into them.

Cleburne's staff communicated with the other divisions to his left, leaving Johan free to stay with Cleburne's division. Colonel Fremantle had procured a horse for himself as well, and as a foreign military observer, he remained to the side of the division to have a clearer view of the action. Johan rode with the English Colonel for the first hundred yards, but when he heard the first shots of Cleburne's skirmishers, he bid the Colonel adieu and rode forward through the ranks of infantry to be at the front of the fight.

Johan's black horse wove through the ranks and did not flinch when the Confederates delivered their first volley into the Union battle line. The Yankees responded, and though their volume of fire was less, several Confederates fell. What took the Yankees by surprise even more was that only a portion of Cleburne's front line had fired in the initial volley, and the second volley was delivered just as the Yankees began to reload.

Upon the firing of the second volley, Cleburne ordered the entire division to charge. Bayonets gleamed in the sunlight that came down between the trees as 8,000 Confederate infantry charged forward. The two unfortunate Yankee brigades buckled and ran as Cleburne's men crashed into their front ranks.

Cleburne's division and all the Confederate divisions to his left were the beneficiaries of Loring's impulsiveness to begin the attack early, for McClernand had begun to reorient his entire Corps to face Loring. McClernand reacted fast to the threat from Loring, but his fast reaction put him in a compromised position to face the 25,000 other Confederate troops en route to attack him. The key to the action against McClernand's Corps was to hit him from almost every side, including the Vicksburg side that Pemberton's men manned. So far, McClernand had been attacked on three sides.

The first two Union brigades Cleburne's division encountered were routed easily, but this bought time for an entire Union division to form a defensive line. Johan was near the front of Cleburne's division as they exchanged fire with that Union division. What gave the Confederates a slight advantage was the fact that the gray-clad troops had more tree cover than the Yankees. Men from both armies fell and formed neat, ghoulish lines of dead and dying men on the ground. The original plan devised by Beauregard envisioned all five Confederate divisions facing McClernand, to attack simultaneously, but Loring's attack on his own initiative threw the entire plan into disarray.

Johan felt like he had a clock ticking in his head. Though the Union division they faced was taking the worst of the fighting every minute, the Confederates were held up; it gave the Yankees time to redeploy their men and a better chance of wrecking the Confederate battle plan—hell, it was already wrecked.

Being a Colonel in battle entailed different responsibilities than those of a second lieutenant or a Captain. Though Johan was not officially part of Cleburne's chain of command, he felt as connected to it now as he did during his time with the Louisiana Tigers. Perhaps serving with another Stonewall, the Stonewall of the West, had something to do with that.

Bullets buzzed over Johan's head as he worked his way to Cleburne. The Irishman waved his sword in the air, imploring his men to keep pouring it into the Yankees. "Ah, Lutze. How does our left flank look?"

"We are not in true contact with Walker at the moment, but I can see some of his troopers. It seems for once we have the numerical advantage over the Yankees, and it is dressing up our shortcomings for now."

The sound of hundreds of rifles going off every second made the conversation difficult for the two men to hear. "Colonel, you know we are losing valuable time. We must keep moving. Grant has probably figured out what we are trying to do by this point, and he will throw everything he has at us."

Johan knew what Cleburne was getting at. The longer the Yankee division held them up, the more likely Grant's counterattack was, and a possible catastrophe for the Confederates. "What do you need me to do?"

"Find Walker. We need as much of his division as he can spare to help us break these people."

Johan's horse thundered through the forest at a dangerous pace in his quest to find Walker. By the time he found Walker, his and Cleburne's divisions had fully linked. Walker, though engaged with a couple of Union brigades as well, could shift a few regiments over to Cleburne. It made an immediate impact on helping to turn the Union division's flank. Satisfied with his work, Johan raced back to Cleburne to update him.

"Good work, Colonel. I can tell the Yankees had to shift over some men, and our boys are having a pronounced effect on their front line now." He gestured to the Union line, which was now noticeably thinner and putting forth much less firepower. "We must act decisively and remove the enemy from that position."

Orders were issued, and begrudgingly at first, Cleburne's entire division moved forward while still delivering a punishing fire into the Union line. But even as the Confederates advanced, the Union troops held firm and maintained their rate of fire.

"Charge!"

Smoke hovered over both the Confederate and Union forces as Cleburne's entire division and Walker's reinforcements charged forward with bayonets leveled. Cleburne was at the front of his division, leading his men, when disaster almost struck. A Yankee minnie ball struck his mount in the torso, and as blood sprayed out of the animal's severed artery, the poor beast fell over and launched Cleburne from the saddle.

Johan did not know how he managed to turn on time to see Cleburne go down. Still, he spurred his mount towards Cleburne immediately and without regard to the Union infantry zeroing in on him for being a mounted officer. As he rode up to Cleburne, he leaped off the saddle and was relieved when he saw the general pick himself.

Handing over the reins, Johan helped Cleburne to mount. "She is all yours, Sir." In pain but trying his best to ignore it, Cleburne thanked Johan and rode forward again to lead his division.

The battle raged as the Confederates tried to close the gap between the Yankees and Johan. They fell in with a nearby regiment, the 32nd Mississippi. With his saber in his right hand and his revolver in his left, Johan asked a sergeant, as he was ramrodding his rifle, what unit he was with.

In a strong Mississippi accent, the sergeant replied, "Why, Colonel, this is the 32nd Mississippi of Lowery's brigade."

"Well, Sergeant, I hope you are alright with a Louisiana Colonel tagging along today."

"Pleased to have you, Sir."

The 32nd Mississippi bravely advanced with the rest of the division while taking heavy rifle fire from the Yankees. Several bullets found a target, and as over a dozen men fell, Johan tried not to think about whether any of these men had wives, children, or families waiting for them to return home. Sadness filled him as he knew men whose families had been on the North American continent longer than the United States had existed, and fell on the soil of their home state. But despite the continued losses, like their sister regiments, the 32nd Mississippi of General Lowery's Brigade closed the gap with the Yankees and unleashed a punishing volley.

Rage and battle lust filled Johan as he tried his best to direct the men forward, yelling encouragement as loud as he could. As the regiment was about to make contact with the Yankees, they released their volley, and it was like a wind swept away part of the Union line. But the Yankees, though stunned, held their ground, refilled their line, and a vicious bayonet fight ensued.

Johan had been in so many battles that he knew there was only one thing for him to do at that point, and it was to kill the Yankees. He slashed a Yankee private across the face with his saber and shot another at point-blank range in the chest. Half-deafened by all the rifle fire, Johan could still hear the sound of a ticking clock in his head and screamed a few words to move his men forward.

As a Yankee drove the tip of a bayonet at Johan's belly, he deflected it with a quick flick of his saber and angrily shot the man in the face. Ignoring the man's brains spraying everywhere, Johan emptied his revolver into three other Yankees and holstered that revolver to retrieve another. With blood all over his face and uniform,

Johan continued to cut a path of destruction with his troops through the unending Yankee line.

The chaos of the battle caused Johan to shift all his focus to the 32nd Mississippi, and after he had spent all 12 rounds that his revolvers had loaded, he made deadly use of his sword, all the while urging whatever troops near him to push forward. There was a tendency for Johan to lose himself in a fight, and today, the ticking clock in his head forced out any other thoughts.

It was then that he found himself next to a man carrying the flag of Cleburne's division, set with a blue background with a white circle in the center. And that man fell as a bullet made a neat hole in the chest of his uniform jacket. The only thing for Johan to do was grab the flag, which he did. Forgetting his sword, he grabbed the flag and led the men of the 32nd Mississippi forward.

***

10:25 AM, Pemberton's Vicksburg Headquarters

It was the same story all over again. General Pemberton had listened to a superior, this time supposedly Beauregard, and had been unsuccessful against Grant. His besieged troops had performed well that morning in surprising the Yankees and taking several fortified positions, but the sheer numbers of counter-attacking Union troops had reversed all his gains. Worst of all, he had clearly heard the sound of battle coming from the Snyder Mills area, but now that battle had obviously drifted back towards the Big Black River. Pemberton had probably inflicted twice as many casualties on the Yankees as they had inflicted on him, but he knew he could not afford losses he could not replace. If he kept it up like that, in another two or three weeks, he would no longer have any more combat-effective troops.

A door to the room opened, and a young captain entered. In mid-salute, the captain began, "General Pemberton, I don't mean to be rude, Sir. But General Stevenson sent me to tell you there is a hell of a fight raging from the railroad all the way south to the river. Sir, it looks like Beauregard is delivering on that promise, and General Stevenson requests permission to launch a general attack, Sir."

It took a moment for Pemberton to absorb the shock of Stevenson's request. "General Stevenson is sure? Have you seen anything to confirm or deny what he sees?"

"Sir, I saw it with my own eyes with the General's field glasses. Sir, that Yankee Corps on the Southwest is getting hit from almost three sides. If we attack now, hell, we might destroy an entire Union Corps."

So many emotions went through Pemberton's mind, and he desperately wanted to avoid another fiasco like Champion Hill. However, he knew doing nothing would only result in his Army of Mississippi dying a slow, painful death. "Tell Stevenson to attack with everything, Captain. And tell him I'm coming as well, but do not wait for me to get there to start the attack." Pemberton wrote out a quick order and handed it to the Lieutenant. "And son, implore him to throw in everything he has. Hold nothing back."

***

If there was ever a doubt about Cleburne's loyalty to the Confederacy or ability as a general, the late morning of a very hot and dry June 1, 1863, put all those doubts to rest. Atop the black mare Johan had given him, Cleburne not only turned the left flank of the Union division, General Landram's, but he also led the charge that broke their center. As a divisional commander, one of Cleburne's most important roles was to decide when to commit his reserves. That time had come, and Cleburne deployed the five regiments of his 1st Brigade, Govan's Arkansas Brigade. Being from his home state, the men of the 1st brigade were fiercely loyal to Cleburne and were, without a doubt, his most reliable troops. Cleburne personally addressed the brigade and led the charge himself, which finally broke McClernand's Corps in half. The 32nd Mississippi played a crucial role in breaking Landram's final line as well, and with that line collapsing, McClernand had to immediately react and pull forces that were facing Vicksburg to plug that gap and the other problem spots that were occurring all along his line.

McClernand had terrible luck on June 1. After he pulled forces away from facing Vicksburg, Pemberton launched an all-out attack on his lines, notably with some Louisiana regiments, but the Union troops that had been pulled were out of place and too far away to help either repulse the Confederates from Vicksburg or Beauregard's wing.

With the Union line in disarray, Cleburne, after he cut through Landram's division, turned and hit Lindsey's from behind as they were engaged with Walker. And like dominoes, McClernand's entire line began to unravel.

Johan continued to lead the charge with the men of the 32nd Mississippi. As he charged forward into the camp of McClernand's Corps, he was thrown backward and felt as though someone with a steel bar had hit him in the face. He managed not to fall to the ground, but his face streamed blood, and the world spun all around him.

"Steady as she goes, old chap," said a familiar voice in an English accent as strong arms steadied Johan on his feet.

The left side of Johan's face felt like it was on fire, and he had trouble seeing out of his left eye. "Fremantle, what happened to you being a neutral observer?" Johan laughed at his own joke as he spat out blood.

"Well, my friend, I was watching you Confederates and the Yanks slaughter each other, but when I saw you take a bullet to the face, I couldn't just leave you to your own devices. Come on, I saw a surgery tent not too far back. Let's see if a doctor can patch your boyish face right up."

***

1:15 PM, McClernand's Headquarters

It was all too surreal for Cleburne. Almost 20 minutes ago, all the fighting in his sector had come to an almost complete stop when a Union officer carrying a white flag gingerly approached Cleburne as a dozen rifles were pointed at him. And just like that, General McClernand requested terms of surrender.

General McClernand stood disheveled yet dignified as he handed his sword over to Cleburne. The Union General was a proud man, a man who was a lifelong politician before the war and a man who aspired for the White House in next year's Union Presidential election. But that dream had died with several others today as the XIII Corps in Grant's Army of the Tennessee effectively ceased to exist.

Cleburne saluted his now prisoner. "General McClernand, I regret we must meet under these circumstances, but I will commend you and your men for the stubborn defense of your position today. Feel no shame in the outcome of this battle, for your men did everything possible to prevent their defeat."

McClernand angrily shook his head, "If it is all the same to you, General Cleburne, I have nothing that I wish to add to this travesty. Let us get on to the business of surrender." And so, they did. Somehow, part of Beauregard's plan had worked in destroying the XIII Corps. McClernand once had 20,000 men under his command, but attrition on the battlefield and Grant constantly stripping away regiments, then entire brigades, left only 15,000 at the start of the day he could actually depend on to fight.

Earlier that morning, Beauregard had located Loring's division, but to his chagrin, Loring had been killed minutes into the battle he had instigated. Beauregard had salvaged the situation, and the Loring division played a crucial role in the morning's events. Most importantly, Beauregard was able to have several of Loring's regiments retake part of the railroad, and he was able to close the trap for most of McClernand's Corps. As many as 4,000 Yankees were able to escape, but with 11,000 men killed, wounded, or captured, McClernand suffered an almost 75% casualty rate. It was a disaster for Grant, but the battle was not over.

Colonel Fremantle, the diplomat, as always, walked up to McClernand and saluted him. "General, Sir. Forgive me for the introduction under these circumstances. I am Colonel Arthur Fremantle of Her Majesty's Cold Stream Guards."

McClernand shook his head in disbelief and, in a rough voice, said, "They have you Englishmen doing the rebels' bidding now as well. And I thought you British wore scarlet jackets."

Fremantle shrugged and looked down at his gray jacket, "I thought this ensemble would be a little less conspicuous, shall we say. If you do not object, Sir, I am here at your service."

A frustrated McClernand could still hear the sound of Grant's counterattack on the other side of Vicksburg, but Grant might as well have been 100 miles away. Dejected and soul-deflated, McClernand acquiesced to Fremantle's request and walked away, now unofficially under the Englishman's supervision.

Cleburne knew he had just achieved the single most significant victory of any western Confederate army, but there was still plenty of battle left to fight. The sound of battle to his northwest clearly indicated that the battle was far from over and that he had to act to prevent this victory from being reversed.

The fighting on the southeastern side of Vicksburg was over, and now the monumental task of redeploying 5 Confederate divisions to counter Grant was underway. General Beauregard, for his part, stabilized Loring's division and appointed General Buford, one of the brigade commanders, as acting divisional commander.

Wasting no time, Beauregard put into action the rest of his plan. Being closest to Johnston's wing, Beauregard sent Buford with his division across the Southern Railroad and deployed them towards Johnston. There was still a gap between Buford and Johnston, which was filled by part of the 6,000-man cavalry force under General Forrest.

Forrest had been given explicit orders by Beauregard and launched a ferocious attack on Sherman's flank while he was attacking what became known as Johnston's Corps. The Confederate cavalry on both of Johnston's flanks acted as a screen, and Johnston began to disengage from Sherman and sift his corps to the southeast to link with Buford's division.

One of Beauregard's greatest strengths was his organizational skills. With the Vicksburg front now cleared of Union forces south of the Southern Railroad, General 'Red' Jackson's cavalry began to lead wagon trains loaded with supplies along the two roads that entered Vicksburg from the south.

When the first Confederate defenders saw wagons filled with supplies rolling down Warrington Road, they initially thought the Yankees were playing a trick. That attitude changed when General Jackson himself rode up and addressed them.

"Hell, boys, can you stop whistling Dixie for a minute and help clear the damn road?"

The young Confederates moved as General Jackson asked, but one boy of about 16 walked up to Jackson with tears in his eyes.

"Son, since you are not helping to clear the road, what is troubling you?"

"I'm sorry, sir. " The boy raised a shaking, empty hand and touched the side of Jackson's saddle before pulling away his hand. "I'm going to get back to work, sir. It's just that these last two weeks have been a living hell for us, and I think we all believed that we had been abandoned. But here you are, sir. You are like our guardian angel come to save us."

"Hate to disappoint you, son. But I think the angel of death is closer to the mark. Now, back to your post."

Chapter 14

June 1, 1863, 2:00 PM, Grant's battlefield HQ, Snyder's Mill

General Grant put down the paper and shook his head. "Damn." For all intents and purposes, McClernand's XIII Corps had ceased to exist. Sure, a few thousand men had escaped to McPhearson, but there was no way to sugarcoat the disaster that had occurred south of the Southern Railroad.

"Well, no crying over spilled milk."

Both Generals Sherman and McPherson entered the tent, and Grant put down the report.

"Sherm, Mac. How do we stand? How soon till we can launch the counterattack?"

McPherson answered, 'Well, sir, I would say give it more than another hour. In an hour and a half, we will have all the divisions deployed and our batteries ready to sweep that ridge. The Rebs have launched a substantial cavalry attack from each of Johnston's flanks, but it appears to be more of a spoiling operation meant to buy time for the Rebs to dig in further and bring up more reinforcements.

Sherman's gruff voice filled the tent. "I just received word that General Hurlbut has disembarked and is on his way. Almost 80% of the XVI Corps has now arrived from Memphis. So, despite whatever transpired with McClernand today, we have now replaced his entire Corps with fresh troops."

The map on the table had Grant's full attention. "Alright, well, we know this will be a grinder, but if we do it right, we can dislodge Johnston and hand him a major defeat by the end of the day. To review, Mac, your boys will man the trenches, or McClernand's survivors under your command will man the trenches. Your boys will make up 1/3 of the attack deployed on the right, and Sherm, you will be on the left with the other 2/3. Try as hard as you can to find the edge of their flank and turn it. I will help Hurlbut assemble his Corps, and half of his men will act as the battering ram when we identify Johnston's weak point. The other half will be with the rest of your Corps, Mac, facing the Southern Railroad. We will take heavy losses for sure, but we can hand Johnston a worse defeat than at Jackson by the end of the day."

***

2:45 PM, Beauregard's Battlefield HQ

"Why, Colonel," Andre hobbled over to Johan. "There is something about you that looks different. Did you get a haircut?"

Johan narrowed his eyes at Andre and tried not to laugh, "No, Lieutenant, I just thought for the hell of it to get shot in the face. That way, I could have some orderlies sew my cheek back together, all the while hearing some poor devil get his leg sawed off."

Producing a small flask and handing it to Johan, Andre smiled warmly, "Well, cuz, I'm just glad that Yankee bastard didn't aim two inches further to the right. Ready to go see Beauregard?"

They reached Beauregard's headquarters and got less than two minutes with the General. "Well, Lutze, looks like you took a good one there. Lieutenant, get yourself back to Pickett and ensure he swings over far enough to link with Buford. Colonel, you have done well with Cleburne; if you are up to it, I will return you to him.

"I won't say I feel my best, but I'm doing better than many of our boys."

"Well, you two see to your assignments then. Everything points to Grant hitting us with a massive counterattack, and we need every gun on the line."

Johan secured a horse for himself, and, as a colonel with a massive stitched-up scar on his face, he found most of the men he met along his ride accommodating when giving directions to General Cleburne. The trauma to his head was more than just his flesh wound, and as his horse bounced him around more than once, he felt sick as the world spun around him. Johan had suffered a concussion and was not going to feel better anytime soon.

Arriving at Cleburne's headquarters, two of his staff officers recognized Johan and took him to see the general. "Colonel, good to see you. It looks like they patched you up fairly well. How does it feel?" He asked sympathetically.

"Well, General, the whole left side of my face hurts like hell, and my cheekbone feels like it has a deep bruise. But I'm lucky compared to others I've seen today."

"Right, you are Colonel. A mini ball hit me last year." He pointed to one of his cheeks. "That ball went through my cheek and out my open mouth. Took a couple of teeth with it as well. That's why I grew out my whiskers." He paused and then grabbed a rifle and an ammunition pouch that had been put to the side. "I wanted to thank you for your help this morning, Colonel. I desired to make sure you got this interesting rifle back as well."

"Thank you, sir. This Spencer Rifle has proved its worth over the last month. General Beauregard said he expects Grant to launch a massive attack against us. Where will you have me?"

Cleburne called for a Captain to come over. "Captain, you know where Gibson's brigade is?" When the Captain responded with a yes, Cleburne continued, "Good." Then he turned to Johan, "Since we freed up a portion of the Vicksburg line, I have been able to absorb some of the Vicksburg men into my command. Gibson has several

Louisiana regiments, and I think you will be right at home fighting with your bayou state brethren."

"Thank you, Sir. Since I am going that way, is there anything you want me to convey to Gibson?"

"Being that you are a Colonel, look over the fortifications and have the men address anything you see. Other than that, we hold the line and kill as many Yankees as we can."

***

3:30 PM, Grant's attack on the entire Confederate line

Every cannon Grant possessed that was not facing the Vicksburg entrenchments was facing Beauregard's line. Several dozen cannons had been lost with the destruction of McClernand's Corps, but that still left Grant with over 100 guns to point at Beauregard. As those guns began to fire upon the Confederates, Porter's ships on the Mississippi intensified their bombardment of Vicksburg and any Confederate entrenchments within their range.

For close to an hour, Grant's 100 guns and Porter's ships bombarded the Confederate lines, which now resembled a U-shape running along Vicksburg's Northeast section, then along the Southern Railroad and turning north, paralleling the Big Black River towards Snyder's Mill. Thousands of artillery shells fell all along the quickly assembled Confederate fortifications, and the Southerners began to take heavy losses from the bombardment.

Beauregard did his best to organize his forces for the attack. The Railroad was the east-west axis of his line, and thousands of Confederate infantry hunkered down on the south side of the tracks and were well sheltered from the bombardment.

Pemberton almost cried when he saw the first supply wagons entering the city from the south. Without wasting any time, he coordinated with Beauregard and began shifting his forces from the southern flank of Vicksburg to integrate fully with Beauregard's command. The morale of the Vicksburg defenders surged widely as news of McClernand's defeat and the arrival of Beauregard's supply wagons circulated.

Foodstuffs and thousands of percussion caps, .58 caliber rifle cartridges, and artillery shells entered the city and changed the entire dynamic of its defense. Pemberton, now with a fresh supply of artillery ammunition, ordered every gun either facing the Mississippi or Grant's army to return fire. So even though Beauregard was limited in his own artillery in terms of number and others in transport, Pemberton was able to mitigate the Union artillery fire by responding with over 150 of his own guns.

General Johnston, having received instructions from General Beauregard to shift southwards, used his own cannons to respond to Grant and coordinated with Forrest to begin shifting Pickett's division to the south. In contrast, Breckenridge began to pull back to the Big Black River crossing to prevent Grant from trying to cross the river and attack Beauregard's right flank or rear. As these divisions shifted out, a few thousand of Forrest's Cavalrymen took up positions as skirmishers along Johnston's old line in case Grant decided to take advantage of the Confederate movement.

Even as Union shells fell all around Vicksburg, Pemberton's Army of Mississippi, with its newfound energy, rushed forward and reinforced its northern entrenchments and the railroad line as well. Cannons that had been entrenched south of the railroad were also brought forward and deployed along the railroad line, some responding to Grant's own guns. In contrast, others were concealed in anticipation of the main Union attack.

Johan saluted Colonel Francis Campbell, commander of the 13th Louisiana. "Well, Colonel Lutze, as you can see, we are entrenching along the railroad." He paused as an artillery shell flew overhead. Taking a brief interest in Johan's facial injury, Campbell continued, "And I see you saw some action earlier today."

The day's heat had begun to irritate Johan's wound. "Yes, sir." He spoke slowly, his jaw aching. "I am a member of General Beauregard's staff and have worked closely with General Cleburne, sir. But given the circumstances of the battle, I thought I could be of use here to my fellow Louisianians. I have served under General Jackson in the Louisiana Tigers, Virginia, and I have my rifle as well."

Colonel Campbell smiled and extended his hand to Johan, "Lutze. That name rings a bell. Was your father Colonel Paul Lutze in the 18th Louisiana, and your brother Captain Lutze?"

A pained grin crossed Johan's face as he shook Campbell's hand, "Yes, sir."

Recognition blossomed in Campbell's eyes, "Shiloh was our little spot in hell last year. The 18th Louisiana was in our brigade at Shiloh. Your father, he was a brave man. When Colonel, now General, Mouton was wounded at Shiloh, your father took command of the 18th Louisiana. I wish I could describe to you how terrible the fight at the Hornet's nest was, Colonel. My God, even during this siege, I don't think I have ever witnessed fighting as intense and terrible as that day. Your father took command of the 18th and helped lead the final charge to take The Hornet's Nest. I remember how all the regiments of our brigade were all tangled together, and your father took command and led us to victory. Many, including him, paid dearly for that victory. So, sorry for the long story, Colonel, but I will always have a place for a Lutze in my regiment."

The railroad served as a natural fortification for the Confederates, and Johan busied himself all along the regiment's section of the railroad line. The one glaring issue the Confederates faced was the lack of a platform or steps for troops to use the railroad as a proper fortification. Logs, gravel from the track, and any other practical material were employed to make it easier for the men to step on and keep their balance while firing over the track and into the Yankees when they came. As the Union cannons continued to roar and send shells all along the Confederate line, Johan put the men of the 13th Louisiana to work. He even spoke to officers from the regiments on either side of the 13th, the 16th, and the 19th Louisiana, and showed them what he was having his men do.

Scores of Negro laborers pitched in as well. Most of these men were enslaved and conscripted by the Confederate army as laborers. Johan was amazed at how eager these men were to help, even though they were enslaved, and significant progress was made in preparing the railroad line. Though there was a social distinction, Black and white Southerners felled trees and dragged the logs to the railroad bed to stack them to build an impromptu stepped platform.

About an hour into the work, the Union artillery began to die down, and Colonel Campbell found Johan and spoke to him one final time, "Colonel, I think the time for the enemy assault is near. I like your idea of keeping our best shots on top of the platform while the other boys stay below and load the guns. That's a hell of an idea."

Johan wiped his face with his sleeve, "I wish I could take credit for that, Sir. At the Battle of Fredericksburg, General Longstreet's corps deployed that tactic, and it worked exceptionally well."

Johan was one of the few men under Beauregard's command with a breech-loading rifle. The vast majority of the Southern troops were armed primarily with Springfield, Enfield, or Austrian Lorenz muzzle-loading rifles. It was a gamble, but his plan would allow a steady rate of fire from the 13th Louisiana while only a portion of its troops were exposed to enemy fire. It had worked before in Virginia, and Johan prayed his idea would work now.

The forest was cleared several yards away from the railroad on the north side, and as Johan took his position on the tracks, he and the men around him saw the mass of blue-clad troops begin to advance. Artillery still thundered deadly projectiles into the Southern defenses, but at a much lower rate since not all of Grant's guns could shoot without the risk of hitting their own men.

Bayonets glittered in the day's waning sunlight, and the crunching of thousands of boots on the forest floor sent a shiver through Johan's body. Confederate officers called out encouragement all down the line and ordered their men to hold their fire.

The Confederate infantry mainly consisted of battle-hardened veterans like Johan, but any man would have been a fool to say that the spectacle of the Union host was not daunting. The clear cadence of the Union drums added to the dread of their advance, and yet the Confederates held their fire. They were so close to the Confederate line that the men could make out the various features on the Yankees' uniforms. Having done everything he could to assist Campbell, his face throbbing, Johan looked over his Spencer Rifle one last time and aimed at a Union officer riding horseback. He knew it was just a matter of time.

At three hundred yards, the few Confederate field pieces that were deployed along the railroad began to fire into the ranks of incoming Yankees. Beauregard had wisely husbanded his artillery during the Union bombardment so that he would have some guns left to use against the Yankee infantry. And their effect was immediate. Huge holes opened in the Union battle line as almost a dozen cannons fired canister and grapeshot into the Union ranks.

Parts and pieces of body parts, blood, equipment, and blue uniforms flew into the air, forming ghoulish clouds over the ranks of advancing Yankees. And like earlier at Snyder's Mill, the Yankees kept advancing, impervious to their losses.

When the Yankees had advanced within 250 yards, the command was given to fire an initial volley and then to fire at will. The entire Confederate line unleashed its volley, and the Yankees fell by the hundreds, but they still kept coming.

Johan had 10 of the seven-round magazines for his Spencer, and he went to work on the Yankees. Smoke hung over the battlefield and obscured the view, yet Johan was patient and followed his own plan to seek out Union officers. His first shot cleared a blue-bellied officer out of his saddle over 200 yards away, and though he did not unhorse the second man he aimed at, he saw the man clench his arm and knew it was a hit.

He emptied his first magazine and cleared it from the rifle, knowing four of his seven shots had found their mark. Loading his second cylindrical magazine into the rifle's stock, Johan looked along the section of the railroad he was responsible for. He was amazed at the rate of fire his fellow Louisianas were able to maintain using his method, with some men shooting while others loaded. But when he looked back at the Yankees, they were only a hundred yards away and beginning to return their rifle fire. There was no more time to pick out targets casually, and Johan aimed at the mass of oncoming infantry and began to discharge his rifle quickly.

Though under a hail of gunfire, the Yankees continued their advance while shooting and reloading. Men all along the Confederate line fell, and though others continued to take the place of the fallen, the Yankees' numbers were clearly winning the contest.

At 50 yards, the Yankees charged. Joahna lost all sense of time and place and mechanically fired his rifle into the mass of charging Yankees. Many of the men of the 13th Louisiana who had been acting as loaders jumped onto the tracks to put as many bodies as possible on the line. And it worked in the sense that staggering numbers of Yankees fell, but their numbers were so great that they reached the railroad tracks and began to climb.

Johan and the men around him jumped onto the tracks and began firing down into the Yankee horde. All along the railroad, the other Confederate units reflexively did the same, and a bloody fight ensued with the Yankees attempting to scale the tracks and being successful in several places.

With his rifle empty and no time to load, Johan pulled out his two revolvers and, with one in each hand, fired point-blank into the mass of Yankees. But very quickly, his revolvers were empty, and Johan, with a bayonet on his Spencer, did his best to hold his portion of the line together and command and guide what troops were left near him.

As one Yankee corporal rose onto the tracks and bayonet pointed at him, Johan subconsciously went through the bayonet drill in his mind, and after feigning to the man's right, he swung over and stabbed the man in the thigh. All sympathy was gone as Johan then pulled out the bayonet, only to impale the man in the chest.

The top of the tracks was filled with both Confederate and Union troops, and one Yankee officer pointed a revolver at Johan's chest and stared in shock when the gun misfired. A slash to the man's throat ensured that the Yankee captain would never be a threat again.

The battle ebbed and flowed as all do; within an hour of the main attack beginning, Beauregard had committed all his available reserve troops to plug the holes along the railroad. With it being the last of his reserves, he knew that he was gambling on the very survival of his army. There was no other choice, and the creole knew this situation was highly likely.

But Beauregard's gamble paid off because, by 6:00 PM, Grant had called off his attack. The Yankees had suffered immense casualties, though the Confederates had not escaped from the battle unscathed. The day belonged to Beauregard, but at the cost of much of his army being mauled. It was true that an entire Union Corps had been destroyed, but Beauregard was well aware that Grant had been receiving reinforcements all day and that he would undoubtedly attack again tomorrow, June 2.

Chapter 15

June 2, 1863, 4:00 AM, Confederate White House, Richmond

President Davis sat at the table and reread General Beauregard's message. "Mr. President, we attacked General Grant's army today. Our losses are high, but we achieved several objectives in today's victory. Grant's losses are severe and have significantly weakened his force. The XIII Corps under McClernand was annihilated, and its defeat alone netted some 6,000 prisoners. Two roads approaching Vicksburg from thc South were opened today, and a steady flow of materials and supplies has entered the city. I entered the city this evening to show the people and brave soldiers defending Vicksburg that their government has not abandoned them. A new defensive line has been established paralleling the Southern Railroad, and we fully expect Grant to attack in great force tomorrow. We shall hold! Gen. Beauregard."

There was a knock at the door, and secretaries Benjamin and Seddon entered. Davis handed Seddon the telegram, and once he had read it, he handed it over to Benjamin. When both secretaries finished reading, they looked back at Davis.

"Do you believe Beauregard is being truthful?" asked Davis in a tired voice.

"I think so," responded Secretary Benjamin. "This is the version of events that puts him in the best light, but I believe it's truthful. Somehow, he managed to get one over on Grant."

Secretary Seddon agreed, "Grant is probably irate that Beauregard got the best of him, and I would wager Beauregard is correct in his assessment. In all likelihood, Grant will throw everything he has at

Beauregard today. Hopefully, Beauregard used the night wisely, and his men are entrenched and ready for the fight."

***

June 2, 1863, 5:00 AM, the War Department Telegraph Office, City of Washington

President Lincoln stood over the telegraph operator as the man wrote out the message. It was a painstaking process, but in the third year of the war, Lincoln had made a second home for himself in the War Department telegraph office. When the operator finished writing out the message, he handed it to Lincoln.

The President walked over to a corner of the room to read the message in privacy when Secretary Stanton waltzed in, followed by General Halleck.

"How bad is it?" asked Stanton gruffly, almost but not entirely forgetting that Lincoln was technically his boss.

The shake of the head signaled Lincoln's displeasure. "Well, it's not another Chancellorsville, but without a doubt, it seems Beauregard was somehow transferred from the Carolinas without our knowledge and managed to move an entire army in secrecy and attacked Grant at dawn yesterday morning."

Fuming, Stanton grabbed the paper from Lincoln's hand and read it. "God Almighty! Did he lose an entire corps?"

Halleck also read the note: "Even if we ordered Grant to withdraw, that order would not reach him before he launched his attack today."

Stanton put a hand through his gray hair, "So Grant was lucky and able to replace his losses. What now? Are we confident he can take the city? If this report is anywhere near truthful, he suffered close to 16,000 casualties yesterday. How much of a price are we willing to pay to take Vicksburg? Can we even keep Grant in command?"

Tapping a finger to his cheek, Lincoln voiced his opinion. "Grant was whipped. There is no two ways about it. But he still remains in the field. Beauregard cannot surprise him again; besides, he cannot replace the men he has lost. This campaign will be a tough grind, but we can still win decisively if we are willing to make the sacrifice. General Halleck, your thoughts?"

"Mr. President, Grant does have his shortcomings, but he is the best man for the task of capturing Vicksburg at the moment. I agree with you; this campaign will devour men and material, but if we can close the Mississippi to the rebels, we will have made this war that much harder for them to win. Grant can sometimes require supervision, but I propose we stay the course. Guns, supplies, and men are what will win this campaign. And we have an infinite supply of all three compared to the rebels."

Stanton looked visibly unhappy, but Lincoln did not care. "Alright," he sighed. "This war, I swear, is destroying an entire generation of our boys. Nevertheless, we stay the course, and even if Vicksburg must be leveled to the ground, we do it. And one last thing," he paused to give a side-long glance at the telegraph operators and crumpled the note in his hand. "This news does not leave this room."

***

June 2, 1863, 5:15 AM, Beauregard's Headquarters

General Beauregard looked over the map one last time. With a sigh, he took a deep sip of coffee, courtesy of McClernand's captured supplies. Across from him were Generals Cleburne, Pemberton, Forrest, and Johnston, each nursing their own cup of coffee. In all, these generals had 10 hours of sleep between them.

"Well, Grant is coming. Given his history, I would expect a great effort from him today. He will undoubtedly have to pause his offensive operations and reassess his options if we can hold the line. I would pray he would abandon the siege, but as Lincoln is the spawn of the devil, I doubt we will be so lucky."

Johan stood towards the back of the tent, drinking coffee as well, and contemplating Beauregard's plan for the day. In all, the plan was simple. Hold the railroad line against Grant. Fending off Grant's army would not be a simple undertaking, though.

The meeting ended, and while Pemberton and Johnston left the tent, Cleburne and Forrest remained with Beauregard. The Creole general looked over and motioned for Johan to come forward.

Forrest took a quick look at Johan and remarked, "Damn, Colonel. Not only does it appear like you were shot in the face, but from the looks of it, you had less than an hour of sleep."

"You are mostly correct, General Forrest. I had an hour and fifteen minutes of sleep."

There was a good laugh among the four, and as the pleasantries continued, Beauregard patted Johan on the shoulder. "I have heard very complimentary reports on your conduct yesterday, Colonel. No one will ever doubt your or anyone in your family's courage. But today, Sir, I need you to be more judicious in risking your safety." The rigor and stress of the last several days showed in Beauregard's face and eyes. "We won a victory yesterday over Grant. But it was a costly one. Take care of yourself today."

Johan departed Beauregard's headquarters with Generals Cleburne and Forrest a short while later. The camp around them bustled with activity. Gray-clad men of European and African descent hurried about as final preparations were made for Grant's attack.

Several men in gray and butternut leading horses approached General Forrest. As a black man handed Forrest the reins to his horse, the General turned and raised his hat to Johan and Cleburne, "General, Colonel. Good luck, and kill as many of those Yankee bastards as possible." Forrest mounted his horse and looked at Johan again, "Colonel Lutze, those two Krauts you sent me. Well, unbeknownst to me, and probably you, those two German bastards know how to ride and fight. Apparently, they served under the Austrian Emperor and strongly dislike anything French or Italian. You should see how they use those damn sabers!" And then Forrest rode away with his entourage.

Johan continued walking with Cleburne to where their horses were tied. The Irishman laughed, "General Forrest might be blunt to a fault at times, but he has never lied to me. But above all else, that man is a devil of a fighter. I garner praise that is overloaded at times, but that man has earned every bit of his reputation. But alas, are you ready for your assignment today, Colonel?"

The sights and sounds were almost overwhelming to Johan. As they walked by a field hospital, there was still a score of men on stretchers or lying on the ground, still awaiting treatment. Johan knew many would not make it through the day, and his head wanted to spin as he heard some unfortunate soul screaming all his worth that a limb was being amputated.

"Colonel?"

"Oh, sorry, Sir. Yes, I know being in a reserve brigade is the appropriate spot for me today. Since yesterday, I have found that my thoughts have been wandering quite often. General, could I ask you something?"

Cleburne nodded, "Of course, Colonel. Is something troubling you?"

The fact that Cleburne was so intuitive and sincere again convinced Johan as to why Cleburne's division and now corps were so loyal to him. "When I was back in Virginia, I made some suggestions to my godfather, President Davis, that he was not very keen on. One of my ideas was to enlist negroes into the army and offer them and their families emancipation for their loyalty to the country. And then now, like so many other times over the last couple of years, I see so many negros, by the hundreds, with my own eyes, working without malice or complaint alongside our white troops. And more often than not, they are impervious to the dangers they face. I guess what I am saying, sir, is that this war has changed much, yet these men, sons of the South, have willingly done their duty."

Cleburne paused momentarily to size up Johan, "Colonel, that is an idea I have wrestled with myself for some time. It is a contradiction, really. As we fight for our own rights, we, as a country, withhold the rights of so many of our fellow men. Colonel, it's an issue we cannot escape, especially if we desire to be victorious in this war."

Johan spent much of the early morning contemplating General Cleburne's words. As he worked his way to his assignment for the day, he allowed some introspection to creep into his mind. There was no kidding himself; he had been born and raised in a life of wealth and privilege. His family's plantation on the German Coast of Louisiana had operated and run on slave labor. No matter how well he got along with the family servants, as was the popular term, and how several of the servants had a hand in raising him, they were, at best, second-class citizens in the eyes of the law.

And yet, the issue was exacerbated by so much Yankee propaganda, which was just that, propaganda. The common conception of the South, which Johan had witnessed up North, was that every Southern plantation was run like the one dramatized in the rag *Uncle Tom's Cabin*. So many Yankees Johan had crossed paths with thought every plantation had its own Simon Legree, and the abuse, beatings, and even rape of slaves was the common and accepted practice.

It was not true, for the most part. Johan remembered a childhood in which most of his playmates back home were black, and for good measure, many of the authority figures in his life were as well. And then there was Pierre. How he, Andre, and Johan had caused so much havoc as little boys, virtually terrorizing the plantation with their escapades. Ultimately, however, none of those factors changed the truth; Johan's family owned Pierre and the rest of his people.

And then there was the tragedy with Andre and Mary. The events of that night would forever haunt Johan. How could one night change everything in one's life? Andre had certainly not been the same since. Sure, he was still his unapologetic self, but the joy Andre had been filled with and known for was forever gone the night Mary and her and Andre's unborn baby had died. Pierre had lost a sister, Andre, the love of his life, and the daughter he would never know. But who was there to cry over the death of a black plantation slave and her mixed-race unborn child?

Soon after, Johan finally agreed to his father's wishes to venture into law for a time. But his motivation had not been to protect his family's estate or to personally enrich himself. He wanted justice, and he wanted it for people who were often deemed too unimportant to receive the protection of the law. And as fate would have it, it was how Tesa came into his life.

The early heat of the day brought Johan back to reality. The dead could not be brought back to life, whether it was five years ago or today. And today, there would be many more deaths than on that stormy night in Louisiana. The constant boom of Grant's artillery foretold of the fight that was to come.

Today, Johan was assigned to an ad hoc reserve division that was part of Cleburne's Corps. Liddell's Arkansas Brigade and Gibson's

Louisiana Brigade formed the backbone of this division. And Johan knew they would be needed before the day was done.

***

8:00 AM, The Southern Railroad

For two hours, over 100 Union guns pounded the Confederate line along the Southern Railroad. Throughout the night, white and black Southerners had toiled away with fortifying the Confederate position along the railroad in anticipation of Grant's counterattack. From General Beauregard to any sergeant in the Army of the Mississippi Valley, it was apparent what Grant's most likely course of action would be. Drive the Confederates entrenched along the Southern Railroad and destroy Beauregard's newly formed army while once more isolating Vicksburg from the outside world.

Johan reported to General Gibson and, using his latitude as a staff officer for Beauregard, convinced the General to let him go to the railroad to get a feel for Grant's plan of attack. As a measure of goodwill, Johan promised not to get involved in any fighting, only to observe and report.

Afterward, reporting to General Liddell of the Arkansas brigade and borrowing a field glass, Johan ventured to the rail line and looked north. The Union artillery had reached a crescendo, and as quickly as it started, it ended. That was the clue everyone knew signaled the Union advance.

The Confederates could hear the cries of the wounded and dying stranded on the battlefield from the day before. After the fighting ended on June 1, Beauregard sent a messenger under a flag of truce to request a cease-fire from General Grant. That way, the wounded and dying of both armies could be retrieved from the battlefield. That request had been denied, and all night, the Confederate line had to listen to countless men slowly die in agony.

There was no customary drum roll to announce the advance of the Union line. Instead, Johan, like his compatriots, watched in grim fascination as thousands of blue-clad Yankees emerged from the tree line, marching in perfect step with bayonet-tipped rifles.

Johan would never forget the feeling of not seeing any Union troops, but only hearing the soft sound of thousands of boots hitting the forest floor. Like some grim dream, the forest was in its natural state, and the next moment, a wall of dark, blue-jacketed soldiers emerged.

Like the previous day, the Confederates held their fire as the Union divisions headed toward the Confederate defenses. The Confederates could feel the thump-thump of men marching in step towards the railroad, and all the defenders shared in a moment of trepidation. This was the moment that the entire campaign hinged on: would Beauregard's army withstand a stand-up fight with Grant after he had a day to prepare his army and bring in massive reinforcements from all across the region?

After counting a second time, Johan confirmed that he counted 16 Union regimental flags. It was as if there were to be a repeat of Shiloh. Beauregard and Grant would face off again on the second day of a great battle, with many troops on both sides being Shiloh veterans.

During the night, brave Southerners of every color ventured out into the battlefield within a couple of hundred yards of the railroad. They retrieved any soldier, Union or Confederate, who was still alive. Additionally, with small security detachments accompanying them, work crews felled trees and underbrush to create a larger buffer between the railroad and the dense forest. It was hard, back-breaking work that ran through the night. However, the brave handiwork of these men was about to be displayed.

At three hundred yards, the Confederate artillery all along the railroad opened fire, and the two Union Corps advancing on the railroad began to suffer heavy losses. But these men earned the respect and admiration of many Confederates by their sheer tenacity and bravery. Large bloody holes would be blasted into the Union lines, and the well-trained and disciplined Midwesterners would close ranks and continue to advance. At two hundred yards, the Confederate infantry opened fire, and Johan knew it was time to return to his new division. Mentally, before he left, he looked up and down the Confederate line to ascertain if there were any potential weak spots. There was one spot, in particular, he did not like, mainly due to its elevation, where the Northern side of the railroad's ground was level or even elevated higher than the railroad. If the right Union Officer came along, that weakness in the Confederate line would be exploited. By all looks, it was time to get word to General Gibson that the division needed to be ready to move at a moment's notice.

Johan gave General Gibson a crisp salute. "General, I found a spot that will probably require our attention." He then promptly described its location. "Sir, General Cleburne is in command of this section of the line today. Do you wish for me to report to him?"

Gibson smiled as the gunfire to their north picked up. "Yes, Colonel. Tell General Cleburne his Louisiana and Arkansas brigades are ready!"

General Cleburne had placed himself on elevated ground roughly in the middle of his deployed forces. According to General Beauregard, Cleburne put himself at too much risk, being no more than several dozen yards from the fighting. But Cleburne knew that if Grant broke through his line, the resulting Union tidal wave would be catastrophic to his army and the nation's morale.

Cleburne and Johan nodded at each other. Beauregard's new regulation discouraged officers from saluting and making other gestures that might attract a Yankee sharpshooter's attention. Turning his attention back to the battle, Cleburne scanned the battlefield, ascertaining Grant's true objective of the day. Hundreds of rifles were going off every second, and as Cleburne's infantry poured a punishing fire into Grant's men, the bluebellies continued to advance and had more horrific casualties. However, as the Union line advanced, it became more confident and returned great volleys of fire.

Cleburne pointed to the feature Johan had noticed before and spoke, "Colonel, how does Gibson's Louisiana/Arkansas division stand?"

"They are on excellent footing, sir. I know they are barebones as a division, sir, but those two brigades can deliver blows harder than expected on any units their size or larger."

Cleburne smiled, "Good. We will need them soon." He looked at the section of railroad that curved out, creating a small bulge in the Confederate line, and allowed a few Yankee troops to take up position and fire down into the Confederates. Pointing, Cleburne turned to Johan, "That section of railroad that acts like an island, that is where the Yankees will throw everything."

The prediction was accurate. As the morning crept by, it became apparent that Grant was not simply throwing troops at the Confederates in hopes of a quick victory. He was feeling out the Confederate line in force, patiently waiting to find the weak spot to throw everything at.

However, this reconnaissance in force served another purpose: It simply ground down Confederate forces and drained their ammunition reserves. For close to two hours, Johan stayed by Cleburne's side, watching the wave of blue troops crash into the Confederate weak spot.

It was almost noon when Cleburne decided to act. "Colonel, retrieve General Liddell and his division and bring them here. Grant has committed the attack here, and we will throw him back here. Be quick, Colonel. The Yankees are going to throw everything they have at us."

It had been agonizing for Johan to watch the fighting without participating. But that feeling came with no longer being a regimental officer and transitioning to a staff officer. Certainly, there was the desire and thrill of fighting the Yankees, but as a staff officer, he had to bring greater perspective and a more strategic approach to battle.

Johan rode his horse hard to General Liddell and could hear the tempo and intensity of the battle increasing behind him. Grant had made his big play for the day, and this afternoon's events would decide the battle and possibly the fate of the South.

General Liddell returned Johan's salute, "Well, Colonel, I take it that General Cleburne requires us."

On a day when it mattered greatly, both reserve divisions were ready for deployment when Johan located Liddell. Being the professional Liddell was, no time was wasted, and the two brigades were assembled and began their quick march to the front line. The reserve division seamlessly deployed from columns to battle line and charged into the teeth of battle with bayonets drawn.

As Johan entered the fray with his division, Cleburne himself had already rallied a couple of regiments that had nearly broken and fled from the fight, and atop his mount, he waved his saber emphatically. The whole Confederate line was at the breaking point, and though the losses suffered were horrendous for the Yankees, Grant's strategy was clearly working: wear down the rebs and then throw everything at their weakest point.

Being atop a horse had its advantages and disadvantages in any given battle, but Johan did not let any thoughts of presenting himself as such a prime target, especially for sharpshooters, distract him.

Sword in his right hand and pistol in his left, while he wrapped the reins around his left wrist, Johan let his mouth gape and almost lost his reins as he watched in awe and horror as Liddell ordered a volley into the mass of Union troops that had breached the Confederate line. As a wave of Yankees fell, Liddell ordered a charge, and a few thousand Confederate infantry slammed into the stunned mass of Yankees.

But these blue-bellied veterans, to Johan's surprise, barely flinched. Rather, these professionals shrugged off their dead and wounded comrades and fought back the Confederate onslaught with hand-to-hand combat.

Sharpshooters aside, being atop a mount allowed Johan to help direct the troop movements until Liddell had ordered a charge. When the two bodies of troops slammed into each other, Johan rode the Confederate wave and savagely used his sword to dispatch more than a few Yankees. But he did not go unscathed. As he slashed one man across the face, another instead came up and almost succeeded in impaling him in the leg.

What saved Johan with a painful but more or less surface wound and not deep tissue trauma was his horse shifting just slightly as the Yankee committed to the attack. With faster reflexes, the pistol was swung around, and Johan's Yankee attacker was met with a bullet to the chest.

As the fighting devolved into an all-out brawl, Johan became separated from his horse and again assumed command of a company that had lost its commanding officer. It was grim work, with Johan managing several times to rally his men and release a volley into the never-ending stream of bluebellies.

Not long before, Johan had seen General Cleburne atop his own mount furiously encouraging his men to hold. The dice were cast, and practically speaking, Cleburne and, to that effect, for the South.

But the fight would never end. Grant sent wave after wave of troops against Cleburne on the track. Johan kept drilling it into his company to maintain discipline and to continue pushing the Yankees to the edge of the entrenchments. The fighting was brutal, with men from Arkansas and Louisiana now providing the reserve brigade with firepower. It was chaotic and impossible to discern how the general battle was unfolding, but Johan knew that he and the men needed to hold this land by the end of the day.

It was the hottest part of the summer afternoon when the lack of water and the sizeable amount of blood loss in his leg dropped Johan to his knees. The battle at the bulge on the railroad had been ferocious, and as the Confederates committed the last of their reserves, Grant kept throwing more and more brigades and regiments into the battle. Grant just needed one more push, and his army could very well break through Beauregard's line.

General Pemberton knew the tactical and strategic position his garrison would face if Grant defeated Beauregard's army. With Beauregard's blessing, Pemberton manned most of his defenses with a bare-bones force and, with 6,000 of his best troops, launched an all-out attack just north of the Southern Railroad.

Pemberton's initial attack that early afternoon of June 2 captured several Union entrenchments and surprised the Yankees with the tenacity of the Confederate attackers. The Army of Mississippi, Vicksburg's garrison, was highly motivated by the results of the previous day's battle and the sheer number of supplies Beauregard had arranged to be delivered into the city. To top it all off, Beauregard had ridden down the main street of Vicksburg all the way to the courthouse to show the soldiers and citizens of Vicksburg they had not been forgotten.

Eventually, Grant's army savagely counterattacked and retook several of their lost positions. But Pemberton's attack had served its purpose as his men returned to their rifle pits. They had bloodied Grant's men and fought them to a draw, all the while, vital troops for Grant's attack on the railroad were withheld to deal with Pemberton.

Two black orderlies retrieved Johan by stretcher and took him to a hospital tent away from the fighting. Barely conscious, his leg wound was cleaned and stitched by other black orderlies, and Johan began the laborious effort of rehydrating himself. As he fell asleep again, the late afternoon faded into evening, and Grant's army began to limp back to their entrenchments. Though the siege of Vicksburg would continue, the Confederacy had achieved one of its first undeniable victories west of the Appalachian Mountains.

Chapter 16

June 3, 1863,
The White House, Washington City, Noon

President Lincoln put his face in his hands. "My God." The paper fluttered from his hand onto the floor and revealed the ghoulish truth of war. Looking out a window, Lincoln put a hand through his hair and looked at General Halleck. "25,000 men, General. 25,000 men in two days. Then there were the 4,000 he lost at the end of May. What will the country say? What will they say? This is just a month after Chancellorsville. Within a month, two of our largest armies have suffered a combined 60,000 casualties."

Halleck stood rigidly, trying his best to maintain his composure. "These reports are troubling, Mr. President." He gestured to the report lying on the floor.

Secretary Stanton picked up the report and crumpled it. "Obviously, this is bad. But not on the level of Chancellorsville. What now? Do we continue with the campaign? Reports indicate Lee is building a massive force near Fredericksburg. Even if Grant were ordered to withdraw from Vicksburg, any sizable portion of his army would take several weeks to be redeployed to either middle Tennessee or Virginia."

Lincoln looked at Halleck and Stanton. "No, I will not have an army that was battered and mauled yet still hold its ground at the end of two brutal days of retreat. That has happened too many times in Virginia over the last year. Out West, we have been winning the war. The last two days, we clearly were not victorious. But Grant's army is intact and holds its ground. The campaign for Vicksburg will continue. The question is, what is to be done about Grant?"

Halleck answered before Stanton could. "Mr. President, I have had misgivings about General Grant's leadership. After Shilo, I took control of our forces in Tennessee to give a steady hand at command. But, Sir, if Grant has proved anything since last year, he is tenacious. Any setback he has is followed up with the force of a hurricane. I favor leaving Grant in command at Vicksburg. Our losses have been heavy; there is no denying that fact. But Beauregard has played his hand, thrown his best punch, and his army has also suffered heavy losses. He cannot replace what he has lost. We can. It might take longer to subdue Vicksburg than originally hoped for, but I say we see this thing through with Grant at the helm."

A mischievous smile cut across Lincoln's face. "Secretary Stanton, your opinion, Sir?"

Clearly unhappy with how he had been maneuvered into a corner, Stanton shrugged, "Even if there was the desire to replace Grant, we have no one else qualified at the moment to take his place. Hooker is in command in Virginia, Rosecrans in Tennessee, and Banks in Louisiana. Who would replace Grant? Sherman, his friend?"

"Well, gentlemen," Lincoln said with some animation, "it appears Grant is still our man at Vicksburg."

June 5, 1863, Confederate camp, outskirts of Vicksburg, Evening

The train ride from Mobile to Jackson had been a long one for Paul Lutze and his three companions. At Jackson, they were given horses and a security detail to ensure they reached General Beauregard's headquarters. On top of everything, Paul had to ride a horse for the first time with his new prosthetic left leg.

Many who knew the Lutze family swore that, in one moment, Paul resembled his mother's French ancestry and, in the next, his father's German roots. He was tall, with an angular face, deep blue eyes, and hair darker than Johan's. And over a year after Shiloh, he had relearned to walk with his new prosthetic leg, thanks mainly to losing his left leg below the knee, which gave him a much freer and broader range of motion than many others who had lost legs above the knee.

Presenting his pass to another picket line, the purpose of Paul's mission was within reach of being accomplished. There was Confederate cavalry all about, and a few men volunteered to bring Paul and his small entourage straight to General Beauregard.

The ride to Beauregard's headquarters took most of a day of hard riding. Even with an escort, Paul and his men encountered several Confederate mounted patrols, and each time he had to present his pass and verify his identity. Undeterred, at 9 PM, Paul walked into the barn, which served as Beauregard's headquarters.

"General Beauregard," Paul saluted, his new gray uniform dusty from the long ride from Jackson. He then handed an envelope to the commander of the Army of the Mississippi Valley. "President Davis sends his regards and thanks for your victory over General Grant."

An exhausted Beauregard gave a slight smile. "Thank you, Major Lutze. President Davis and I have not seen eye to eye much of this war. But we all strive for victory over the enemy. And now I have the pleasure of hosting another Lutze."

Paul and Beauregard talked for more than an hour. Telegraph service had been restored to Jackson, and Davis had a dispatch waiting for Paul to deliver to Beauregard when his train arrived. Davis had other instructions for Paul. He was to retrieve General Johnston and bring him back to Richmond so he could take command of the new IV Corps of the Army of Northern Virginia. As part of his latest assignment to the Confederate Secret Service Bureau (CSSB),

Paul was tasked with compiling a dossier on Grant and a general study of his army and operations. Beauregard was apprehensive when Paul first brought up this topic, for though he had a good relationship with Paul's brother, Colonel Lutze, and cousin, Lieutenant Breaux, there was still a sense that President Davis was keeping a close eye on him. But Paul won Beauregard over by appealing to his scientific leanings and explaining that the CSSB was a professional intelligence organization and that they were in the process of analyzing all Union field commanders.

Once his meeting with Beauregard was over, Paul left the barn. As he stepped outside, a man wearing a gray jacket approached him. "Excuse me," the man said in an English accent, "I am Colonel Arthur Freemantle of Her Majesty's Coldstream Guards. If I understand correctly, you are Major Paul Lutze, brother to the honorable Colonel Lutze and cousin to the scoundrel Lieutenant Breaux?"

Laughing and extending his hand to the Englishman, Paul exclaimed, "Major Paul Lutze. Nice to meet you, Colonel Freemantle. I am still getting used to my brother being called a Colonel. But Andre is indeed a scoundrel. He still owes me $20."

Freemantle laughed, "That puts me in good company, sir, for that unabashed Frenchie owes me $15." Both men had a good laugh, and Fremantle led Paul through the Confederate camp and to a structure that had once been a farmhouse but had been quickly expanded and modified into a hospital. Despite it being past 10 PM, dozens of men lay on stretchers or litters outside the building, and orderlies tended to a handful of injured men.

To Paul's surprise and gratitude, several older women were assisting with the wounded men. More than one of these women had visible blood on the fronts of their dresses and were hard at work assisting in the medical care of the wounded Confederates. Even more surprising, Paul saw these women working and speaking with several black orderlies. It gave the older Lutze brother both a sense of both hope and trepidation. The people of the South, of all genders and races, were rising to the occasion in the fight for their country. But there was a blending of social order and roles, a development that could be hard to unwind when the war ended.

"This way, Major Lutze, I know the corner they have your brother in."

Paul followed Freemantle's lead into the hospital. The initial step forward was the hardest for him. He remembered his nightmare from Shiloh a year ago. There were times when he swore he felt his missing lower left leg, but his prosthetic rubbing across the stump of his leg gave him a very painful reminder with every step that his lower leg was indeed gone.

The two men maneuvered their way inside the dimly lit hospital to a side room where officers were housed. Johan sat up in his cot to Paul's relief, and Andre sat on a log next to him.

Paul immediately noticed the ugly wound on Johan's right cheek, but his brother looked to be in good spirits otherwise. "Well, Johan, I know you outrank me, but that scar does improve your ugly face."

Gingerly getting out of the cot, Johan walked over to Paul and hugged his older brother. "Glad to see you, Paul. It's been a long time."

After more pleasantries were exchanged, Paul prodded Johan for information. "So, tell me, Johan, why did Beauregard threaten to arrest you if you left the hospital before tomorrow morning?"

Andre laughed out loud, "Because after fighting like a madman and getting scoured in the leg by a damn Yankee, the Colonel bled like a piggy and damn near died. For whatever reason, General Beauregard values having us on his staff and thought it wise not to risk another staff officer or high-ranking officer being killed over nothing. Ol' Johan has since been the model patient."

"Thank you, Andre." Johan rolled his eyes, his face still showing signs of pain. "Along the Southern Railroad has been mostly quiet since the end of June 2nd, so I figured, what's the harm in spending three days in this lovely establishment and letting my face and," he gestured to his leg, "other injuries heal up before I go back on duty."

"But don't worry, Paul. Your brother is too beaten up to return to the field, so General Beauregard has a mountain of paperwork for Johan to tackle once he is cleared for duty tomorrow morning."

Freemantle chuckled as the exchange continued, "You Confederates are such an interesting yet uniquely diverse lot. There are your Louisiana bushwhackers, and then there are the refined gentlemen like General Johnston, and then there are the men such as Generals Cleburne and Forrest. I tell you, Captain Lutze, you would never see this in Her Majesty's army. Men treat their officers as if they were the best of friends in this army, and I have heard of officers elected by their regiments. Yes, the Confederate States are a unique collection of peoples and cultures."

June 6, 1863, 7:00 AM, Beauregard's Headquarters

While Johan had spent the better part of his adolescence training for a military career or working in the field of law, Paul had been trained to run his family's plantation and other business operations. It was not something he found exciting at first. Still, after he decided to apply his intellect and creativity, Paul learned he had a knack for numbers and logistics in large-scale agricultural endeavors. Then, of course, the war had come along.

After his maiming at Shiloh and his subsequent return trip home with Pierre, things had only gone downhill for Paul's family. Papa had died at Shiloh, and Momma had died only months before from yellow fever. To top it all off, New Orleans had also fallen to the

Yankees in the first half of 1862, and the Lutze family home soon after was burned to the ground by marauding Yankee forces.

Those were some trying months after the city had fallen. Many of the household servants had run away at that point or were scooped up by the Yankees for any number of forced labor jobs. It was a minor miracle that Paul had gathered his wife, Hellena, their children, Angella, Charlotte, and Johan's fiancée, Tesa. Eventually, even though he was missing part of a leg, Paul found a way to get his family through Union lines.

It had taken some time and considerable expense, but Paul resettled the family in Mobile and rented a modest two-story home through luck and his negotiating skills. At the time, despite lacking any meaningful income, Paul had secured the house with cash he had been able to smuggle in the children's luggage. Adding to the family's good fortune, Paul was able to draw on a deposit account he had set up at a Mobile bank a couple of years earlier to cover the family's living expenses for a few months. The modest house had only two bedrooms, which, given the circumstances, no one argued with. Paul and Hellena took the largest bedroom, while Tesa became a live-in governess and slept in the children's bedroom. There were few luxuries Paul could afford, but he had a roof over the family and food on the table every night.

With Tesa able to stay home with Hellena and the children, Paul felt confident about finding employment, even if he had to be paid as an apprentice. No sooner had he found a job working for a blockade-running operation when the CSSB (Confederate Secret Service) knocked on his door. Before the ink on the contract was dry, Paul was on a secret mission inside New Orleans. And now, he was outside of Vicksburg, a hairsbreadth away from the fighting.

Paul was accompanied by Eric McCown, his most able man this morning. Eric was young and a redhead, barely 150 pounds at almost six feet tall, but the young man was bright and energetic, an essential trait for a CSSB agent.

When the two men entered Beauregard's headquarters, Paul recognized two generals meeting with Beauregard. One was older, with thinning gray hair and a refined manner.

Joseph Johnston returned Paul's salute, then looked to the dark-haired general next to him, "General Pemberton, I believe an admirer of mine has arrived."

Paul smiled nervously and knew it was time to play diplomat, "General Johnston, that is true. Last night, General Beauregard briefed me on your operations before he took command of this army and your performance during the battle. Sir, not only did you give the Yankees a bloody nose, but you enabled General Beauregard's plan to be realized, and you played no small part in the destruction of McClernand's Corps. Rest assured, my report to the President will bring attention to your actions, Sir."

Johnston's tired face showed the slightest relief. "That is good to hear, Major Lutze."

Paul grinned, "Sir, in this war," he lifted his left pant leg to show the prosthetic coming out of his boot, "we will all experience setbacks, but it is what we do after that counts."

"Could not be truer," chimed in Pemberton.

"Yes, Sir," Paul jumped at the opportunity to switch topics. "General Pemberton, since I will be returning to Richmond with General Johnston this evening, could I borrow some of your time? The President understands the hardships your garrison has been facing and would very much like to know what he can do to help."

***

"You know, Colonel, for someone a few inches away from missing some essential anatomy, you seem to be moving well."

Johan had to stop himself before he opened the barn/headquarters door. "Lieutenant," Johan said as he gingerly patted his groin, "if I didn't know any better, I would say you are a rat bastard of the first order."

Andre opened the door for Johan, "A couple of generals have already made that observation," he said with a laugh.

When Johan entered the building, he saw Paul in a corner with a piece of paper and a pencil, talking to a general—it looked like General Pemberton. Beauregard and Johnston were talking by one of the few tables in the headquarters, looking over a large map of the Vicksburg area.

Beauregard looked up and grinned when he saw Johan saluting. "And the younger Lutze returns to the fold. Well, Colonel, I have eagerly been waiting for you." Beauregard gestured to a short chair and a barrel that served as a desk, with a stack of papers atop it. "If you want to be properly trained and integrated into my staff, Colonel, I can't have you getting yourself shot at the trench line. Besides, those papers have your name written on them."

Andre took the opportunity to retrieve some dispatches and promptly left the barn. On the other hand, Johan took everything in stride, sat at his makeshift desk, and got to work. Reading through the paperwork and signing and completing reports as needed, Johan observed that the campaign had settled into a stalemate, with the Confederate entrenchments running from Vicksburg and then for miles along the Southern Railroad. Grant, having had enough frontal assaults for a time, had his army reposition itself to face Vicksburg and the railroad. Over the past few days, the Yankee army had begun digging new entrenchments and working methodically toward the railroad. It was as if both armies were besieging each other.

Reading through reports and requisition forms, Johan saw that Beauregard was moving heaven and earth to get supplies into Vicksburg. Geography was king in war, and with the Mississippi in Federal control and Grant dug in north of the city, only two roads entering Vicksburg from the south were viable to bring in supplies. It seemed that everything Beauregard could get his hands on was being sent into the city: ammunition, percussion caps, clothing, water, beer, and foodstuffs. This undertaking consumed an enormous share of the Confederacy's limited resources.

Putting a hand through his hair, Johan considered another report and put it in the pile for General Beauregard to review. The paperwork seemed to multiply nonetheless as Beauregard reorganized the Army of the Mississippi Valley. General Johnston was set to leave that evening for Richmond with Paul, which gave Beauregard the impetus to reorganize his army into three roughly equal-in-strength corps. Most of Pemberton's Army of the Mississippi was designated 1st Corps; Cleburne was given 2nd Corps, which included his division along with a Louisiana division from Pemberton and other various brigades; and then Breckenridge was given 3rd Corps, which was primarily composed of his division and Pickett's.

"Ready for a break," Paul's voice broke Johan's concentration. The older Lutze brother had a barely noticeable limp as he pulled up a worn chair across from Johan. Staff officers were constantly entering and leaving the barn, but a time had passed when there were relatively few men other than the Lutze brothers in the barn.

Johan took the flask from Paul, took a deep sip, then passed it back to his brother. "Must be hard duty working for the CSSB. Did Uncle Jeff buy that bourbon for you?" Johan grinned. "I haven't tasted something that fine in a while."

"A parting gift from the shipping company I worked for before I joined the CSSB."

"You mean the blockade-running company you worked for," Johan said in jest. "They must have really appreciated your work."

Paul nodded. "They did, but I think they liked the idea of having a friend in the CSSB." Looking around the barn, Paul pulled an envelope from his jacket and handed it to Johan. "Tesa sends her love."

The letter rested in Johan's outstretched hand like a holy relic. Had it only been just over a year since he had seen her? "Thank you, Paul. I know you have much to do today before you leave for Jackson, but I would greatly appreciate it if you could deliver my response to her."

"That's what I am here for, little brother. Among other things."

***

Eric McCown shadowed Paul most of the day as he met with most of Beauregard's staff, Corps commanders, and General Forrest. Forrest was the hardest to track down of all, and Paul was amazed at the man's energy, tenacity, and willingness to be unconventional.

When Paul tracked him down in the late afternoon, Forrest had just returned from a reconnaissance in force. "Well, Major, I don't have much time to talk," as Paul followed him around the corral Forrest's men had built to house several mounts, "but I am headed to Jackson tonight myself. Why don't I take my men along and accompany your party to the station? You can talk to me as much as you want, as long as we don't run into any Yankees."

Paul took Forrest up on the offer, and soon after, when he was heading to the tent Johan had moved into, Colonel Freemantle found Paul and Eric.

"Major," Freemantle shook Paul's hand and was introduced to Eric. "Nice to meet you as well, Sergeant McCown. Well, Sir. I understand you are headed back to Jackson tonight and shall be making your trek to Richmond."

Looking at Eric, Paul grinned, "Why, yes, Colonel. As you probably heard, General Johnston will be accompanying me, and General McClernand will as well."

"If it would not be a further inconvenience to you, Major, I would very much like to accompany you. I have taken leave from Her Majesty's army to tour the Southern States and am compiling my travel journal. It would seem I need to travel the rest of the southeast of the Mississippi to complete my work."

***

The constant musketry and cannon fire did not even slightly bother Johan. Neither army was inclined to attack the other, so the day was filled with each side returning cannon or sharpshooters picking off unwary men. But none of that mattered while Johan took a short break to read Tesa's letter in private.

"Angella and Charlotte keep Hellena and me busy most of the day. There is so much to do that my mind is occupied and racing to do the next task most of the day. But at night, when the house is asleep, and my thoughts are to myself, I think of my sweet Johan."

"My love, this war is terrible, and I know you must do your duty for your home and your people. But do not let this war consume you like poor Jacques, who ran away to Virginia. Please do what you must, but remember who you are and return to me when possible. My heart is yours, always. Tesa."

The letter still smelled like her. Johan had to will himself not to put the letter to his nose again, wanting to feel as if he were with her one more time. With the current campaign, he knew asking for leave was out of the question. But maybe this winter, there would be an opportunity for him to spend some quality time in Mobile.

That evening at army headquarters, there was much activity and fanfare as General Johnston made the final goodbyes to the Army of the Mississippi Valley staff. The chief of staff, Major-General Mackall, was to remain as the chief of staff for Beauregard. However, Colonel Johnston, the aide-de-camp, was to travel with General Johnston to Virginia and serve as the chief of staff for the new IV Corps under Johnston.

Colonel Freemantle was also in attendance, with a subdued General McClernand by his side. The Yankee general had been a model prisoner since his surrender on June 1st, and Beauregard and most of his staff had no desire to embarrass the general further. In fact, it was hoped that McClernand's traveling to Richmond to meet with President Davis would bring a new dimension to the war and put more political pressure on Washington.

Johan found Paul tightening the saddle of his horse. "Heading back, I see."

Turning, Paul grinned at Johan, "It's a critical time in this war, Colonel. The President requires quick and effective action from the CSSB."

"Can't argue with that." Johan held out an envelope to Paul. "If you could pass this along."

"Who do I need to deliver it to?" Paul asked in a teasing tone as he took the envelope. He then reached over and hugged his little brother. "I promise not to tell Tesa how much you cried when you read her letter. Now you take care of yourself, Colonel. Grow out that beard some more, and for God's sake, stop getting yourself shot."

"Sorry to interrupt," General Cleburne said as he walked forward, his frame casting a long shadow in the rapidly setting sun. Both Lutze brothers saluted as Cleburne gestured for them to stop. "None of that right now," he chuckled. "No need for formalities." He produced an envelope and tapped it with a nervous finger. "Major Lutze, it is my understanding that you shall be passing through Mobile on your way to Richmond. If it is not inconvenient, might you deliver this correspondence for me?"

Taking the letter, Paul assured the Irish general, "Certainly, General Cleburne. Whom shall I deliver this to?"

Cleburne looked uncomfortable for only the second time, while Johan knew the general. "Major, I have spent much time with your brother, Colonel Lutze, in the past few weeks. There was a particular conversation we had one night that made me realize one must set aside fear and uncertainty when it comes to matters of the heart. I will be forever in your debt if you could deliver this letter and my affections to Susan Tarlton."

Chapter 17

June 8, 1863, 6 PM, Brandy Station, Virginia, Louisiana Tigers Encampment

Jacques Lutze had no idea why his brigade, the Louisiana Tigers, had been invited to attend a cavalry review with Generals Jackson, Longstreet, and Lee in attendance. General Jackson wasn't even technically the Corps commander of II Corps anymore; that title belonged to General Ewell. Still, apparently, the golden boy Johan had made himself a hero to the army's top brass, and since General Hood's division was in attendance representing General Longstreet's Corps, why not have II Corps represented as well? Jacques didn't understand the politics of the army, and he felt no inclination to attempt it. That was the realm of Paul and Johan.

It wasn't that Jacques felt ill will toward Johan or even Paul. It was just that their lives were so different from his, and they had always talked about this war in ways that made no sense to the 16-year-old Jacques. There was one reason Jacques was fighting. And that was to kill Yankees. Let the generals and the ass-kissers like Johan strategize and position the army and supply him with bullets for his liberated breech-loading Sharps Rifle. If they put Jacques on any battlefield, he could deliver dead bluebellies.

"Still cleaning that rifle?" Sergeant Poisson asked as he sat down next to Jacques.

Jacques responded without taking his eyes off his rifle, "You had to stand through that review today. Don't you want to shoot somebody?"

Poisson laughed, "Oh, come on, boy. It wasn't that bad."

Jacques looked to Poisson, "Oh, Generals Lee and Jackson were as nice as can be. When they inspected the brigade, they had nothing but wonderful things to say about Saint Johan and the Apostle Andre." He smirked when he saw Poisson's face. "I know. The whole damn regiment has those two up on this damn pedestal. It's just that I am not one of them. Why would they want us at some damn cavalry review?"

Poisson sighed, taking a sip from his canteen. "Alright, son. Given that we have the same great-granddaddy, I will take the time to teach you a few things."

"Go on ahead, Sergeant."

"Being in this army, or any other army, is more than just how many enemies you can kill. Half of winning a battle and having your army ready for the next one is having your men believe in themselves and their officers, especially their commanding general. You weren't around last year when we were in the Valley with Jackson or Seven Days, Second Manassas, Antietam, and Fredericksburg. With General Lee leading this army, it is unstoppable. That's what that review was about today. So, all those dandy cavalrymen could feel invincible. But it was also to let General Lee and General Jackson know they are ready for the campaign ahead."

Jacques put his rifle down and asked, "Do you want me to be all patriotic like you?"

Poisson shrugged, "No. I've been around you long enough to know there will be no convincing you of that. Look, Jacques, we are a team. Now, I know you made a good showing of yourself at Chancellorsville when you shot the Yankee Colonel and Captain at 500 yards. But you acted like you were the lone wolf, an asshole the whole time. The boys want to accept you. Hell, you walked half of the way here from Mobile. You have passion within yourself, Jacques. But turn it into something more. You ain't the only one whose home is burned to the ground or has half their family dead or missing."

Jacques loosened his grip on the rifle; his hand began to ache as he had gripped the weapon so hard. It took great effort for him to hide the moisture in his eyes. "I just hate the blue-bellied bastards."

With a pat on Jacques's knee, Poisson stood up, "I know, son. I know. But look, come on over and grab some grub. And if you are lucky, you might even hear the story of how your brother getting shot in the ass saved the life of General Jackson." Sergeant Poisson then handed Jacques a cartridge box.

Intrigued by the story and the gift Poisson was offering, Jacques stood and accepted the leather box. "What's this?"

Poisson smiled, "Even if you are a tad obnoxious, your last name carries some weight. That cartridge box holds just over 40 cartridges for your fancy rifle."

Jacques was taken aback by the thoughtfulness with which someone had obtained hard-to-find ammunition for a rifle that was not standard issue in the Army of Northern Virginia. "Who do I have to thank?"

Poisson smiled as he put his arm around Jacques's shoulders. "Just come sit around the fire with the boys, and you will figure it out."

As the two of them walked to join the rest of the company, Jacques conceded that he might be more open to making friends in this army.

***

June 8, 1863, 6 PM, Mobile, AL Train Depot

When the train reached the Mobile train depot, Paul Lutze was ready to pass out. It had taken the better part of the day to reach Mobile, and

Paul was ready to be home. He had sent a telegraph message in Jackson, alerting Hellena to his anticipated arrival.

Paul had quite the entourage with him, more so when he had left Mobile for Jackson. Eric and the two other agents had traveled with him from Mobile to Jackson. Then, there was General Johnston and his aide, Colonel Johnston. The two companions Paul had not counted on were General McClernand and Colonel Fremantle.

Paul was behind schedule in his mission for President Davis, but felt it was easy to justify the delay. General Johnston had played a significant role in the victory outside of Vicksburg, even if Grant was still entrenched and willing to continue the campaign.

Letters from Generals Lee and Longstreet had been hand-delivered to Johnston by none other than Johan and Andre. Those two had no small role in convincing Johnston to stay for Beauregard's attack on Grant. And now, Johnston would return to Virginia, able to hold his head high, even though he had been effectively demoted from Department commander down to Corps commander. Rather than resign, the man had done the honorable thing. And that Paul was thankful for.

General McClernand was deeply melancholy, and Paul could not blame him. Hell, Paul felt he would probably feel the same if the circumstances were reversed. However, it seemed that the Englishman, Colonel Fremantle, had established an unexpected friendship with the Yankee general. And if that could carry on all the way to Richmond, all the better. The train came to a stop, and Paul and his small entourage gathered their things and stepped off.

The carriage Paul often hired for the family was waiting at the train station, but to his surprise, so was another. By coincidence, Paul was very familiar with Susan Tarlton's family, for they had given Paul his first employment in Mobile. Susan herself had become good friends with both Hellena and Tesa. And the fact that the Tarlton family carriage was waiting beside his own told him that Hellena had received his message and relayed it to the Tarltons.

With little fanfare, Paul, Generals Johnston and McClernand loaded into the Lutze family carriage, while Sergeant McCown, his two agents, and Fremantle loaded into the Tarlton family carriage. They were shortly at Paul's home.

Hellena and Tesa greeted the entourage as they arrived at the Lutze home. Paul went through the formalities of introducing everyone, but made sure to give Hellena a loving kiss when he first approached her.

"I missed you." He spoke softly as Hellena led the party into the one formal room of the house.

Hellena Lutze's family hailed from southwestern Germany before settling in Louisiana a century earlier. She was of average height for a woman, with blonde hair and piercing light blue eyes. Her face was pleasing to Paul, but what had made him fall in love with her was her kindness and her smile. She was honest to a fault at times, but Paul appreciated that in a woman, for he was all too familiar with the fact that wives often hid their true feelings within the social circle in which he was raised.

"As did I," Hellena spoke softly. "I know it was only for a few days. But it felt like an eternity."

To Paul's surprise, he saw Susan Tarlton and her brother, David, speaking to Tesa Hofmann, Johan's fiancée. "Hello, Paul," said David fondly. "When Hellena messaged Susan about helping to transport everyone and their luggage, we couldn't say no. We also knew you could use some reinforcements for a large party at such short notice."

Back at their rented home, Paul put a nervous hand through his hair when he saw all the food prepared at the table. "This is quite the spread here. How can I repay you both for all the help you have given me tonight?

Susan, a dark-haired woman in her early twenties, smiled sweetly. “I think you'll find my price very reasonable, Paul. Sit next to me during dinner and answer some questions I have about a particular Irish general you may have become acquainted with.”

To Paul’s delight and surprise, the dinner went off well. For such short notice, it was practically a miracle. General Johnston was the guest of honor, and David Tarlton had no trouble stroking Johnston’s ego. Eric McCown and his two agents remained quiet for the most part, keeping a close eye on General McClernand, who was seated next to Colonel Fremantle. The English Colonel was polite and very appreciative of this being the first night in a while of having a proper dinner and a roof to sleep under.

As the Tarlton family's servants served dessert, Tesa brought the Lutze children, Angella and Charolette, down to greet the guests before they were put to bed. The girls met a Bona Fide hero in General Johnston, and the girls' joy and kindness lightened the night's mood.

As the evening was winding down, Susan turned to Paul, “It appears your mission was fruitful, Paul. Are there any generals you became acquainted with?” She asked with a mischievous smile.

Paul grinned. “Well, I did speak with almost every general in the new army that General Beauregard organized. But a particular one of Irish extraction left quite the impression on me.” He slid his hand into his jacket and handed the envelope to Susan. “General Cleburne sends his regards and has requested that I deliver this to you; you made my job very easy tonight, Susan.”

***

June 9, 1863, 2 AM, Mobile, Alabama, Lutze Home

Colonel Fremantle and two of Paul's agents stayed the night in the Lutze home, sleeping in the common area. Tesa Hofmann slept in the girls' room that night as usual to give the guests some privacy. The two generals were guests at the Tarlton home, and Tesa was thankful that Susan had made those arrangements.

Between the moonlight that leaked through the window and the oil lamp at her small table, Tesa read Johan's letter over and over. Her emotions resembled the waves of an ocean, constantly rising and falling. It had been late December of last year, just as the family had settled in the home in Mobile, when they received news of Johan missing in action at Fredericksburg and presumed dead. It had been earth-shattering to Tesa. Several years earlier, she had lost her husband to yellow fever after four short months of marriage, but it now appeared she had lost a fiancée as well. And then, in early May, like Lazarus raised from the dead, Johan not only reappeared but also saved the life of General Jackson.

Tesa missed Johan dearly and cried when his first letter from Virginia reached her. It was like a terrible nightmare had ended, and all Johan could say about his time in a Union prison camp was, "I would rather have visited New York under much different circumstances and with you by my side, but I made the most of my stay."

Johan's down-to-earth sense of humor had drawn Tesa to him in the first place. His ability to put a positive spin on even the most catastrophic events amused her to no end. But his letter tonight was filled with love and longing. "*I've tried to write as often as possible. The business of this war is never-ending, and I always seem to get caught in the middle of the worst conflagrations. But have no fear, love; I have emerged once again mostly unscathed."*

Tesa wanted to laugh and cry at Johan's ridiculous understatement. According to Paul, Johan's idea of being mostly unscathed was a mini ball hitting him in the face and only a few inches shy of exiting the back of his head.

"Every night, when I lie down, my final thoughts are of you. Someday soon, in the waking hours, we will be with one another again."

***

June 9, 1863, 8 AM. Brandy Station, VA. The 'Louisiana Tigers' Hayes Brigade

Jacques heard artillery as the first light of day ran across the morning sky. Given that yesterday had been the grand review of General Stuart's command, the sound of the distant cannons could have been the crews cleaning their cannons, Jacques wanted to believe. But as darkness completely retreated, the young sharpshooter knew something was wrong.

The Louisiana Tigers were encamped on Fleetwood Hill in somewhat cramped conditions. They were placed next to General Stuart's headquarters, which somehow made them an unofficial honor guard. Or that was what senior members of Stuart's staff claimed the day before. General Hood's entire division had marched back to Culpeper Courthouse after the review, as there was no suitable accommodation available for the 7,000-strong division around Brandy Station. Jacques was thankful that he would not have to march several miles to General Ewell's headquarters only to turn around and march back to Brandy Station the next day.

By around 8:00 a.m., it was clear that a significant engagement was underway. The sound of rifle fire was unmistakable, coming from the north and east of Brandy Station. And General Stuart, being the cavalier he was, rose to the occasion, assembled his horsemen, and rode off to fight the Yankee threat.

Few Confederates at the time knew that the Army of the Potomac had a new commander of its cavalry Corps, General Pleasonton. For the last several days, General Hooker, who was still in command of the Army of the Potomac, had been receiving substantial intelligence that a large Confederate cavalry force was assembling near Culpepper Court House, and he desired Pleasonton to find the gray cavalry and destroy it.

Pleasonton's plan was straightforward. He would divide his 11,000-man force into three independent wings and simultaneously attack Stuart from multiple directions at the same time. The first Union cavalry wing, led by General Buford, made contact with Confederate pickets on the western bank of the Rappahannock River around 4:30 AM and advanced. With all its ferocity, this attack led Stuart to take most of his 9,500-man command and his attention away from other sectors of his defensive line.

General Stuart, taking almost all his horsemen and riding east to face the Yankee threat, left Brigadier General Harry T. Hayes, commander of the Louisiana Tigers, in a quandary. As reports began to flow back to Stuart's headquarters, which his brigade was encamped next to, it became evident that a significant cavalry action was taking place. The Tigers were encamped on a ridge that offered a view in every direction for several hundred yards, which was excellent for defending against an infantry brigade. And as much as Hayes wanted to render aid to General Stuart, the brigadier questioned how much his infantry could assist Stuart in the open terrain versus cavalry when Fleetwood Hill was more suitable for defense.

As the morning wore on, Stuart's adjutant, Major Henry McClelland, the cousin of Union General George McClelland, found himself the sole staff officer left on Fleetwood Hill as Stuart ordered every available regiment to assist in repelling General Buford. Fleetwood Hill was the nerve center of Stuart's command, and now, no mounted units were left to defend it. Additionally, there was no horse artillery, but plenty of supplies and ammunition were left exposed and vulnerable.

Frustrated by the lack of communication with Stuart's command, General Hayes approached Major McClelland, and the two men agreed to deploy the Louisiana Tigers all along Fleetwood Hill in case any other surprises emerged. Hayes, an experienced infantry commander, advised McClelland that his Louisiana troops should not be deployed conspicuously. The reasoning was straightforward: if the Yankees liked surprises, Hayes would be more than willing to return the favor to the blue-bellies.

Major McClelland's fears of further danger were not unfounded, for none other than Generals Lee, Jackson, and Ewell rode up to the crest of Fleetwood Hill to observe the rest of the day's actions. A short time before 11 AM, a few scattered pickets informed the Confederates atop Fleetwood Hill that a second Union cavalry wing, led by General Gregg, had emerged from the forest just south of the Orange and Alexandria Railroad and the Caroline Road that passed through the crest of Fleetwood Hill. Gregg should have been at Fleetwood Hill hours earlier, but had been delayed for a litany of reasons. Nevertheless, according to his scouts, there was no Confederate presence on Fleetwood Hill that could stop his nearly 3,000-man division from capturing and destroying Stuart's headquarters and perhaps capturing some high-value Confederate prisoners.

With 1,500 of his infantry against 3,000 Yankees, General Hayes had his entire command fix bayonets and lie flat on the ground to conceal their numbers from the Yankees. Major McClelland also assisted with the ruse by sending couriers to warn General Stuart of the peril Fleetwood Hill was in and by having a lone cannon, commanded by a Lieutenant Carter, fire a handful of shots to create hesitation in the head of the Union column.

Yankee scouts were undeterred by the one Confederate cannon and informed General Gregg and his subordinates that there was no other Confederate defensive presence on Fleetwood Hill. Like a predator sensing blood in the water, General Gregg ordered his command forward at a charge.

Brigadier General Wyndham commanded Gregg's lead brigade, which charged up the western slope of Fleetwood Hill. The 1st New Jersey led the charge and had General Stuart's headquarters in their sights. Colonel Kilpatrick commanded the second brigade, which swung around to attack the southern and eastern sides of Fleetwood Hill.

Sergeant Poisson hushed Jacques, who itched to stand up and shoot the Yankee horsemen. "Not now, boy. Wait for General Hayes to give the command."

The hell with waiting, thought Jacques. His vision was exceptional, and he could see the mass of Yankee horsemen beginning to ascend Fleetwood Hill. Five hundred yards, four hundred…

"Company," called out an officer. All along Fleetwood Hill, General Hayes's entire 1,500-man command stood to the shock of Gregg's oncoming Yankee division. "Ready, aim!" Jacques, as a sharpshooter, had to wait no longer. His rifle at the ready, he located his first victim, aimed, and fired his Sharps rifle. The first casualty on either side in the battle of Fleetwood Hill was Lieutenant Colonel Brodrick of the First New Jersey Cavalry, with a bullet to his left lung. He would die almost instantly from Jacques Lutze's well-placed shot.

"Fire!" Came the command from General Hayes. In near unison, almost seven hundred rifles went off, mauling the front ranks of Wyndham's and Kilpatrick's commands. Stunned momentarily, the Union cavalry slowed, regrouped, and continued its charge up Fleetwood Hill, as thousands of Union cavalry troopers were now committed to the fight. At 200 yards, the order to fire came again, and this time, the second half of Hayes's Tigers fired their rifles. The First New Jersey, which had been leading Wyndham's brigade, effectively ceased to exist after the second Confederate volley.

Gregg's command slowed to a near stop after the second volley. Hayes had played a masterful trick by creating two volleys quickly and having half of his command participate in each one. But as the Yankees began reorganizing and ascending Fleetwood Hill again, there would only be time for one last volley, this time from the entire brigade, before Gregg's entire cavalry division was upon the lone Confederate brigade and General Lee.

Jacques had taken a position on a large boulder and systematically fired and reloaded his breech-loading rifle. The Sharps Rifle was a single-shot breechloader that used cloth or linen cartridges and metal percussion caps, like most muzzle-loading rifles used by his compatriots. However, with a breach-loader, he could fire an impressive seven rounds per minute. And each of his rounds found its mark. So far, Jacques knew he had felled at least three blue-bellied officers and four or five enlisted. But as the Yankees charged forward after the second Confederate volley, Jacques became unsure how long his brigade would last against several thousand mounted troopers armed with sabers. To his astonishment, Old Man Lee stood stoically just a few dozen yards away, with Generals Jackson and Ewell at his side, both with pistols drawn.

When Gregg's division was within 50 yards of the Confederate infantry line, Hayes ordered the last volley. This time, all 1500 Tigers fired in unison, crippling the First New York and First Maryland

Cavalries. Hundreds of Yankees fell with the third volley, and the carnage from all three volleys combined was severe. To make matters worse for the Yankees, two regiments of Confederate Cavalry sent from Stuart immediately after the third volley slammed into Gregg's surviving men. To their credit, the Gregg's Yankees fought like demons despite the trauma they had just endured. However, it was to be a losing fight, as all the Yankee momentum had been lost, and severe losses had been incurred.

Meanwhile, with the battle's confusion, some of the couriers Major McClelland had intended for General Stuart ended up near General Longstreet's First Corps headquarters near Mount Pony. These dispatch riders had wild stories about the fight at Brandy Station, and somehow one of the messages was interpreted to mean that General Lee's headquarters at Culpeper Courthouse was under threat. This led Longstreet to release General Hood's entire division, and two brigades took only rifles and ammunition and more or less ran north to save their beloved commanding general.

The battle around Brandy Station raged, and though General Stuart countered every action by the Yankees, the Confederate general was taken aback by the ferocity and nature of the attacking Yankee cavalry. Buford's division steadily pushed back the bulk of the Confederate cavalry to the eastern edge of Fleetwood Hill while, despite heavy losses, Gregg pushed from the south.

The Louisiana Tigers, atop Fleetwood Hill, faced a dilemma: limited ammunition. They had unleashed three shots per man in volley, but the men in the brigade carried an average of 15 to 20 cartridges per man. Following the review of the previous day, there had been no opportunity to supply the brigade with adequate ammunition, and now every shot had to count. Luckily, the Confederate cavalry, with some direction from Major McClelland, twice funneled a few Union cavalry regiments up Fleetwood Hill only to have the men from Louisiana deliver a couple of volleys into their ranks.

However, as the battle dragged on into the afternoon, the attrition of losing so many troopers began to catch up with the Yankee troopers.

***

June 9, 1863, 2 PM, Gregg's Command, Fleetwood Hill

George Armstrong Custer gasped in horror when over a thousand Confederate infantrymen stood from their concealment on Fleetwood Hill and delivered several volleys into the lead regiments of General Gregg's division. The First New Jersey had effectively ceased to exist after the second volley.

Custer stayed in the fray and even rallied the First Brigade, whose commander, Colonel Wyndham, was killed early in the fighting. "First Brigade," yelled the young Captain Custer, "Rally to me!" And the First Brigade rallied to the aide-de-camp of General Pleasanton. The men of the First Brigade had no choice but to listen to Custer since most of their senior officers were either dead or wounded.

First Brigade rallied just in time to be hit by two Confederate Cavalry regiments on the crest of Fleetwood Hill. The young Captain from Michigan led what was left of the brigade down Fleetwood Hill in a rolling fight with the Confederate cavalry. As fierce as the Confederates were, the First Brigade kept its composure and fought the Confederate horsemen hard. Custer took out more than one gray-clad trooper with his saber, and he constantly waved it over his head to rally his troops to him. By the time the First Brigade reached the bottom of Fleetwood Hill, the rest of Gregg's division had joined them, and the entire division charged up the hill again.

As delighted as Custer would have been in any other circumstance to have so many reinforcements, he felt utterly powerless as the whole division charged up Fleetwood Hill, only to be met by a volley of rifle fire from the Confederate Brigade entrenched on the hill.

The battle had become a general melee as Union troopers with sabers and pistols fought off the Confederate cavalry and began firing at the massed ranks of Confederate infantry. At a distance, the single-shot muzzleloaders gave the Louisiana Tigers an advantage over the Yankee cavalry. But when the distance was closed, the Yankee troopers could rapidly fire their pistols' six rounds into the Confederate ranks and cause much mayhem.

Custer ignored the fact that he was only a Captain and took command of any units near him that appeared to need a commander. The thrill of battle exhilarated the young man, and he felt that maybe there was a chance the Confederate line on Fleetwood Hill could be broken.

The bugler mounted next to Custer practically flew out of his saddle as his head exploded. With the back of his gauntlet, Custer wiped the brain matter from his face and leveled his revolver to see a hundred yards away, a Confederate sharpshooter standing on a boulder while he reloaded his rifle in seconds.

Seeing no point in letting the man reload unmolested, Custer drew up his revolver and cocked back the hammer. To his dismay, the Confederate moved with speed and agility that Custer was not expecting, and Custer looked in disbelief as the young man fired his rifle directly at him.

Captain Custer did not feel the bullet's impact. The bullet barely missed him, hitting his mount instead, and seconds later, Custer found himself flying through the air. Landing hard, Custer surprisingly still had a revolver and pointed it in the direction where the young Confederate had been to repay the favor. Custer knew that the shot was dubious at best, but he could not allow such an act to go without some type of response.

To his dismay, the sharpshooter was no longer there. So much for revenge.

"Sir," a young corporal gave the reins of a fresh mount to Custer. "General Gregg has ordered a tactical retreat."

Custer acknowledged the orders, but why now? "We can break them," he said out loud.

"Sir, there are reports of an entire Confederate infantry division approaching from the west."

***

As Custer and what was left of the First Brigade fought to extract themselves from Fleetwood Hill, multiple regiments from Hood's division arrived near Fleetwood Hill. Earlier in the day, when reports had reached Longstreet that General Lee was in danger, Longstreet jumped into action and sent what units he could to assist General Lee. At the time, General Lee's headquarters were not endangered. Still, by the time the first brigade from Hood arrived, multiple Union cavalry companies were in the vicinity and shooting at the home of General Lee and General Ewell, and their staffs had been in that morning.

The third Union cavalry wing to attack the Confederates was General Duffie's, whose division was supposed to swing around the southern tip of the Confederates and attack from the west. According to General Pleasanton's plan, Duffie was to attack simultaneously with Gregg and Buford. Unfortunately, Duffie got lost in the early hours of the morning, and his attack was delayed. However, his division was able to sweep aside Butler and Wickham's divisions, and his troopers ended up at not only Fleetwood Hill but also by Mount

Pony, General Longstreet's headquarters, and Culpepper Court House, General Lee's headquarters.

General Lee had initially wished to conceal his infantry from the prying eyes of the Union Cavalry. Still, with the battle hanging in the balance, threatening his campaign before it had even begun, Lee took no chances and sent couriers to Longstreet.

***

June 9, 1863. 5 PM Fleetwood Hill

It had taken over 12 hours of hard fighting, but the Battle of Brandy Station was over. Jacques had to sit down and tuck his hands under his knees to keep them from shaking anymore. He had lost count of how many times the Yankees had charged up that damn hill, but they had been repulsed every time. The over 60 rounds Jacques had fired from his rifle played no small role in stopping the Yankees. And almost every shot had found its mark. It's what Johan would have proclaimed as a target-rich environment.

General Lee had never wavered from his spot just a short distance from Jacques in the battle for Fleetwood Hill. And the young sharp shooter couldn't understand it. The old man was the commanding general of the Army of Northern Virginia and should have gotten the hell out of there. And the thought occurred to Jacques. Maybe that was why that old man was the Confederacy's best and most beloved general. Could that be why this army was willing to march to the gates of Hell and take on the devil himself if Lee asked them?

Jacques ignored the footsteps behind him until the man cleared his throat. Rolling his eyes, Jacques stood and turned around, only to see General Lee standing just a few feet away from him. Jacques quickly saluted and apologized, as the mounted Jackson and Ewell both let out soft laughs a short distance away.

The general gave a slight smile and returned Jacques' salute. "Corporal Lutze, I believe you have earned that title after today's work. Many in this army, including your wing and Corps commanders, also seem to hold our Louisiana troops in high regard." Lee paused and extended his hand, holding the corporal's stripes. "Son, your brother left his mark on your brigade and this entire army. But you are blazing your own path quite effectively. Keep up the good work, and there will always be a place in this army for a man that can handle a rifle like you."

Sometime later, after the generals had ridden off to inspect the battlefield, Sergeant Poisson and several other men, including the Irishman Murray and the Creole LaRoux, came to congratulate Jacques on his promotion, which had been bestowed upon him by General Lee himself.

Poisson grinned from ear to ear when he saw Jacques's face. "So, how was it to talk to Marse Robert? He even shook your hand for all that fine shooting."

The flushed face gave away how uncomfortable Jacques felt. "He watched me the entire battle. I'm glad I didn't stop to scratch my ass too often. I just told him I thought the idea was to shoot as many Yanks as possible, and he thought that was a most excellent way to look at things."

The men laughed, and Poisson patted Jacques on the shoulder. "Why, boys, I think we have a new convert to the church of Lee!"

Chapter 18

June 9, 1863, 11 PM.
White House, Washington

Lincoln rubbed his temple while General Halleck tried to explain away the day's events. "Alright, General Halleck, I know this is not a crippling setback, not like Chancellorsville, thank the Almighty. But let's not kid ourselves. Generals Hooker and Pleasanton are trying to dress this operation up as nothing short of a grand victory over Stuart. But don't have one of your horses piss on my leg and exclaim that it's rain coming down."

Secretary Stanton cut in. "How bad are the losses? Has the Army of the Potomac lost its mounted screening force?"

Halleck shook his head. "We suffered some losses; the rough count is approximately 4,000, with around 1,000 of those being captured. All the reports I have received speak highly of our troopers, especially those under the command of Buford and Gregg. And our boys showed they were equal to the Confederate horse soldiers. They gave as good as they got until they ran into an ambush at Fleetwood Hill. And how were these men supposed to know a Confederate infantry brigade had dug in on top of that hill and was ready for us? According to all the reports I have read, it appears that the Confederate brigade was present for the grand review the day before and was there again this morning by chance, perhaps because they had encamped there the night before. The rebels were lucky that the infantry brigade was there, for Stuart was being pushed back everywhere. We almost had the bastard."

The emotion in Halleck's voice was sincere. With this war, Lincoln was subjected to a never-ending line of people offering him nothing but empty promises and nonsense. But Halleck, for all his faults, was being truthful. The Army of the Potomac's new cavalry commander, General Pleasonton, had approached both Generals Hooker and Halleck with a bold plan to disrupt Stuart's cavalry buildup or even destroy it. It was a big swing, and a miss, or that was how the newspapers would describe it once they learned about the engagement. However, Lincoln knew that the Union cavalry had proven that man for man, they were equal to the Confederate horse soldiers.

"General Halleck," Lincoln spoke with tiredness but warmth in his voice, "Today was a hard day for your horse soldiers. Although they were driven from the field, they came close to capturing General Stuart and his entire command. We can't dwell on the what-ifs." Lincoln looked at the map on the table and continued, "So, we thought Stuart was at Culpepper Court House, but he was at Brandy Station instead. And despite our losses today, his command sustained significant losses. But what else do we know now? Can the other Confederate infantry brigades be verified? Was General Lee actually on top of Fleetwood Hill during the battle? What are Lee and Stuart up to now?"

With a look and a nod from Secretary Stanton, Halleck responded to the president, "Mr. President, it is difficult to surmise what the rebels are planning. But given all the intelligence, the facts suggest Stuart is planning another raid outside of Virginia, most likely in southern Pennsylvania, like last year. As for the Army of the Potomac, it appears that General Lee has undertaken a significant reorganization of the Army of Northern Virginia. According to the Bureau of Military Intelligence, Lee has taken on this reorganization for one or two reasons. First, he plans another invasion of Union territory, with Stuart serving as his screening force. As seen by the Bureau, the more likely scenario is that Lee will send more than one Corps, or up to one-third, of his army to the western theater. The

Army of Northern Virginia would then be compelled to take up a defensive line well south of the Rappahannock."

"I favor this scenario as well, Mr. President." Stanton proclaimed assertively. "Beauregard might have given Grant a bloody nose a week ago, but that campaign is back to a slow, drawn-out affair that will slowly drain Beauregard of resources and see Vicksburg reduced to ash. Beauregard cannot beat Grant with the forces that he now has. And Bragg in Tennessee is barely holding his position against Rosencrans. I would say give the Army of the Tennessee another month or two, and it will outflank Bragg and be in Chattanooga. Bragg has sent his best troops to Beauregard in Mississippi and urgently needs veteran troops to replace those he has sent away. If I were Jefferson Davis, I would send an entire Corps to Bragg and replace him with either Lee or Jackson."

Lincoln pondered Halleck's and Stanton's remarks: "The news from the western theater is encouraging, but I wish to stop brushing aside each disaster in the East like it does not matter. I would be the first to rejoice if General Lee decided to dig in behind the Rappahannock, but let us not count on that assumption. We have all read the reports of massive troop movements of Rebel troops throughout the South. They are planning something, and we need to determine its nature quickly. Anything else you gentlemen care to share with me? Any other surprises?"

Halleck, the consummate professional, hid his annoyance at Lincoln's slight rebuke: "A dispatch came across my desk just before I left to get to this meeting. It seems we captured a few prisoners of considerable value during today's battle. The most notable is a rebel officer named Frank Hampton."

The first indication of Lincoln's attitude change was his grin from ear to ear. "Would that be the brother of General Wade Hampton? Of General Stuart's command?"

***

June 10, 1863, 12 PM, Train en route to Virginia

As much as Paul tried to focus on his work, it was next to impossible for him to do so. His report was just as much a work in progress as it had been when they had left Mobile the previous day. But for a brief shining moment in this god-forsaken war, he did not care.

"I would say a celebration is called for here," said a voice in an English accent.

Paul looked up to see Colonel Fremantle holding out a bottle. Taking to his feet, Paul smiled as he took the proffered bottle into his grip. "Thank you, Colonel. When one is told the news that they are to have a child, whether it be their first or third, it changes the way one views the world." Paul paused, emotion thick in his voice, "It is a contradiction in many ways, my friend. I have seen significant suffering in this war, both up close and from afar. Many would even say that bringing a new life into this land ravaged by conflict is irresponsible."

Fremantle smiled as he pulled out two cigars and offered one to Paul. "But the birth of a child can also be a testament to your belief that a bright and joyous future is worth fighting for."

***

June 14, 1863, 6 AM. Port Hudson, Louisiana

It did not matter to Sergeant Pierre Landry whether it was night or day; the nightmares blended the light and the dark. The nightmares were so bad that he hated to go to sleep at night, because when he closed his eyes, all the horror of that day never left his mind. It had been that way since the first Federal assault on the Confederate fortifications around Port Hudson on May 27th. The 1st and 3rd Native Louisiana Guards, Blue-clad Union regiments formed from both free men of color and former slaves native to Louisiana, had shown nothing but gallantry as they attempted to storm the Confederate defenses. They had paid dearly in blood that day for little gain, and the same occurred this morning with what had to be an even higher butcher's bill.

The two black regiments were put under the command of General Dwight, and like the other failed attack of May 27th, the men of the 3rd Native Guards marched and died bravely in the open terrain before the Confederate entrenchments. The regiment had been told the name of the main Confederate redoubt, which was their objective. Fort Desperate seemed to be a suitable name for the predicament Pierre found himself and his men in.

Despite the continuous rifle fire from the Confederate entrenchments, Pierre urged his squad forward to their objective. General Banks, the overall Union commander of the Port Hudson Operation, had decided in his strategic brilliance to attempt another mass assault on the Confederate fortifications. The attack that morning began with a massive artillery barrage on the Confederate positions, followed by massed infantry assaults across the entire front of the Confederate fortifications. And predicably, this assault was bogged down just like the one that occurred on May 27th.

A cannon boomed with the distinctive sound of canister shot, and Pierre and his men instinctively dropped to the ground again to avoid what was essentially a gigantic shotgun blast. Unfortunately for Private Leon, he was not fast enough, and Pierre heard a metal projectile thud into the private's flesh. The young man screamed before his body thudded to the ground.

"Hang tight, boys!" Pierre called out as he crawled through the mud with what remained of his company, seeking cover. This was easier said than done for the negro sergeant, for he was over six feet tall and two hundred pounds of lean muscle. Across the open field, the Confederates had set up abatis, felled trees with sharpened ends or branches pointed toward the attackers. As the men moved to find cover behind these felled trees, Confederate sharpshooters continued to fire, and several bullets violently hit the felled tree Pierre attempted to find cover behind. However, more than one of Pierre's men was struck by the sharpshooters, and they lay still with their lifeblood running out as Private Leon still lay screaming in the mud.

By this point, Pierre had abandoned his rifle and crawled slowly towards the injured private. With bullets and artillery shells buzzing overhead, Pierre reached Leon and immediately saw his severe thigh wound that was oozing blood. Leon was gripping his leg tightly as Pierre crawled up to him and gritted his teeth so as not to cry out any more from the pain.

Pierre placed a gentle hand on Leon's shoulder. "How bad does it hurt?"

On his back with his face upwards towards the sky, Leon blinked to fight back the tears. "It hurts, Sarge. Damn, it hurts. I don't want to lose my leg."

"Alright, Leon. Stay with me. I'm going to put a tourniquet around your leg. It will hurt like hell, but then I'm going to get you out of here."

Leon nodded, and Pierre pulled out a strip of leather from the man's pack and tightened it around Leon's thigh above the wound. The young man screamed as Pierre tightened the makeshift tourniquet, but by the time Pierre finished, the flow of blood out of the wound had stopped.

"Company on me," called out Peirre. Even as he issued the command, his men were still pinned down by the heavy Confederate fire. He had seen most of the other companies from their regiment obliterated, and Pierre knew that meant their regiment's losses would be particularly high today. He just had no intention of sticking around for his men to fire a couple of volleys at the Confederates, only to have none of his men survive the day. This attack had been a bad idea from the start, and having his men slaughtered would do nothing to save the day for General Banks's ill-planned attack. It was time to get out.

Slowly, the men from his company crawled or stayed close to the ground and began the painful withdrawal process. With a pat on Leon's shoulder, Pierre half-crawled and dragged Leon behind him. The young man cried out in pain a few times, but he did what he could to ease the burden on Pierre, as there were several hundred yards of open field they would need to traverse before they were out of range of the Confederate guns.

To Pierre, it felt like the longest day of his life. As his men and he made the slow retreat back to their starting point, other men from the 3rd Louisiana joined them as the Confederate fire did not let up. Occasionally, solid shot artillery would be fired, and one time, the man 30 yards ahead of Pierre and Leon was vaporized by one unlucky shot. The retreat was through a virtual hellscape of dead and wounded black soldiers clad in dark blue. Almost nowhere was there solid or dry ground, so every step was in mud, with the occasional man-made or natural obstruction forcing several detours. Twice, Pierre had to pull Leon through a ditch, the only benefit being that they were mostly protected from Confederate fire.

It did not even register to Pierre at first when they had finally cleared the Confederate guns and were safely back to Union lines. In all, he had led 20 men back, most of whom had some degree of wounds or injuries. Not until he had helped get Leon into a hospital tent to see a surgeon did Pierre realize how much his right knee ached. Sitting on a log and stretching out his injured knee, he removed his field cap and wiped his face with a bandana.

His hands shook so badly that it took him some time to steady them before he took a sip from his canteen and splashed water in his face to wipe away sweat and mud. No one could ever justify to him why today's attack would have been a good idea. His regiment and the other infantry brigades would suffer from General Banks's incompetence alone today. There had been no lack of courage; if anything, all of the men in the attack, black or white, had been the bravest men Pierre had ever witnessed in action. And all for nothing.

A voice broke through Pierre's thoughts. "Are you Sergeant Landry?"

Pierre looked up, then stood, coming to attention as a surgeon, obviously a white officer, addressed him. "Yes, Sir. Sergeant Landry at your service, Sir."

The Surgeon smiled weakly, "None of that is necessary, Sergeant, especially after that hell you all went through today. It might have been ill thought out, but my God, no one can say there was a lack of courage on your men's part." He paused to wipe a blood-smeared hand across his brow, "We finished working on Private Leon a short time ago."

Pierre tensed, expecting the worst. He brought Leon to the triage area of the field hospital and, out of exhaustion, wandered away until he found a tree log to half fall asleep on. Now he prepared himself for the bad news this doctor was about to give about Leon's leg. It was to be another soldier he was responsible for who was to die or lose a limb. Pierre just knew.

"How is Private Leon, Sir?" Pierre asked as his voice quavered.

"Well, Sergeant, it was a nasty leg wound. The canister took a good-sized chunk out of his leg. But you saved his life by getting him to us. I think with some luck, he should be able to keep the leg."

“Thank you, Sir,” was all Pierre could speak as the day's emotions overpowered him.

***

June 14, 1863. 7 PM, General Beauregard’s Headquarters, Mississippi

Johan concluded the Sabbath by reviewing another stack of paperwork. It had been over a week since he began spending every day at work in Beauregard’s headquarters, but Johan did not mind. Just this week, he learned a great deal about how an army operates and how challenging logistics are. Though being a line officer was much more dangerous, it was easier in some ways. You were usually ordered to either attack or hold a position, and you executed the order. As a staff officer, one had much more responsibility than a company or line officer would command.

A good part of his day was writing General Beauregard’s orders to the corps and divisional commanders. It also made his head swim when, within a few days, he realized that orders had to be as direct as possible; otherwise, misunderstanding would creep in, whether it was legitimate or merely an excuse for a commander not to do what he was commanded to do.

Somehow, in the middle of the wilderness outside of Vicksburg, Johan felt he and the other junior staff officers were producing enough paperwork to produce several books. He tried to put things in perspective as he shifted his seat to take the pressure off his injured leg. The Army of the Mississippi Valley was not only newly formed, but it had just fought its first major battle. Mountains of paperwork were to be the norm for the foreseeable future.

The newly constructed, more secure main door to the barn opened, and Generals Beauregard and Forrest walked in and made it straight for Johan at his makeshift desk. As he rose to greet the generals, each man signaled for Joahn to remain seated and pay attention.

"Colonel Lutze," Beauregard smiled as he spoke, "You have been extremely diligent with your work this past week and have obeyed my orders not to get involved in the fighting along the railroad and, most importantly, not to get yourself shot again. How are your two injuries faring? Do you feel that you are on the road to recovery?"

The two men obviously required Johan's services for something, and the young Lieutenant Colonel knew it would be best to be forthcoming. "Well, Sirs. My face still hurts, and I am growing out my whiskers to help conceal my injury. Regarding my leg, the injury appears worse than it is. So, I can confidently say I can take on any task you may have for me."

General Forrest grinned from ear to ear. "You see, General Beauregard. We need more men like this young Colonel here. He volunteered before we could even assign him a mission. This is just the type of officer I need, damn crazy enough to work for me."

General Beauregard saw the look of concern on Johan's face and smiled, "Do not worry, Colonel. The task envisioned for you is tame, by most standards. It will also give you a chance at a limited command.

Despite enjoying the confusion on Johan's face, General Forrest knew he had to fill him in more. "Colonel, could you finish your work in 20 minutes? Great. Well, meet me by the coral in 20 minutes; that way, we will still have daylight to work out some details.

The following 20 minutes flew by for Johan, mainly because he finished the document he was working on, distributed his unfinished paperwork to junior staff officers, and painstakingly gave instructions on how General Beauregard preferred his orders written and organized. Satisfied that things were squared away as best as possible, Johan left the army headquarters to meet General Forrest.

Johan found Forrest at the coral and Andre by his side with a wide grin. "Colonel," Forrest began after he let his two junior officers tease one another for a moment. "I have filled in your cousin, Lieutenant Breaux, but I will tell you now. A moderately sized wagon train of 25 wagons is heading to Vicksburg tonight. It will bring food, medical supplies, and ammo to General Pemberton's command. That is the easy part. I have already deployed several mounted companies to ensure there are no Yankee bushwhackers and to facilitate your entry into Vicksburg with minimal attention. The hard part will be the return trip. General Pemberton has compiled a list of severely sick or wounded men who will be removed from Vicksburg by your wagons and transported to Jackson. I know, this operation will take a few days, but it is important."

Forrest paused and waited to see if Johan had any questions. When the general saw that there were none from Johan, he continued, "This is perhaps the most important part of the mission. Several of the men we will be retrieving from Vicksburg are officers. One in particular is General Bowen. Generals Pemberton, Beauregard, and even Johnston hold him in high regard. From all accounts, he is competent in his role. So good, he got himself wounded the other day when he led his men in a hand-to-hand fight to take one of Vicksburg's redoubts back from the Yankees. On top of that, the poor man has contracted what appears to be dysentery, so that General Bowen will be out of the fight for a while."

Nodding to himself, Johan knew why special effort was being devoted to rescuing a young but wounded general. The Confederacy was losing generals on the battlefield at an alarming rate, and something had to be done to ensure that a year from now, there would still be some generals left. "Understood, General Forrest. When is the departure?"

Forrest turned to look at the western horizon. "Can you believe that the summer solstice is almost upon us? The wagons are being loaded and assembled on two parallel routes to enter southern Vicksburg. They leave in an hour."

Andre had procured himself and Johan mounts, giving Johan enough time to run back to his tent and grab his necessities, bedroll, and Spencer rifle. Invigorated by the mission that General Forrest had personally assigned to him, Johan even laughed at most of the jokes Andre told as they rode to where the wagon train was assembled.

It was the first time Johan had ridden a horse since the battle of June 2, and when he was dismounted at the assembly point, he knew his leg would still need a few more days to heal before he felt confident riding a horse any great distance.

At 8:30 PM, all sunlight was gone, but there was a fair amount of moon and starlight that night. It was not ideal, but given the supply situation within Vicksburg and Grant's unrelenting daily attacks upon the city and Beauregard's army, the Confederates could not wait for anything approaching ideal to resupply Vicksburg.

Johan approached the second wagon in the convoy and asked the driver if he could ride with him to Vicksburg. A middle-aged black man in Confederate butternut sat in the driver's seat and held the wagon's reins loosely when he saw the Spencer rifle Johan had strapped over his shoulder. "Colonel," the driver said in a mostly respectful tone, "If you actually know how to shoot that rifle, I won't turn you down."

Tying his chestnut gelding to the wagon's rear, Johan noticed an oil lamp mounted to the back and modified it so it would not give off an excessive glow. Quickly, he saw that other wagons were outfitted in the same way, and Johan concluded someone must have come up with the trick to prevent the lamp's light from penetrating too great a distance. Spies were everywhere, but the last thing he wanted was to have the wagon train ambushed and caught strung out for miles. That would be a recipe for disaster.

Sitting down next to his driver, the wagon train was soon moving, and Johan, speaking softly, started a conversation with his driver. Not only was this another negro serving in the Confederate army, but he was also wearing a butternut-colored uniform.

As the wagon rolled forward and got onto the dirt road, Johan struck up a conversation with his driver. "I don't think we had the opportunity to introduce ourselves to one another properly. I am Lieutenant Colonel Lutze. Oh, none of that," he waved off the driver, trying to salute him. "What is your name?"

"Name is David, Colonel. If you were curious, I worked for General Forrest before the war. Then he offered me freedom if I served him during the war. So here I am."

"That's quite understandable," Johan said after he had taken in everything David had mentioned. "Well, David, how do you feel about doing most of this riding in the dark and on these roads?"

Knowing he was being tested in a friendly way, David explained the operation from a driver's perspective: " If you know General Forrest as I do, there are probably a few hundred of our boys out here tonight not only making sure that the roads are passable but also to make sure no Yankees were waiting to pounce on them. Our boys will ensure there ain't no blue-bellies around for miles in any direction, but I am more worried about these roads still being intact. Even if the roads are rough but still passable, that will determine when we make it to the streets of Vicksburg."

Chapter 19

June 15, 1863. Evening, Winchester, Virginia, Louisiana Tigers

The last three days had been a whirlwind of violence for Jacques. He was now the veteran of three battles, all major Confederate victories. With the conclusion of the Second Battle of Winchester, Jaques could say that this was the best he had seen his brigade perform.

It had been an exhausting three days of battle, with the Louisiana Tigers playing a crucial role in every stage. The previous evening, the Tigers had charged across 300 yards over open ground and, after fierce hand-to-hand combat, had routed the Yankees at Apple Pie Ridge. As the brigade charged and slammed into the Yankees, Jacques felt out of place, as he was unable to stand and deliberately pick and knock his targets off one by one. It hadn't been that type of fight; it was one for the bayonet. And Jacques, like every other man in Hayes's Tigers, did his duty and used the bayonet tip more than once in that fateful action.

But today, Jacques had made up for the lack of shooting on his part the previous day. He did not even know if it truly had been his shot, but the commanding Yankee General Milroy had been captured when his horse had been shot from under him. It only added to the completeness of the Confederate victory when over 4,000 other Yankee troops had been taken prisoner.

The brigade lauded Jacques and proclaimed him the best marksman in the Army of Northern Virginia. Jacques wasn't too sure about that distinction either. There had been a lot of troopers firing their rifles in the battle, and unless someone came up with a way to examine bullets and determine the gun from which they came, it would always be a mystery in his mind who shot out General Milroy's mount.

With a victory as decisive as Second Winchester and General Ewell's first battlefield action since his severe wounding and subsequent loss of his leg at Second Manassas, the Second Corps thought it was time for a celebration. An extraordinary number of supplies had been captured, and the whiskey supplied by the United States Army was a very fitting gift for most of the men in the Louisiana Tigers.

Jacques was not drunk, or at least he did not think he was. Thanks to Cousin Andre, he had been whiskey drunk before, but tonight, he just felt good and happy, slowly sipping on the whiskey in his metal cup.

A friendly pat on the shoulder from Sergeant Poisson and a few other men from the company put an authentic smile on Jacques's face. "Why, boys," said the shaggy-looking private with an Irish accent, Murray, Jacques could barely understand as he put an arm around Jacques, "Why, lads, not only did he shoot the Yankee General off his ass today, I think the ol' boys below grew some hair!"

Not sure exactly what was being referred to, Jacques took it in stride as the company, and then it seemed most of the regiment patted him or tousled his hair. Perhaps he was now truly accepted by these men as one of their peers.

"Don't let it all get to your head," Poisson grinned. "We need you to shoot many more blue-bellied generals off their horses."

Much later that night, when the festivities had died down, Jacques, Sergeant Poisson, and a few other men sat around a glowing campfire. "Sarge," LaRoux spoke in French, "now that the Shenandoah is cleared out of Yankees, what do you think they will have us do next?" Another man chimed in, "There is some talk that things in Tennessee and Mississippi aren't looking so good. They could use all the help we could send."

Poisson puffed his pipe and considered his words. "That's a good question, boys. I don't have the faintest idea, but I'll make sure to ask General Lee tomorrow morning when we have breakfast together." He paused as a few of the men snickered at the joke. "Tell y'all the truth, I think we are heading through Maryland right into Yankee Pennsylvania, just like we tried last year. We are here right now and can cause a hell of a lot of havoc for the Yankees, especially if we can cut loose in Pennsylvania. And even if they were to send us to Tennessee or even closer to home, how long would that take? Hell, Jacques, how long did it take you at the beginning of this year to make it to Virginia from back home?"

"A long time," was all Jacques cared to say. He had traveled part of the 1,000-mile journey by train but had walked a fair distance from the Gulf Coast to Virginia. "Probably the better part of four to five weeks."

"Yeah," continued Poisson, "boys, this war is about logistics, or the lack thereof on our side. But if I were President Davis, I would give every man, rifle, and horse I could spare to General Lee and tell him to go terrorize Pennsylvania and dare any Yankee army to take their best shot at us."

***

June 16, 1863. 10 AM, Vicksburg, Mississippi

The wagon train had made a mostly uneventful journey to Vicksburg via the two southern roads that led into the city, which were still under Confederate control. And Johan was shocked at the condition of the city he found. As a young boy, he had visited Vicksburg with his family when they had journeyed upriver from south Louisiana to visit Uncle Jefferson and Aunt Varina. The town had been relatively prosperous atop the bluff overlooking the Mississippi River. There had been much wealth in Vicksburg, and the antebellum charm of the city nearly had Johan enthralled.

But now, Vicksburg was no more than a bombed-out crater —a ghost of its former glory and a living metaphor for its downfall. The defenders of Vicksburg largely managed to keep the city streets free of debris. Still, Johan did not think he had seen a single building in the city undamaged by the Union artillery fire, and quite a few homes and buildings had been claimed by flame.

The people of Vicksburg came out to greet the wagon train, braving the constant artillery fire that would frequently hit something within the city. Luckily for Johan, his wagon drivers were experienced professionals, and they wasted no time parking their wagons and directing the soldiers who came to help unload, giving clear instructions on what each wagon contained.

His back hurt more than any other part of his body, but Johan went into action when several women gathered around the wagons and discovered that food was one of the items being delivered in this convoy. Initially, there was no shouting or pushing by civilians, but word spread quickly that food was included in the day's delivery. The crowd swelled from a dozen or so people to several hundred very quickly, with most of the citizens present being women, often accompanied by a small child. And the murmur of a few hungry women turned into a chant by scores of desperate people on the verge of attacking the wagons in search of anything to eat.

Fearing a riot could break out, Johan stepped between a wagon loaded with foodstuffs and the crowd, ensuring his pistol holster was visible. "Good people of Vicksburg," Johan spoke loudly as he addressed the crowd. "General Beauregard, after much work and great cost, has sent this wagon convoy to help relieve some of the many depredations that have been forced upon you. Our supplies are limited, but let me assure you, I will stay here as long as I need to ensure no one in this city goes hungry today."

The crowd seemed to settle down, and with the help of some garrison troops and the never-ending boom of Yankee cannons providing background noise, Johan initiated a distribution system that General Beauregard had directed him toward. It was far from a perfect system, but with ten wagons dedicated to the civilian population of Vicksburg and other soldiers, Johan helped distribute flour, bread, boiled meat, and a variety of household goods that General Beauregard had procured for Vicksburg.

Johan had to rely on the honor system, hoping people wouldn't line up more than once. There would also be no turning away of anyone, whether young or old, rich or poor, black or white. All the people of Vicksburg were suffering mightily under this horrific siege. Still, the people of Vicksburg self-policed, and several citizens allowed older adults or young mothers to cut in line to ensure that the most vulnerable received food for the day. To Johan's relief, this was not the first convoy of its kind to reach Vicksburg, which also helped keep the line from becoming unmanageable.

Most of the supplies in the wagons were for the troops defending the city. Food, uniforms, percussion caps, and ammunition for rifles and artillery were unloaded from most of the 15 other wagons. Johan did his best to imitate Christ when he fed the 5,000 with a few pieces of bread and fish.

Once the supplies for the civilian population had been distributed and the other wagons were being unloaded efficiently, Johan felt confident asking a sergeant supervising some of the garrison troops for directions to General Pemberton's headquarters.

The sergeant, a weathered man around ten years older than Johan, did not hesitate. "Kingston," the older man called out.

A young private handed off his load to a comrade, hurried up to the non-commissioned officer, and asked how he could assist. Soon enough, the young man led Johan to a once fine home that, though still standing, had several windows blown out and a large hole in the roof on one side.

After dismissing his escort and knocking on the front door, Johan was led to General Pemberton's office. Several officers were moving around and working inside the home. Still, upon arriving at General Pemberton's office, which had once been the homeowner's study, he was relieved that no one else was in the office at the time.

Johan saluted the Confederate General of Northern extraction and handed over a thick folder whose flap was tightly secured. Pemberton received the folder and looked at it closely, and Johan filled him in, "General, those dispatches are from General Beauregard and his staff. You will also find a general breakdown of the supplies that were delivered today. And a report that General Forest had one of his aides copy is also included in there."

Pemberton, whose dark hair and beard were beginning to gray, looked worn out and tired but smiled with his reply to Johan, "Thank you, Colonel. I know that General Beauregard is sending these supplies to us with great difficulty. There is no doubt that these supplies are fulfilling the physical necessities for the citizens of Vicksburg and my men. But even if General Beauregard could only send one wagon, the people of Vicksburg would still be grateful, knowing they had not been forgotten."

"We will do all that we can for Vicksburg, Sir. I must leave soon to attend to the loading of General Bowen and the other wounded. Nevertheless, General Beauregard has insisted that I ask you personally whether you are lacking any additional supplies or resources. If you were to give me a written list, I would ensure that it is delivered to General Beauregard."

A thoughtfully written list was in Johan's possession when he left Pemberton's office. It was neither overly long nor overly concise; Pemberton did not see the need to request items he knew would never materialize. Taking his meeting with Pemberton as a positive development, Johan walked carefully towards a home that was serving as a makeshift hospital as more Union artillery went off and exploded in the distance.

Arriving at the home, several of the convoy's wagons were already lined up in the street in front of the once palatial house. Greek columns, originally whitewashed and wrapped around the front porch, gave the home a spectral appearance, even in the middle of the day. Vicksburg, perched on a bluff overlooking the Mississippi, allowed its residents to excavate tunnels into the rock and build small, cave-like shelters as artillery bombardments intensified. This day was not one of those days, and so several wounded Confederate soldiers were either sitting or lying down on the porch. But the smell of blood, rot, and death assaulted Johan's senses the most.

Now that the supplies had been delivered to the city, the second half of Johan's mission began in earnest. Soldiers from his convoy and healthy troops from within the town began helping load the injured soldiers into the wagons. Johan stayed focused as he talked to one of the doctors who helped run the makeshift hospital. After their brief conversation, Johan remained on the porch as he waited for the doctor to lead General Bowen out.

David's wagon had by now pulled up to the house, and Johan tipped his hat in recognition to the man. During their ride to Vicksburg, David had been told who their special passenger would be, and the man had quickly set up the wagon to transport an invalid after the provisions were unloaded.

Several wounded or sick soldiers had by now been loaded into the wagons. More than one soldier was missing an arm or a leg. There were others whom Johan was not convinced would survive the journey.

"Colonel Lutze." Johan turned to see a pretty but tired woman in a once fine dress addressing him. She appeared to be a few years older than Johan, and her smile made him think of his mother. "My name is Mary Bowen, the wife of General Bowen."

After giving the woman a slight bow, Johan smiled, "Mrs. Bowen, I have heard much about you and your efforts to help care for the sick and injured defenders of Vicksburg. I assure you we will take every care and precaution in caring for your husband."

General Bowen was soon brought out on a stretcher by two orderlies who followed Johan to David's wagon. Mary Bowen remained by the general's side the entire time, holding his hand and giving the injured man comfort. It ended up taking a fair amount of time to get the general on his stretcher into the wagon. Two other men were loaded in as well, and Mary Bowen took her place beside David as the wagon train began its slow exit from Vicksburg.

Mounted on his horse, Johan felt a little more confident that he was healthy enough to make the ride to Jackson. He issued the orders for his wagons and escort to form, and by early afternoon, Johan and his small command had departed from Vicksburg and were en route to Jackson.

June 17, 1863. Late evening, Jackson, Mississippi

Johan's back and injured leg were incredibly sore, but he thanked God that his convoy had made it to Jackson with no incidents along the way. Granted, General Forrest's cavalry had been out in force and ensured that the roads to Jackson would be clear.

Johan's primary mission had been accomplished in bringing General Bowen to Jackson safely. He had done it. Johan commanded almost 100 men and completed his mission with no loss of life among his mounted escorts. There was no doubt that the mission had been successful, but Johan knew that the success was mainly due to the active patrols General Forrest had established.

The chestnut mare he had ridden from Jackson, he had decided to name Gertrude. Why Gertrude? He could not say anything other than that her sweet demeanor reminded him of his German grandmother, Gertrude von Lettow Lutze. Faithfully, Gertrude the mare followed him as he walked her to where a temporary stable had been built to hold officers' mounts overnight in the city.

"Colonel," Johan heard someone speak in a clear Austrian accent. "You are a hard man to locate."

To Johan's surprise and delight, Karl and Fredrick, illuminated by moon and torchlight, walked onto the road beside him. Each man wore Confederate gray, which still seemed out of place to Johan since he had spent so much time in the Army of the Potomac with these men in Union blue.

"It's good to see you two," Johan spoke with happiness as he returned the men's salutes. "You two should have been in the cavalry all along," Johan said as he motioned to the riding boots each man wore. "Glad to see General Forrest has put you two to good work. And speaking of General Forrest, is he in Jackson tonight?"

Karl gestured down the roadway, "In fact, Colonel Lutze, General Forrest sent us to find you."

A short while later, Johan and his companions arrived at the Bowman House Hotel, a three-story brick building that had partially burned down the previous month and been hastily repaired. On the first floor, in what must have served as a meeting room and ballroom, Karl and Fredrick brought Johan to what had become General Forrest's headquarters.

General Forrest dominated the room not only with his height, but also with his piercing blue eyes, which let everyone know he was in command and that his word was final. This headquarters setup was less formal than General Beauregard's, but that did not concern General Forrest. He was here to fight and kill Yankees.

Johan was not short by the day's standards, but General Forrest's six-foot frame made him look up to one of the most feared warriors in the Confederacy. "Colonel," Forrest looked up from the table that was serving as his desk. A large map was displayed on the table, and Johan saw that it showed both the Mississippi and Eastern Louisiana along the river. And Forrest immediately noticed Johan's interest in the map.

"Well, Colonel. First, I will congratulate you on a successful mission."

Johan shrugged, "General Forrest, I thank you for the compliment, but my mission was uneventful because of the work and vigilance of your men."

Forrest grinned, acknowledging Johan's statement. "You are much more intelligent than that Frenchie cousin of yours, Lieutenant Breaux, claims. Now to business," Forrest pointed to the map. "You have spent quite a bit of time with General Beauregard over the last month and have been exposed to quite a bit of sensitive intelligence by working on his staff. Could you describe the strategic situation our forces in the Mississippi Valley now face?"

There were many in Yankee circles whose first instinct would be to discredit the intelligence and honor of General Forrest. For after all, the man had made his fortune as a slave trader. Were not men such as Forrest scum? Being a Southerner from a once-wealthy family, Johan knew the true story was much deeper and more complicated. But wasn't everything dealing with race, class, and wealth complicated in the South? Nevertheless, it was time to answer the question that he knew Forrest already had an answer for.

"Well, General, we are stuck—no point in pretending otherwise. We knocked the hell out of Grant at the beginning of the month, took out an entire Corp. However, he immediately replaced those troops, and he has been fighting a battle of attrition with us ever since, a battle we cannot ultimately win. We currently have the upper hand, but that will not last forever. We face the same dilemma General Pemberton faced before our army arrived. How long can we keep Vicksburg out of Yankee hands without destroying or entrapping all of the forces under the command of General Beauregard? And then there is Port Hudson, in my home state. From the limited dispatches I have seen, they are not in much better shape than we are."

General Forrest's piercing blue eyes took in Johan, and the man nodded his agreement. "Yes, Colonel. That sums it up. Now the question is, what do we do about it? How long do we try to hold on, to keep the river open for our people and deny its use to the Yankees? And how long are we to drag out this misery to kill even more Yankees? Can we force their hand somewhere, have them make a mistake that is too costly?"

It was then that Johan realized almost every man in the room was focused on General Forrest and himself, even as General Cleburne and a handful of his staff walked up to the large dining table that displayed the map.

Cleburne patted Johan on the shoulder, "Now consider my question, Colonel. How good a general is Banks? Indications are that he has 40,000 men besieging Port Hudson. How capable a general is he with that force?"

Johan had become accustomed to this back-and-forth in conversation that the two generals before him liked to use. However, it still took him a few moments to refocus his thoughts and remember his time in the Shenandoah Valley a year ago in Stonewall Jackson's army.

There was no way for Johan to be diplomatic about his opinion. "Sir, I believe that scoundrel cousin of mine, Lieutenant Breaux, drunk and naked, would be one hundred times the general Banks is, sir. Hell, we captured so much of his supplies last year in the Valley that both us and the yanks called him Commissary Banks."

With a glint in his eye, Cleburne grinned at Forrest and gave Johan one more pat on the shoulder before he pulled away. "Colonel, one of the benefits and drawbacks of being a staff officer is the inherent flexibility of your role. Now, General Beauregard is at Vicksburg, and you are here in Jackson in our company."

Johan looked at Karl and Fredrick, both of whom remained still as statues in the presence of two generals. However, the look on their faces led Johan to believe that they knew what was about to happen. "Well, General Cleburne, it appears that you and General Forrest have another task for me to accomplish."

Cleburne looked to Forrest, "We have a sharp one here, General." There was a twinkle in Cleburne's eyes as he faced Johan. "I have disengaged my home division and a good bit of my Corps from General Beauregard's defensive line. With the assistance of General Forrest, I am going to take my men for a quick march into Louisiana, all the way to Port Hudson, to visit General Banks and to break out General Gardner and his command. The 13th Louisiana will be joining this adventure, but unfortunately, its commander, Colonel Francis, was wounded the other day. Though his wounds are not life-threatening or severe, he will be out of action for a time. So, I am left needing a replacement for him, without rearranging the entire chain of command for half of my forces. And Colonel, that leads me to congratulate you on taking command of the 13th Louisiana and helping to blaze the path to General Banks.

June 18, 1863. North Carolina/Virginia Border. Noon

Paul Lutze stood at attention as another trainload of soldiers departed. Uncle Jefferson was a good man, but as President, he had gained a reputation for favoring family and friends with promotions and assignments that many of his detractors questioned as invalid and unwise.

However, there was no question that Paul was confident in his abilities. When one was trained to run the family plantation and knew numbers and logistics better than most, that confidence was unmistakable. But creating an entire Army Corps from nothing was something else altogether.

General Johnson was a proud man, and somehow, by the grace of God, Johan and General Beauregard had convinced him to set aside his ego and put the country first. However, General Johnston was in a unique situation: not only had he been commanding the Army of Relief, now renamed the Army of the Mississippi Valley, but he had also been the department commander. President Davis had removed Johnston from command of his army, but he had also removed him from command of the department and had, more or less, demoted him to corps commander. And not only was General Johnston a corps commander, but he was also the corps commander of the army he had put together and commanded only a year ago.

And yet General Johnston was showing remarkable growth, which was the only thing that Paul could call it. At Vicksburg, Johnston graciously remained with Beauregard and helped design the battle plan that led to the victory over Grant. And now they were in the Carolinas, forming together a corps that would become the IV Corps of the Army of Northern Virginia. There were stranger things that happened in this war, and Paul could attest to that. Paul's artificial-cork leg, he would have thought, would make him ineligible for active Army Service, and here he helped get all the logistics together for this new Corps. Only time would tell if the gamble would pay off.

June 19, 1863, Early Morning, Ramond, MS

The plan derived by Generals Beauregard and Forrest was bold because it had to be. General Forrest was in overall command of the expedition, while personally leading a cavalry screening force. General Cleburne was to follow with 10,000 hand-picked men in two separate but parallel marching columns. These two columns were to travel through the interior of Mississippi, hidden from prying Yankee eyes, then to link up at St. Francisville, Louisiana, and assist General Forrest in breaking out General Gardner from Port Hudson. Once Gardener was extracted, his force would hurry to St Francisville, where most of Cleburne's men would wait in ambush for General Banks's army that was sure to follow. It was not a perfect plan by any stretch of the imagination, but it was better than the alternative of General Gardner's men starving and being forced to surrender.

The 13th Louisiana marched in column along the forested Mississippi road as the sky began to lighten that morning. For Johan, this was a new experience because he had never commanded a regiment in the field before; he had only served as a junior officer. Luckily, he had fought with these men almost three weeks ago around Vicksburg. And during this war, it was common for unfamiliar commanding officers to assume command on the battlefield after the death of the previous commander, whether he was a captain, colonel, or general. Luckily, Colonel Francis's injuries were not severe enough that he would be out of action for long. It did seem, however, much to Johan's relief, that the men of the 13th Louisiana were confident in his leadership for the current expedition.

Like most Confederate units, this regiment didn't march in perfect step or in perfect order, though they moved efficiently and with purpose. It was the middle of summer in Mississippi, and the men realized that, with the need to march over ten miles a day, the sooner they started their day and the more miles they marched before the heat of the day set in, the better they would handle the march as a whole.

General Forrest had given Johan a mount for this expedition. And so far, with it just being the second day of this march, he could not complain about his gift. A three-year-old mare, Johan could not quite call her coat cream; it almost had a golden hue, and he was happy with that. Her gate was smooth, she seemed intelligent enough, and not finicky around other men. Was that all you could ask for in a war horse?

Johan knew the business of war, and he wasn't worried about what he needed to do. But there was that doubt in the back of his mind. An idea that the men of 13th Louisiana would think that he was an impostor. Leading a regiment on a march was one thing, and leading that regiment in the heat of battle was something else altogether. Though if one looked back at the events of June 1st and 2nd, there was no doubt that he could fight, which gave him some respectability among the men of the 13th Louisiana. But did he have the charisma and the respect of the entire regiment for these men to put their faith in him to lead? There was only one solution to this predicament: lead with confidence and lead by example.

Though his wound from the fighting around Vicksburg still bothered him somewhat, Johan did not spend the entirety of the previous day on his horse. Of the ten miles they marched, Johan marched at least two with his men. Maybe it was not much in the grand scheme of things, though it did show his men that he was willing to endure anything that they had to endure. That came in handy that night when Johan put in physical effort to help set up the camp and their defensive positions around the encampment. And like the veteran troops they were, the 13th Louisiana efficiently set up camp and broke it down in the morning. And with little incentive, his men were in the same mind as him. They were marching back into their home in Louisiana to save as many of their fellow Louisianians as possible and to stop the looting of the state by General Banks.

"Oh, there you go looking official and important looking," Andre chuckled as he brought his horse up next to Johan's. "You look right at home being a colonel and all that. Now, don't get too excited, they might want to make you a general next."

Johan didn't even have anything to say at first. He returned a salute to Andre, who had given maybe an approximation of one. It was a miraculous victory that his cousin had even remembered to salute a superior officer. But who would be worried about those kinds of details? With a laugh, Johan responded, "Well, Lieutenant, once we have marched a few days, I will make that promotion request to General Forrest. I'm sure nothing could go wrong with that. Not like he or his cavalry would have anything better to do."

Andre replied, "We have been mighty busy, Colonel. General Forrest did say we've done a good job of clearing out the Yankees. Every once in a while, we come across a couple of blue bellies who aren't that eager to stick around and see who else is coming. So here, we have hundreds of miles of territory to cover for you ground pounders. I would think tonight your Louisiana boys might show me some of their appreciation and share some of their refreshments that they brought along."

"So, you boys are earning your keep," Johan said as he chuckled. "Lieutenant, if you keep up the good work, who knows, you could be a Colonel one day."

By the look on Andre's face, Johan didn't know whether Andre was sincere or playacting, "Colonel, for all that is holy, never put a curse like that upon me." With those words, Andre rode off.

The men of the 13th Louisiana could clearly see the smile on Johan's face. There was only one Andre Breaux in this world, and he seemed to be enjoying himself as a soldier. Johan wondered when the flying pigs would come around.

June 23, 1863. Early Afternoon, Waynesboro, Pennsylvania.

It was the farthest north that Jacques Lutze had ever been, but it was also the farthest North the army of Northern Virginia had ever advanced. The battle of Brandy Station and the Second Battle of Winchester were the precursors of what would occur in the coming days. With the Shenandoah Valley cleared out of all Union forces except the garrison at Harpers Ferry, the invasion route to the north was open.

Jacques had started this whole mess as a way to kill Yankee officers. And now here he was in Pennsylvania, invading honest-to-goodness Yankee territory. But the day wasn't over by a long shot. Sergeant Poisson had said as much; the army had to keep moving, especially the Second Corps. Those were General Jackson's orders, and they would stick to them.

The Louisiana Tigers were the tip of the spear for the Army of Northern Virginia, and this afternoon was no exception to that rule. In the distance, Jacques could hear the crack of carbine fire. That meant there would be some skirmishing ahead, but carbines sounded different from rifle fire to Jacques. The idea was to fight the Yankees deep in their own territory, and skirmishing cavalry in the distance meant that the Yankees did not have infantry nearby, Jacques hoped. So far so good, if the cavalry brigade attached to General Ewell could clear out the Yankee horsemen, Second Corps could march several more miles today.

The officers kept the columns moving past Waynesboro even as another company of gray-clad horsemen galloped past. If there were to be a fight for Second Corps, they would have deployed into battle lines, so the fact that they kept marching either meant all Yankee cavalry had been driven off or General Jackson was pushing General

Ewell to make as many miles as he could in a given day. Several non-commissioned officers shouted encouragement to the passing cavalry and their own troops as well, in an apparent attempt to keep up the spirits of all the Confederate forces.

When Sergeant Poisson finished with his exultation, he turned and winked at Jacques. "See that, boy? That is how you keep the army moving. It's a tough pace General Jackson has set for General Ewell, but if we keep this up, we will be in Chambersburg tonight."

"Why, Sergeant," Jacques asked in a playful tone, "what on earth are we going to Chambersburg for?"

"The road to Harrisburg!"

As Poisson answered, the entire brigade shouted, "Huzzah!"

***

Not only had Jacques spent his entire life in Louisiana, but he had also called that war-torn state home for the last two years. He had walked part of the way from Mobile to Virginia to join the army of Northern Virginia, and what he saw along the Chambersburg Pike truly astonished him. Pennsylvania was not devastated as much as Louisiana or Virginia. In fact, these farms were well-kept and prosperous, offering excellent opportunities for Confederate soldiers to forage.

The war had been raging in Virginia for two years now, and the soldiers of the Army of Northern Virginia, especially those of the Louisiana Tigers, were stunned by the plenty they saw in Pennsylvania. For many men, putting any political or social issues aside, seeing the prosperity of Pennsylvania firsthand, convinced them that this war was Mr. Lincoln's war, and it was a war of conquest and plunder. But, unsurprisingly, his compatriots had been given strict orders from General Lee himself. These orders were issued to every Corps, divisional, and brigade commander, with clear instructions. Civilian and private property were to be respected, and any requisitioning was to be done through official channels. Confederate quartermasters and provisioners were to visit all the farms in that area, especially those along the roadway, pay in Confederate dollars for any supplies taken, and issue receipts. General Lee wanted to show that the Confederacy was indeed a civilized nation that did not make war upon the defenseless and helpless, including women and children.

As the Second Corps marched down the Chambersburg Pike, it was very apparent to Jacques that Lee's system would be enforced. Still, it would be hard, if not nearly impossible, to ensure it was perfectly implemented. Many of the soldiers within his brigade would help themselves to any fruit or vegetables that grew close to the roadway. Even family farm animals were sometimes spirited away before a commissary officer could come and pay for the animal and bring it to the quartermaster.

But Lee's men were not mutinying. They would never abandon Marse Lee and ignore his orders. However, the men had great fun, and once the cat escaped, they would play with Confederate commissary officers. Several men, including Sergeant Poisson, often gave the commissary officers misleading information about the whereabouts of certain sheep or cattle.

It was all in good fun and further boosted morale in Lee's army. This was the strongest that Lee's army had ever been, and they were now taking the fight to the enemy in Yankee home territory. Of the significant actions Lee had commanded over the last year, Sharpsburg was the only clear non-decisive victory Lee had achieved. And they had not been defeated at Sharpsburg; he had fought McClellan to a standstill.

The one thing that unsettled Jacques was the number of farmers and field hands who just watched in silent fury as the Confederate army marched past their farms. A fair number of these farmers had sons or relations fighting in the Union Army or had already been casualties of the war. Jacques and his comrades were aware, however, that a large proportion of the farmers were German or of German ancestry, which led to their being known worldwide as the Pennsylvania Dutch.

The men from Louisiana did not take long to make their own fun. Known for their sarcasm and humor, they lost no opportunity to tease the "Dutch" farmers again and again. Often, while the Louisiana troops marched past, some of them, who were German immigrants or had German immigrant parents, would ask, "Alles gut, ja? and Wo sind deine Männer? Which, translated, meant, "Everything good, yes? And where are your men?"

In most of these instances, Jacques stayed quiet. It felt good to finally be able to give the Yankees the taste of their own medicine, but he did wonder what would come of this adventure that Lee was taking his entire army on. Jacques had complete faith and trust in Lee's leadership. Under Lee's command, Jacques had now fought in three major battles: Chancellorsville, Brandy Station, and Second Winchester, all of which were decisive Confederate victories. General Lee had never led the men wrong. But why did Pennsylvania feel so off, so different from all the other battles he had been in? Why did he feel like he was going to meet his impending doom here?

After they had marched about five miles past Waynesboro, General Jubal Early, whose division General Hayes and the Louisiana Tigers were attached to, took a more extended break from the march. They were in a beautiful country; the Dutch or German farms were well kept, and, to the surprise of many Confederates, some of these farms —the barns and outbuildings-were actually larger than the homes the families lived in.

The Tigers took a break on one of these properties as the afternoon sun sat in the middle of the sky. It was a hot June day, and

Jacques took a moment to appreciate that they were not in war-torn Virginia and that he had a fresh apple for lunch. He leaned against a fence post as he listened to his compatriots cut up, gamble, pass around a flask that someone had managed to bring along for the journey, and just in general be the rowdy outlaws they were from Louisiana. But the owner of this farm, who appeared to be a German as well, stood with a staff in hand and sternly watched the Confederates as they dismantled his fence and led away some of his livestock.

To many of the men in the Louisiana Tigers, this was just the spectacle they needed to end their boredom. First one man, then several, spoke to the owner in broken German, some deliberately to irritate him as much as possible.

As the exchange continued, Jacques sat back, looking in amazement. This man with only a staff as his protection stood in the midst of these Confederate troops and even dared to correct their grammar as they insulted him.

Being the youngest of the Lutze brothers, Jacques had gotten away without studying as much German as Paul and Johan. Like any good Louisiana boy, or so he thought, French and English were the two most essential languages that he spoke. But whether he wanted to admit it or not, he could speak German, and the urge hit him to talk to this man who was brave enough to take on the entire Confederate army that was encamped on his property.

Jacques stood and approached the man, then gave a friendly smile as he tipped his hat. Slowly, Jacques put the words together and spoke to the farmer in German, "Don't take it too personally, Sir. It is all in good fun. Most of these men, their homes have been either attacked or destroyed by the Yankees. The men who supposedly run your state. Though the appearance of our boys might seem both laughable and scary at times, these are good men who will not molest you at the very most, simply tease you because you live too far north of the border for their taste." Jacques pointed to the corporal stripes on his jacket's sleeve. "It doesn't give me much authority, Sir, but it does give me enough to keep these boys in line."

The German farmer raised an eyebrow as a boy in a gray and butternut uniform addressed him in perfect German. "Well, lad," the farmer said in a mostly cheerful voice. "I am surprised to see one of your lot fighting with these brigands. You might be polite, but I can guarantee your friends are not who you think they are."

***

So far, there had been little Yankee infantry to be found on the march into Pennsylvania. There was constant skirmishing ahead of Ewell's lead brigade, but this was apparently the Jenkins Cavalry Brigade, screening the II Corps' approach to Harrisburg.

They camped in Chambersburg, or more accurately, on its outskirts. II Corps might have been north of the Mason-Dixon line, but for Jacques, it still felt warm. But be that as it may, they were following General Jackson's commands, marching straight to Harrisburg.

Jacques sat around the campfire with the rest of his platoon while he ate a chicken leg. The other men feasted on a variety of chicken and sausage, and, according to Sergeant Poisson, this amounted to a scrumptious feast.

"Don't eat that bird too fast, boy," Poisson spoke as he took a big bite out of a leg himself. "And I haven't eaten this good in a while. So, savor it as best you can."

Jacques swallowed a large piece of chicken before he replied, "Honestly, sir. I can't remember the last time I had chicken either."

Poisson took another bite. "Well. You can thank our Yankee host."

Several other men around the fire chuckled in acknowledgment as they enjoyed the supply bounty provided by the Yankees and the food that had been "requisitioned". From Jacques' viewpoint, he was thankful that this was the best he had eaten in a very, very long time. Food had been scarce in Louisiana and Mobile ever since the Yankees had taken New Orleans, and then his journey from Mobile to Virginia hadn't exactly been easy or filled with joyful adventure.

After Chancellorsville, there were the mountains of supplies they had captured from the Yankees, and after Second Winchester, there had been another bonanza in captured supplies. Jacques had periods where he'd eaten better over the last few months, but this adventure into Union territory was paying huge dividends for the Confederacy and its most famous army.

Despite the days of marching, Jacques was starting to put on weight. Many of Jacques' comrades were also filling out their once loose uniforms. Murray the Irishman's shoulders looked as large as a bull's, and LaRoux appeared to have gained at least five pounds. But despite his youth compared to the veterans he marched with, Jacques knew this campaign was about more than taking chickens and cows from Pennsylvania farms.

Sergeant Poisson read Jacques' eyes and surmised what the young Corporal was calculating in his head. How long before we get to Harrisburg?

It was all on track, according to Sergeant Poisson. "Well, Corporal, that is knowing how General Jackson had his march last year in the Valley Campaign. I know he's no longer our Corps commander. But he's the one who's been giving orders to General Ewell these days. Tomorrow will be a hard march. So will the day after. But that will get us to Harrisburg before General Hooker can. Then, the goal is to take the city."

This campaign had started at Fleetwood Hill in Virginia, and now the Louisiana Tigers were camping on the outskirts of Chambersburg,

Pennsylvania. Whatever was to happen, this showdown in Pennsylvania was already shaping up to be different from any other in the entire war so far as the Army of Northern Virginia was concerned.

Jacques had fought in 3 battles to date: Chancellorsville, Brandy Station, and Second Winchester. Chancellorsville had been a ferocious and confused affair. While Jubal Early was the divisional commander for the battle, Hayes had commanded the Louisiana Tigers. They had been given the task of conducting a delaying action against a couple of Union Corps. Brandy Station, on the other hand, it was by accident that the Tigers were even at Fleetwood Hill when the battle had begun.

For Second Winchester, that had been General Ewell's coming-out party. The newly promoted Corps commander had used his entire Corps brilliantly against a single Union division, more or less annihilating it. General Milroy, the Union commander, had even been captured. Many believed this was thanks in part to Jacques, who supposedly shot the horse out from under the Union General. Four thousand men of General Milroy's division were either killed, captured, or wounded, giving the Yankees a 50% casualty ratio for the battle. Those were good statistics —or results, whatever battle you fought when you were able to destroy half your enemy's army.

But all three of those battles had occurred in Virginia. And now General Ewell was the tip of the spear for the invasion of Pennsylvania. With a blanket underneath the stars, Jacques slept well at night, or as well as we could. The Army of Northern Virginia was marching into Pennsylvania, ready to make war on the Yankees that had invaded and ravaged the South for the last two years of this war.

The Confederates of Hayes' brigade woke up early the next morning. And like the veteran troops they were known to be, they were marching on the road as the sun rose in the east, continuing their march to Harrisburg. A couple of hours into the march, the Tigers had already marched several miles as they passed by more Pennsylvania

Dutch, or German farms. And who would pass by the Tigers as they marched, General Ewell himself and several of the staff officers. Jacques could freely admit it to himself; he was a true believer in the Confederacy. He had been completely converted at this point, and it wasn't just the corporal stripes there on his sleeve. Enthusiastically, as all the other men did, he cheered as General Ewell rode past strapped to his horse, peg leg and all.

There was only one General Ewell. Hell, Ewell was certainly playing the part of General Jackson in this campaign. Ewell had lost a leg at Second Manassas and, almost a year later, was back in action and performing brilliantly. And he wasn't just driving the Yankees out of southern territory. Ewell was taking the fight to the Army of the Potomac. Jacques could not be happier about that. In fact, he could not wait to bring the war to the Yankees who had been so eager to bring the flame and the sword to the homes and towns of the South.

Chapter 20

June 25, 1863, Early Morning
Confederate White House, Richmond, Virginia

Colonel Paul Lutze. Welcome to the Confederate White House." One of President Davis's household staff invited Paul in. "Come on in, sir," the servant said, and Paul obliged. Inside the grand foyer, he was met by none other than Uncle Jefferson himself.

"Paul," said President Davis. "So good to see you," Davis grasped Paul's right hand with both of his.

Paul smiled at his adopted uncle as he shook his hand. "It's good to see you, Uncle Jefferson."

Davis smiled warmly, "We have been busy, but all of that will come back to pay for itself. Please, come into my office."

A few minutes later, they were seated in Uncle Jefferson's office. President Davis sat behind his desk, with Paul seated in the chair before him. "So, how goes the organization of the new corps?" Uncle Jefferson asked.

"Well," Paul said as he put a hand through his hair. He fidgeted with his cork peg leg to help him gather his thoughts intelligently, "There have been challenges, for sure. But believe it or not, Uncle Jefferson. The men are in high spirits. Most of these men have seen action together in some way, shape, or form in the Carolinas. There is a rudimentary command structure in place as well. I mean, again, we're creating a whole corps out of nothing, but many of these regiments and brigades have worked together before. We will still be a new corps, but it could be worse, you know, we could be taking men from across the country who had never worked together before and attempt this project with them. The majority of these troops are from the Carolinas or Georgia. The transition has been mostly smooth. And the fact that General Johnston is fresh off a victory in Mississippi with General Beauregard goes a long way in giving validity to this command."

President Davis looked with his one good eye and placed a hand atop a stack of papers on his desk. "Yes, sometimes I wonder if I was too hasty in relieving General Johnston of command of his department and his army in Mississippi. And transferring General Beauregard from the Carolinas to Mississippi was a risk, but they seem to have pulled off a minor miracle. Well, the closest thing to a miracle." Davis paused to contemplate, "And as much as I would have loved Beauregard to achieve a complete victory over Grant, the victory that he did win has bought us some time in Mississippi and cost Grant dearly."

"That's true, Uncle Jefferson, I'm not claiming to be some grand military strategist. But I think in time, we might be forced to retire from Vicksburg and give up the fight to Grant. But I think we have cost his army dearly. Hell, Beauregard destroyed an entire Corps of Grant's on the first day. That, by itself, forced the Yankees to rework many of their plans." Paul's pause added urgency to his words. "But you had me here for a reason, Uncle Jefferson, and I won't beat around the bush anymore, Sir. What can I answer with any certainty for you? Hopefully, my relay of the facts will help you. I have already heard the gossip about other members of your family and the public's reception to them. I know it's gossip, Uncle Jefferson, but I wanted you to hear it from me."

President Davis shook his head, "No, Paul: you, your brothers. A few of my older nephews, and perhaps my brother, are the only people I would let get that familiar with me. But I appreciate the honesty. What else do you have? I wish more men could talk to me honestly, like you do. From the depths of my soul, I want to win this war for our people. And I fear that too many give me the information I want to hear, not the information I need to hear."

Paul gestured with an open hand, "I will always be honest with you, Uncle Jefferson. At least for what I see the truth to be. Since the events at Shiloh and New Orleans last year, I have been forced to confront many uncomfortable truths."

Davis nodded, remembering two of his close friends, Albert Sydney Johnston and Paul Lutze Sr., both of whom had met their deaths at Shiloh. "Well, at least you are more diplomatic than your brother was." He chuckled, "I might have said some unkind things to your brother. And he said them right back. But I still gave that scoundrel an embrace before he went off to Vicksburg with General Beauregard."

Paul grinned, "He told me about that exchange. Believe me, Uncle Jefferson, Johan is doing everything he came to prove you right in your decision. Uncle Jefferson, Johan might be opinionated, but he believes in telling the truth. And those reports are as truthful as you could hope for in a war situation that we are in."

Davis nodded, "Yes, Paul, I gave those reports great attention. I very much appreciate the input from Johan and you on those dispatches. Beauregard and Johnston together achieved perhaps one of our few truly decisive victories that we have had in the Western Theater. Grant was hurt and hurt badly—25,000 casualties in two days. My god, I could not imagine the same happening to us. Grant, despite his losses, could not justify them because Vicksburg never fell. However, not only did he replace those men almost immediately, but he is also back to his old tricks. Your report proved one thing over many others: that Grant is unrelenting. If the Yankees had more generals like him, we would be in serious trouble."

"Johan told me about the first day's fighting. Beauregard filled me in on the second day of the battle along the railroad. Luckily, the General seemed to have learned from his mistakes at Shiloh when he faced Grant the first time. The second time was still a close call. But at least we all recognize what the game is going forward. Grant will be methodical and thorough. That massive Yankee army will do its utmost to wear down General Beauregard, and Beauregard is going to try to hold on as long as he can to keep that river open."

"I can tell you, Paul, every day that the river is open. It allows more troops and supplies to pass over from the Trans-Mississippi. And perhaps most importantly, it gets us closer to full recognition from the Europeans, especially the French. I know it!"

"If I may be bold, Uncle Jefferson, can we really count on European recognition?" Paul's question hung in the air.

Davis sat silent for a moment. "I hope so, Paul. But unfortunately, I believe we must rein in our expectations. Between you and me, I think the British have no stomach for this war. And unfortunately, I see their position. They have sent thousands of reinforcements to Canada. But if our Yankee friends decided to turn their attention against them, the best the British could do would be to conduct a fighting retreat in Canada. They would more than likely lose Quebec. And then British Canada would be divided into two, maybe three parts. Their navy could give the Yankees some trouble, but would they be willing to lose a quarter to a third of their navy and much of their merchant marine? So that they can lose Canada? There is no benefit to the British Empire to get involved in our war. I would not take that deal, and neither would most of the people that I know."

"It does beg the question of what the stance of Napoleon is," Paul said with some excitement. "Since General Johnson and I arrived in Richmond, I've heard more about the French adventures in Mexico. Is it true that Maximilian has been offered the Mexican throne?

President Davis sighed. "He's playing coy about it, and so is Napoleon III. But from what Secretary Benjamin has told me, it seems Maximilian is waiting for the right moment to seize the throne. But the French are facing a tough fight in Mexico right now. And even though we are getting some support from them in terms of supplies and weapons, their main effort will be to pacify Mexico.

Since they are having such a time of it, I would assume they want their army and navy in Mexico itself. Not in the Confederacy."

Paul Understood Napoleon III's game all too well. Use the Confederacy as a buffer against the United States, giving it just enough support to keep the Union from intervening in Mexico. "Will they give us official recognition? Believe me, personal recognition from the French would go a long way for our cause."

Davis had a distant look in his eye. "Lincoln has essentially threatened France with war if it were to recognize our government. But if we were to have more decisive victories on the battlefield…" Davis trailed off. "We need more time, and we need to convince the French that we will stand on our own two feet. They are using us, but I will certainly use them when the time comes."

"I don't know when we'll have to deal with Vicksburg, Uncle Jefferson. We've certainly bought some more time there. At least we can show the French we still control part of Mississippi, for now."

"Well, Paul, I know you have much work to do. I appreciate you taking the time to come here and meet with me. Will you and General Johnston be joining us for dinner tonight?"

"I believe so, Uncle Jefferson. He has had a busy day like me. Most of the troops that will form this Corps are now on the outskirts of Richmond. It seems the Yankees are making some noise from fortress Monroe. Before we head north, we might need to take a serious look at what they are doing. However, with us responding in force, it could play to our advantage. But I know if we want to link up with General Lee in any reasonable amount of time, we will not be able to linger here for long."

"That I know, Paul. Go to your duty, meet up with General Johnston." Davis extended a letter to Paul. "Please give this to General Johnston. And make sure he knows that he and his wife are cordially invited to dine with us tonight. And he is to bring along any of his senior staff that can be spared for the evening as well. And please tell General Johnston that Secretary Benjamin will be in attendance.

Paul smiled. “Well, sir. I'll let the general know.”

***

General Joseph Johnston was one of dignity and decorum. After all, he had been the highest-ranking officer to enter Confederate service from the old army, but had a year already passed since Seven Pines? A few bitter thoughts entered his mind as he remembered his last battle as commanding general of the Army of Northern Virginia, or the army that became known by that name. His injuries from that fateful battle still bothered him at times. But how life had changed in just a short time again!

He still harbored some resentment toward President Davis over his dismissal from command of the Western Department. The Battle of Jackson had been a confused affair, which made General Johnston want to ask the president how he would have fared in that situation. That question would not do any good now, for that past dispute was water under the bridge.

When General Beauregard first arrived in Mississippi, General Johnston was taken aback at the speed at which President Davis had chosen his replacement. There was a brief period when Johnston considered leaving the Confederate army altogether. But then there were those two rascals from Louisiana, Colonel Lutze and Lieutenant Breaux.

Each man had presented him a letter. Lieutenant Breaux presented Johnston with a letter from General Longstreet; meanwhile, Colonel Lutze handed Johnston a letter from General Lee himself. The message in both letters was clear: Lee and Longstreet felt that Johnson was being maltreated and empathized with him. But they asked them to set aside his ego and pride and do what was best for the country.

General Beauregard wasted no time. He reorganized the army and even renamed it the Army of the Mississippi Valley. However, Beauregard, being the friend he was and trusting Johnson's judgment, asked him to stick around for the campaign about to launch. And when Beauregard presented his plan, Johnson couldn't resist. And after two bloody days, Beauregard and Johnston had achieved perhaps the most significant Confederate victory to date west of the Appalachian Mountains.

Much had changed in how the war was fought since First Manassas, and Beauregard displayed how much he had grown as a commander with a plan that was elegant but simple. Johnston was to attack from the northeast towards the Black River with Pickett and Breckenridge as division commanders. These two divisions were to attack with everything they had, push forward, and, by all appearances, make it look like this was the main Confederate attack. Grant and Sherman would overreact and overcommit to pushing back Pickett and Breckenridge. Johnson's wing of the attack would gradually fall back once Grant and Sherman had committed most of their forces to pushing back Johnston. But when Johnston's two divisions had pulled back just enough, entrenched Confederate artillery would tear into Grant and Sherman's unsuspecting troops. But the main attack came south of the Vicksburg Jackson railroad. McClernand's Corps was effectively isolated below the railroad, and there, Beauregard sent most of his troops to attack. McClernand's Corps was annihilated, and Beauregard's staff estimated that at least 10,000 of McClernand's troops outright surrendered. And it was the Irishman General Patrick Cleburne who led his division in the attack that broke McClernand's line and sealed his Corps' fate. By the end of the two-day battle, Grant had lost 25,000 men. But the

Confederates had only suffered 10,000 casualties combined in those two days of heavy fighting.

The campaign had settled into a slow grinding battle of attrition from there. When Johnston had taken his leave of Beauregard, most of the Confederate army was entrenched along the Jackson-Vicksburg railroad.

Just days after the battle ended, Paul Lutze arrived at General Beauregard's headquarters. At first, it was hard for Johnson not to suspect Paul Lutz of spying for President Davis. The older Lutze brother soon proved his worth and loyalty. Now, Johnson was in Virginia with the Corps that had been organized in the Carolinas with Paul Lutze's help. What made this experience even more surreal was that General McClernand, the Union general captured at the battle of Vicksburg, accompanied Johnston on his train ride from Mississippi to Virginia, along with the British Colonel Fremantle. And to make everything ever the more improbable, Johnston was back at the home of President Davis, having dinner with his family.

President Davis smiled at General Johnston and his wife. "Well, General Johnston, I'm glad you and your wife were able to make it here tonight. Varina was telling me today how excited she was for you two to come here for dinner. It has been a long time. And the people of Virginia remember your service from the first two years of this war. You brought victory then. And let us toast to more victories to come!"

Johnson returned the toast, for it was plain to see tension remained between himself and the president. Both men were trying to put their best foot forward tonight. In the newspapers, Johnston was credited, along with Beauregard, for the victory in Mississippi, and his presence in Virginia was explained as the president assigning him a new command, a new "army" in fact. But they both knew the truth: Davis had fired Johnson and Mississippi, and Johnson had come within a hair's breadth of resigning from the army.

Mrs. Davis looked to Paul Lutze, “My dear Paul, it's been a long time since I've seen you. I know with your injuries from last year, mobility is an issue for you at times. And I'm glad to see how much progress you've made. And it's also a pleasure to have another Lutze boy in this house, not arguing with my husband this time.” Varina chuckled, “Though, I do believe the president benefits from having grounded conversations from time to time with those who have only known him as Uncle Jefferson.” The First Lady of the Confederacy patted President Davis’s hand lovingly as she spoke.

“Aunt Varina, grounded is a polite way of characterizing Johan. He is honest to a fault at times, but that is the beauty of my brother. A lie spoken tortures his soul, but that means he will always say what he believes to be the truth.”

“If I may add, Mrs. Davis,” General Johnston interjected, “your godson is one of a kind.”

After dinner was finished, President Davis, General Johnston, Secretary Benjamin, Secretary Seddon, and Paul congregated in the president's parlor. Each man had a drink, and President Davis once again offered a small toast to Johnston. “General Johnston, tomorrow the newspapers will be announcing your campaign, and I wish to congratulate the new commander of the Army of Ohio.

It was perhaps Davis's biggest gamble of the war. Publicly, the force Johnson had raised in the Carolinas, roughly 20,000 men, would be called the army of Ohio. The idea behind this was that terrified northern civilians would call for the diversion of Union troops to Pittsburgh and the Ohio area for protection, even though Johnson had no intention of going there. In fact, Johnson's force would officially be known as the IV Corps of the Army of Northern Virginia - Pennsylvania.

After taking a sip from his glass, Secretary Benjamin asked General Johnston what his plans for the coming days were. Johnson's answer was straightforward. Deal a sharp blow to the Yankee forces outside Richmond and then head north, with the goals of capturing Harpers Ferry and then linking up with General Lee in Virginia.

"After that, Sir, "General Johnson continued, "the direction of the campaign is out of my hands. The enemy forces harassing Richmond can be easily brushed aside, and our overwhelming numbers can take Harpers Ferry with little loss. But, once my army joins General Lee's, it'll be up to him to decide how we are utilized."

Secretary Seddon here decided to interject, "General, once you have joined General Lee, that would make the Army of Northern Virginia four Corps strong with nearly 100,000 troops in Pennsylvania. The enemy from the north seems to have no trouble forming armies of this size. However, this will be the first time we have an army of this size, and it will be in their territory. With four strong Corps, I believe this would give the perfect opportunity to deal a decisive blow to the enemy."

President Davis and General Johnston looked at each other for a moment. Once they had been good friends, in fact, when this war began, they were on the best of terms. Things changed right after First Manassas, when Johnston did not pursue the Union army, and the relationship between the general and the president had continued to degrade ever after. And it seemed with the defeat at Jackson and Johnson's subsequent firing that their relationship was beyond repair. But fate sometimes intervenes, and with Johnson and Beauregard's combined victory in Mississippi, a new opportunity presented itself.

The President looked to Paul and then spoke, "Well, General Johnston, I don't mean to keep you any longer. I know tomorrow you and your new Corps, or must I say, your army, will have a hectic day. But I wish you and your men the best of luck and Godspeed. I cannot relay to you how desperate I am to have this war end and for our nation to achieve its independence. I do not doubt that General Lee picked the right man to lead the IV Corps.

Even though the night had been pleasant so far and Paul had enjoyed the company of the president, Aunt Varina, and General Johnson's wife, it always felt a bit tense, and now he could feel that tension leaving the room.

"Well, thank you, Mr. President," Johnson said graciously. "Your family and the Secretaries of State and War have given my wife, Lydia, and me the most gracious hospitality and respect tonight. Please appreciate that. Mr. President, I know our vision for this war hasn't always been aligned, but now you are a true patriot in every sense of the word.

"Thank you, Joseph," David said with a bit of affection in his voice. "We have had to sacrifice so much with this war, which leaves me with a proposal for you, Sir. Your army or your Corps plan to do a demonstration against the Yankees tomorrow outside of Richmond, after which you will march to the train depots to the Shenandoah and then march on Harpers Ferry. When your Corps is ready to make that march through the Shenandoah, I hope you would not mind if I could accompany you? And no worries, Sir, this is your command, not mine. My only wish is that when we achieve a decisive victory on Union soil, I am there, and then a letter written in my hand can be delivered to President Lincoln. My greatest hope is that with his army defeated in the field, he will see reason and agree to an armistice with us. And perhaps if God were to look down upon us, he would be willing to meet me as an equal, and we could end this war for once."

The room sat in shocked silence, especially Paul, who had no idea that Uncle Jefferson was to propose such a thing. But General Johnston, being the gentleman that he was and showing growth as a man and a general, replied, "Mr. President, I could think of nothing better but for my men to see their president marching and riding beside them. Sir, to them, your presence would be like General Washington to their grandfathers.

Chapter 21

June 26, 1863, Evening
St. Francisville, Louisiana

It had been over a year since Johan Lutze had set foot in Louisiana. In the spring of 1862, he had taken leave from the 6th Louisiana in the army of Northern Virginia, and he made his way home to see his dying mother. With an hour to spare, he made it, and he was able to say goodbye to the matriarch of the Lutze Family. It had also been the last time he had seen his father, Paul Lutze Sr., who fell at Shiloh only a few months later.

On the calendar, it had been a year, but for Johan, it felt like another lifetime. To add to his mental recollection and anguish, the war had only started two years ago, and the year before that, he had been a cadet at the Louisiana Military Institute with General Sherman as the commandant.

The 13th Louisiana, 43rd Tennessee, and various other regiments in Cleburne's small army spent the better part of a week marching through rural Mississippi, partially along the Natchez Trace, partially along secluded country roads. The small Confederate army passed by many towns and farms that had been visited by General Grierson and his troops during his great cavalry raid two months ago. Much of Mississippi's interior was still devastated, though some places they passed through were beginning to rebuild what they could. At first, in many of the farms and towns they passed by, the locals, black and white, were hesitant to come out as soldiers marched by. But slowly the word spread that these troops were dressed in gray and butternut.

With several rebel battle flags clearly flying at the head of the column, the local population's attitude changed radically. Many small farmers and plantation owners came out to the soldiers as they were marching and offered them food and water. This touched many of Johan's men, for they knew that these people were giving away what they could ill afford to part with. But the presence of this small Confederate army in the middle of Mississippi meant something. It meant that these people had not been forgotten by their government.

As this detachment continued to march South, many locals asked where they were marching to. And the men of the 13th Louisiana, along with the other regiments marching in this column, politely but with a smile said, "South."

Andre appeared earlier to check in on Johan and his regiment, though not much had changed since that morning. When the regiment crossed into Louisiana, many of the men felt it was a spiritual experience. These men of the 13th Louisiana were returning to their home state to defend their families, homes, and communities.

With the state border behind them, Johan turned to Andre and asked the time. Johan's cousin pulled out a fine German pocket watch. It obviously had been pilfered from a dead Yankee. Andre, in mock seriousness, looked at the time.

"Another watch?" Johan asked.

With a smile and a short flourish, Andre put away the timepiece. "If you'd like to know, Colonel," he said with a laugh, "I traded away my old one." Andre then pulled out two Colt Navy revolvers and handed them to Johan. "Consider this your gift, Colonel, for finally being allowed to take men into the field. And who knows, you might even look like you know what you're doing."

As multiple ranks of men marched close by, Johan and Andre let out a unified chuckle. Every day of this march since it had begun just south of Vicksburg, these episodes between Johan and Andre would occur. Johan had clearly shown the ability to lead and was a competent commander. But there was something about Lieutenant Breaux that the men had the satisfaction of knowing that even their officers put their pants on one leg at a time.

"How much further distance to Saint Francisville?" Johan asked Andre.

"Not much further," Andre replied. "I rode into town earlier with a strong detachment, and it didn't take me long to retrace my steps down this road and find you. Which reminds me, Colonel," and Andre said that with a chuckle. "When I saw General Cleburne, he instructed me to guide you along with the regiment behind you, to where he wants you to camp. Some of the regiments are going to encamp within the city, but the regiments that will be involved in the breakout of General Gardner will go outside the city."

Johan nodded in agreement, "You should not argue with that logic. Well, Lieutenant, would you care to bless us with your presence and guide us to our assigned spot?"

"Certainly, Colonel." Andre soon fell back, mounted it was easy to do, and took up conversation with several of the men marching up and down the forested road. The men had been instructed not to make much noise so as not to alert Banks and his army to their presence, and with at least some Confederate regiments already in St. Francisville, many of the Louisiana boys were delighted to have one of General Forrest's officers to converse with. They were in high spirits, but officers like Andre had a way of having them believe they could accomplish anything. Of all things, Andre was making the army fun. Johan did his best to maintain a military bearing while grinning, as his cousin, formerly a bushwhacker, was now a responsible officer under General Cleburne's command. And that was one thought that Johan never thought would cross his mind.

***

The 13th Louisiana and the 43rd Tennessee camped about a mile outside of Saint Francisville at the Greenwood Plantation, which the

Matthews family owned. This included the matriarch, Miss Matthews, who had been a widow for almost 20 years; her son, Charles Matthews, who was nearly 40; his wife, Penelope; and several children. With the family's cooperation, the 13th Louisiana and 43rd Tennessee were encamped past the slave quarters in a fallow field near the wood line.

The two regiments arrived with perhaps an hour of daylight left and then quickly established camp. The Matthews family and what was left of their servants were very accommodating to the two Confederate regiments, and the regiments were able to eat a good meal that night, much of it salted beef and some vegetables from the garden. The plantation could not give much materially at that moment, but the fresh food made all the difference to the men.

Johan would have preferred to stay in camp with his regiment, but the Matthewses insisted on hosting the senior officers for dinner that night. And of course, General Cleburne was present as well; he had made the trip from Saint Francisville to dine with the Matthews that night.

But both Johan and Andre knew that General Cleburne was at the Greenwood house for more than just dinner. As they entered the house, one of the Matthews boys, approximately 10 years old, led Andre and Johan to a study where Mr. Matthews was reviewing a map with General Cleburne. For the next 30 minutes, Mr. Matthews provided detailed instructions to General Cleburne, Johan, Andre, and several senior officers from the 43rd Tennessee on the terrain and geography around Saint Francisville, Greenwood, and Port Hudson.

Johan and Andre sat next to each other for dinner. After a brief conversation with Mr. Matthews and a good night to the children, they both took their leave and found General Cleburne back in the study of the plantation house.

General Breckenridge was with General Cleburne in the study; apparently, he had arrived during dinner. However, this meeting was abbreviated, in which General Cleburne reviewed his plan with Johan and Andre, the commander of the 43rd Tennessee, and General Breckenridge. When all present affirmed their understanding of General Cleburne's intentions, they bade each other good night.

But before Johan and Andre could leave, Cleburne extended his hand to Johan's cousin. "General Forrest," Cleburne stated to Andre, "has communicated to me how useful you've been in this campaign so far, so please take this as a sign of my appreciation." In Cleburne's outstretched hands were three captain's bars. Andre's competency had earned him a promotion.

Upon returning to camp, Johan called a meeting of his company captains. With Andre acting as an adjutant of sorts, Johan got to business right away with his five company captains. Pleasantries done, Johan began, "Alright, everyone, I know we have marched a long way from Vicksburg. And now our sacrifice pays off." He gestured to a large map Mr. Mathews had provided. "We need to be ready to march out by seven in the morning. The 13th Louisiana, 43rd Tennessee, and the 6th and 7th consolidated Arkansas regiments will be the infantry force that opens the gap for General Gardner to escape from Port Hudson. Mr. Mathews and his oldest son will arrive in the morning and serve as guides for our small ad hoc brigade. General Breckenridge will have overall command of our force, while General Cleburne will command at St. Francisville. We have cavalry encamped a quarter mile away on either side of us, and that will be our screen. Tomorrow, we march and get into position and conceal ourselves. The morning of June 28th, at dawn, marks the breakout. General Forrest will create the necessary distractions all along the Union line, and we will tear open a hole with the Tennessee and Arkansas boys. General Gardner is going to sally out with no heavy equipment or wagons, only with the men who are healthy enough to walk and carry a rifle. The hope is that 4,000-5,000 men can break out of Port Hudson with him. Once they reach us, we withdraw to St.

Francisville, with General Forrest providing our screen. Any questions?"

The company captains had a few questions, and Johan answered as best he could. Luckily, these men were veterans, and they knew Johan was giving them the information that he had.

Captain King, Company I commander, asked, "Alright, Colonel. I assume we have to keep the men quiet tomorrow as well. And let's say we make it to our assigned position. And Gardener's men actually make it to us. Are we to fight our way all the way back to St. Francisville?"

Johan took a moment to give a thoughtful response to Captain King, "Banks' men are solid veterans, but he is incompetent. Trust me, last year in the Shenandoah, General Jackson was brilliant, but we were helped a lot by Banks not knowing what the hell he was doing. His boys will fight hard when we attack, even with surprise on our side. The plan is that once Gardner and his men have broken through, we can disengage while confusion overtakes Banks, and the cavalry can then insert itself between Banks and us. Then it is just a matter of marching back to St. Francisville and joining General Cleburne's welcoming committee for Banks."

***

June 27, 1863. Outside Richmond, VA.
Army of Ohio (IV Corps)

Ever since General Lee had brought the army of Northern Virginia into the Shenandoah Valley and across the Mason-Dixon line, the sizable federal army at Fortress Monroe had been steadily pushing forces forward to harass the Richmond defenses. But that harassment ended on the morning of June 26th. In the first official action of

General Johnston's new command, almost half of his force, 10,000 men, had deployed and attacked the Union probing forces at several locations. Johnston had even deployed 15 artillery pieces to support these attacks. The fighting had only lasted a few hours, but there were a few instances where the combat had been quite fierce. But the loosely organized union brigades that had been harassing Richmond did not expect 10,000 infantry and 15 guns to hit them like a bolt of lightning first thing in the morning.

After General Johnston and Paul Lutze had finished their dinner at the Confederate White House on the evening of the 25th, Johnston went back to his headquarters. He affirmed that orders had been issued to the brigades assigned to participate in the attack the following morning. The troops, in fact, had been put in position that night, and at dawn, the attack began. By 9:00 AM, the fighting was effectively over. In Johnston's first victory back in Virginia, with all forces engaged, in the engagement the Confederates suffered at most 70 casualties. In comparison, the Confederates inflicted around 200 battlefield casualties on the Union, while capturing another 200 men. Johnston could have pursued further, but that wasn't the purpose of this operation. He applauded his men, so to speak, and outside Richmond, he had achieved a clear victory. The Union forces that had been harassing Richmond promptly withdrew and retreated toward Fort Monroe. With the harassing Union forces suffering such a sharp drubbing, Richmond could now be confident it would not be harassed while General Lee's army was in Union territory.

Paul had spent the morning delivering dispatches and helping to position the brigades for their attacks. But most importantly, when the Yankees began to retreat and vacate the battlefield, Paul helped ensure that the Confederate troops, on the verge of charging wildly after the Yankees, were stopped. Skirmishers went forward to convince Union forces not to return, and the battlefield was cleared of weapons, prisoners, and wounded, after which Johnston's men promptly marched back to Richmond. That afternoon, most of the Corps boarded trains and began the journey to the Shenandoah Valley.

The work never ended for Paul. He was now officially on General Johnston's staff, a senior officer, and still had duties to fulfill within the Confederate Secret Service. But most of his time was dedicated to logistics. And even though a short battle was fought on the morning of the 26th, Paul spent most of the day getting two of Johnston's divisions loaded onto trains and heading West to the Shenandoah, and then getting his third division, commanded by General Kirkland, marching and heading to Fredericksburg. And to add to the complication, President Davis came along with General Kirkland.

It had taken most of the 26th for General Kirkland's men to march to the train, load it, and ride the rest of the way to Fredericksburg, and this was able to be accomplished because Kirkland's men were not involved with the fighting outside of Richmond. Again, this was achieved with some foresight. Johnston needed his entire Corps to be mobile and concentrated at the right places at the right time. Kirkland therefore set off marching that morning, and then, when the fighting concluded, the rest of Johnston's men headed West.

After Kirkland's men had marched several miles north of Richmond, they found the trains waiting for them. It was well into the afternoon by the time the entire division was loaded and then transferred, rolling towards Fredericksburg. To Paul's chagrin, with a small entourage, President Davis boarded the train as the engineer began to take it northward.

General Kirkland was at first taken aback when he saw what looked like civilian hangers-on or even newspaper reporters boarding his train car at the last moment. Exhausted and limping from the day's exertions, Paul wanted to laugh when it was Uncle Jefferson who had sneaked onto the train. While General Kirkland was speechless, Paul gave a slight bow, not wanting onlookers to see him saluting someone in plainclothes.

"Greetings, General Kirkland, Colonel Lutze," President Davis said with a tired smile. "I hope I am not imposing by tagging along with a few friends." He gestured to the half dozen soldiers who had accompanied him.

"Mr. President," Kirkland said, somewhat confused, "you are more than welcome to accompany us on our journey."

Word soon spread throughout the train that the president was accompanying the division. As the train made its way through the northern Virginia countryside, more than a few farms and homes could hear the rebel yell coming forth from the passing train.

***

June 28, 1863. Dawn, Mechanicsburg, Pennsylvania. The Louisiana Tigers

The night before, the Louisiana Tigers were told to sleep lightly and be ready to move out early. Before dawn, they awoke, prepared their rations that they had cooked several days before, and were marching as the first rays of sunlight hit the road. General Ewell had made it very clear that everyone in II Corps had to pull their weight today and that speed was essential.

Many considered General Ewell a Jacksonian successor. So far, with the Louisiana Tigers' performance at Brandy Station and the entire Corps' triumph at Second Winchester, Ewell had flawlessly played the part of Jackson. And like religious dogma drilled into the heads of monks, Jackson had drilled into both Generals Ewell and AP Hill the necessity of speed in this campaign. Since Jackson was traveling with General Hill's III Corps, he corresponded with Ewell every day and was kept abreast of II Corps' movements. Jackson finished every dispatch to Ewell with the instructions to move effectively, quickly, and with brains.

Ewell's plan was straightforward from a Jacksonian perspective. Jenkins' Calvary would be the first to leave that morning. With not quite a full moon but a waxing gibbous moon, just before 4:00 AM, the moon had risen, and the first of Jenkins' men rode for Harrisburg. Riders were dispatched in groups of 200 to 250, with over a dozen scouts sent ahead of the main column.

Jenkins was relying entirely on surprise and moxie in this operation. Around 15 scouts were sent ahead of the initial body of troopers, and in the early hours of the morning, they secured bridges, neutralized pickets, and scared off patrols. The only way Jenkins could succeed in his mission was if the defenders in Harrisburg were caught off guard. Speed was the paramount requirement for Jenkins' troopers. There were farms to plunder along the way to Harrisburg, but the orders were clear: make it to the south bank of the Susquehanna and secure it along with the entrances to the covered bridges, pry out the Union forces that were on the south bank, and then hold until the infantry arrived.

Many viewed these cavalry troopers as nothing better than raiders, but Jenkins had nearly 1600 men, and that was what Ewell had on hand to work with, whether he approved of the arrangement or not. That was until midnight on June 28th.

Two regiments from General Stuart's cavalry division made their presence known at Mechanicsburg and almost began a firefight with General Jenkins' and Ewell's pickets. At 1 AM, none other than General Wade Hampton made an appearance at Ewell's temporary headquarters for the night.

After the Battle of Brandy Station on June 9th, General Stuart had been granted authorization by General Lee to conduct a ride around the Army of the Potomac, like he had done twice in 1862. Due to the intensity of the fighting at Brandy Station, Lee gave Stuart broad authority but also a strict operational structure to follow. Lee wanted to avoid another near-disaster that Brandy Station nearly became if not for the Louisiana Tigers being encamped on Fleetwood Hill. By luck, almost 1,400 crack infantry encamped on Fleetwood Hill had decimated unsuspecting dense Union cavalry formations and inflicted thousands of casualties. If Stuart were faced with a similar situation again, there would be no infantry to bail him out.

His command still rode a wide arch around General Hooker and the Army of the Potomac, but Stuart had shown uncharacteristic reserve when he launched his operation. Granted, he had captured a Union wagon train outside of Washington, but he remembered that his main job was to be the eyes and ears for General Lee. It also helped that there were almost 4,000 fewer Union cavalry under Hooker's overall command when Stuart began his ride.

Stuart was desperate to get the bulk of his cavalry back into contact with General Lee, and there were over one hundred captured wagons to get to Lee's quarter master. However, the capture of Harrisburg was important enough that he sent General Wade Hampton and the 1st Virginia Cavalry, Fitz Lee's regiment, to assist in the city's capture.

The majority of Jenkins men, about 1,200, set out at first light, and their goal was to ride hard to Harrisburg and seize the two bridge entrances south of the city that spanned the Susquehanna River. Jenkins had three clear objectives: first, seize the approaches to the bridges by surprise, which included the railroad bridge and the foot traffic bridge, and take these approaches with as few casualties as possible, and then hold out until the first lead elements of Ewell's infantry arrived and were able to relieve them.

After careful reconnaissance by veteran scouts, when the first 300 of Jenkins' men were within a couple of miles of the bridges, the formations split into two groups of 200 and 100 each and galloped to the covered bridges. As the leading group attacked the Union camps and entrenchments all along the south bank of the Susquehanna, 20 men entered each of the covered bridges, trampling over the guards on the South Bank of the river and pushing aside and riding over anyone who got in their way inside the bridges. Fort Washington, a hastily erected fortification atop a hill just to the southwest of the bridge entrances, was captured by the third group, which consisted mainly of mounted infantry. After a brief skirmish, the Union troops at Fort Washington were driven off. There were several artillery pieces arrayed throughout the fortifications, and the Confederate victors at Fort Washington promptly turned these guns towards Harrisburg and, near the bridge's openings on the north bank of the Susquehanna, began firing them.

However, the 200 men storming the approaches to the bridges could not gallop through the covered bridges. They had already traveled 15 miles that morning and were nearly spent by the time they reached the Susquehanna. But Jenkins' veterans had prepared for this and had been warned that once they entered the bridges, they were not to venture far into either bridge. Still, only a handful were to enter to ensure any Union forces were retreating to Harrisburg proper. Amid the absolute chaos inside the bridges for the Confederates, fortune was on their side. It was early in the morning, and civilian foot traffic was nearly nonexistent, leaving the Union troops flat-footed and unprepared for an attack. Only 40 men would enter the bridges, while the Union militia stationed there was in complete panic.

For almost 10 minutes, there was pandemonium on the part of the militia due to the carnage that Jenkins' men inflicted with such ferocity. With pistols and sabers, the Confederates inflicted well over 100 Union casualties in those 10 minutes. There was a purpose to the controlled chaos the Confederates implemented: to create confusion within the Union command. Those first minutes of the attack were critical, and the Union chaos allowed for more Confederate troops to funnel into the battle.

General Darius Couch, the commander of the Department of the Susquehanna and the defenses of Harrisburg, was an experienced commander. He commanded the Second Corps of the Army of the Potomac at both Fredericksburg and Chancellorsville, and, ironically, was the roommate of General Stonewall Jackson while they both attended West Point. When he received word that the Confederate forces had not only entered the covered bridges and had established a strong position on the southern bank of the Susquehanna, he wasted no time. Militia forces were gathered and rushed to contain the incursion. But the general would soon find out that too much precious time had been lost.

Despite the initial confusion, the Union counterattacks were ferocious. Couch sent infantry into both covered bridges, but they were met by now dismounted Confederate cavalry that were primarily armed with either Spencer or Sharps rifles. The Confederates put these rifles to good work, and 40 men were able to turn both covered bridges into killing zones as tightly packed Union infantry tried to overrun the Confederate skirmishers. After the second attack, the Confederate troopers withdrew from the bridges, but they had bloodied Couch's inexperienced New York and Pennsylvania militia with losses of almost 200 men.

The covered bridges were perhaps the worst place to fight a battle, given the enclosed and confined nature of the bridges. Both were well-suited for a small handful of men to hold up thousands of men. But with the bloodbath of the second attack and the Confederate withdrawal from the bridges themselves, Couch decided not to send men into the death trap a third time.

General Early's division followed after all of Jenkins' men had moved forward around 5:15 AM, which made them the first division to arrive at Harrisburg and relieve Jenkins' men. Early's first brigades arrived around 8 AM that morning, without a minute to spare. Accompanying Early were some of Ewell's artillery, which added to the firepower needed to hold the bridgeheads. Couch had methodically fought and positioned his green federal troops and state militia in preparation to throw back the Confederate cavalry from the bridgeheads and annihilate them. Still, the battle had shifted from destroying the Confederate bridgeheads to simply keeping the rebels out of the city proper.

Rhodes' division followed soon after, along with Johnson's division. Most of Ewell's Corps was now engaged on the bridgeheads south of Harrisburg and on the riverbank west of the city, shooting down into Harrisburg. This would be Ewell's primary focus, and it would force General Couch, commanding Union forces within Harrisburg, to send off most of his troops to the south of the city.

Ewell was making a convincing demonstration to Couch. This operation was meant to bloody the Union forces in and around Harrisburg, spook them, and force General Couch to commit the vast majority of these forces to face General Ewell and what appeared to be his entire Corps. As the morning progressed, Ewell ensured that his next action was visible. Johnson, minus his Louisiana Pelican brigade, marched down the south bank of the Susquehanna to the east with the 1st Virginia Cavalry as his screening force. As Johnson went further south, he made every effort to find a place to ford the great river. Couch was forced to respond to this operation as well, and thousands of troops had to be diverted from Harrisburg to have the strength to stop a division-sized Confederate force from crossing the Susquehanna south of Harrisburg.

But the most dangerous part of Ewell's plan involved General Issac Trimble's ad-hoc division. Ewell had three divisions in II Corps, his divisional commanders being Early, Johnson, and Rodes. Each division shed a brigade, so that Trimble now commanded the Louisiana Tigers from Early, the Pelicans from Johnson, and

Ramsuer's brigade from Rodes. With local guides and Hampton's Legion to act as a screening force, Trimble and his men marched some ways down the Chambersburg Pike. But then they veered off to the north and the northeast, for General Ewell's plan was for them to swing around Harrisburg, separate from the rest of Second Corps. Several miles north of the city, there was a shallow point in the great river which Hampton's scouts deemed practical for Trimble's force to ford across. Once across, the men were to march around the northwest corner of Harrisburg. This strike force would have minimal supplies and no artillery. These were Ewell's most elite shock troops, and the plan entailed that they spent the entirety of the 28th marching to the Susquehanna, crossing it, and then getting in position that night to be ready to attack on the morning of June 29th. At dawn, the Louisiana shock troops would attack the loosely defended rear of Camp Curtin in Harrisburg, where the fortifications were least developed and where most of the tents and troops faced the bridges over the Susquehanna, toward either the South or the southeast. It was an audacious plan, but if it were to work, Ewell's demonstration south of Harrisburg at the bridges had to be convincing. The troops under Trimble would approach undetected and attack with fury at dawn, aiming to drive into the heart of the Union command and logistics center in Harrisburg. With Ewell tying down the majority of Union forces in Harrisburg, the idea was that, within an hour of the Louisiana troops' attack, the city's defenses would collapse.

Jacques had no part in planning out Ewell's campaign; his job was to take orders and march with the rest of the men of the 6th Louisiana. They might have been north of the Mason-Dixon line, but many of Johnson's men marching in the Pennsylvania heat felt like home in Louisiana in late June 1863. It was easier for Jacques to keep his thoughts to himself that day; Trimble's brigades had been explicitly told to keep the chatter and their equipment as quiet as possible. Their mission depended on absolute secrecy and on avoiding detection by Union pickets or patrols.

The roads in Pennsylvania were well kept, and there were even some mechanized roads that Trimble's men could march on. Jacques and Sergeant Poisson looked at each other in disbelief more than once as they marched on miles of well-kept and well-paved Pennsylvania roads. The irony of it all was not missed by those two or the men with their company or regiment, and many of the men saw clearly how well the Pennsylvania roads held up, even with all of the summer rain that had fallen over the last several days. The well-maintained Pennsylvania roads were providing the Confederates with a superhighway to the back door of Harrisburg.

By the early afternoon, the Louisiana brigades could hear sustained artillery fire to their south and west. That meant the rest of the Corps was now at Harrisburg, beginning the great deception. It was all the motivation the Louisiana boys needed to quicken their pace. They could not let General Ewell down.

They had a march of over 15 miles to reach the ford across the Susquehanna, where they could cross without the water being more than knee-deep. The men still took special care to ensure their rifle cartridge boxes were well above the waterline. Several men removed their shoes as they crossed, while those without shoes did not have to stop. Jacques treated his Sharps rifle as if it were a relic of the true cross. That rifle served him well in the later days of Chancellorsville, Brandy Station, and then Second Winchester. It wasn't as fancy as Johan's rifle, but Jacques was confident he had put his rifle to much better use than his older brother and had shot many more Yankees than Johan.

By the time the men put their shoes back on, adjusted their cartridge boxes and their rifles, and filled their canteens in the Susquehanna, it was dark and past 10 PM. Conversation was sparse, but many of the men felt ill at ease with both the lack of sound and conversation and the presence of any Union or Confederate forces around them. The inverse should have been true, but for these veterans, many felt they were walking into a trap. It was unnerving that they encountered no Union patrols or pickets. However, Hampton's Legion had lived up to its reputation and had done its job well that day, and there were no pickets or union patrols to worry about for some time.

The three infantry brigades followed a series of winding country roads and passed several well-to-do farms. The well-kept fields, in some ways, impressed the invading men more than the farms they had encountered when they first entered Pennsylvania. The terrain was mostly hilly with farms and woods scattered throughout. No Confederate battle flags were visible, and General Trimble had even managed to bring along captured stars and stripes that flew with the head of the column. Technically, the three brigades were breaking the rules of war masquerading as Union forces, but the stakes were so high that Trimble and his three brigade commanders were willing to take the risk.

The moon was nearly full that night, providing excellent light for Trimble's men. It also allowed the cavalry escort to position itself behind a well-placed farm with orchards and some light woods, to screen Johnson's men until daylight. There were still five miles to march to the final resting spot before the battle in the morning. Still, with the darkness of the night providing cover, there was renewed hope that this gambit would succeed. They had crossed the river well north of the city, and the Yankees were none the wiser of it.

Jacques was exhausted; he put down his bedroll and lay upon it. The captain told them they would only get a couple of hours to rest, and Jacques swore that as soon as he closed his eyes, he was awoken by Sergeant Poisson. The Sergeant pushed him again to get up and get ready. In the east, they could see the first rays of the sun rising, and they knew it was time to take their positions. Quietly and professionally, the two Louisiana brigades and Ramsuer's North Carolinians lined up in battle formation and fastened bayonets to their rifles. The ranks were dressed, and the officers and their NCOs whispered the final commands. It took Jacques a moment to remember that he was a corporal himself, and he passed the word along to a couple of his buddies.

Softly, General Trimble's command to advance was issued. The three brigades, arrayed in two battle lines with the Tigers as the lead attack element, stepped forward. It was 4:45 AM on the morning of June 29th, 1863. In the distance, Jacques, Sergeant Poisson, and the rest of their company could hear the cacophony of General Ewell's artillery. That was part of the deception, as Ewell had assembled all of his artillery south of Harrisburg, which made that morning witness to the most extensive bombardment Pennsylvania had seen in its history up until that day.

Trimble had no way of knowing, but Ewell's plan had worked brilliantly so far. Jenkins' men had ridden hard on the morning of the 28th and, exhausted, with at least a third of their men falling behind with tired mounts, over 1500 men stormed the Union fortifications. It seized the bridgeheads on the western bank of the Susquehanna. Panic had engulfed the city. The commander of the Union garrison at Harrisburg, General Couch, who had only two months earlier been a Corps commander in the army of the Potomac, did not panic himself. Green federal recruits and state militia charged forward to evict Jenkins and his men from the easy victory they had won on the western bank of the river. Jenkins and his men were far more organized than the inexperienced union officers could have predicted, and their initial assault was hit with volleys of carbine fire from Jenkins's men in the covered bridges. As the Union casualties piled up, Couch took control and realized that if he was to pry Jenkins out of his bridgeheads, Union artillery had to be appropriately deployed.

At the same time, the federal and state forces carried out their duties methodically. No more made charges to displace the Confederates.

And though General Couch was correct, and this decision he later came to regret, ironically. Couch spent that moment on what Ewell had desperately wanted him to pay. Time. Various brigades and regiments were brought forward, and precious ammunition was expended. Artillery was brought up, and a tremendous artillery duel had commenced. However, the Union forces were at a significant disadvantage, with Ewell having all of his artillery massed on Washington Heights with a full view of Harrisburg and for miles around.

Couch was no coward, but he also had no desire to throw away the lives of men needlessly. Although Jenkins surprised the militia and the predominantly green troops guarding Harrisburg, Couch was proud of their response, reorganization, and counterattack against Jenkins. After close to three hours of fighting, Couch knew he had suffered several hundred casualties. It was also clear that Jenkins had suffered heavily and had far fewer men than Couch.

When Ewell's artillery arrived and began to fire down at the masted troops that had assembled to assault Jenkins and into Harrisburg itself, Couch realized he had been hoodwinked. As Confederate artillery fired down on Couch's men, Confederate infantry brigades began to appear and relieve Jenkins' men within the space of an hour. At least 5000 Confederate infantry had appeared and were deploying into the battle. Couch was no fool, and he could clearly see these Confederate troops were crack infantry from the Army of Northern Virginia. After another 30 minutes, a handful of Couch's officers were able to identify the Confederates as belonging to Ewell's second Corps.

By the time the sun set on June 28th, Couch, who commanded maybe 12,000 troops total in Harrisburg, knew he was facing almost an entire Confederate corps, nearly 20,000 men. Couch commanded the state militias of Pennsylvania and New York primarily, along with some inexperienced recruits who had not yet seen battle. Meanwhile, he knew he was facing a veteran Corps of the Army of Northern Virginia, perhaps some of the best troops the Confederacy could field. Before the sun set on June 28th, Couch knew he was in serious trouble.

Chapter 22

June 28, 1863, Dawn
Port Hudson Louisiana

In his desperation, General Gardner, the commander of the Confederate garrison at Port Hudson, had sent more than one request to General Johnston in Mississippi: either send reinforcements to Port Hudson or send a relief force to allow him to withdraw the Confederate garrison. The response Gardener received shocked him, not only because of who had sent the message, but also because of what it ordered him to do.

Perhaps it had to do with Beauregard being a Louisiana native and an early proponent of fortifying Port Hudson. However, about a week before, General Gardner had received the dispatch that had been smuggled in through the Union lines that surrounded Port Hudson. General Beauregard was sending a relief force, and Gardner was instructed to prepare his men and coordinate with the Vicksburg relief force.

When a man on a small river boat sailed into Port Hudson two days ago, Gardner was even more shocked. There were no written orders for this soldier, and his message came directly from General Forrest. The Wizard of the Saddle, as he was also known, was in Louisiana and was approaching with a small army whose sole purpose was to extricate Gardner and his men from Port Hudson. Thus, General Forrest ordered Gardner to prepare whatever men were capable of hard fighting and marching, and to suggest what section of the Union lines were the most advantageous for this breakout attempt. After consulting with his staff, Gardner sent his message to General Forrest, along with several suggestions. Gardner, on his own initiative, had studied extensively the possibility of his small army making a breakout, and in his response to General Forrest, General Gardner made it clear where he believed the best terrain for this mission was.

The plan was not ingenious or elegant; it was desperate. As much as it pained Gardner to admit it, he knew all of his 7500 troops couldn't accompany him. Over 1,000 of his men weren't fit for duty and were in the hospital or otherwise incapacitated. There were also his artillerymen and the medical staff. Hard decisions were made; many of the wounded men, knowing they would not be able to make the march, volunteered to man the walls and the artillery. By the time Gardner had assembled his breakout force, it was slightly over 5500 men.

Banks launched his campaign to capture Port Hudson with more than 40,000 men. But due to the terrain and geography around Port Hudson, and the defenses Gardner had expertly erected, Banks had no way to mass these men in one place. There were miles of trenches and rifle pits that had to be manned, and Banks relied on his numbers and artillery to keep Gardner hemmed in, or so he thought. Throughout the campaign, Banks's army had suffered exceedingly high casualties, with over 10,000 to date. That meant before the end of June, Banks had already lost 25% of his army to death, disease, and injuries. However, of the less than 40,000 men Banks now had under his command, perhaps 10,000 troops would be manning the Union entrenchments at any one time.

After careful reconnaissance, Gardner's staff determined that the eastern sector of the Port Hudson siege lines was the weakest point in Banks's entrenchments. While bluffs overlooked the Mississippi River in the western portion of Port Hudson's defenses, the terrain in the eastern sector was more broken, swampy, and hilly. The union entrenchments were not uniform or continuous, and in some sections, relied on isolated fortresses with no direct connection to the trench lines or rifle pits. Often, the entrenchments themselves were only three feet high, with fallen trees, fence rails, barrels, and sandbags added to increase height and stability. The rolling terrain also made communications challenging for Union forces. With the cover of darkness, Garner would mass his troops here and launch an attack where the Union was not expecting.

The operation was going to be risky, that was without question. That Gardner knew, with the assistance of Cleburne and Forrest, that with this breakout, he had a chance of preserving thousands of his troops to fight another day. If the breakout was not attempted, Garner would have perhaps a few weeks of supplies left to keep his Garrison afloat. The decision had been made, and the breakout was ordered.

***

General Breckenridge's ad-hoc brigade of the 13th Louisiana, 43rd Tennessee, and Cleburne's consolidated Arkansas spent the 27th of June marching from the Greenwood Plantation to their assigned position for the night of the 27th. With Mr. Matthews and his son acting as guides, Breckenridge was able to navigate his almost 1,700-man force along back roads and trails, which avoided coming anywhere close to Banks's forces.

The men of the 13th Louisiana were in high spirits as they leisurely marched and methodically moved towards their destination, rather than a desperate sprint that would exhaust them. Orders had been issued to keep talking to a minimum, and Johan did not have to remind the men of this. He had inherited a veteran, well-disciplined regiment, and he was grateful for it.

The 43rd Tennessee marched behind Johan's men, and Andre spent most of his day riding between the two regiments, ensuring that proper spacing was kept and that stragglers returned to their appropriate units. Mr. Matthews led the way for this column, while his oldest son, Charles Jr., led the consolidated Arkansas on another trail.

The men remained in good spirits for most of the day, and even though they made multiple detours to avoid detection. Several small waterways and streams had to be crossed along Thompson's Creek, which delayed the Confederate march by over an hour. However, by the time the sun was setting on the 27th, Breckenridge had all of his force assembled and ready to attack the Union siege lines at first light.

***

General Gardner chose the Sandy Creek sector as the location of his breakout attempt. As 5,500 of his healthiest troops were assembled and packing lightly, with each man carrying over 50 rounds of ammunition, the men who were to stay behind kept campfires lit and manned the walls. Some men walked along the fortifications all night until the first rays of the morning light, all to give Banks the impression that Gardner was not even considering a breakout.

The moon was nearly full, and this gave General Forrest's cavalry light for most of the night and the advantage of being correctly positioned when the first light of day appeared on the eastern horizon. And that was the signal for Forrest. As the morning sun began to illuminate the Union camp, Forrest attacked with a fury that led Banks to believe his entire northern front was under attack. All along the Union line, as men awoke and disregarded their stacked rifles and busied themselves with breakfast, hundreds of Confederate cavalry would attack and mow down dozens of unsuspecting, tired Union troops.

And though Forrest's attack was real, the conclusions Banks reached were incorrect. Rather than have competent officers go and ascertain for themselves where an attack could be originating, Banks decided that the bluffs near the Mississippi were where the Confederates were concentrating for their attack, with a possible breakout attempt in mind. His logic was somewhat sound if made in a vacuum; the bluffs would have been the shortest route to St. Francisville and Bayou Sara from Port Hudson. Banks could not have been more wrong.

***

Before dawn, General Breckenridge assembled his three regiments in line of battle and ordered bayonets to be fixed. The sound of General Forrest attacking up and down the Union line was the signal for Breckenridge to attack.

The 13th Louisiana and the Consolidated Arkansas 6th & 7th were the lead regiments, with the 43rd Tennessee as the reserve. Johan pointed two fingers forward, and the 13th Louisiana obeyed his hand signal and began to march forward. That was the first command Johan gave as a regimental commander in a battle. As the commanding Colonel, he had to use his sword as well to direct his men, but also kept his Spencer rifle slung over his shoulder. With hand gestures and a low voice, he guided his men forward. "Steady, boys," his voice carried over the marching troops. "Steady. Another two hundred yards to go."

The three regiments of Force Breckenridge tried their best to keep formation, but the uneven ground made this next to impossible. With much foresight the night before, General Breckenridge had positioned his men so that the sun would be to their backs during sunrise and in the eyes of the Yankees.

Using the uneven and swampy terrain and morning mist to conceal their movements, Force Breckenridge moved with speed, and when it was only fifty yards from Federal lines, the order was issued to halt.

Johan raised his sword and, in an authoritative voice, commanded, “First rank, aim! Fire!” Every Confederate let out a rebel yell, and the first rank fired a volley at nearly point-blank range into the Union camp and fortifications. In the area around Sandy Creek, the Union formations were isolated in places, allowing Force Breckenridge to destroy an entire Union regiment completely within minutes.

***

Sound had strange ways of traveling on a battlefield, but General Gardner’s men heard an unmistakable Rebel Yell and multiple volleys of rifle fire. Gardner did not waste time to ensure he was hearing Breckenridge or any other Confederate formation. He issued the order for his men to advance into and along sunken Sandy Creek.

The sides of the creek bed were tall, and Gardner urged his men forward, giving no thought to the possibility of Union troops attacking from the height of the creek walls and ambushing his breakout force. Regardless, the orders remained the same: keep moving along Sandy Creek and the adjacent and parallel roads that led through the Union lines. Banks was an incompetent general without a doubt, but Gardner knew that broken clocks were right twice a day. In case Banks caught a bout of competency, Gardner and his men would be well out of the Union lines before Banks could do anything about it.

***

Chaos reigned throughout the Force Breckenridge attack. The morning sun did help in giving more visibility, but things became so confused that more than once, friendly Confederate forces fired on one another. However, these regiments were well-disciplined and motivated to deliver a decisive blow to the Yankees. With extreme effort on behalf of General Breckenridge, his three regiments reformed and knifed through multiple isolated Union regiments.

The first Yankee regiment the 13th Louisiana engaged was so thoroughly routed that Johan had no idea which regiment it was, given that most of its officers were killed in the initial volley. Nevertheless, Johan shouted out orders and reformed the regiment after a sharp bayonet fight. Forward they moved in unison with both the 43rd Tennessee and the Consolidated Arkansas on the right flank. They had to rendezvous at Sandy Creek with General Gardner's breakout force. Once the two Confederate formations linked, Johan and his men could start going back in the direction that they came from to St. Francisville.

Though the attack began at dawn, it took over two hours to locate General Gardener in the swampy and hilly terrain around Sandy Creek. It took Mr. Mathews of Greenwood Plantation to ride onto Sandy Creek itself and, at much personal risk, locate General Gardner. Although Gardner was making good time, Banks' subordinates took the initiative, and several hundred men had to form a rear guard for Gardner. As Union units became more organized and aggressive, several hard-fought fights were carried out, and Gardner's rear guard was slowly being bled out.

When the 13th Louisiana made contact with Gardner, Johan felt both relief and anxiety. As rank after rank of bedraggled Port Hudson defenders passed him by, Johan could hear and feel the ground shaking from the firefight that was occurring not far away.

Ordering several ranks of skirmishers forward, Johan went with them, and after advancing 75 yards, they came into contact with Union forces harassing the rear of Gardner's formation. As Johan's skirmishers thinned the ranks of the Yankees and diverted their attention, he brought up the rest of the 13th Louisiana. Two well-placed volleys encouraged these Union regiments to fall back rather than be annihilated. Johan took the victory where he could and ordered his regiment to begin slowly falling back with the rest of Gardner's men who were to their left flank. It would be a miracle, Johan thought, if half of that small army escaping Port Hudson would survive.

***

June 28, 1863, Early Morning.
Market St, Harrisburg, Pennsylvania

The horse carrying Jason Harrington rode at a near gallop to his family home, a three-story red brick Federal, in the 200 block of Market Street. In the early morning, Confederate cavalry had arrived and begun a vicious battle with Union forces on the western bank of the Susquehanna. Though Union forces on the west bank had fought bravely, Confederate artillery was now emplaced on Washington Heights overlooking the city, and a steady bombardment was underway by the Confederate guns.

Harrisburg had been in a near panic that morning as hundreds of demoralized blue-clad Pennsylvania and New York State militia troops retreated in panic over the two bridges that spanned the river. Thankfully, the Confederates had not yet attempted to force the bridges, but their artillery was making it nearly impossible to organize or accomplish anything in Harrisburg itself.

Jason's mother, Eleanor Harrington, was standing on her front porch when Jason arrived. "Mother!" he shouted at her, as dust flew from his recently acquired Pennsylvania militia lieutenant's uniform. "What are you doing out here?"

Mrs. Harrington, now in her fifties and five years a widow, was every bit the independent woman and gave a scornful look to her middle child, "Not one government or army official has given any of the citizens of this city any answers to what those rebels mean to do. Are they about to breach the city's defenses?" At that moment, an artillery shell whistled overhead, and several dozen yards later, a neighbor's carriage house went up in an explosion and flames. "And what of the artillery of those scoundrels?"

"Mother," Jason said calmly. "I am expected back at regimental headquarters, but you must not worry yourself at this instant. We have the rebels stuck on the other side of that bridge, and they have no way of getting across. The only thing they can really hurt us with is their artillery, which was deployed much too fast on Washington Heights for my liking. I would say you are safe for the time being. Did you manage to get Clara on the train to Philadelphia?"

The front door opened, and a young African American woman stepped out, dressed in a well-made yet unadorned dress. She answered for Mrs. Harrington, "No, Jason. Because of the Rebel attacks this morning, the trains were suspended for non-essential travel. General Couch has proclaimed that while the Rebels are in the vicinity of the city, the railroads will be used for military purposes only."

The look of concern on Jason's face was obvious and pressing, "Clara, listen to me, do not go far from here at all. Civil order has already broken down in some parts of the city, and no one knows what the Rebels may do. Stay here, please. If I could arrange a wagon ride for you to Gettysburg, where Audrey is, I would. But there are reports of Rebels around that town as well. Promise me you will not venture from this house. You and the other colored people within Harrisburg are in the gravest of danger now."

Clara stood up straighter and looked Jason in the eye. "Thank you for your concern, Jason, but I will stay here. This is my home, and I will not run from it."

June 28th, 1863. 10 AM, St. Francisville

Inside the study of the home, General Cleburne looked at each of his brigade commanders: Generals Wood, Polk, and Deshler. "A courier arrived from General Forrest 15 minutes ago. General Gardener by the Grace of God made it out of Port Hudson with several thousand men. His army and Breckenridge have linked up and have been fighting a rolling battle with Banks most of the morning. General Forrest assures me that soon he will have his cavalry completely between our fugitives and Banks's pursuing Yankees."

General King asked, "Do you want me to go forward with my brigade? My boys seem fresh, and" he looked at the map, "There is the Port Hudson-St. Francisville Road. There are so many stream crossings in there and ravines. Seems like a perfect spot for an ambush."

Cleburne shook his head. "No, General, we will concentrate almost everyone here. General Forrest should slow the Yankees down enough to allow Generals Breckenridge and Gardner a clear escape. But I want Banks to see those men entering the town. They are the bait. General King, do send a couple of companies of skirmishers forward to Grants Bayou. Hit Banks there, make him deploy, then fall back. Have your boys keep doing that until they make it back here. Now, let's take a look at the earthworks and barricades. In an hour, I want all three brigades deployed."

An hour later, as Cleburne's brigades deployed for the ambush, General Forrest rode up with several men behind him. Forrest and Cleburne saluted one another. "General Cleburne," Forrest smiled, "It took most of the damn morning, but we have Gardner's and Breckenridge's men marching hard on the Port Hudson-St Francisville Road. For every 100 yards they are covering, Banks is only getting 50,"

"How many did they save?" Cleburne asked, his voice tinged with trepidation.

Forrest smiled, "From what I have heard, Gardener has a few thousand men. Maybe 4 or 5,000. Patrick, I think we have pulled this thing off so far."

"We can only hope," Cleburne spoke as he looked East and South. A rolling thunder of musketry could be heard trickling through the forest.

***

Rifle fire crackled as Pierre Landry took cover behind a tree and reloaded his Springfield rifle. He pulled out the ramrod, replaced it, and attached the percussion cap to the rifle. More bullets whizzed past his face, and he saw another man from the Louisiana Native Guards get hit by a large bullet and fly backwards. Pierre swung forward and fired his rifle in the direction he saw the muzzle flash, not the smoke from the gun that fired it. Immediately as he pulled back behind the live oak, three bullets hit where he had been standing in rapid succession.

"Company C, on me!" Pierre called out. Thirty yards ahead, a small bridge running across a deep stream bed had provided an excellent opportunity for a Confederate ambush. And as Pierre's company rallied to him to form a skirmish line and return fire on the Confederates, the attackers melted away into the nearby dense forest and swamps. Within a few more minutes, the firefight was over.

"Sarge," one of the young Privates called out to Pierre. A young private was low to the ground and had his rifle at the ready. "I think them rebs are gone."

A white officer came forward, using the trees and underbrush for cover, and scanned the bridge ahead with his field glasses. "Sergeant Landry!" the young officer called out. Pierre came and crouched down next to the young captain. With no theatrics, he handed over the field glasses. "Tell me what you see."

Pierre scanned the terrain ahead. "Johnny Reb is gone, Captain Harrington."

With a sigh, Captain Joshua Harrington took out a map and glanced back at the terrain ahead. "This is the second ambush this morning. And Johnny Reb packed a hell of a lot more firepower into this one than the last." Harrington looked to Pierre and said, "I am thinking of deploying companies A and B into skirmish lines up to that bridge. Once the regiment is past the bridge and the land opens up, I will deploy additional companies into the skirmish line."

Pierre smiled inwardly. Captain Harrington was a young and inexperienced officer. But he was also intelligent, brave, and considerate of his men. Pierre could not say this about all of the white officers in the 3rd Louisiana Native Guards. The captain was the real deal in Pierre's view. Before the war, he was enrolled in a Lutheran seminary in Gettysburg, Pennsylvania. The young Captain was a true believer; he did not just preach to the men and cite Bible verses, he practiced what he preached and treated each soldier in the 3rd Louisiana Native Guards as a man, nothing more, nothing less.

"Captain, Sir," Pierre said in a low voice. "Perhaps it could be wise to send a company to that low rise to the right of that bridge," Pierre pointed to the terrain that worried him. "Have the men dress ranks so we are not so strung out."

Harrington gave the approach to the narrow bridge another glance. "Good call, Sergeant."

The bridge was crossed without incident, and Captain Harrington, the temporary commander of the 3rd Louisiana Guards, cautiously moved his regiment forward. That was how brutal the day's fighting had been so far. The regiment's Colonel and three other officers had been seriously injured enough that Captain Harrington had been put in command for the day.

Pierre was no military genius by any stretch of the imagination. Still, he could not reconcile in his mind the orders that General Banks continued to issue regiments and brigades, and what he had seen that morning. At sunrise, the Rebels had attacked Union lines from inside and outside Port Hudson. Things were confusing, but Pierre knew enough about the area's geography that the 3rd Louisiana was being funneled northwest, away from Port Hudson and toward St. Francisville. General Banks had slowly fed one regiment after another into the advance, and Pierre just felt the entire army was being fed piecemeal to the rebels. More than once, behind the regiment, he heard gunshots coming from the forest that came too dangerously close to the road.

A few hours after noon, General Banks had a large portion of his army on the Port Hudson-St. Francisville Road. Speed was most critical, and when couriers left dispatches with Captain Harrington, Pierre could clearly see the captain's distress. With no cavalry to speak of to screen or scout for Banks's army, it would be up to the 3rd Louisiana Guards.

By mid-afternoon, the brigade was deployed in line of battle in the available space before St. Francisville. The 1st Louisiana Guards were on the left, the 3rd Louisiana Guards were in the center, and then there was a white regiment from Indiana on the right.

At a fence line ahead, figures in gray could be seen by most of the regiment. Captain Harrington, centered on the regimental colors, gave the command, "Skirmishers forward!" The Indiana regiment and the 1st Louisiana nearly simultaneously issued the same orders, which soon left almost 400 skirmishers in front of the brigade, advancing and engaging the Confederates.

The Brigade continued the advance, per the orders of some colonel Pierre had never heard of. The thought would not leave his mind. If they had done so well today, then why were so many officers for the brigade either wounded or killed? Why was this operation looking more like a pursuit of an army that had outfought and outsmarted its opponent?

Pierre did not let the thought linger long. He had his own responsibilities to worry about. As the regiment continued to march, they stepped over blue- and gray-clad bodies, but Pierre could count, and there was no question that there were many more blue-clad bodies scattered on the field than Confederate.

The regiment was moving at a good tempo, but orders came from Captain Harrington for the regiment to halt. Soon, the 1st Louisiana and the Indiana regiment did the same. Pierre was standing next to the young captain, and he soon became alarmed. Harrington sat mounted while he argued with an officer from the brigade commander's staff. "Can't you see the barricades set up facing us from the town? And the woods, you don't think Johny Reb would have anyone positioned inside the tree line? Any further, the brigade can be enfiladed by the rebs on three sides."

"Captain, the orders come from General Banks himself. Those orders are unequivocal: destroy the Rebel formations within St. Francisville and take possession of the town."

Pierre could feel the hair on the back of his neck rising. The regiments to either side of the 3rd Louisiana had continued marching for a short distance, allowing Pierre to step out of formation and look at the wood line on the regiment's flank.

As Captain Harrington and the brigade staff officer continued to argue, Pierre read the vegetation of the forest like it was a book. Everything appeared normal to Pierre, and he wondered if, after two hard-fought ambushes/skirmishes with the rebels, he was a tad skittish. Ultimately, he did not care if he was. He was a sergeant major for a reason, and it was his job to be alert and keep his men alive. He stared long and hard at the tree line only a few hundred yards away on either side of the regiment and, for a moment, convinced himself the only rebels they had to deal with were the ones the skirmishers were fighting with just ahead towards St. Francisville.

It should not have caught his eye, but it did. The afternoon sun shone gloriously for the briefest of moments on just the wrong spot. Metal glinted in the forest. Pierre did not want to believe his eyes, but he knew better and acted without hesitation. Luckily for many of the men of the 3rd Louisiana Native Guards, Pierre's order to dive for cover saved countless lives on the warm Louisiana summer evening.

There was no warning from the forest, only ferocious volleys delivered into both flanks of the regiment. Though many men listened to Pierre's warning and dove for cover, there were still many who were too slow to act, and the Rebel rifle fire felled dozens. The 3rd Louisiana and its two other sister regiments were pinned along with multiple other brigades behind them. Pierre kept his composure and ordered his men to hold their position and return fire. This was easier said than done.

The Confederate rifle fire was reminiscent of the earlier assaults on Port Hudson and the rebel response to them. As blue-clad black Union soldiers lay in the prone position to return fire, they were left in an unenviable situation because it was challenging to reload a muzzle-loading rifle while in the prone position. Nevertheless, the men of the 3rd Louisiana comprehended almost immediately that attempting to stand and fight out of this ambush would be tantamount to suicide.

As bullets whizzed overhead and continuous smoke and thunder rolled over the regiment, Pierre continued to shout orders and crawled to where he had last seen Captain Harrington. Inch by inch, Pierre crawled to the captain, through dirt, mud, and blood. With his rifle slung over his back, Pierre dug his hands into the soil, trying his very best to be as flat as possible to the ground. The vibrations from the thousands of rifles going off repetitively made the ground tremble underneath him.

He first found the brigade staff officer. Though Pierre thought his orders had been wrong-headed, he knew the man was only doing his job. And that job had cost him the top part of his skull. Pierre was forced to pause next to the dead officer as he saw the earth before him open up as large wooden splinters tore great gashes in the soil. With a final look at the blank eyes of the young officer, Pierre made it to Captain Harrington's horse.

"Captain," Pierre called out, fearful that he would find something just as bad as what he had seen from the other officer.

"Sergeant," called out a weak voice from the other side of the horse that lay still on the ground. Pierre's heart leapt, and with agility like a swamp cat, he jumped over the top of the horse and landed on the other side. There, he found Captain Harrington with his left leg pinned under the dead horse. Harrington smiled when he saw Pierre, "Sergeant, praise God. You are still the most dependable man in this army. Could you do me a favor and help get this dead horse off my leg?"

Pierre quickly looked over at the captain and saw cuts all over his face and dark blood coming from his right shoulder. "Captain, you are hit," was all Pierre could muster.

"Yes," replied the captain with a hollow laugh. "Now help me out of here before it becomes even worse. And my God, what is happening to the regiment?"

Not wanting to agitate the captain further, Pierre thought it best to handle one crisis at a time. Quickly, he examined the captain's shoulder and put a field dressing on it, or the closest he could come to a field dressing. Then, as bullets still sliced through the air overhead and often found a new victim, Pierre went to the saddle of the dead horse and positioned himself. “Alright, Captain, I’m going to pull up as much as I can, then you pull out that leg.”

It was easier said than done, especially as a battle still raged around them. After his third attempt, Pierre crouched as low as he could and lifted from the saddle. Even a dead horse was heavy, but Pierre was able to lift the dead beast in the right spot, with just enough inches of clearance so that the captain let out a roar of pain but was able to pull out his injured left leg.

Both men took cover behind the captain’s dead horse as the battle raged around them. The men of the 3rd Louisiana Guards took cover in anything they could use, whether it be depressions in the ground, dead comrades, or broken equipment. The Confederate rate of fire had slowed, but it was heavy enough that any man who dared to stand and shoot or run invited the angel of death to come and visit him.

Using the dead horse as cover, Harrington, in severe pain, drew his revolver and scanned the battlefield with Pierre. “Sergeant,” the captain said after each man had arrived at the same conclusion, “I believe the proper military term for this predicament that we find ourselves in is nothing short of us being royally screwed.” Pierre agreed.

The fighting did not let up, and General Banks led the bulk of his army forward despite Confederate resistance. As Banks brought forward more regiments and entire brigades, the Confederates in the woods on either side of the road were flushed out, and Banks ordered an all-out assault on St. Francisville.

For General Cleburne’s men, the Battle of St. Francisville was the equivalent of Fredericksburg in December 1862. Massed Union Brigades marched right into prepared Confederate positions and paid by the thousands. In fact, on this bloody day of June 28, 1863, Banks would suffer 6,000 casualties, his most significant single-day loss of the entire Port Hudson Campaign.

The battle at St. Francisville shattered the 1st and 3rd Louisiana Native Guards, and for no good reason in Pierre's eyes. Captain Harrington, having the musket ball and not a feared mini ball dug out of his shoulder, was given another horse, only to have that shot from under him as well. Two other officers who took command of the 3rd Louisiana were also killed when General Banks ordered the withdrawal from the field. A First Lieutenant now led the regiment. With darkness falling, Pierre stayed behind with two trusted men so that they could find Captain Harrington in the carnage and bring him back to camp. Or that was the plan.

Chapter 23

Gray Hurricane
June 28· 1863, 11:30 PM. St. Francisville, LA

The shooting had died down, and Pierre stood still watching his two companions lead a couple of wounded men by moonlight out of the hellscape that Pierre crouched in. There were dead Union soldiers everywhere, and it angered Pierre to no end that for the hundreds of boys, black and white alike, this sacrifice had gained nothing. Granted, he knew General Banks would spin this battle into a great victory, that he had captured Port Hudson and routed an entire Confederate relief force, and had the Confederate prisoners to show for it.

But Pierre knew that no matter how Banks spun this catastrophe to the Yankee press, he felt that this battle had been unnecessary and had only served the ego of Banks. What the hell were they fighting for? As Pierre slowly stalked the battlefield and used the moonlight to look at the faces of the dead and wounded, the sergeant wondered again and again what he was fighting for. General Banks had not even the decency to accept General Cleburne's ceasefire that would have allowed for the collection of Union dead and wounded. Pierre struggled to keep specific thoughts out of his mind, but why did it seem like a Confederate general had more thought and understanding for the well-being of Union troops than General Banks himself?

Pushing those unwelcome thoughts aside as the smell of death and human waste nearly overtook his senses for almost the tenth time today, Pierre anxiously looked in a few more places for where Captain Harrington could be.

Pierre saw a horse that he thought looked familiar, and he weaved his way through the sea of dead and wounded blue-clad bodies. When he was less than 20 yards away, he saw a figure leaning against the beast move and point a revolver towards him.

"Come any closer, and I will blow your goddamn head off, you human vermin. Have you no decency for the dead? Are you not ashamed?"

Pierre smiled, even when wounded, defeated, and exhausted; Captain Harrington never lost sight of what was right. "Captain," Pierre said in a low voice, "I have come to get you the hell out of here."

Captain Harrington was young and dashing, as many ladies in New Orleans would have testified, and he sported dark blonde shoulder-length hair that made him appear to be closer to six feet tall than he really was. But now, the young man who was covered in blood, mud, and other filth held on to Pierre as he limped with a painful knee injury. The two men together did not make great time, but Pierre promised himself that even at the cost of his own life, this righteous young man would not be left to die.

The walk was challenging for Captain Harrington, Pierre knew that. The two men continued down the Port Hudson-St. Francisville Road, neither saying much to the other. But there was no need for that. Harrington showed obvious gratitude to Pierre, and he was willing to shoulder any burden to get this young man back to safety. And as the minutes ticked by, St Francisville slowly faded behind them, and the blue-clad bodies on the ground became fewer.

As the road narrowed and the woods edged closer to the sides of the road, Pierre kept up his encouragement of the captain in a low voice. "One step after another, Sir. One and two, one and two. You see, you are doing it!"

Pierre was almost carrying Harrington by now, and the young man struggled to offer any assistance. "My name is Joshua, Pierre. With just the two of us, we don't need all of the formalities. And with what I'm putting you through, it is the least I can do."

"Well, Captain Joshua," Pierre said, winking and smiling in the moonlight, "I am Sergeant Pierre."

Something moved up ahead in the road, and Pierre and Joshua halted. His revolver at the ready, Joshua stood prepared and ready to meet his fate.

***

Andre had not slept much over the last few days, and after the main battle had finished with the sunset, he had spent a great deal of time harassing the retreating Yankees and retrieving war booty. The horse he was pulling behind his own was no different, other than being exceptionally stubborn. As he wound his way along the road in the moonlight, he could see two figures walking down the road. One was taller than the other, holding his companion up, which meant the man was obviously injured.

As the two men approached, Andre became deadly silent and drew and cocked his pistol. When they were only a short distance away, he ascertained that they were Yankees. And then, he heard the tall one speak. He was encouraging the other, enticing him to continue forward. And Andre knew that voice; it could only belong to a man he had known his entire life. Emotions Andre had not felt in a while swelled through his very soul, and he knew he had to act. He dismounted his horse and slowly walked towards the two approaching men.

The injured man raised his revolver and spoke threateningly to Andre, which only put a smile on his face. In French, he spoke out to his brother by choice and love, "Pierre, please tell your agitated friend to put down his gun. Tell him if I wanted to shoot him, I had plenty of opportunities to do so."

***

Pierre stood dumbfounded as none other than Andre Breaux appeared in the moonlight with two horses in tow behind him. The slouched hat and cigar in his mouth proved to Pierre beyond a shadow of a doubt who he was seeing before his eyes.

Captain Harrington was half delirious, but lowered his gun when he saw that Andre's weapons were holstered and that Pierre had shown no fear. "You know this man," he asked, almost out of breath.

Pierre smiled as he gently let go of Harrington and stepped forward, only to be embraced by the man who had been married to his sweet little sister Mary. When the two men stepped away from each other, Pierre asked, "How are you doing, Andre?"

With his characteristic chuckle, Andre replied, "Well, judging by the looks of your friend, not bad at all, Pierre. Well," Andre looked to the moon, then ahead to St. Francisville. "Seems like we both have business in the opposite direction. Glad you are alive, Pierre."

Emotion caught in his voice. Pierre nodded, "Same to you, Andre."

"Looks like your officer is pretty beat up. Tell you what: you take this extra mount I have and take him back to your camp.

"Andre, I'm sorry, I can't. I appreciate the offer, but it's too dangerous for all of us."

"The hell it is. No, come on, let's get this Yankee on a horse."

Soon, Captain Harrington was mounted with Pierre holding the reins, and Andre remounted. Satisfying himself with another look over the area, Andre approached Captain Joshua and put out his hand, which the captain took. "Your blue-bellied boys fought hard today, Sir. I've never seen more courage than I did from your men. It's a shame you have to fight for that idiot, Banks. We whipped him last year in the Shenandoah, and we whipped him here today. Shame he can't learn and must waste the lives of so many good men." Andre looked to Pierre, "Take care of yourself, my friend. I pray that one day, this tragedy will come to an end."

And as if he were never there, Andre Breaux rode into the night, towards St. Francisville. Captain Joshua sat stunned. "Pierre, if I did not know any better, I would say we were just visited by a ghost, or even the Angel of Death itself."

"No, Captain Joshua, what we saw was a man. One of the most decent men one could ever hope to meet."

***

June 29, 1863, 5:30 AM. Harrisburg, Pennsylvania, Military Hospital

When the rebel artillery commenced before dawn, Mrs. Eleanor Harrington and Clara Coleman arose and, after dressing quickly, left the Harrington family home and hurried to St. Michael's Lutheran Church on Second St. The church had been converted the previous day into a military hospital, and with the continued fighting on June 29th, Mrs. Eleanor knew there would be a great need for medical assistance and nurses.

By 5:30 in the morning, both Mrs. Eleanor and Clara were helping to bandage wounds and, at times, just comforting citizens of Harrisburg who were not injured, but whose homes were either destroyed or damaged by the Confederate artillery. The sound was stupendous as well. Clara had never before seen or heard a battle before yesterday, and the artillery alone had made her feel claustrophobic, even though the rebel cannons could not reach her.

But this morning was different. The rebels obviously had more guns, and their fire was never-ending. Clara was able most of the time to count between the different cannons firing, and there was only a 10-15 second gap between each rebel cannon going off. And the longer the barrage lasted, the more people came to the church for treatment or safety.

One particular soldier had no visible injuries but mentioned to Clara how he had hit his head, and since then, he had not felt right. He complained of a headache that made him feel dizzy and of the light itself bothering him. Clara realized the young soldier had a concussion, so she gave him a wet towel for his head and put him in a dark corner of the church to get some rest. The young man thanked her profusely, and Clara kept her emotions inward. It was obvious that she was black, and most of the people here were white, but that young man in blue and the other thousands protecting Harrisburg were what stood between her and the rebels sending her south to be a slave.

After a while, the makeshift hospital began to take on a rhythm, and Clara approached Mrs. Eleanor. "Long morning," the German-born Matriarch of the Harrington Family said to Clara.

With a yawn, Clara replied, "It's not even six in the morning yet. Is the whole day going to be like this?" She paused, thinking she heard a strange noise from the Northeast.

A young blue-clad soldier ran into the church. His shirt was undone, and he had a wild look in his eye. Clara immediately felt her stomach sink. "The Rebs are in the city!" The young man exclaimed. "They are in the city, I tell you. I just came from Camp Curtin, and the Rebels hit us there at dawn. They are coming this way! Thousands of them! Run while you can!"

The hospital's head doctor, an army major, was an older man who took charge. "Bar the doors. Guards!" he called out. "Make sure all of the windows are secured. They will take no one from this hospital!"

Mrs. Eleanor took Clara's hand and held it tight. "It will be alright, Clara. It's probably nothing."

Clara appreciated Mrs. Eleanor's support. But Clara knew that the youngest Harrington boy, Ezekiel, was stationed with the state militia at Camp Curtin. Clara prayed that the boy would be unharmed, no matter what happened today.

***

June 29, 1863. Northwest of Harrisburg, PA. 4:45 AM

The men of General Trimble's strike force were roused early in the morning. Every action was carried out with a sense of urgency, yet the utmost effort was made to stay quiet and keep noise to a minimum. Before dawn, as the ranks of the Louisiana Tigers, Pelican Brigade, and Ramseur's brigade assembled and moved into line of battle, the boom from General Ewell's artillery gave the signal to proceed.

The artillery was much louder and consistent than it had been the day before, and Jacques could feel the ground tremble beneath his feet, even though they were a far distance from Washington Heights and where General Ewell had all his artillery arrayed. The men around him checked their weapons, and a few even cracked some inappropriate jokes. Murray the Irishman cracked a joke that Jacques believed he might go to hell just for hearing it. Private Henri LeRoux snickered and added his own commentary, which made Sergeant Poisson begin to recite the rosary. Jacques could not keep his composure and chuckled softly as Murray made an inappropriate gesture. Apparently, Jacques was now an ordained official member of this unholy alliance.

Word soon passed that General Trimble himself was nearby. A tall, and some would say angular man, the war had been brutal on his health, and by will alone, he had recovered enough from his previous injuries to be able to make this campaign. If anything, he seemed to have lost his sense of anger and anxiety and was content with however the day would unfold.

The ranks began to quiet, and General Trimble became visible, exchanging words with a Louisiana soldier here and there. He stopped at Sergeant Poisson and then looked to Jacques and his two accomplices. “Well, men. It looks like you have done this before.” He paused and looked at Murray and LeRoux, “But I do not think you have done all of the acrobatics you seem to be so enthusiastic about. The logistics of it all would be complicated. But let me know if you ever get the chance.”

Murray gave some unintelligible response, which even made the at times austere Trimble smile. The general then looked to Jacques, “Corporal Lutze, is it? They tell me you are the one who unhorsed General Milroy at Second Winchester. That was some inspired shooting. We will need your skills more than ever today.” He put a hand on Jacques’s shoulder and gave a firm squeeze.

Stepping away, Trimble then addressed the brigade, “Men, you have been chosen for this task because you are the finest troops the Army of Northern Virginia has. Wherever you are on the field of battle, the enemy retreats. I expect no different for today.”

There were no loud cheers by the men assembled, but they expressed their appreciation for the general in standing straighter and looking forward with a confidence that they could beat anyone on the field before them. Trimble then came back to Sergeant Poisson, who stood in the front rank. “Sergeant, would you do me the honor of carrying the colors today?”

“It would be my honor, Sir.” Poisson brimmed with pride as the Confederate battle flag was handed over to him.

Satisfied, Trimble stepped back and drew his sword. “Gentlemen, the time has come to send the clearest of messages to Mr. Lincoln and his cronies in Washington." With a signal from his hand, he then let out the command, "Skirmishers forward!"

Jacques and Murray stepped forward with the other skirmishers of the two Louisiana brigades and surged forward, rifles at the ready, into the morning mist. Daylight was barely visible as the skirmishers advanced rapidly. General Trimble allowed a few seconds to pass by before he ordered the two Louisiana brigades forward. "Tigers! You are the center and hammer of this attack. Pelicans, dress the flank. Boys, maintain alignment and keep pace. We have several hundred yards to go before we are within range. Forward men!"

There were perhaps two hundred skirmishers that led the attack and disappeared into the morning fog in front of Trimble's main force. The grass padded the skirmisher's footsteps, and occasionally, the sound of metal rubbing or clanking could be heard. One could feel the division's anticipation as yard after yard was steadily covered. Jacques more than once caught himself holding his breath; there were several hundred yards of open ground to cover before the attack could really start, and all it would take was for one Union sentry to spot them and sound the alarm.

There was a ticking clock in Jacques's head that he tried his best to ignore. Every step the skirmishers took meant nearly another yard covered, and the outskirts of Camp Curtin became all the more visible. The men spoke not a word; the only sounds were their boots pounding into Pennsylvania soil and the clank and rub of metal against canvas or leather. A rhythm developed, one that Jacques thought helped the yards melt away.

And then, it was like the mist parted like the Red Sea. Three hundred yards from Camp Curtin, Jacques felt he was center stage in a play he had no desire to be in. Clear morning daylight engulfed the skirmishers, and to their shock, there was still no response from within Camp Curtin. It was clearly visible to the Louisiana skirmishers: neat rifle stacks, men lazily getting out of their tents and having breakfast, and, most of all, hardly any guards along the camp perimeter. And then everything changed. A lone sentry paused in his steps and looked gapemouthed at what he saw. Seconds later, he raised the alarm. But to this young man's horror, the Confederates were only 200 yards away at this point.

The order came. "Men, ready, aim!" Jacques had his Sharps rifle loaded and ready, and as he saw Union troops hurriedly trying to organize, he picked out one officer who seemed a bit more animated about getting his men in order. "Fire!"

***

Private Ezekiel "Zeke" Harrington was bone tired as his guard duty rotation came to an end. With the Confederate attacks on the city yesterday, the troops at Camp Curtin were put on standby and given so many changing or contradictory orders that much of the camp's manpower was spread out. Units were often sent to multiple locations due to miscommunication.

He wanted to eat, and maybe even take a nap if he could. He looked over the field to the north of the camp and was nearly able to tune out the artillery bombardment by the bridge landings. But then he had to look again, and then a third time. Something glittered in the morning fog. Then it was unmistakable. In the forms and shapes that he saw, he knew what his eyes told him. Several hundred men led an unmistakable Confederate advance, and then the mist opened up once more to reveal thousands of battle-hardened Confederates. Ezekial knew the battle had been lost before the first shots rang out. But that did not matter. Whatever the cost, he would stay here with his comrades and make these invaders pay dearly for invading his home state.

"Ready," came the call from the Confederate officer leading the skirmishers. "Fire!" And indeed, a wall of fire erupted from the Confederate skirmishers. And too many of those shots found a target. The captain, who attempted to rally Zeke's company, was taken by a shot to the chest as he raised his sword up in the air. Pandemonium spread throughout Camp Curtin as the Confederate skirmishers began delivering shot after shot into the Camp.

And then a major was unhorsed, followed quickly by a captain. As Zeke hurriedly rammed the cartridge down his rifle, he wished he were back home. He aimed and fired. The smoke from the rifle obscured everything.

There was no mistaking what his ears heard. The entire Confederate force let out a roar that seemed to be inspired by Satan himself, and as the skirmishers thundered towards camp, the main body let out two volleys in rapid succession. There was pandemonium inside the camp, and men gathered in twos or threes, and sometimes by company, but all of this effort would not be enough to stop the thousands of Confederates who appeared out of nowhere.

Zeke ran because his life depended on it. Bullets whizzed by his head, and two of the men who were running beside him went down. His small group came upon an industrious supply colonel, using any available soldiers to form a barricade of wagons and whatever solid objects they could get their hands on. Joining an impromptu assembly line, Zeke stacked wooden crates after another between two wagons in the hopes it would help slow or even stop the Confederates.

A short while later, this hastily assembled barricade was tested. At first, a handful of rebels approached the barricade, but they were quickly thrown back. Zeke, with calm that even surprised himself, would fire his Springfield rifle, duck behind the wagon next to him to reload, then swiftly reemerge to fire again and again at the rebels. More than one rebel fell to his shooting, but the easy defense soon ended.

Dozens of Confederates approached the barricade from the front, and the disciplined fire of these troops began to take its toll on the mostly green Union defenders. Though the young Union troops fought hard, they were increasingly pinned down, and their return fire was less effective. For Zeke, it did not matter. If they could hold on and give the rest of the units inside Camp Curtin time to rally, maybe the rebels could be thrown out of the city.

But it was not meant to be. As Zeke crouched behind the wagon, trying to load his rifle as sweat poured into his eyes, he heard that demonic rebel cry again, but from behind the barricade, not in front. Again, he heard bullets whiz past his head, and splinters exploded off the wooden wagon sides as bullets impacted. The resistance at the barricade collapsed almost immediately, and the colonel who had led the valiant effort in constructing and defending the barricade went down when a bullet hit him near the chest. Zeke was running once more, south toward Harrisburg proper.

***

The exhilaration Jacques once felt when he shot a Yankee officer was no longer there. In battle, he had become a machine with his Sharps rifle. He had taken careful aim at the Yankee colonel behind the barricade and knew his shot had hit in the shoulder, still a serious injury, and not in the center of his chest. Working the lever of the rifle, Jacques pulled out the spent paper and inserted a new paper cartridge along with a percussion cap. He had done this exercise so often that, in seconds, his weapon was ready again for the next target.

Most of the Yankee soldiers at the barricade had the brains to run when they were outflanked. But there were a stubborn few who decided to stay. Murray and Jacques dispatched a number of these men, with Jacques's Spencer rifle firing over twice as many bullets per minute as Murray's.

With the obstruction cleared, Confederate officers pressed their men forward. Soon, General Trimble was in the confusion as well, mounted now and helping to reorganize Confederate units and facilitate the push forward. Sergeant Poisson was right beside him, waving the Confederate battle flag.

"To me, men!" Trimble shouted as he waved his sword and pointed. "We must keep moving. The Yankees cannot be given any time to reorganize. Follow me!"

In a great mass, Trimble's ad-hoc division surged through the rest of Camp Curtin. Union forces were too scattered and unorganized to slow the Confederates for any length of time. At times, a few dozen men could organize into a battle line and fire into the Confederates. Still, every time these brave souls were overwhelmed by their sacrifice, they bought the disintegrating army and the city only a few seconds.

Union troops began surrendering en masse, many unwilling to be victims of this tragedy for the Union cause. The blue-clad soldiers could not stand up to the gray hurricane of Ewell's Corps.

The few thousand Union troops that had managed to escape Camp Curtin ran into Harrisburg proper with the Confederates close behind them. To the shock of many of Harrisburg's citizens as they began to awake, they saw blue-coated Union troops running for their lives as thousands of Confederates flowed into the city,

***

When General Ewell's artillery barrage began at dawn, General Couch had gone to South Harrisburg to help direct the bridge landings into the city. With reports of Confederates capturing Wrightsville and apparently a whole division sent to reinforce them from Ewell, Couch had been forced to send 3,000 of his best troops to shore up the defenses of Columbia, which was just on the other side of the Susquehanna from Wrightsville. Later that morning, when Couch received word about the surprise and catastrophic attack on Camp Curtin, he knew General Ewell had hoodwinked him.

At first, only a few dozen men had run past Couch's headquarters; within minutes, hundreds were running past, most with shocked, terrified expressions on their faces. And then, another messenger reached Couch. Confederates were flowing into northern Harrisburg itself. Ewell's artillery barrage had not ceased as well, and the Confederate infantry on the western bank looked as if they were preparing to cross the covered bridges in force.

It pained Couch to the core to know what he had to do. To preserve the force that he still had under his command, to prevent the useless slaughter of so many young and inexperienced Pennsylvania and New York troops, he ordered his small army to withdraw from Harrisburg.

***

The Pennsylvania State House was a red-brick federal-style building that was not grand in any sense. Refined Greek columns lined the front entrance as Sergeant Poisson, Jacques, Murray, and LaRoux walked through the front entrance to the building. What had usually been a bustling government enterprise was now a virtual ghost town. The solemn group climbed several flights of stairs and entered the cupola that stood atop the statehouse.

Jacques took down the Stars and Stripes and the Pennsylvania State flag, respectfully folded them, and set them aside. In his hands, Poisson held the Confederate battle flag and looked up before he attached the flag to the rope and then, with speed, hoisted it.

***

The road to Lebanon, Pennsylvania, was crowded with blue-clad Union forces, but that was okay for Jason Harrington. It meant that these men had survived the catastrophe of Harrisburg. A report of Rebel cavalry in pursuit put Jason in an uncompromising mood.

"Company halt!" He commanded. For these men, he was utterly at a loss as to which unit they belonged to or who their officers were, but Jason did not care. The two dozen men more or less came to a halt and turned to face this young officer. "Alright," the fact that these men had listened to him surprised him. Maybe sounding like you knew what you were doing translated into men having some faith in you? "Reb cavalry is not far behind us. We set up skirmishers on both sides of the road. Let's put some obstacles in the road as well; they can be anything we find. Abandoned wagons, fallen trees, something that will slow down the rebs. If they pursue us, they will learn a bloody lesson indeed. Questions? Alright..."

Before he could finish, a private with a disheveled uniform raised his hand, "Need a drink, Lieutenant?"

Jason blinked more than once when he saw his cousin, Zeke, smiling at him like a fool. A loveable fool. "I think I will borrow your canteen, Private Zeke."

***

June 29, 1863. 9:00 PM. Harrisburg PA

General Ewell read the message a second time, and there was to be no mistaking General Jackson's orders. "Hooker's army is ready to converge on Gettysburg. These orders come directly from General

Lee: Move your Corps with absolute haste and get them to Gettysburg without delay. Our army must fully deploy to meet this threat. If we fail, Hooker can then destroy the army in detail."

Ewell, sore from being strapped to a horse all day, called in one of his staff officers and handed him the message from General Jackson. The young officer read it and looked back to General Ewell. "We have much to get done tonight, Sir."

After rubbing his temple, Ewell looked back at his young staff officer, "Yes, it will be. Draft the orders, and have someone find General Stuart and ask him to come here. We must coordinate this march properly, or everything we have gained will be lost. We have not even begun to catalog the wagons we have captured. Nevertheless, we must act now, so find General Stuart, and let us begin our preparations to bring these captured supplies with us. And," he signaled to the staff officer, "Tell division commanders I want this Corps on the march for 7 tomorrow morning."

Epilogue

June 29th, 1863. Early afternoon, Harrisburg, PA

The streets of Harrisburg were subdued ever since the Confederate battle flag had been hoisted above the statehouse. Jacques and his companions walked down the streets of Harrisburg, taking in the sights of a city that had known no war until a few days ago. Sergeant Poisson had assigned their group the mission of finding a suitable campground for the 6th Louisiana for the night.

***

After the fighting had died down, General Hayes, the commander of a Confederate unit known as the Louisiana Tigers, gave his word that no one would be molested inside St. Matthews Church. Only then did the colonel running the impoverished hospital within the church allow the two double doors to be unblocked and the church to reopen to the public.

At first, everything that morning had continued to progress as it had before, except there was an influx of Confederate wounded and many times more Union injured or dying. Clara worked side by side with Mrs. Harrington, cleaning wounds, comforting soldiers, and even assisting with surgeries. Many of the surgeries were amputations, and the colonel, who asked only to be called Dr. Caldwell, performed his work with skill and compassion for the seriously injured men he treated.

Clara quickly developed a deep respect for the man as he worked competently and spoke to all his nurses with dignity. Clara was treated no differently than any of the other women working in the church hospital, and she realized that with every procedure or operation, Dr. Caldwell was teaching her something.

However, during one of the surgeries, the young man died on the operating table, and after that, Clara had to step outside. On the steps of the church, she sat down while Doctor Caldwell took a seat next to her. The pain and loss that Clara felt, the unfairness of everything, of that poor young boy dying for no good reason, it simply overwhelmed her. As she cried, the fatherly Dr. Caldwell put his arm around her and told Clara what a service she had been today, and the Christlike work she had done by holding the young man's hand as he passed away.

"But it wasn't enough to save him," Clara said, fighting back more tears. "It wasn't enough."

A rude whistling sound cut through Clara's thoughts. She and Dr. Caldwell looked up to see four rough-looking, plainly dressed white men staring her down. Each man was heavily armed and looked at Clara with complete disdain. A horrible feeling washed over her.

It was obvious Dr. Caldwell felt the same way, and as they both stood on the church steps, he motioned for Clara to stand behind him. "I am Colonel Caldwell, United States Army Medical Corps. How may I help you, gentlemen?"

One of the men, his skin darkly tanned and his brown beard almost down to his chest, spoke first, "Yes, you can, Colonel." He spoke with disdain in his voice. "Hand over the negress and we will be on our way."

"Excuse me?" Rage filtered through Dr. Caldwell's voice. "I will do no such thing. I am a Colonel in the Army of the United States. You have no authority to ask me anything. And second, this woman is as free as you or I. I will not be handing her over. Not now, not ever. You understand."

Another man, this one with dark hair and more arrogance, spoke up, "Colonel, if you were unaware, you are a prisoner of war. You have no authority here. Second, that there is a darkie. And there is only one place for darkies where we come from."

"I beg your pardon." Mrs. Eleanor had come outside and stood beside Dr. Caldwell, the two of them shielding Clara from these would-be kidnappers. "You gentlemen will leave now. This is a house of God, and right now it is serving as a hospital filled with northern and southern boys. I would advise that you leave now before you learn of how bad a mistake you are making."

The slave catchers all laughed, and one man spat tobacco on the church steps at Mrs. Eleanor's feet. "Step aside, ma'am. We don't want you getting hurt."

"How dare you!" Mrs. Eleanor said indignantly. "What right do you have to come here, profane the house of the Lord, a house that is now treating the wounded of both armies that have just fought in this terrible battle? Have you no shame?"

"Ma'am," spoke the leader. "Just hand over the bitch, and we will be on our way. No need to make a fuss."

Clara stood up straight when he heard the name she was called. "If I am what you call me, sir, I at least know who my father was. You, sir, act like there might have been several candidates for your mother to choose from."

The violence the men unleashed took all three natives of Harrisburg by surprise. Doctor Caldwell was pushed aside while one man struck Mrs. Eleanor, and two others grabbed Clara and attempted to drag her down the steps of the church. Clara screamed as she tried to fight off the two men, but they were much stronger than her and more willing to use violence. When she had been dragged to the street, one of the men began to put shackles on her. It was the last thing he ever did.

A rifle shot rang through the street, and the man forcing the shackles around Clara's ankles flew backward. Stunned, Clara pulled back and ran up the Church steps to Mrs. Eleanor, who was sporting what would soon be a black eye.

When Clara looked back at the street, the three remaining slave catchers had their hands up as four Confederate soldiers had their guns pointed at them. An older man walked forward; he had three stripes on his sleeve, and Clara knew that meant he was a sergeant of some type. Revolver in hand, he snarled at the three men still alive, "Who is next? Please do something stupid, because then I would have a free hand to kill the three of you."

The slave catchers stood in shock, frozen in place. And then Clara saw him—a young man with blond hair and dark blue eyes. Smoke still blew out of his rifle as he mechanically reloaded and pointed his weapon at the leader of the slave catchers.

"You have no right." The leader of the slave catchers said.

"The hell I do," The sergeant spoke authoritatively. "And if you don't get your ass out of here, my sharpshooting friend here will make sure you end up worse than your friend over there. So, what will it be? Do I kill all of you now, or do you go and never come back here?"

It took some time and the intervention of General Hayes, but the three remaining slave catchers were thrown out of the state by orders of General Ewell. As the dust settled, Sergeant Poisson realized they had not made much progress in finding appropriate accommodations for his men.

When Mrs. Eleanor overheard the conversation, she gladly agreed to let the 6th Louisiana camp in and around her property. That night, meat and loaves of bread that had been saved for a future date were distributed to the men of the 6th Louisiana. Hundreds of men camped in and around Eleanor Harrington's property, and by the strangest of accidents, Mrs. Eleanor found herself providing for a small part of the Confederate army.

Clara kept to herself, and when she went outside, she mostly stayed near the kitchen and stable area. As the summer sky darkened into night, she found herself drawn to the fire to see how these Confederates lived and acted. And then she saw him. The young man, who might not even be her age, had golden hair and deep, sad, dark-blue eyes.

He interacted with the other men and would even crack jokes with them. The men who had accompanied him when she was rescued all seemed to like him and treated him kindly. But there was still a reserved way the young man carried himself.

***

By midnight, most of the Confederates encamped on the Harrington property were asleep, except for Jacques. The fire from earlier had died down, and Jacques sat by himself, half-awake, staring at the embers of the dying fire. It had been a hellacious day, and he struggled to rationalize everything within his mind.

He hated the Yankees, at least the ones that wore blue and claimed it gave them the right to do whatever the hell they pleased. But he hated bullies and injustice, and he had witnessed that firsthand today from his own people. Slavery wasn't something new to him; he had been around it his entire life on the Lutze family plantation. But the enslaved blacks he had grown up with, his parents had always referred to them as servants, not slaves. In fact, it was accurate to say he had been raised by African women as much as he had been by his own mother. But to see men treat that girl the way they did today…it moved something within him. If it hadn't been for Sergeant Poisson,

Murray, and LeRoux, Jacques would have killed the other three slave catchers.

"Mind if I join you?" The voice cut through the quiet night air.

Jacques looked up in surprise and saw the girl from the church. He stood, the polite thing to do for any woman, and replied, "Of course, ma'am. There is plenty of room," and he gestured to the bench the men from the company had dragged over to the fire.

Clara smiled, and as she sat, she gestured to the spot next to her. "There is plenty of room for two." Unsure of himself, Jacques sat next to her but kept a very respectful distance between the two of them. He was so nervous he could not see the smile on Clara's face. "My name is Clara, by the way. Clara Coleman." She put out her hand, and Jacques took it hesitantly, unsure of himself.

"Clara is a beautiful name." The two looked at each other for a moment, and Jacques belatedly remembered, "My name is Jacques. Jacques Lutze."

"I wanted to thank you for what you and your friends did for me today."

Jacques spent a few moments thinking of a poetic response. None came to his mind, partially because he was so enamored with the prettiest girl he had ever seen. So, he answered in the most honest way he knew, "There might be a war going on, Ms. Clara, but that doesn't mean decency has to die with everything else."

Moonlight shone down, and Clara saw the contradiction within Jacques' eyes. On the surface, there was an intensity she could sense that was ready to pounce on any threat or enemy. But beneath the surface, she sensed something else—a young man, vulnerable but with his walls up. A breeze blew through, and both shivered despite the summer night. Clara moved closer to Jacques, and he did not pull away. In fact, Clara could sense that he moved ever so slightly closer to her. "Tell me about your home, Jacques. How a young man from

Louisiana came all the way to Harrisburg, Pennsylvania, to make war on us Yankees."

"Well," Jacques sighed. "It's a long story. I'm not even sure if I really believe everything that has happened to me over the last year."

"We have time," spoke Clara, voice barely above a whisper.

The two talked for some time. They told each other their life stories and what had brought them to Harrisburg at this time. Generally, they avoided politics, and having each other as a companion did something for both the young man and the young woman. They fell asleep at some point, Clara's head resting on Jacques's chest, when Poisson nudged the young man awake early in the morning.

In a very short time, the 6th Louisiana was assembled on Market Street in front of the Harrington home and the other neighbors. Orders were being issued hurriedly, and before the sun had entirely arisen, it appeared that the Tigers and the rest of Ewell's Corps would be leaving Harrisburg. Jacques had not seen Clara since Sergeant Poisson had roused him, and that pained him. Never had he felt more like himself just being able to talk with the young woman all through the night.

Mrs. Harrington came onto her front porch to see off the Louisiana Tigers. General Hayes himself and the entire brigade saluted the Harrington Matriarch before they set off on their march. It was all surreal. Ewell had occupied Harrisburg less than 24 hours before he was to abandon it.

Jacques stood in the outside rank and gave Mrs. Harrington one last look. And then Clara was beside him with something in her hand. "Good morning, Jacques," she said with a hint of shyness in her voice.

"Good morning, Clara."

Sensing her time was short, Clara placed an item in Jacques's hand. “I know we only met yesterday under…trying circumstances. But I wanted to give you this, as something to show my gratitude and affection.”

A photograph of the most beautiful woman he had ever known sat in his hand. To take this photograph, Clara must have spent a small fortune, especially given the salary she earned as a house servant for the Harringtons. Jacques spent a moment looking at the photograph, as though he were committing it to memory. Reverently, he placed it in his breast pocket and looked back at Clara. “This I will treasure above anything else in this world.” That was all the young man could say.

Forsaking cultural norms and whatever rumors were bound to follow, Clara stepped forward and kissed her sweet Jacques. It was the first kiss either of the young lovers had ever had, and the entirety of the Louisiana Tigers let out the Rebel yell as Jacques stepped closer and took Clara by the waist.

When they finally separated, Clara had tears in her eyes. “Try not to get yourself killed.”

His deep blue eyes showed an intensity that made him mean every word he spoke. “When this is all over, whatever happens, however the dice may roll, I will come back for you.”

Clara nodded. On one hand, she had no idea how she had fallen for some young Confederate boy from Louisiana, a boy whose family had owned people like her. But on the other hand, Clara knew her life would never be the same after meeting Jacques Lutze. “And I will be here, waiting for that day.”

The End

ABOUT THE AUTHOR

By day, J. A. Quarles owns and operates a landscaping company in southeast Louisiana, where summer temperatures routinely flirt with the unimaginable. By night—and on those rare weekends when the heat loosens its grip—he turns to the world of Alternate History writing, steadily crafting the stories that have intrigued him with the questions of what if something happened differently? He and his wife share their home with their beloved "gray ghost," the couple's much-adored fur baby and her fur-sibling. But most importantly, their home is filled with the joy and laughter of two of the most wonderful children in the world.

Justin's love for storytelling began in second grade, when he wrote and illustrated his first book, The Troll King, as part of an after-school tutoring program. Handwritten and hand-drawn in the early 1990s, the book found its way onto the school library shelf—an experience that left a lasting imprint on his imagination and solidified a lifelong devotion to all things fantastical.

Much has changed in the decades since that first creation, but writing has remained his constant. Justin attended the University of New Orleans and received a bachelor's degree in history, and after that began graduate school but never finished, much to the chagrin of his thesis advisor. In both undergraduate and graduate work, he focused on the American Civil War and World War II.

Justin's grandfather, the original JAQ, served in the US Navy in World War II in the Pacific Theater aboard an aircraft carrier. The USS Kadashan Bay was hit by a Japanese kamikaze in the Battle of Leyte Gulf, and the crew of the ship suffered no fatalities. This story alone perhaps gave Justin his first insight into the "what ifs" of history. Because this one event had such a profound effect on his family, or the very existence of it at all.

Through the shifting seasons of work, school, friendship, and marriage, he has continued to write and examine the human experience through the lens of alternate history. Authors such as Peter Tsouras, Harry Turtledove, James Rosone, and Max Lamirande have helped shape his creative compass and shown the path to building good, well-written, and well-researched alternate history.

Follow the author at www.jaquarles.com

www.historiumpress.com

www.ingramcontent.com/pod-product-compliance
Lightning Source LLC
LaVergne TN
LVHW041309150826
845673LV00008B/2816

* 9 7 9 8 9 5 0 0 7 8 1 4 9 *